It was too late

Sir Justin's hand closed over Isabelle's mouth just as her eyes flew open to see him sitting beside her on the bed, and the scream that naturally followed was thoroughly muffled.

"Do not," he warned, his voice low and firm as he placed a cloth over her mouth and quickly tied it behind her head. Isabelle tried to strike him, but found that her hands and feet were already tied. "I mean you no harm, and I do not wish to hurt you. If you will but trust me a little, I vow, on my honor, that all will be well." Then, picking her up, he carried her to the chamber's one window, out of which a rope dangled. "I've wanted to tell you this past month, but never found the chance. I find you very beautiful."

Isabelle had always been rational. Always. But in the wake of Sir Justin calling her beautiful, rationality disappeared, and he had tossed her over his shoulder and carried her all the way down the length of her uncle's grand manor house before it even occurred to her that she should put up a struggle…!

Dear Reader,

In the third book of her medieval BRIDE TRILOGY, *The Bride Thief*, Susan Paul, writing as Susan Spencer Paul, tells the story of the youngest Baldwin brother, Justin, a delightful rogue who is being forced by his brothers to marry or lose all he possesses. Justin, however, neatly sidesteps the marriage that has been arranged for him and falls for his intended's cousin instead, a woman much more worthy of his love.

A young woman puts herself smack in the middle of the investigation of her father's murder, despite opposition from the local sheriff, who would rather she butt out, in 1996 March Madness author Lynna Banning's second book, *Wildwood*, a terrific new Western. And in *Tempting Kate*, longtime Harlequin Historicals author Deborah Simmons returns to the Regency era for her heartwarming tale of a haughty marquis who falls in love with the penniless daughter of a local earl, after she shoots him by mistake.

We are also delighted with the chance this month to introduce our readers to a new Western series from award-winning author Theresa Michaels. The trilogy opens with *The Merry Widows—Mary*, the tender story of a marriage-shy widow who opens her heart to a lonely widower and his little girl.

Whatever your tastes in reading, we hope you'll keep a lookout for all four books, wherever Harlequin Historicals are sold.

Sincerely,

Tracy Farrell
Senior Editor

Please address questions and book requests to:
Harlequin Reader Service
U.S.: 3010 Walden Ave., P.O. Box 1325, Buffalo, NY 14269
Canadian: P.O. Box 609, Fort Erie, Ont. L2A 5X3

SUSAN
SPENCER
PAUL

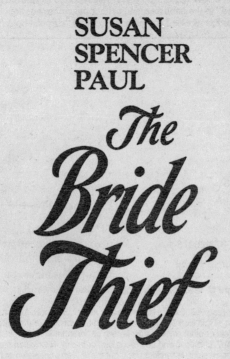

The
Bride
Thief

Harlequin Books

TORONTO • NEW YORK • LONDON
AMSTERDAM • PARIS • SYDNEY • HAMBURG
STOCKHOLM • ATHENS • TOKYO • MILAN
MADRID • WARSAW • BUDAPEST • AUCKLAND

ISBN 0-373-28973-1

THE BRIDE THIEF

Copyright © 1997 by Mary Liming

Books by Susan Spencer Paul

Harlequin Historicals

*The Bride's Portion #266
*The Heiress Bride #301
*The Bride Thief #373

*The Bride Trilogy

SUSAN SPENCER PAUL

lives in Monrovia, California, with her husband and two young daughters. She started her first novel when she was in her early teens, but eventually put it aside, unfinished, in favor of more important interests...such as boys. Now happily married and—somewhat—settled down, she's returned to her love of the written word, and finds it much easier to finish the books she starts.

Dedicated with love and gratitude to my
wonderful mother-in-law, Betty Joyce Liming.

Prologue

England, May 1426

It had been exactly nine years and seven months since Sir Hugh Baldwin, the earl of Siere, married the lady whom he then, as now, loved deeply and completely. She was, in his admittedly biased opinion, the most beautiful, charming, intelligent, witty and desirable woman presently alive on God's earth, and he counted himself the most fortunate of men to have made her his. It was understandable, then, having spent the past several weeks abstaining from his conjugal rights while this same woman recovered from the rigors of birthing their fourth child, that the earl had eagerly anticipated this particular night, when Lady Rosaleen would at last be able to rejoin him in their marriage bed, and more understandable, having embarked upon that pleasurable encounter, that he should fly into a furious rage upon being almost immediately interrupted by his steward. The steward, who steadfastly remained outside his master's chamber door despite the dire threats hurled his way, insisted that the earl attend to the missive that had only just arrived from **his** eldest brother, the venerable lord of Gyer. Fortunately for the steward, the lady

Rosaleen found the situation thoroughly amusing, and sent her irate husband down to his working chamber to see to his sudden and unwelcome task, promising that she would repay him tenfold for his attention to duty when he finally returned to her.

"I'm very sorry, my lord," said Robert, the steward, as he followed his master into his working chamber, "but it cannot wait. The lord of Gyer requires an immediate reply."

"The lord of Gyer is making a damned nuisance of himself!" Hugh informed his stoic minion as he paced the chamber, dressed in nothing more than a velvet robe. "It's the *middle* of the godforsaken night! He probably had a spy here for weeks, just waiting for the moment when Rosaleen and I would shut our chamber door before he sprang. What a pestilential lot of relatives I've got." Swinging about, he pinned his steward with an angry glare. "Couldn't *you* have taken care of it, Robert? Forged my name or something? You know how much I hate this sort of thing."

Spreading the parchment missive flat upon his master's working table, Robert gave a calm, long-suffering sniff. "Please, my lord. The lord of Gyer's servant must be on his way at once with your reply."

"Damnation," Hugh muttered, falling with a thump into the chair behind the table. "I'm going to kill Alex the next time I set sight on him. What in the Fiend's name does he want, anywise? I *hate* being a nobleman."

"That's not what you said last week, when Lord Farron was christened."

The earl of Siere made a face of disbelief. "Of course I wasn't unhappy with it while Farron was being christened. What man is going to be unhappy when hundreds of people are cheering at his newborn son? Are you going to tell me what Alexander wants, or must I read this damned missive myself?"

Straightening, Robert folded his hands behind his back. "It regards your younger brother, Sir Justin. The lord of Gyer is displeased with his behavior of late and wants you to find him a wife."

"F-find him a *wife?*" Hugh repeated, choking over the words. He gaped at his steward. "By the rood! Why in God's name does he want me to do it? Alex is the eldest in this family. Let *him* find Justin a bride."

"But you're the highest-ranking, my lord. The lord of Gyer was right to put the matter in your hands."

"Highest-ranking," Hugh said with a snort. "That's as good an excuse for shrugging trouble onto another man's shoulders as I've ever heard."

"My lord…"

"Oh, very well." Hugh took the document up and began to read it. "I've got better things to do than sit down here arguing. What's Alex's complaint, then? I thought Justin was doing well at Talwar. And he and Christian Rowsenly have made Briarstone profitable, have they not?"

Robert cleared his throat discreetly. "The lord of Gyer seems to believe that they've turned Briarstone into a brothel, my lord. He's not very pleased with the reports he's had."

Hugh lifted his head. "A brothel? Have they, now? Well, what's wrong with that?" His voice took on a defensive tone. "It was very nearly a brothel when I had the managing of it, before I married Rosaleen and got forced into becoming the earl of Siere. Nothing wrong with brothels, though you may not be in the habit of visiting them. I spent some of the best years of my life running in and out of brothels while I was naught but a soldier for King Henry, may God rest his soul."

"Aye, my lord," said Robert, staring calmly down his nose at his increasingly irate master. "I'm certain that's true. But one of the duke of Gloucester's closest advisors stopped at Briarstone to spend the night and was displeased to be asked by the guards at the gate how much money he wished to spend for his pleasures. Sir Justin drove him off at sword point when the gentleman refused to pay anything. Needless to say, he returned to London and complained to the duke, who in turn complained to your brother, Sir Alexander, who—''

"Who decided to shove the matter into my lap," finished Hugh, more thoughtfully. "I can scarce believe Justin would do such a thing. He's ever been most sensible, very like Alex. Surely there's a better way to calm the lad down than by shackling him with a wife. Ever since that Feltingad wench turned him down—''

"Lady Alicia Sherringham, my lord."

"Yes, her," said Hugh, waving a hand about. "Alicia Sherringham. Dim-witted wench if I ever saw one. Justin had a lucky escape when she ran off with that furrier from Carstairs. I hear she chattered the man into an asylum before twelve months were out. I'd hate to see Justin end with a similar fate."

"But Sir Justin grieved for her, my lord," Robert reminded him. "Remember the tournaments he attended that first year after she left him?"

"Aye," Hugh said grimly. "And during the three years after that. It was as if he courted death. He was none too pleased when Alex and I finally arranged to have him disqualified from such events. 'Twas another year before he spoke to either of us, and even then he was bitter. Perhaps…" He fell silent, thinking. "It may be, Robert, that Justin needs a wife. Who have we got available in the way of brides?"

Chapter One

June 1426

Three days left. Only three. I wonder if she'll ever forgive me?

The view from his chamber window did nothing to ease the tension that had shadowed Sir Justin Baldwin like a plague for the past month, since he received the missive sent by his brother, the earl of Siere. London, spread out before him like a crazily patterned tapestry, wasn't the sort of inspiration that gave a man—any man—an overwhelming feeling of confidence. Of course, it didn't help that he hated cities and towns. If he'd been home at Talwar, or even at Briarstone, everything would be different. With space to move and clean air to breathe, he might be able to think clearly enough to avoid his chosen course, but here, bound tight in London's stench and madness, he could barely think at all.

She'll forgive me. She must. If I had more time to woo her gently, I would. But with only three days left...

Pushing from the window out of which he had spent the past half hour gazing, Justin moved to stand before the polished steel mirror in his rented chamber. His dim reflection gave him little pleasure. His hair was overlong, he thought, frowning and running his fingers through the dark strands to smooth them. He should have had it cut—*would* have had it cut, if he'd had more notice. But with so little forewarning about the match that had been arranged for him, he'd been fortunate to achieve London as quickly as he had. Not that it mattered. The bride who'd been chosen for him had greeted him with less enthusiasm than Justin, himself, exhibited.

"I owe you for this, Hugh," Justin said aloud, softly. "I most assuredly do. Could you not at least have chosen a willing lady for me?"

A knock fell on his chamber door, and at his spoken invitation, it opened.

"Good day, Chris," he said in greeting as Sir Christian Rowsenly, the lord of Briarstone, made his way into the room, dressed in finery that equaled Justin's.

"Almost time," said Sir Christian. "Are you ready?"

Ready? Justin thought silently. Oh, yes, he was ready, whether he wished to be or not. If he failed in this final attempt, everything he had spent so many years working for would be taken away. Lost to him completely. All for the lack of a bride. Thus the duke of Gloucester had commanded, at the earl of Siere's bidding, and thus it would be.

"Yes," he said, bending to pick up his light dress sword. With a sure movement, he sheathed the beautiful weapon, which had been skillfully fashioned by his own hand. "I'm ready. 'Twould not help our cause to keep Lady Evelyn waiting. My friend," he said as he approached Sir Christian, setting a hand upon the other man's shoulder, "I thank you for all you have offered to do to aid me in this matter. Only promise that you will take every care this day. If Lady Evelyn or her father should discover our intent before we have done, I will not want you sharing my rightful punishment."

Sir Christian's smile was fully amused. "You don't think I'll let myself be caught? Come, Justin, be serious, I pray."

"I know you'll be your excellent self, as you ever are," Justin replied with a weary sigh, "but as everything that could have gone wrong with Lady Evelyn has, I fear I'm not optimistic about the rest of this unhappy venture."

"Never fear," Sir Christian said reassuringly, motioning for Justin to proceed him through the open door. "All will be well. You set your mind and skills toward charming the lovely, stubborn Lady Evelyn, and I'll dedicate mine toward taking care of the rest. Depend upon it."

An hour later found both men bowing, by turns, over the hand that Lady Evelyn smilingly offered.

"My lord, Sir Justin," she said. "How kind of you to visit me again, so soon."

The words had their intended effect, despite her gentle manner, and Justin inwardly cringed. He felt like a damned dog, sitting by her door night and day, and could only imagine how Lady Evelyn felt—probably like some prize calf at a fair being handed away to the highest bidder. She'd borne the matter admirably, and much more kindly than he would have done. Finding herself so suddenly betrothed to a complete stranger by the duke of Gloucester's command must have been, for a beauty of her renown, quite an unpleasant shock. Until now she'd held court to an impressive assemblage of admirers, every one of them more suitable as a husband than Justin knew himself to be.

She was beautiful, educated, intelligent. At least Hugh had done that much in choosing a wife for him. And yet, Justin wondered if Lady Evelyn knew what she would lose if she married him. Talwar, with its simple comforts that appealed to Justin's own nature perfectly, was like a stable compared to the grand wealth of this home where Lady

Evelyn had been raised. Was that why she so firmly resisted the match? He was afraid it was only a small part of the reason.

"Thank you for receiving us, my lady," he said, adding to her father, Baron Hersell, Sir Myles, "and thank you, my lord, for your long suffering in this unusual matter."

Then, aware that the action would probably be viewed as extraordinarily rude, Justin walked past Lady Evelyn and Sir Myles, fully ignoring their surprise, and strode across the room to where another lady, dark-haired and plainly dressed, sat at a small table behind a stack of large leather-bound books. Seeing his approach, which she'd clearly expected even less than Lady Evelyn and Sir Myles, the girl flushed brightly and clumsily slammed shut the particular book in which she'd been making entries.

"Lady Isabelle." Justin took the cold fingers she shakily proffered. Her heavy skirt caught beneath her chair as she awkwardly attempted to stand, causing her to stumble forward. Justin set a hand upon her waist to steady her, and the girl's color became a fiery red.

"Sir Justin," she murmured with what sounded like horror, her sapphire eyes wide.

Justin bowed over her hand. "It is a pleasure to see you again. I hope this day finds you well?"

"Oh, yes. Yes. Thank you."

"Will you have a glass of wine, my lord?" Lady Evelyn asked behind him, displeasure clear in her tone.

Justin smiled into Lady Isabelle's worried eyes. "Will we have the joy of your company, as well, this day, my lady?" he asked, holding fast the fingers that she attempted to tug free.

"Oh—I don't think—"

"I fear that my niece is too occupied with her work to join us, Sir Justin," Sir Myles stated over Justin's shoulder. "Isn't that so, Isabelle?"

"Isn't she always?" Justin murmured, too low for anyone but Lady Isabelle to hear. He released her and stepped away, turning to Sir Myles with a pleasant smile.

"Have you received the satisfaction you sought from the duke?" he asked as they walked together toward the table where Lady Evelyn was filling golden goblets with wine.

"I regret to say, my lord, that I have not. I spoke with Duke Humphrey yesterday, as I promised you I would, but I remain unconvinced of the legality of his dictates. To that end, I've sent a missive to France for the duke's brother, John of Lancaster."

Justin's brow furrowed. "John of Lancaster? How can he have any say in the matter? His concerns are only for France, as England's regent there. Surely he would not gainsay the duke of Gloucester in any such domestic matter as this."

"This may be true," the baron admitted kindly, accepting the goblet his daughter handed him. "Nonetheless, I will await word from him until I make my final decision."

"But that may be many weeks, my lord. I have been commanded to wed before this month finds its end, three days from now, else I lose all that I hold as my own."

Sir Myles's smile never wavered. "I understand, my lord, and I appreciate your concerns, but I cannot—will not—force my daughter to wed you or any man unless she freely consents to do so. It was her mother's final wish that Evelyn be allowed to have a husband of her own choosing. 'Tis an oddity, s'truth, but I gave my oath of honor and cannot turn from it."

Justin's steady gaze moved to Lady Evelyn's lovely face. "And you, my lady. Every day for the past month I have come, asking the same question. Has your heart experienced a change since yesterday? Do you have a different answer for me?"

The expression in her eyes told him that he was the

most desirable man on God's earth, while her lips said, "You must know how flattered I am by your declarations, my lord. I can think of no finer fate than to be wife to a man such as you are. And yet, if I only had a little more time to think on the matter… You could not wish me to come to you, to wed you, unless I can bring my whole heart?"

There it was, Justin thought. The same as every day. They must believe him to be a fool ten times over. He felt the trap being laid out as surely as if Lady Evelyn and Sir Myles were spreading a net on the floor beneath his feet. They were a cunning pair, he admitted, but come the morrow, they would know who it was had played their game the better.

"Nay. I would not."

"Perhaps," Sir Myles said lightly, "if Evelyn could be more certain of your regard for her, Sir Justin, such a step might become easier for her to take. After all, you were chosen for each other by the duke and your brother, the earl of Siere. It is understandable that any maid, under such like circumstances, would question the sincerity of her betrothed's feelings."

"I have come every day to ask Lady Evelyn to become my wife," Justin told him. "If, after twenty-seven proposals, my desire to wed her is not evident, I cannot think that a hundred more would make the matter clearer."

"But you would not be making such proposals if 'twere not for the duke's command," Sir Myles argued, while Lady Evelyn blushed prettily. "If there were some way that you might make your own feelings in the matter more sincere, I'm certain Evelyn would feel secure in becoming your wife."

Justin's eyebrows rose. "More sincere?"

"Certainly," Sir Myles said pleasantly, setting his wine goblet aside. "If you truly desire to make Evelyn your wife, could you not prove it by perhaps gifting her with some evidence of that desire? The dowry she brings to her marriage will be exceptional. A suitable marriage gift from you, in turn, would be proof of your consideration for her as a bride.''

"Father, please," Lady Evelyn protested. "You make it sound like the veriest extortion. I'll not be bought, nor bargained for. I want only to be certain of Sir Justin's honest hope to wed with me, nothing more. Is it too much to ask, when we are to be bound together for life?''

"Nay, of course not," Justin assured her, praying that he sounded fully sincere. He had never been good at plotting and deception, but if he failed in this, all would be lost.

"Perhaps," Christian said gently, putting his own wine goblet down, "we should leave Lady Evelyn and Sir Justin to discuss the matter more privately." He turned to Sir Myles. "I've been fascinated by the architecture of your fine home, my lord. Would you be so kind as to let me examine it more closely? There are a good many improvements here that I should like to have made at Briarstone, and I would very much appreciate it if you could explain the workings of some of them."

With a bow, Sir Myles acquiesced. "A wise consideration, my lord. Indeed, perhaps Sir Justin and my daughter will be able to find their way more readily without company present. I will, of course, leave Isabelle."

"Father, nay," Lady Evelyn said quickly. "We have no need of an attendant."

Sir Myles gave her a wry smile. "Haven't you, my dear?" To Justin he said, "We will leave you for half an hour's time. No more."

"I am grateful," Justin replied. "Thank you, my lord. You will have no cause for worry. I vow it on my honor as a knight of the realm."

The baron was apparently reassured, and shortly left the chamber with Christian following behind. Justin waited

Chapter Two

Don't trust her, my lord, Isabelle thought from her chair, keeping her eyes firmly on the page before her. *Don't trust either of them. 'Tis only your land they want, only the power and influence they might gain by wedding themselves to your family.*

With all the strength she possessed, Isabelle willed him to heed her silent plea.

"More wine, my lord?" Evelyn offered in the beguiling manner that never failed to charm.

"Nay, I thank you," Sir Justin replied, and Isabelle whispered a sigh of thanks. Evelyn was captivating enough without the aid of wine, and Sir Justin would need every faculty undimmed if he was to avoid the neat trap that Sir Myles and his daughter had set for him.

He was different from the other men who courted her cousin. Entirely, wonderfully, different. Not only in his splendid physical frame, so tall and muscular, or in his face, which was by far the most handsome Isabelle had ever seen, but in his manner. Where other men praised Evelyn's beauty with gallant words and poetry, Sir Justin spoke his admirations plainly, simply. Where other men hid behind masks of elegance and propriety, Sir Justin was open and honest, as clear as a bright day.

The next moment, she heard him add, "Will you not offer some to your cousin, who labors so greatly?" and, as Isabelle stiffened with panic and dread, he continued, even more gently, "Indeed, never once have I seen Lady Isabelle when she has not been busy with your father's accounts. What wonderful diligence."

Drawing in a breath through parted lips, Isabelle lifted her head, already knowing that he was looking at her. His kindness, though well-meant, was a torture for her. When her uncle and cousin had finally finished toying with him, when Evelyn at last agreed to be his wife, Isabelle knew she wouldn't be able to bear it any longer—seeing him, suffering his gentle manners and kind ways, his pity. He was simply staring at her, she saw. Not smiling, not frowning. Simply looking into her eyes from across the room.

"Your father," he said slowly, holding her gaze, "is most blessed to have such a considerate niece."

"You speak truly," Evelyn replied with the sweetness she generally reserved for such public displays. "I don't know what we would do without cousin Isabelle. She's an angel in every way. She knows very well that Father expects nothing from her in turn for his care of her and Senet, yet she insists upon relieving him of the most tedious duties." She strolled toward Isabelle carrying a goblet, the tight smile on her lips giving full warning of what Isabelle had in store as soon as Sir Justin departed. "You've spoiled us terribly, Isabelle, dear," she said, setting the goblet with slow care before the pile of books. "And you've been working so hard. Wouldn't you enjoy a rest? Perhaps a walk in the gardens?"

Oh, no, Isabelle thought. She couldn't save Sir Justin Baldwin entirely from her uncle and cousin, but one thing she *could* do was not leave him alone to battle Evelyn's deft machinations. A few minutes alone under the heat of Evelyn's seductive persuasions and his marriage to her would be as good as done.

"Thank you, Cousin," she said, dipping her quill in the inkpot and bending over her work again, "but I'll just finish this first."

Isabelle didn't need to see Evelyn's fury. She could feel the heat of it where she sat.

"Leave your cousin to her work," Sir Justin suggested in a voice filled with surprising tenderness. It was the first time Isabelle had heard him use a lover's tone on Evelyn. "Come and sit with me, my lady. We have much to discuss."

From the corner of her eye, Isabelle could see him touch Evelyn's elbow, could see Evelyn turn, smiling, toward him.

"You speak truly, my lord," Evelyn agreed with open pleasure. "There is nothing I should like more."

Tucking her hand beneath his arm, he led her a distance away, to a couch at the opposite side of the chamber, so that Isabelle heard very little of their conversation. Making the best pretense she could of concentrating on the figures before her, Isabelle watched them—him—fleetingly, moment to moment, as she dared. She had never seen Sir Justin behave in such a way before, with such deference and charm, and the sight made her heart sink. He had fallen under Evelyn's spell, just as every other man who courted her had. Evelyn, for her part, was masterful; shy, smiling, daintily colored with maidenly blushes.

At last, after what seemed an eternity, Sir Justin stood and pulled Evelyn to her feet. "I'm grateful for your candor, my lady, although I realize how difficult it must have been for you to speak of such matters. But have no care for that, I beg you. Now that I fully understand what you require to be made comfortable regarding the question of our marriage, I shall be able to proceed accordingly."

"You have gladdened me beyond words, my lord," Evelyn murmured, her eyes shining. "If I can believe that the man who would be my husband truly cares for me, then my decision to wed will be willingly and, aye, joyfully made."

She lifted her face to receive his kiss—an invitation that just as well as sealed their betrothal—and Isabelle, her heart twisting painfully in her chest, lifted her head, to watch, as well.

Sir Justin smiled sweetly at the upturned face and closed eyes before stepping back and bending low to kiss Evelyn's hands. Straightening, he met her bewildered expression and said, "It is past time that I take my leave, for I would never bring you harm in any measure, nor make your father worry. You have made me the happiest of men, my lady. Indeed, you have given me a gift beyond price, for which I shall ever be thankful. By this time tomorrow, I will have proven the depths of my feelings for you. I vow this by all I hold dear."

Isabelle began to slowly release the breath she'd been holding, but when Sir Justin suddenly turned on his heel and strode toward her, the air came whooshing out in an embarrassingly loud rush. Horrified, she was hardly able to make sense of his words when he at last stopped before her and asked, "May I ask a great favor of you, Lady Isabelle?"

Dumbly, she nodded, unable to form even the simple word "Yes," on her lips.

He smiled. "Will you do all that you can to finish your work here very soon? There will be cause for celebration shortly, and I'd not wish you to miss a moment of it. For any reason." With a bow, he added, "I look forward to our next meeting. Good day, my lady."

He bade Evelyn a similar farewell, and took his leave. The moment the door shut behind him, Evelyn turned to Isabelle with a triumphant laugh.

"Perfect!" she declared, her richly ornamented skirts whirling as she made her way toward Isabelle. "Just as Father said it would be. Absolutely perfect. Do you not agree, Isabelle?'' Setting her beautifully feminine hands on the tabletop, she leaned forward. ''What? No congratulations, Cousin? Come. Wish me happy. Let me hear the words from your lips. Say them, Isabelle! I want to *hear* you wishing me happy.''

It was unfortunate, in Isabelle's opinion, that she had not yet learned how to master her temper. Since her parents' deaths four years before, she'd learned many things—how to beg for help, how to plead and crawl—but her temper, unhappily, had remained untouched by every misery that either her cousin or her uncle had visited upon her. *Very French,* her father had often said of her temper, approvingly. *A thing to be conquered,* her mother had always added with despair.

Her stony silence enraged Evelyn, as it always did, and the stinging slap that followed seemed, to Isabelle, just what she deserved for being so stubborn.

''You stupid little mouse,'' Evelyn said with seething anger. ''I've seen you looking at him, watching him. Sir Justin is handsome, is he not? Handsome, and well-favored in every way. And he's *mine.* If you think a man like that would ever look at a repugnant mouse like you, then you're stupider than I ever imagined. Now say it!'' Another slap, harder this time, knocking Isabelle back slightly. ''Tell me you're happy for me, Isabelle!''

Evelyn was one of the most beautiful women in London. In all of England, so it was said. Isabelle recited the fact calmly in her mind, while her eyes registered, with deep satisfaction, that in this moment, mottled and enraged, Lady Evelyn was as ugly as the heart she hid.

''Bitch!'' Evelyn cried furiously, childishly. ''How can you smile? I *hate* you! I hate looking at your unsightly face every day, sitting here as if you had a right to such comfort, as if you were a queen, instead of naught but a beggar!''

She raised her hand again, and Isabelle straightened, preparing to receive the coming blow.

"Evelyn! Leave Isabelle be. Will you never learn to leave her in peace?" Sir Myles closed the chamber door behind him **as** he entered the room. "She has work to do, and I want it finished by day's end. Leave her be."

"She's making me crazed, as she ever does," Evelyn said angrily. "Why can't you make her behave as she should?"

"Isabelle's behavior doesn't concern me at the moment," Sir Myles told her curtly. "Our guests have just taken their leave. Tell me what happened with Sir Justin."

Evelyn seemed not to hear his words. Still holding Isabelle's gaze, she said, "It's only pity, Isabelle. 'Tis why he's so kind, why he deigns to speak with you. Only pity…for a small, unsightly, insignificant mouse. You *know* it's true." She laughed when Isabelle closed her eyes against the pain the words wrought. "Aye," Evelyn said, more softly. "'Tis worse than death, is it not? You've too much pride, mouse."

Sir Myles grabbed his daughter's arm, turning her about. "Sir Justin?" he prompted.

Evelyn's smile was wide, brilliant. "He's ready to give me anything I want to make me his wife. Tomorrow, he promised, he'll prove the depths of his devotion to me. He said that he understands perfectly what needs to be done to make me comfortable in our marriage."

"God be praised," Sir Myles murmured fervently. "Well done, my daughter. Well done. I had thought he would surely run away when you made him wait so long for your answer. It's been a near thing, I vow."

"I would have made him wait until the last day, if you'd not been so insistent in the matter," she said haughtily, pushing free and returning to the table where her wine goblet sat. "'Tis an insult to be given to a man—any man—in such a coarse manner. Sir Justin is fortunate that

I find him so favorable, else I'd never have agreed to the match.''

"Oh, no, my dear," her father countered, accepting the goblet she handed him. "I'd not have allowed you to let such a prize as Sir Justin Baldwin get away, no matter if you'd found him wholly unacceptable. An alliance with one of England's wealthiest and most powerful families is naught to be trifled with. I gave you your moment of revenge, my sweet, but never should I have let you throw away such a boon." He lifted his cup to her in tribute. "Wedded to a Baldwin! Who could have foreseen such a miracle befalling us? You'll have everything your heart desires."

"And you," said Lady Evelyn, "will have the influence you have long craved. I expect you to remember what I've brought you, Father, and to be ready to repay me in the future."

"Repay you? What nonsense is this? You're soon to become one of the most envied women in all of Britain."

"Being the wife of Sir Justin Baldwin will have its certain pleasures," Evelyn admitted, "for he is well-favored in face and form, as well as in his relations. Howbeit, a duller man I've yet to meet. Lady Alicia told me what she suffered at his hands years past, before she found the courage to break their betrothal. He constantly wearied her with his dull manners and vexing conversation, and, despite his skills as a lover, she could not bear the thought of spending her life with such a tedious husband. I'm of no such mind to suffer the same."

Sir Myles gave a careless shrug. "I care not how you amuse yourself in your marriage, Evelyn, nor with whom you do so. I only ask that you keep your name, and reputation, unsullied."

"And *I* only ask, dear Father, that you stand ready to lend me aid as I require it. I'll guard your interests, my lord, if you'll help me to guard mine."

With a smile, Sir Myles put his cup forward to lightly tap the one in Evelyn's hand. "Agreed," he said, and, laughing, they both drank.

"He is *not* dull!" Isabelle was on her feet, one fisted hand crushing her writing quill. She was as furious as she'd ever been in her life—more furious than she'd realized she could be—and when her cousin and uncle turned to her, shock on their faces, she repeated, "Sir Justin is not dull!"

After a moment of stunned silence, Evelyn began to laugh, while the baron's face darkened with anger.

"You've no say in the matter, my lady," he said sharply. "Indeed, you've no say in any matter. Be silent and finish your work, before I'm led to punish you for such intemperate speech."

"I'll not be silent!" she said hotly. "You sicken me. Both of you." Her gaze moved over them with unveiled disgust. "Sir Justin Baldwin came here in truth, speaking honestly, in every word and deed a gentle man. Can you think it any better for him to be forced into an unwanted marriage? Yet he has behaved toward Evelyn, and yourself, i'faith, with naught but kindness and good intentions. How can you speak so ill of such a man?"

"By the rood!" the baron swore angrily, setting his goblet down with such crushing force that red wine spilled over the table and onto the floor. "You'll not speak to me, or to your cousin, in such a froward manner!"

"Oh, Father," Evelyn said between gasps of laughter. "'Tis too funny! Can you not see? She's in *love* with him! Isabelle—" more laughter, gusting harder "—Isabelle's in love with Sir Justin! Would he not be horrified to know of it? Can you not envision his face if he knew that such a—such an *ugly* mouse was in love with him?"

Sir Myles was too occupied in scowling at Isabelle to pay his daughter notice. "You're wrong," he said to Isabelle, "if you think I'll ever let you wed. Save yourself trouble, my girl, and heed me well. Keep your thoughts on money and numbers, not on men. If you value your brother's life, and your own, then understand what I say.''

But Isabelle couldn't. Her unfortunate temper had taken control, and she was furious. For days now, as they played their game with Sir Justin, it had been simmering. Each afternoon, when he arrived and so urgently pleaded his cause, only to be turned aside by their cruel lies, it had grown hotter. Isabelle had spent four long years suffering and laboring as nothing better than a slave in her uncle's house. Now, every insult, every unkindness, seemed to well up and burn. Holding her uncle's gaze, raising her fist, she crushed the writing quill in her hand, mangling the instrument with labor-strengthened fingers until it was beyond use. Without expression, she dropped the broken quill on the open ledger.

Even Evelyn stopped laughing.

The silence that ensued was complete, until at last Sir Myles said, ''That was unwise, Isabelle. I shall have to punish you. You shall abide in the cellar without food or drink until that account is finished. If it is not done by morning, when the banker arrives to meet with me, I shall write Sir Howton a missive regarding Senet—''

''He has naught to do with this!'' Isabelle cried furiously, taking one step toward her uncle.

''You're wrong, my dear,'' Sir Myles replied calmly. ''He has everything to do with it. You will go to the cellar and finish with that account before the sun rises in to-morrow's sky—'' he pointed at the book with a hard finger ''—else Senet will return here to London, where he shall be made to rightfully labor for his care, in the lowliest manner I can arrange. I make you my promise on it.''

''Send him to White Tower, Father,'' Evelyn suggested with purring satisfaction. ''Have them put him to work cleaning out the garderobes. Or, better yet, offer him as a suitable gong farmer.''

The image of her beloved younger brother slaving daily at such a horrible, filthy task—emptying latrine pits—rapidly cooled Isabelle's fury. She could just imagine her uncle doing such a thing to bend her to his will. He was a cruel man, as wicked as sin in most of his dealings. She'd been too closely involved in his world for too long to take the threat lightly.

Swallowing the angry words she longed to say, Isabelle stepped back and slowly sat in her chair. Her uncle's soft chuckle told her that he understood her surrender, and she bowed her head.

"Most wise, my child. Most temperate. I shall have a new writing quill brought to you in the cellar, and plenty of candles and ink to work by. When you have dutifully finished your task," he said, savoring the words, "and when I have approved it, you will be released."

Chapter Three

It was late before Isabelle was finally let out of the cellar and led, by a lone servant bearing a candle, through night-darkened halls to the small room that was her bedchamber. Exhausted, hungry and cold, her bones aching from long hours spent crouched over her uncle's accounts in the cellar's dampness, she wearily prepared for sleep. In a few short minutes she had removed her clothes and put on the one nightdress she owned, unbraided her hair and brushed it, and washed her face and hands. Gratefully lying down beneath her covers, she muttered a few words of prayer, crossed herself once and, pushing all troubling thoughts of Senet aside, fell asleep.

So deeply did she slumber that at first she mistook the voice for a dream—the same dream she'd had nearly every night since she first met Sir Justin Baldwin. But in the dream, Sir Justin, being a creature of her own making, never actually said anything, and this time, his fourth whispered invocation of "Lady Isabelle" at last pierced the fog of her sleep-ridden brain with realization. By then it was too late. Sir Justin's hand closed over her mouth just as her eyes flew open to see him sitting beside her on the bed, and the scream that naturally followed was thoroughly muffled.

"Do not," he warned, his voice low and firm. "I mean you no harm, and I do not wish to hurt you. Be quiet and all will be well."

"What—?" she cried when he lifted his hand.

"Hush," he commanded. The next moment, he placed a cloth over her mouth, ignoring her struggles while he quickly tied it behind her head. Isabelle tried to strike him, but found, to her increasing dismay, that her hands were already tied, as were her feet. She screamed again, this time into the cloth, and Sir Justin took her head in his hands, holding her still as he bent over her, eye-to-eye.

"My lady," he said patiently, "I wish you would not. There is no cause for such distress, and if you do not cease, I will have to make you insensible, which I profess I am loath to do. Already I regret the necessity that made me bind you. If you will but trust me a little, I vow, on my honor, that all will be well." Then, picking her up, he carried her to the chamber's one window, out of which a rope dangled. Stopping suddenly, he looked down at her, the thoughtful expression on his face fully at odds with the rampant fear that possessed Isabelle. "I meant to say this before," he told her, "but forgot. Chris says my mind is ever scattering." Sitting on the sill, balancing her on his lap, he swung one leg out the window. "I've wanted to tell you this past month, but never found the chance. I find you very beautiful."

Isabelle had always been rational. Always. Even during those unfortunate moments when her temper got the better of her. *Very English,* her father had said disapprovingly. *May God be praised,* her mother had said with thanks. But rationality, in the wake of Sir Justin's calling her beautiful, disappeared as if Isabelle had never known it, and the stupefying result was that he had tossed her over his shoulder and carried her all the way down the length of her uncle's grand manor house before it even occurred to her that she should put up a struggle.

Sir Christian Rowsenly—a man she would never have thought capable of such a heinous crime as kidnapping—was waiting for them on the ground.

"It took long enough," Sir Christian whispered tightly, bringing forward two saddled horses. "I was afraid you'd been discovered."

"She wasn't there," Sir Justin replied, handing her over to his friend while he, himself, mounted one steed. "I thought perhaps you'd mistaken which chamber was hers, or that Sir Myles, being rightfully ashamed at keeping his own niece in such a mean place, had lied about it when he took you through the dwelling. I was going to search her out when she at last arrived, and then I had to hide and wait until she had prepared for bed and fallen asleep."

"I don't want an explanation *now*," Sir Christian told him, lifting Isabelle into Sir Justin's waiting arms. "God's feet. If the ward sergeant catches us we'll be drawn and quartered. Let's get us out of London, right quick."

"Aye, and so we will," Sir Justin agreed, ignoring Isabelle's squirming as he tightly tucked her up against his body and wrapped her within his cloak. With one strong arm he held her captive, with the other he guided his horse to the cobbled street that faced her uncle's home.

"Go to sleep," he advised her quietly as they set out toward what Isabelle knew to be the direction of Bishopsgate. "The guards at the gate have been paid to let us pass without notice, and 'twill do you no good to make a disturbance. You are full weary." The fingers that held the reins skimmed lightly over her cold cheek in a reassuring caress. "Sleep, if you can, Lady Isabelle. Our travel this night will be long, but I shall hold you safe. No harm will befall you, I vow."

He must have heard the groan she gave, for even as the horses began to move more quickly he smiled down at her, so that she saw the whiteness of his teeth in the darkness. "Sleep," he repeated. "There's naught else you can do for yourself at the moment."

Which was true, Isabelle thought an hour later as she fought, and failed, to keep her eyes open. True to his word, they had passed through Bishopsgate and out of the city without being questioned, and had been riding north since. There was nothing she could do to help herself until they arrived at whatever their destination was, save to let her body claim the rest it begged for. Soon enough she would discover why she had been taken, and what Sir Justin wanted her for. Better to be rested and fully aware when that time came than too weary to think.

It was easier than she thought to relax and let herself slide into slumber. Sir Justin's body was warm, his grip strong and sure. The horses were moving at a steady pace, neither too fast nor jarring. She was more than half-asleep when she felt the cloth around her mouth being loosened and pulled free. Bare fingers and a thumb gently vised her cheeks, rubbing for a few moments to soothe the numbness away, and then her head was tucked more firmly against Sir Justin's shoulder.

"Is she asleep, then?" she heard Sir Christian ask.

"Aye," Sir Justin replied just as Isabelle, with a yawn, willingly gave truth to the word. "She's asleep."

Isabelle awoke the moment she was pulled from the saddle on which she'd been riding. The sensation she experienced, at first, was similar to drowning, and she flailed as if to save her life.

"I have you," Sir Justin said soothingly, somewhere near her ear. "Hush, now, my lady. I have you."

His arms cradled her and she subsided, groggy and bewildered. Her head fell against his shoulder as he carried her from the cold damp of dark night into the warmth and dryness of some dimly lit place.

"Where are we?" she murmured sleepily.

"A monastery in Cambridge," he answered. "I'm taking you to a chamber where you may rest peacefully and in comfort. There is naught to fear."

"I do not wish to sleep," she told him, blinking to clear her eyes. "I wish to know what you mean to do to me."

"Do to you?" he repeated with what sounded to Isabelle like bewilderment. He glanced at her before giving his attention to a man in dark robes, who approached them holding a candle.

"You are Sir Justin Baldwin?" the monk asked, his face unseen beneath the folds of his hood.

"Aye."

"All has been made ready. Come with me."

"Father!" Isabelle cried.

The monk turned. "Yes, daughter?"

"This man has taken me from my home, without my consent! Help me, I beg you."

There was a sympathetic nod. "Aye, and so we shall, daughter, if that is your wish. You will be free to leave this place in the morn as it pleases you, either with Sir Justin or without. No harm shall come to you while you bide here. I give you this promise on the holy vows I have taken before God." He turned and walked away.

Sir Justin followed, carrying Isabelle down a long hall and up a number of stairs before at last reaching their destination: a large, clean, well-furnished chamber, warmed and lit by both fire and candle. Placing her in a chair by the fire, Sir Justin knelt and, producing a small knife, cut away the bindings at her hands and feet.

"I regret…" he began as he tried to take her wrists in his hands to chafe them, but stopped when Isabelle yanked free of his touch.

"Leave me be, I pray you, *Sir* Justin." Her tone cast harsh aspersions on his claims to the honorable state of knighthood. To the monk, who stood by the door, she demanded, "Why have I been brought here? My uncle, the Baron Hersell, will be more than displeased to know of the treatment I have received this night.''

The monk gave another nod and put his hand on the door. "There is wine on the table, and I will have food brought at once. Father Hugo has been praying in the chapel, and will arrive to greet you shortly.'' Then he left, closing the door behind him.

Isabelle turned her angry gaze on Justin, who still knelt before her. "What is this about? Do not touch me!'' She tried to pull her feet away, but the warm grip on her ankles held her fast.

"My lady,'' he said with what Isabelle felt was unmerited calm, "be pleased to put your mind at rest. I have not brought you this long distance, to a monastery, i' faith, to rape or harm you. If that had been my goal, I would have managed it at some other, more advantageous spot.'' When she continued to attempt to pull her feet free, he said, "I am sorry for having tied you. I thought it the best way to keep you from harming yourself unnecessarily. But look—'' his gaze fell to where his fingers gently rubbed her raw flesh "—the rope has done its own damage. If I could take the pain from you, I vow that I would.''

Weary, unwanted tears filled Isabelle's eyes. She hated crying. Worse, she hated feeling out at sea, as if she were clawing at a slippery rock to gain any sort of hold.

Having long been treated as one without value, Isabelle believed that she was, in truth, without value, and so she said, "Sir Justin, I cannot think I will make a very good hostage. My uncle will not make Evelyn wed you simply to secure my return. He will probably be glad to be rid of me.''

He pulled his fingers from her feet and took hold of her wrists, rubbing them as he had her ankles. "I do not want you for a hostage,'' he told her, "and I do not want Lady Evelyn for my wife.''

Despite her every effort not to let them, Isabelle's eyebrows rose.

Sir Justin smiled. "I never thought I would ask for a woman's hand in the accepted manner, but as I'm already kneeling at your feet, I suppose I should. Lady Isabelle, will you do me the honor of wedding with me?"

She stared at him as if he'd stunned her with a blow to the head.

He waited a full minute before prodding, "My lady?"

"W-w-wed?" she sputtered. "With *you?*"

"I've surprised you," he said. "I understand fully how it must seem. But give me a moment to explain, I pray, and all will be made clear."

Standing, he crossed the room and filled a goblet with wine, then returned, pressing the cup into her hands.

"Drink this," he said, and bent to tuck his cloak more tightly about her. "Are you warm enough? I threw some of your clothes down to Chris after you'd fallen asleep, and he put them in one of his bags. I'm sure he'll bring them as soon as he's finished stabling the horses, and then you may clothe yourself more warmly."

"You—" she began, then faltered. Just how often did Sir Justin Baldwin deal in kidnapping? He was apparently very well organized at it. "You seem to have thought of everything." And then she remembered that he had stood in her chamber's shadows and watched her prepare for bed. Heat warmed her face at the realization that he had seen her—*all* of her. With shaking hands, Isabelle lifted the goblet and drank deeply, praying for any measure of sustenance. She'd rather be dead than make a muddled idiot of herself in front of this man.

"I hope I have," he replied thoughtfully. "There was no way to keep you from being distressed in some measure, but Chris and I tried to plan for your comfort, as best we could. I didn't wish to give you greater reason to turn me—my request—aside." There was a chair on the other side of the fire, and he settled into it, wearily closing his eyes. "You are aware, I think, that if I am not wed within three—nay, two days, now, I will lose all that I possess? My lands, my holdings, everything." Opening his eyes, he gazed at her. "Even my horses and livestock. I must have a wife, my lady, else all that I have labored for will be lost to me. I do not care so much for myself, but there are others involved whom I do not wish to see brought low because of my misfortunes."

"But I can do naught to help you," Isabelle told him, lifting one hand in a placating gesture. "It is my cousin, Evelyn, whom you are to wed."

"Not so. She was the bride chosen for me by my brother and the duke of Gloucester, but in the missive I received regarding the matter, it was only stated that I must be married by the first day of July, not that I must be married to her."

"But Evelyn is ready to wed you. I know it has not seemed so, but she, and my uncle, always intended that it should be thus."

"Did they?" His smile was suddenly unpleasant. "I am glad they kept from agreeing to the marriage too soon, for I do not wish to wed your cousin, lovely though she may be."

"But, my lord," Isabelle protested, "neither can you wish to marry me! You know nothing of me, of my family. I have no dowry, indeed nothing to call my own save what my uncle has chosen to give me. It is impossible for me to marry any man."

"'Tis not impossible for you to wed me," he said, sitting on the edge of his chair and leaning toward her. "I have no care for who your parents were, and I do not require a dowry. If you will take me as I am, I will take you, and gladly. I am no great lord, but my home is sufficient, and we could live well and comfortably."

Isabelle's head was spinning. He couldn't mean the

things he was saying. It was impossible. Absolutely impossible.

"My lord, I pray you will be serious, and cease speaking such foolishness. Surely there is another, or many others, whom you would more readily choose."

"Nay," he said bluntly. "Only you. Let us speak the truth with each other. Do you wish to continue living under your uncle's hand?"

The question set her off balance, and Isabelle stared at him in silence.

He held her gaze unwaveringly. "He treats you like a servant. He dresses you in servant's clothes. His own niece. I have never heard him speak a kind or gentle word to you. The chamber that was yours—" he hesitated when she lowered her eyes, and when he continued, his tone was more gentle "—it was in the servants' quarters. Small and spare. And cold. I cannot fathom why he should treat you so ill, when he is blessed with more than enough wealth to easily treat you better. Especially when you continuously labor on his behalf."

It's only pity, Isabelle. 'Tis why he's so kind, why he deigns to speak with you. Only pity...for a small, unsightly, insignificant mouse.

Evelyn's words came back full force, with stunning pain, and Isabelle murmured, "You pity me. You wish to marry me out of pity."

He moved so silently that Isabelle hadn't realized it until he was kneeling before her, lifting her chin in his hand so that her eyes met his.

"God's truth, nay. It is so that I did not want a wife, but if I must have one, I would have her come to our marriage with cause of her own, wanting as much as I to make what we can of it. Lady Evelyn has no need of me, no reason to build a life with a man forced upon her against her wishes. But you might. Would you not like to have your own household to manage? Would you not like to be free of your uncle's hand? To wed, to have children of your own? If you marry me, Lady Isabelle, I vow that I shall do all I can to make your life happy and content. We can be partners in all things, and can build a good life together. My home, Talwar, is a small estate, not grand, as your uncle's palace is, but it is sturdy and comfortable, and the surrounding land is a goodly place for raising children. I am not an esteemed lord, as I have told you, but I have enough that you, and any children we give life to, shall never know hunger or discomfort.''

He was a stunningly beautiful man, and the knowledge struck Isabelle even more firmly as he gazed at her. His face was perfect, save for a scar above his brow and a smaller one on his cheek, but neither detracted from the wide set and alluring darkness of his ale-brown eyes, or the aristocratic line of his nose, or the tilt and fullness of his lips. His hair, as richly dark as his eyes, hung thick and waving to his shoulders, which in themselves were amazing to behold. She had never seen a nobleman with such a large, muscular form as Sir Justin Baldwin possessed. He looked more like a hard-laboring smithy than a knight of the realm.

"But why me?" Isabelle shook her head in disbelief. "There must be so many others—"

"Nay," he said once more. "There are not. And if there were, I've no time to find and woo them." Taking the goblet from her unsteady clasp and setting it aside, he gathered her hands up in his. "We would do well together, my lady. I admit that 'tis a strange way to start a marriage, but if we are good and truthful to each other and strive to make what we can of our union, there is no reason why it cannot be as happy and fruitful as other marriages are."

It wasn't right, she thought. Here he was, so handsome and fine that he could have any woman in the world, asking *her* to be his wife.

"There are things about me that you do not know," she

said with open misery. "My family has long been loyal to France. Four years ago, my father was convicted as a traitor." She searched his face for the revulsion she had thought would appear, but his dark-eyed gaze neither faltered nor changed. "He was executed, and all of his lands and possessions were taken from my family. My mother died soon after. Of shame."

A frown settled on his handsome face, and after a moment he ventured, "Gaillard? Isabelle Gaillard? Your father was the Comte Gaillard?"

"The comte was my uncle in France. His titles and properties have since been reclaimed by the crown. My father lived in England, for my mother's sake. He oversaw the Gaillard lands here."

Understanding lit his features. "Ignace Gaillard. Was that your father? Lord Lomas?"

She nodded.

"And your mother was Baron Hersell's sister? Is that how you come to be beneath his hand?"

"Aye. She was his half sister, through her mother." Lowering her eyes to their joined hands, marveling on how strange it was to have any physical contact at all with this man, she said, "And so you understand, my lord, that it is impossible for us to wed."

"Nay, my lady, I do not. I would be honored to have such a wellborn woman for a wife. Will our children not be blessed to receive such a noble heritage?"

Children, she thought. How beautiful his children would be, especially if they took after him, with hair and eyes the color of dark, rich earth.

"But your family would be distressed to have you wedded with the daughter of a traitor."

"My family has no say. After what they have done to me in this matter, I have no care for their sensibilities. I have said that I would be honored to wed one so nobly born, and so do I mean it. I will never speak lies to you,

Isabelle.'' He pressed her hands more firmly. "Will you marry me?"

"It is so sudden. I...I must think on it."

"I fear there is little time for such. Your uncle will be after us soon, if he is not already. 'Twill not be difficult for him to follow after and find us. The men who let us pass through Bishopsgate will readily tell in which direction we rode, especially if Sir Myles pays them well. After that he need only stop at each village on the road to ask whether we passed through, and that will lead him directly here. We must be wed very shortly, before he arrives. Within the hour, i' faith."

"But I do not have his permission to wed. I cannot marry without it."

"What I lack in personal esteem," he told her, "I possess in family influence. One of my brothers is a priest, and he is here and will marry us. Once the marriage is consummated, your uncle would not be able to remove you from my care, unless he went to the duke of Gloucester to have the union annulled." He smiled. "The duke will shortly receive missives from my brothers, the lord of Gyer and the earl of Siere, both of whom will request that the marriage stand as legal. I cannot think even the king's regent will wish to anger two such powerful men as they are."

"C-consummated?" she repeated with a gulp. "Here? *Now?*"

His soft laughter seemed to shiver all the way through Isabelle.

"You needn't worry about that until after you've agreed to wed with me." With a gentle, reassuring squeeze of her hands, he added, "In truth, you needn't worry about it at all. I will never hurt you, Isabelle."

"My brother," she said, thinking suddenly of Senet. "I cannot leave him alone in my uncle's authority. He is but

ten-and-six, and Sir Myles has no care for him, except as
a way of keeping me from being disobedient.''

"Ah," Justin said. "I begin to understand the reason
for your devoted service to your uncle. Your brother will
come to us, then. He has been fostered with Sir Howton,
has he not?'' When Isabelle nodded, he said, "I will continue to train him for knighthood, just as Sir Howton has
done, and he will have all that we can give him to make
his way.''

Isabelle leaned forward. "My lord, do you mean this?''

"On my honor, before God, I vow it.''

The door to the chamber opened, and both Isabelle and
Justin turned. A tall blond man, dressed in brown robes
and bearing a large steaming bowl, entered.

"God's mercy,'' he said, having contemplated them for
a silent moment. "I never in my life expected to see you
on your knees before any woman, Justin. You're clearly
more desperate than I understood. Have you convinced
Lady Isabelle to become your willing wife, or are you yet
trying to persuade her?'' Walking farther into the chamber,
he set the bowl on a low table. "I've brought food,'' he
stated, and stood to his full height, smiling down at Isabelle. "My dear, you are the most welcome sight I've had
in many a year.''

"Hugo,'' Justin said warmly, standing and hugging the
other man. "'Tis good and better to see you again.''

"Aye, and so it is,'' the priest replied, returning the
embrace. "Be pleased to introduce me to Lady Isabelle,
brother.''

"My lady, this is my brother, Father Hugo. He is going
to wed us.''

"*If* Lady Isabelle is willing,'' Father Hugo added, moving forward to take Isabelle's hand. With a warm smile,
he bent and kissed her fingers. "My lady,'' he murmured,
"I am honored. Justin sent me an urgent missive regarding

you, and it is with great pleasure that I meet the woman who has finally captured my youngest brother's heart.''

He was too handsome to be a priest, Isabelle thought. And far too admiring. She could feel herself turning red all the way up to the roots of her hair. "Oh, no, Father, I fear you misunderstand. 'Tis only that he must wed to keep his lands. I've not captured Sir Justin's heart, or any part of him.''

The look that possessed the handsome priest's face reminded Isabelle of nothing so much as the pleased way her uncle looked when he saw the profits mounting up in his account books. Beneath his interested scrutiny she felt, for a moment, like a vastly valuable treasure. "That, my very dear lady,'' said Father Hugo, "remains to be seen. And so—'' he again stood full height "—have you decided which road you'll take? Are you going to marry this knave and go with him to Talwar, or shall I send for your uncle to come and escort you back to London? For me, I should advise trying the first. From what Justin's written me, you've already tried the latter without much satisfaction. Or is he mistaken?''

"Nay,'' she admitted softly, drawing Justin's warm cloak more firmly about her. "'Twas not pleasant to live beneath my uncle's hand.''

"Then you may as well try marrying my brother,'' Father Hugo suggested cheerfully, rubbing his hands together. "He's not perfect, i' faith, but I can promise he's better than most. If he's not good to you, you need only send word and I'll come and make him behave.'' He grinned at his younger brother. "I give my vow on that. Now, what say you? Shall I lend my blessing to a wedding this night?''

Justin's gaze held Isabelle's, questioning. She drew in a long breath and released it shakily. With a nod, she committed herself to a new, unknown life. "Aye. You shall.''

Chapter Four

The marriage took place as soon as Isabelle had been given a chance to eat and clothe herself. Surrounded by men—Sir Christian and several silent, solemn monks—she stood beside Sir Justin Baldwin in the monastery's small chapel and agreed to be his wife. It should have been, she thought afterward, a moment that carried a certain amount of weight, joy or fear or some life-changing impact. But it had been nothing more than a very simple matter. Sir Justin repeated his vows, put a plain gold ring on her finger and, having received it from his brother, passed the kiss of peace along to her by setting his lips briefly against her cheek. And so, in a matter of a few minutes, they were married. At least in the eyes of the Church. What her uncle would think about it, Isabelle wasn't able to imagine.

Father Hugo heartily hugged and kissed her when it was over, as did Sir Christian, who said, "You are a kind and beautiful lady, Isabelle Baldwin. Justin is a fortunate man, indeed. I pray God I will be as blessed someday."

Congratulatory cups of wine were passed and drunk, and then, too soon, Justin was taking hold of her elbow and saying, "There is not much time before daylight. We will bid you all good-night."

Isabelle had never felt so embarrassed in all her life,

standing before a roomful of holy men who surely realized Sir Justin's intent to consummate the marriage.

Father Hugo, setting a reassuring hand on Isabelle's shoulder, said, "Go and tend to this final matter, then, knowing that God has blessed your union. We will send no witnesses with you, for Lady Isabelle should not suffer further distress this night, when she has already so generously done all that has been asked of her." He must have heard the breath of relief that she released, for he smiled warmly and kissed her cheek. "God be with you, daughter. Go now with your husband." To Justin, he added, "I trust you will take every care with your good lady, brother."

"Aye," Justin replied simply, pulling Isabelle toward the door and not seeming to notice how stiffly she went.

"Well," she said as they walked side by side down the darkened hall. "Well."

He chuckled and said, "Indeed."

When he suddenly put his hand on her waist, she nearly jumped into a wall.

"Forgive me," she murmured. "I fear that I'm a little...unused to this." Which was, she thought, a rather weak way of saying that she'd never so much as kissed a man.

His hand pressed against her with light warmth. "There is no need to ask forgiveness, Isabelle. You have never known a man and are afraid. 'Tis understandable, i' faith."

He stopped before the chamber door, which he opened, stepping back to allow her to enter. A simple room had never looked so awful to Isabelle before. She cast a glance at the bed and imagined herself there, beneath this man, her husband, as he made her his wife.

"Come, Isabelle." He took her hand and drew her farther in, closing the door. "Let us have an understanding." Turning her unresisting body by the shoulders as if she were a powerless puppet, he drew her near. "We are all but strangers, you and I, and yet we are also man and wife. I would have you strive to trust me in all things, just as I will strive to trust you.'' He brushed her cheek with the backs of his fingers, gently. ''But such as that will take time, and I would not repay the kindness you have done me this night by forcing you to lie with me before you are willing. When I make you my wife complete, 'twill be because you wish it, and because you have come to trust me. Is this as you would have it, Isabelle?''

''Oh, aye,'' she said with open relief, thankful for a reprieve. ''You are kind, Sir Justin, and I am more than grateful.''

He nodded. ''We will wait until we have achieved Talwar, then, and when you are ready to become my wife in every way, you will let me know. Only promise that it will not be long, for make no mistake—I mean us to be man and wife in every way, and for that I will suffer impatience.''

Isabelle swallowed loudly. '''Twill not be long,'' she promised.

''Then we must now make an agreement between us. I abhor falseness in any form, but even more would I abhor forcing you to an intimacy you do not yet desire. Your uncle will demand proof of our union. You understand this, do you not?''

''Aye.''

''Then, if you wish to have time to know your husband better before you share his bed, you must be prepared to answer accordingly. This thing will be between the two of us only.''

Stepping back, he rolled up the long sleeve of his tunic, uncovering his muscular forearm, then strode to the bed and pulled the covers away to expose the stark whiteness of the sheets beneath.

He paused a moment and looked at Isabelle, who stared

at him in incomprehension until he pulled a small dagger from a sheath at his belt.

"My lord…" she said, as if she would stop him.

"'Tis the only way," he said. "Unless you wish to pursue the matter in the more usual manner?"

Without waiting for an answer, he drew the blade across his skin, on the inner arm, beneath his elbow. Red blood welled bright, and when he held his arm over the bed, a few drops fell. He smeared them with his fingers, then stood back and viewed the stain he'd made.

"I've no experience with virgins," he admitted. "I pray that will be sufficient to satisfy your uncle, and any others who may challenge our marriage."

Isabelle was searching the chamber for a cloth, and at last found a linen napkin. "Here," she said, taking his bleeding arm. "Let me bind the wound. I pray it will heal readily."

"It will," he murmured, smiling as she bent over her work to tie the cloth tightly. "You are a good wife, already," he said. "Taking care of me so. I like it very much. Isabelle?" She lifted her head, and he took her chin in his free hand. "If you will let me, I shall kiss you as a husband should properly do." He didn't wait for permission, but placed his mouth gently over hers and tenderly kissed her, meaning only to give her pleasure and affection. When he lifted his head, he saw, with delight, that she looked dazed.

"Did you like it?" he asked.

She nodded and closed her eyes, and he willingly accepted the offer, lowering his mouth to hers once more, kissing her as chastely as he could, until he felt his body begin to catch fire.

"If we do not stop," he murmured against her lips, "we will be adding proof to the bedsheet." With regret, he stepped away from her warmth and softness. "'Tis verily most promising." He bent and pulled the bedcovers over the stained sheet. "You are full weary, I vow. Lie down and sleep, my lady, and in the morn, if your uncle has not arrived, we will leave for Siere."

"For Siere?" Isabelle repeated, gratefully sinking down upon the bed.

"Aye." He rolled the sleeve of his tunic over the binding she'd put on his wound. "I must present you to my brother, the earl, and make certain that my lands are safe."

She sat up again. "Your brother...when he knows the truth about my father..."

"He will have naught to say on the matter," Justin replied calmly. He sat on the bed and pushed her down on the pillows. "You are my wife now, Isabelle, and I will not give you up. No man will take you from me, be he your uncle or mine own brother or the duke of Gloucester. In time, you will learn to trust me. It is all that I ask of you." With his fingertips, he stroked the hair from her brow. "You have been through much this night. Sleep, if you can. All will be well."

"What of you, my lord? You must be very weary, also."

"In truth, I am. I will sleep there, by the fire, for a time."

"If my uncle comes, will you tell him about Senet?"

"Aye. Is there anything you want from your uncle's home? Any possessions of your own that you value and would have?"

Sadness touched her features, and Justin's hand, yet stroking the hair at her forehead, fell still.

"What is it?" he asked.

"He will never let me have them. And, in truth, all that once belonged to my parents was made forfeit by the crown. Baron Hersell has more right to them than I."

His hand began stroking again. "We shall see."

Weariness made her close her eyes. "I do not wish to

cause you trouble.'' She yawned. ''It is enough to be away from him.''

'''Twill be no trouble. You should have all that is rightfully yours, and though it may be many months in coming, one day you shall.''

But she had already fallen asleep beneath the soothing rhythm of his hand, and didn't hear his vow. Justin sat beside her for a long while, contemplating his new wife and stroking her silky black hair, which was, he thought, extraordinarily long and beautiful. Her blue eyes, which he also thought beautiful, ever stood out starkly against the frame of her hair. When they first met, he had found it difficult to pull his gaze away from her entrancing face. He was not a man to take anything for granted, and he did not do so now with Isabelle. He had done very well in choosing himself a wife, he thought with pleasure. Far better than his brother Hugh had done. Of a certainty, Hugh would be furious when he discovered the truth, as would Alexander, and Hugo would equally fall victim to their wrath for his part in lending his aid in the marriage. But, although he regretted bringing Hugo grief, Justin didn't really care. He had the wife he wanted now—a good, fine wife, for whom other men would envy him— and they would make a life together whether his exalted family bade them well or no.

Chapter Five

She was dreaming that her dreams were real. The man she loved was her husband, and they had the most beautiful children—two boys and a sweet tiny girl—and he loved her. They were walking beside a wide, slow-moving river, their children running before, playing and laughing, and he took her hand. She turned her head and smiled, and he, so handsome and fine, smiled back. She could read his love for her in his eyes. It was there, as clear and constant as the river. She knew the feel of his mouth on hers, the warm, sweet pressure. He loved her, and her heart was full of the knowledge.

"You'll not keep me from searching the place! Get out of my way, holy man, else I'll *strike* you down."

The sound of her uncle's voice seared through her dreams like a blistering heat, and Isabelle sat bolt upright.

"Justin!" she cried, and the next moment his hands found her in the darkness.

"I'm here. Whisper. Take off your clothes and get under the covers. Hurry."

He began to tug at her lacings, and she pushed his hands away. "I'll do it," she insisted shakily and, with trembling fingers performed the task herself.

He stood and moved about the room; she could hear him throwing his boots off and putting on his sword.

"I wish I could remove my tunic," he murmured distractedly in the darkness.

"Where is the slut?" Her uncle's voice boomed louder. "Isabelle! Attend me!"

"Hurry," Justin said, sitting beside her again. "Nay, remove everything, Isabelle. Do not be afraid."

"But—"

Without warning, he took hold of her chemise and dragged it over her head, throwing the garment on the floor beside her other clothes.

"Now, under the covers. Nay, do not lie down yet. Help me, Isabelle." The warmth of his hands fell on her bare shoulders. "Kiss me," he murmured, already pressing hard, hot kisses rapidly against her face and neck. "We must look as if we've been loving. Put your arms around me, sweet. Your hands in my hair."

His mouth came down on hers then, open and moist, and his tongue pushed between her teeth to invade the depths of her mouth. Shocked, she tried to push him away, but he was solid and heavy, as if made of stone, and her distress went ignored. Pressing her down on the bed, he kissed her harder, until Isabelle felt tears of pain stinging her eyes. When he at last pulled away, she gasped for air, and tried to turn away, but he held her face between his palms and ran his tongue over her lips.

"Forgive me," he murmured, placing more stinging kisses on her face and neck.

Finally, as Sir Myles's angry voice neared their door, he thrust his hands into her thick, unbound hair, rapidly disordering it.

"Keep yourself covered," he commanded as he stood. "And trust me, Isabelle."

The next moment he had flung the chamber door open, and in the candlelight from the hallway Isabelle could see that he held his dagger in his hand. Her uncle appeared, his face first angry, and then, as Justin grabbed him by the collar, surprised. He began to say a word, but only air whooshed out of him as he was shoved up against the far wall with the dagger held against his throat.

"Now," Justin said into the other man's face, "did I hear you insult my good lady wife a moment ago, sir?"

"Aye!" Sir Myles sputtered wrathfully. "I'll name her slut and more, i' faith!" Craning his neck, he looked past Justin's broad shoulder until he saw Isabelle sitting in the bed, thoroughly disheveled and covered all the way up to her neck with bed linens. "Harlot!" he shouted furiously. "Jezebel! Ungrateful who—"

The last word died unfinished as Sir Myles choked.

"I will *kill* you for speaking thusly of my lady," Justin told him, seething, pressing the blade closer.

Suffocating, Sir Myles flapped his arms like a helpless bird. "Off," he managed, his bulging eyes pleading desperately with Father Hugo, who stood nearby. *"Off!"*

"That's enough, Justin," his elder brother said calmly. "I do not say he doesn't deserve death, but I'll not suffer murder within these sacred walls."

"Then I shall take him outside," Justin replied evenly.

"Where his men will kill you after you've finished with him. Nay." Father Hugo set a hand on his shoulder, attempting to pull him back. "I'll not let you be killed this night for such a one as this. Leave him be." When Justin gave no proof of hearing his words, he added, "Do you wish to make Lady Isabelle a widow so soon after she became a wife?"

"Nay," Justin admitted. He released Sir Myles and stepped back, warning, "Guard your tongue, and do not speak thus again, else I swear by heaven I will indeed kill you."

Sir Myles put a hand to his throat and breathed with loud relief. A moment passed before he was able to say,

"You—you stole her. You insulted my daughter, and me."

"I stole the wife I wanted," Justin said, "to this I admit. As to your daughter and yourself, I cannot think that any insult I may have given compared to that which was given me."

Sir Myles looked at him with renewed fury. "We gave you no insult! I was willing that my only daughter should become your wife. Evelyn has fully expected to wed you two days from this. How could you mar her name and reputation so? 'Tis worse than mere insult! And to steal my niece from my own home, while I slumbered. With the help of your bastard friend, Sir Christian Rowsenly." He said the name with sour disdain. "I never should have been so generous as to allow that illegitimate whoreson into my ho—"

The dagger went up again, and Sir Myles was once more thrown against the wall. This time Father Hugo had to use both arms around Justin's shoulders to pull him away.

"He's cut me!" Sir Myles cried with horror, pulling bloodied fingers from his throat. "He's—he's nearly killed me! My knights! Attend me!"

"Aye!" Justin snarled, amid a loud clattering in the hall. "And but for my brother, I should have done." He powerfully shoved Hugo away. "Call every man in your service, Sir Myles." Justin pulled his sword from its sheath, holding it skillfully in his other hand even as the blooded dagger twirled like a butterfly in the other. "'Twill do you no good. I will yet kill you, and happily." Raising his voice, he called, "Christian Rowsenly! Attend me!"

"I am here, my friend," Sir Christian said with placid calm as he strode through the crowd made by Sir Myles's men. "Unharmed and well, and wishing you would be less ready to take insults that belong to me." Turning to smile at Isabelle, who was trembling with the awareness that she was starkly naked beneath the bed linens, he said with more gentle reassurance, "My lady, you would do as well to return to your slumbers. This is an interesting display, i'faith, but naught shall come to harm you."

"I want no fight," Sir Myles said. "My niece has proved her ingratitude this night for the years of care that she and her brother have received at my hand, yet I am willing to take her back. Whatever ceremony took place here this night will be annulled, and you may consider your betrothal to my daughter forever broken, Sir Justin."

At this, Justin laughed. "I considered it well broken many days ago, when I realized the game that you and your daughter played upon me. I came to you with honor, and you treated me with naught but contempt. Worse, you sought to steal my lands for yourself by making them a payment for your daughter's hand. But now, my lord, you will suffer the game I have chosen. I have done the stealing, and your niece is my wife. *Mine,* Sir Myles. You will not have her back."

Sir Myles turned nearly white. "I must have Isabelle back."

"So that she may continue to increase your wealth?" Justin asked pointedly, laughing again when Sir Myles's mouth fell open. "Oh, aye, I've learned much about you these past many days, my lord. All that you have has come to you through Isabelle's efforts. You have made her like a slave to gain riches. Now I am the one who shall enjoy her talents, who will have the benefit of the skills she possesses. She will make me rich in ways you've not yet begun to fathom."

"Nay! You'll not!" Sir Myles sputtered. "I'll go to the duke and demand her return. I am her legal guardian, and she did not have my permission to wed. 'Tis all illegal!"

"Is it?" Justin asked, sheathing both his sword and dagger with equally fluid movements. "We shall see." He turned and strode back into the chamber, not stopping until he had reached Isabelle and scooped her, bed linens and all, into his arms and out of the bed. "Look!" he said, his tone daring. "Look and see. I have taken Isabelle as my wife before the Church, and in the way of men. The proof is here, my lord. Can you think the duke will deny it? The law requires nothing more than Isabelle's unforced consent in the matter, and every man who attended our marriage— and Isabelle herself—will attest that she was willing."

Sir Myles stepped into the chamber, staring at the blood-stained sheet as if it were a horror. "You stole her," he repeated weakly. "It cannot stand as legal." He lifted wide eyes to gaze at his niece. "Isabelle, you must come back. Have you no care for Senet?" His meaning was clear.

"You threaten my wife at your peril, my lord," Justin warned in a low voice. "I have never asked my brother, Alexander of Gyer, for anything in my life, but on the morrow I will send him a missive, asking him to use every power he possesses to have Senet Gaillard put into my guardianship. You will know that the lord of Gyer is a man who is not denied what he asks for by either crown or regent. Until Senet is under my hand, you will treat him well, or suffer facing the king's regent with my complaints regarding your care of him."

Sir Myles began to shake. He clamped his trembling hands together in an effort to still them, but when he took another step toward Isabelle, he only appeared to be pleading. "Isabelle, you must come back with me! I'll give you anything. Do anything. Evelyn will be kind. I swear it. You can't want to go with this man. He doesn't care for you. 'Tis only your ways with money that he wants. Can't you see that?"

Isabelle saw it. She'd heard Sir Justin openly proclaim the fact before everyone present, while she sat in the bed and felt as if someone had speared her with a jousting lance. She'd been more than a fool to dream that he might want her for herself, that he might care for her, to let herself believe that he'd spoken the truth when he called her beautiful. Now, held in his arms—not with the value of a person, but only as a prize to be fought for—she was filled with pain. She knew what she must look like, naked beneath the covers, marked and reddened from Sir Justin's kisses, with that deceitful stain on the bed. Mortified at what all who saw her would think, shamed by her foolishness, she wished she could crawl into a hole and hide. But there wasn't a hole anywhere nearby, and so Isabelle took the only refuge she had at hand, closing her eyes and burying her face against her husband's hard shoulder.

Justin's arms tightened about her. "You've had your answer, my lord. Now go."

"Think, Isabelle!" Sir Myles persisted desperately. "Only think. You're no better with him than you were with me. Do you think he'll make anything but a slave of you? Evelyn and I offer you the ties of blood, of family. And matters will change, I vow it! I'll give you a house, and servants of your own. Senet will live with you, as it pleases you. I'll hire tutors for the lad, and buy his knighthood when the time comes. Isabelle," he pleaded. "Please come back with me!"

It was true, she thought, pressing a fist against her eyes to keep the tears from spilling out. She was only exchanging one master for another, going from one place of labor to another. But Sir Justin, at least, had shown her kindnesses that had not been necessary. He'd done everything he could not to distress her. And he had told Sir Myles that Senet would come to them at Talwar—if he had lied about other things, at least he'd not lied about that.

"I'll *not* go back," she managed, weeping. "I will go with Sir Justin."

"Isabelle!"

"Nay!" Justin cut him off. "No more. You will not

torment her further. Leave now. I do not merely ask it of you. Go.''

An angry silence filled the room.

"Very well," Sir Myles said at last. "I will take my men and leave. But heed me, Sir Justin Baldwin. I'll have Isabelle back. I swear it by all that is holy. And you'll come to regret this night and your vile deeds. You will, sir. You *will*."

When he had left, Justin sat on the bed, cradling a silent Isabelle in his arms.

"A dangerous man," Father Hugo commented. "Beware him, Justin, and keep control of your temper. As God's holy word tells us, 'Be slow to wrath, for the wrath of man does not produce the righteousness of God.'"

"But it does get rid of Sir Myles," Justin replied wearily.

"What do we do now?" Christian asked. "Would it not be wise to make for Siere?"

"Aye." Justin turned his gaze upon Isabelle, who still had her eyes closed against his shoulder, although he knew she did not sleep. "Would that we could rest longer," he murmured. "But we cannot." To Christian he said, "We will clothe ourselves and make the horses ready, and then we will ride full haste for Siere, where I will have much to say to my brother the earl."

Chapter Six

Siere was, for Isabelle, a daunting place. Everything about it was grand, as well as on a grand scale. The castle was enormous, with so many stairs and hallways and chambers that Isabelle commonly got lost. The land surrounding the castle was vast, stretching so far that, even when Justin took her to the castle's highest tower and pointed out the direction of the borders, she'd not been able to see the end of it. The town of Siere was really a bustling city and, from the personal wealth of the earl and his lady, Isabelle realized that local commerce must be quite healthy.

Isabelle knew the signs of prosperity when she saw them, just as she knew and understood bankers, money-lenders, traders and businessmen. It took a calm, sure hand to manipulate all of those involved to bring about a city's financial success, and Isabelle was filled with admiration for the one who'd guided Siere along just such a path. Sir Hugh, the earl of Siere, had smiled at Isabelle's shy compliments on the matter and revealed that it was his wife, Lady Rosaleen, who managed Siere and made every major decision. "I'm only here to make speeches," he told her, "and to keep the children occupied when their mother wants some rest. Otherwise, I'm nothing more than the

official bedfellow.'' This he accompanied with a smile so
meaningful that even the memory made Isabelle's cheeks
burn. Of course, it wasn't all true. Lady Rosaleen might
be the one who actually had the managing of Siere, and
did it very capably, but it was Sir Hugh who ruled. He
was an estimable lord, seeming to know everything without being told, heading off trouble before it occurred, always saying the right word at the right moment. Isabelle
had only been at Siere for a week, but in that time she'd
seen Sir Hugh deftly handle a number of his citizen's complaints with the ease and wisdom of a Solomon, and she
had yet to see one person leave the castle whose anger
hadn't been transposed into calm.

The earl had a gift for putting people at ease, which
Isabelle had experienced firsthand when she arrived at
Siere and Justin introduced her to Sir Hugh and his wife.
Exhausted from the long ride, and weary from the rapid
experiences of being kidnapped and married in only a matter of hours, Isabelle had only stared when the earl of Siere
sauntered toward her with a welcoming smile on his lips.
It had taken several long moments before she was able to
mumble some kind of reply, and then, as he stood holding
her cold fingers in his engulfing hand, he'd chuckled with
warm amusement and said, to Justin, ''I gather that you've
not yet explained about Hugo and me being twins. The
poor girl probably thinks that her wits have wandered
away.'' Which was exactly what Isabelle had thought, at
least until Justin explained why it was that the priest who
had married them and the earl of Siere looked to be the
same man.

Sir Hugh had seemingly received the news of Justin's
bringing a different bride to Siere from the one that had
been chosen for him with ease, giving no more evidence
of surprise than the slight lifting of one eyebrow, and yet
Isabelle was wary. He had been all that was kind this past
week, but she had seen him contemplating her often, with

a silent, seeking regard, and it was clear that very little escaped those piercing green eyes. A silent tension existed between himself and Justin, as well, and if the earl wondered why his brother and his brother's new wife didn't share a bedchamber, he never voiced the question aloud. At least, not in Isabelle's hearing.

Lady Rosaleen, fortunately, was a much less bewildering presence. Beautiful, forthright and kind, she had immediately accepted Isabelle as her sister-by-marriage, and had done everything possible to make her comfortable.

"Don't let Hugh rattle you, my dear," she'd said when she took Isabelle to her chamber. "Baldwins tend to be rather intense, and my husband has the added difficulty of being a dreadful meddler. If there's any trouble to be gotten into, Hugh will be the first to get into it. He's not quite as serious-minded as Sir Alexander and Justin are, however, so perhaps that makes up for some of it. Not," she'd added quickly, glancing at Isabelle with a smile, "that there's anything wrong with being serious-minded. Justin is a marvelous man in every way, including his sober nature. But I don't need to tell you that, do I, my dear? Do you love him very much?"

She did, and, sitting before her chamber fire, she'd admitted it, and everything else, to a sympathetic Lady Rosaleen.

"I don't know how it came to be," she said miserably, setting her weary head into her hands. "All the time he was courting Evelyn I loved him, and even now, when I know he only wed me to save his lands and to...to further his own gains, I love him. Evelyn spoke truly when she said that he would be horrified to know of my regard. I am a fool."

"Oh, nay, never," Lady Rosaleen assured her gently, setting a comforting hand on Isabelle's shoulder. "You are weary and distressed, and upset at being taken forcibly from your home and married so shortly after, just as any

woman should be, but you are *not* a fool. I cannot say why
Justin has done what he has, but you may believe that he
would not have taken you unless he held you in some
regard. It may be, my dear, that he cares for you more
than you think.''

But Isabelle found that hard to believe, despite Justin's
continually courteous and gentle manner toward her. She
had only to look in her mirror to see that her face, so plain
and common, couldn't compare to her cousin's, or Lady
Rosaleen's, or those of most other women. It certainly
wasn't the sort of face to inspire love. And as to the rest
of her…well, Isabelle supposed that the most generous
thing that could be said about her was that she was kindhearted. But that, matched with her temper, was probably
far from sufficient to cause any man to want her. And there
was always her unfortunate love of mathematics to consider. Although her skill with numbers was considered
well enough in the way of increasing fortunes, it was seldom a topic that men cared to discuss, especially with a
woman. Only her uncle's bankers and financial associates
had found discussions with Isabelle enthralling, and they
were hardly the sort of men Isabelle wanted to enthrall.
Her husband, now…her husband, she wanted to enthrall,
to entice, somehow…to make him desire her the way he
had probably desired Evelyn. *But how?* she wondered, setting aside the needlework on which she'd spent the past
hour laboring.

The castle was quiet during the afternoons, when the
midday meal had been finished and cleared away. In the
great hall, where the castle ladies gathered to gossip and
ply their needles while the sun yet shone through the tall,
clear windows, servants moved with quiet ease, perform-
ing their tasks with the same efficiency that was to be
found everywhere in Castle Siere. Indeed, not just the castle, but Siere as a whole, seemed to work with all the
elegant beauty of a carillon bell clock.

She was waiting for Justin, just as he had asked her to, just as she did every afternoon. Each day at this time he took her for a walk in the gardens, or sometimes along the river, because, he had said, "We must come to know each other better."

These had been wonderful times for Isabelle, partly because it had been so many years since she had not had to spend her every waking hour inside her uncle's house, laboring over his accounts, and partly because her husband was such an amiable companion. He had not insisted upon any of his husbandly rights during the week that they'd been at Siere, but he was affectionate nonetheless. Surprisingly enough, he liked to walk with her in the same manner that Isabelle's parents had done, which was to link his hand and fingers with hers, rather than to simply offer her his arm to hold. The first time he took her hand in such a manner, Isabelle had been so nervous that she felt her palm growing distressingly damp, and her fingers had been so stiff that they ached, but he had not seemed to notice, although he had loosened his grip slightly, and after a few minutes she'd begun to accept the intimate clasp and relaxed. Sometimes he would embrace her lightly, briefly, and kiss her cheek, doing it without warning and so suddenly that it was over before Isabelle had any chance to respond. Afterward, he would gaze at her in an oddly warm manner before taking her hand in his again and resuming their walk.

Leaning her head back in her chair, Isabelle contemplated the great hall's ceiling. It might be another hour or more before Justin returned from the village, where he had gone with Sir Christian and the earl, and she was weary of needlework. The truth of the matter was, she missed her account books. Oh, she knew they were really her uncle's, but in four years they had come to seem like hers. She knew each one intimately, from the first entry to the last, from every mistaken inkblot she'd made to every crease in the leather bindings. She had filled each page with meticulous care, had tallied every column twice, had... *God's mercy!* Isabelle sat upright, with a hand to her forehead. She must be mad! If Evelyn could only hear her thoughts now, she would laugh long and loud. And with good cause, Isabelle thought with a groan. If anyone could be charged as dull, it was she, Isabelle, and not Justin. She would probably bore her handsome husband into weariness before a year's time was out, God help her.

"Have you an ache, my lady?"

Isabelle dropped her hand to gaze at Lady Rosaleen, who stood before her with her young son, Lord Farron, tucked firmly in one arm.

"Oh, nay," Isabelle replied foolishly. "I was only...thinking."

"Ah," said Lady Rosaleen, seating herself in the chair beside Isabelle's. "I must have looked very similar whenever I used to think of Hugh, before we were wed. We had an exhausting courtship. But that seems to be the way the Baldwin men carry out such things. Sir Alexander held his wife prisoner for many weeks before marrying her to gain her dowered lands, Hugh forced me to labor as a servant at his estate for three months before we were wed, and Justin kidnapped you." Lady Rosaleen laughed. "Poor Willem is the only brother among them who managed to be a gentleman, and he was finally ensnared in marriage to a lady who decided she wanted him for a husband. And a good thing it was, else he'd never have married at all."

Isabelle laughed, too. "Justin has told me some of these stories before. I think I have been the lucky one, after all that you and Lady Lillis went through."

"Aye, s'truth," Lady Rosaleen agreed. "Justin has ever been the most considerate of the men, certainly when it comes to women."

"Father Hugo seemed very kind," Isabelle noted.

At this, Rosaleen shook her head. "Hugo, like his twin brother, loves women. *All* women, regardless of age or condition. I've seen those two charm young girls and elderly grandmothers with but a smile, the rogues. I'll *never* understand how Hugo has managed to stay in the Church all these years. He's worse than Hugh, at times."

Remembering the warm, appreciative gaze that Father Hugo had eyed her with at the monastery, Isabelle had to agree.

"Are you still worrying, my dear, over why Justin wed you?" Lady Rosaleen asked.

Isabelle's smile died, and she lowered her eyes. "Aye," she whispered. "I know I should not care so much, for I can give him what he wants of me. I have just been thinking of how I miss working with my uncle's accounts. 'Twill be good to have some to work on again soon."

"You have not known Justin long, as I have," Lady Rosaleen said gently, "but if you had, you would be reassured, and would know that it is not wealth he wants you for. I have never seen him look at another woman the way he looks at you, with such tenderness and affection. And I have never seen him so content, either, despite his current anger with my husband."

Isabelle lifted her head. "He has seemed angered with Sir Hugh. Is it because of me that they quarrel?"

"Not you, nay, but with matters that may have concerned you at one time. I do not think any man would like to be commanded to wed, do you?"

With a thoughtful frown, Isabelle replied, "He did not seem displeased to wed Evelyn until she and my uncle were so foolish as to give him insult. But for that, he would have married her."

"Would he?" Lady Rosaleen asked. "I do not know if that is true. But let us speak of the matter no more, for I've no desire to test how red you can go." She laughed lightly when Isabelle reddened even further. "My dear, if you have missed working with numbers, would you like to entertain yourself with some of my accounts? I should be exceedingly glad to let you work with any or all of them, I vow, for although I enjoy working them, as well, I've not much time to do so since this little one was born.'' She smiled lovingly at her sleeping son. ''Robert, the steward, once suggested that I give Farron over to the care of a nurse, and Hugh nearly took a whip to him, but he spoke the truth. With Kathryn and Harry just babies yet, and Galen so active—'' at this, she uttered a long sigh ''—I've not much time left for Siere, as I used to. 'Tis a blessing Hugh is so willing to lend me aid.''

''Robert does not care to take over the task?''

''Oh, aye, he does, just as he wishes to take over *every* task, God bless his efficient soul, but he has enough to do in keeping Hugh out of trouble, I fear. 'Twould be unjust to make him do the accounting, as well. I suppose I should let him hire a treasurer, but I've always had the keeping of my own accounts and have never desired assistance until now. Any help that you might be ready to give, dear Isabelle...''

''Oh, aye, my lady,'' Isabelle said at once. ''I should be most glad to repay your kindness to me in any way that I can.''

The countess of Siere smiled warmly. ''Then go to the working chamber that I share with my husband, and see what may be done with the accounts. Stay for as long as you are happy, and when the work grows tiresome, put it away. You have my permission to work there as often as it pleases you, save when my husband is there. I know he would welcome your company, i' faith, but his language is so unchristian at times that I'd never expose you, or any gentlelady, to it.''

It was, for Isabelle, a boon too good to believe. She nearly dropped her needlework as she quickly stood.

"Thank you, my lady," she said gratefully. "Is there anything urgent that needs tending, in particular?"

"The rents are far behind," Lady Rosaleen said thoughtfully, "as are the livestock accounts. Don't touch the household books, however, for Robert does keep those, and most jealously."

"Will you please tell Justin where I am if he should come looking for me?"

Lady Rosaleen nodded and smiled. "I'll tell him. Do not worry on it."

"Robert," said Sir Hugh as he walked into his working chamber, carrying his sleeping daughter in his arms. "Well met. Lady Kate had the audacity to fall asleep while being admired in the village. Can you imagine such a thing?"

Setting down the pen with which he'd been writing, the steward rose from his table. "Good day, my lord," he said, adding, when Justin, holding one of his nephews by the hand, followed his brother into the room, "And also to you, my lord, Sir Justin. May I hope you have at *last* come to discuss important matters?"

"No, you may not," the earl said affably. "We've come to have a friendly, brotherly chat—"

"Oh, have we?" Justin asked with bemusement.

"We have," his brother assured him. "And we won't require a legate, as I'm certain we'll not resort to violence. If we do, we won't need witnesses, either. Be pleased to take Katy and Harry to their nurses, Robert."

Gazing at the small bundle in his master's arms, Robert gave a disdainful sniff. "*Really*, my lord. You cannot mean it. And we *must* discuss these matters." He picked up several pieces of parchment from the table. "The duke demands a reply, as does Sir Alexander, and Sir Myles is threatening to be very disagreeable if he doesn't have some satisfaction soon."

"Sir Myles," said Justin, "may take himself to Hades. I would be happy to aid him in the task."

"Justin…" Hugh said in a warning tone. Then, with a sigh, went on, "Very well. We'll discuss matters. Now please take Katy and Harry to their nurses." He didn't wait for a reply, but set his sleeping child in his steward's unready hands.

"But, my lord!" Robert sputtered indignantly.

"She's only a babe," the earl chided, carefully arranging his daughter's head against Robert's shoulder. "What grave harm could she visit upon you?" With tender affection, he bent to kiss the child's forehead, then straightened and looked his steward directly in the eye. "Never say you're ashamed to be seen carrying my children, Robert?"

The insult hit its intended course, and Robert's nose lifted sharply. "I will never understand your strange sense of humor, my lord," he said, "and I was not aware that my duties included being a *children's* maid." He gave an imperious humph and took young Harry's hand. "Come along, Lord Harold." As he walked out the door, he called back, "If you don't have replies ready for me to send this evening, I'll stand outside your bedchamber door *all* night."

Justin shook his head as Hugh closed the door.

"Alexander would never put up with such familiarity in a servant, you know."

Hugh chuckled and went to pour wine from a nearby decanter. "Alexander can afford to be stiff-necked. If it weren't for Robert, I'd have been committed to an asylum long ago. Will you have wine?"

Justin gave his brother a considering look. "Perhaps. How long is our 'friendly, brotherly chat' to last?"

The earl of Siere filled a goblet for his brother and handed it to him.

"That all depends on you, I think. You might as well say what you've been wanting to these past many days.

I've considered beating it out of you, but somehow the idea of trying to explain that to Rosaleen doesn't appeal."

Justin, smiling grimly, only shook his head again.

"God save me," Sir Hugh said. "I suppose I'll have the headache when this is done. Very well, then I'll say it." Placing his goblet on a low table, he lazily settled his long body into a comfortable chair. "You're angry with me for meddling in your life."

"Angry?" Justin repeated.

"Oh, all right." The earl waved a hand about. "You're furious. I don't think we have to bicker about it. Despite your present feelings toward me, I am not a fool."

Justin's expression darkened. "I'm not in the mood for your careless manners, Hugh. If you're going to be amusing, I'll leave."

"Oh, Justin," Hugh said with a groan. "You make everything so difficult, and ever have. You were somber even as a boy, always skulking about the hallways at Gyer like a silent shadow. You haven't changed overmuch since those days."

"I had good reason to be as I was," Justin told him, sitting in the chair opposite his brother's. "I had Candis to protect from Father, and when he was gone, from Alexander's lack of care and from your and Hugo's dangerous ways. Before Lillis came, Castle Gyer was not a pleasant place for small children, certainly not for our young sister. Or have you forgotten?"

Hugh shifted uncomfortably beneath his brother's steady gaze. "Nay, of course I've not. I realize full well what life was like for you and Candis then, and have long since accepted my own part in what you both suffered. Perhaps, in some misguided way, I've tried too much to take care of you now to make some sort of... recompense."

"Recompense?" Justin repeated with disbelief. "You force me to wed as a way of making recompense?"

"As a way of keeping you from harm, aye," Hugh admitted. "Alex wanted me to find you a bride in the hopes that a wife might settle you down and keep you out of trouble, and I thought—having heard of what transpired at Briarstone with the duke's advisor—well, I thought, perhaps, that he might be right."

"I've told you what happened at Briarstone," Justin said tightly. "*Chris* told you what happened."

"Yes, well. Ahem." The earl cleared his throat. "How was I to know that the fellow had been trying to rape one of the women there? He said you'd taken a sword to him because he wouldn't pay for his pleasures, not that you'd taken a sword to him because he deserved to be gelded. And before you tell me that I should have taken the trouble to ask you about the matter first, I'll remind you that it wouldn't have done any good. Alexander wanted you wed, and would have used any reason to accomplish the goal. You know what he is."

"You're an *earl* now, Hugh, and no longer a mere soldier for the king. You outrank Alexander."

"Ha! As if that has anything to do with it." Hugh took up his goblet and drank deeply. Wiping his mouth with his fingers, he said, "I should like to see you try to stand against anything that our eldest brother decided upon. It's about as simple a thing as hacking a stone mountain to bits with a dull blade. And I'll tell you truly that I thought the idea had merit."

"Did you?" Justin asked in a low tone. "Because you think I needed to 'settle'?"

"Because I don't want you to keep on as you have been, aimless and solitary. You've nearly made yourself into a hermit at Talwar, save those few times when you visited Chris at Briarstone. I realize that what you went through with Lady Alicia was painful—"

"You," Justin said as he abruptly stood, "of all people, should know better than to mention her name to me." He stalked toward the fire, restless, angry. "God save me," he muttered, running his hands through his hair. "Was ever a man so cursed as this in his family?" He fell still, staring at the flames in the hearth. "I was content with my life. It was not my intention to wed."

"Justin," Hugh said gently, standing to join his brother by the fire. "I would never bring you harm apurpose. If I have done so by my deeds, then I pray you will forgive me. I would undo matters if I could, but you are the only one who can do that."

Justin lifted his head sharply. "Undo matters?"

Hugh nodded. "Sir Myles wants Lady Isabelle back. Indeed, he has gone to Duke Humphrey and demanded her return."

"Sir Myles may rot in Hell."

"And so he may," Hugh agreed readily. "I believe you've made your feelings more than clear about that, but unless you mean to slay him and end up being tried for the crime, that doesn't answer the problem. He wants your marriage to Lady Isabelle annulled, and has said that if she is returned to him, he will yet allow you to marry his daughter, Lady Evelyn."

The face Justin made told Hugh everything that he needed to know about the desirability of marrying Lady Evelyn. "Ah," he said. "I see. Ugly, is she?"

"Nay, she is quite beautiful. Extraordinarily beautiful."

Hugh looked at him curiously. "But you did not want her?"

His gaze held upon the fire, Justin shook his head. "Not after I saw Isabelle."

"So it wasn't simply to punish Sir Myles? Or Alexander and me?"

Justin's smile tightened with keen unpleasantness. "Oh, yes, it was that, too. I wish you could have seen the look on your face when I told you who I had taken for my bride. Not the wellborn beauty you'd so carefully chosen, but the ignoble daughter of traitors.'' He laughed. '''Twas worth all the trouble you put me through in London, I vow. I only wish Alexander could have been here, so that I might have seen his horror, as well. A precious *Baldwin* wedded to such a one. S'truth, I would have given Talwar away to see his face.''

''Justin,'' the earl of Siere said in a calm voice, ''if you're saying that you married that delightful creature simply to make a jest of her, I am going to beat you sense-less. And then I'm going to personally return Lady Isabelle to her uncle.''

''You may beat me, or attempt to, if you like,'' Justin said with equal calm. ''I would verily enjoy breaking a few of your bones at just this moment. But you will not take Isabelle anywhere. Not unless you kill me, first.''

The two men stared at each other before Hugh finally pulled away, walking back to his goblet of wine, which he picked up. ''I'm relieved, brother, to know that you're not quite such a fool as you sounded for a moment. Al-though how any man who saw Lady Isabelle could be, I don't understand. She's stunning enough, by the rood. That hair. And those eyes...'' His drifting voice finished the thought. ''Hardly the sort of female one would want to get rid of. Which makes me wonder why you've not yet made certain of your rights to her.''

Justin stiffened. ''She is my wife,'' he said.

The earl uttered a short laugh. ''She is your *bride*. She is not yet your wife. You are singularly unable to lie, Jus-tin, so please don't weary yourself with trying to make excuses. I know what it is to be married to the woman you desire above all others, and separate bedchambers aren't part of such a relationship. But heed me well. Unless you make Lady Isabelle your wife soon, Sir Myles will have every reason he needs to take her back. There is nothing that Alexander or I will be able to do to legally stop him.''

"You must find a way," Justin said. "I took Isabelle by force to make her my wife. I will not also force her to share my bed until she is ready to do so."

Hugh turned to face him. "Then you chance losing her."

Justin's expression hardened. "I cannot make a woman accept me against her will. When Alicia did not wish to…wed me…I…" He was embarrassed by the pain he heard in his own voice, and fell silent.

"You let her run, God's feet," Hugh finished for him, fingering his goblet consideringly. "It was not well done, I vow. Of either of you."

"I am not like you, Hugh. If Isabelle will come to me, it must be of her own accord."

"Then for all your brave words, brother, you may lose her. I'm not ashamed to admit that I bedded Rosaleen while I had the chance, before she could think long enough to say me nay. After that she was mine, just as I wanted, and no man could take her from me. If you wish to keep your Isabelle, then I advise you do the same."

"I'll keep Isabelle," Justin assured him. "Never doubt it. But if you want the matter to be legal, you must be the one to make certain of it. Unless you wish me to kill Sir Myles?"

"Stubborn lad," Hugh said wearily. "Nay, I do not want you felling noblemen to keep your good lady. And, as Alexander and I are the ones who decided to meddle in your life, I suppose 'tis only fair that we do what we can to lend you aid."

"Now we are at last in complete agreement."

"You needn't beat me over the head about it. I've spent the past month sleeping, eating and breathing guilt. Rosaleen's made certain of it."

"I must thank her, then," Justin said impassively. "Now that we have an understanding regarding Robert's 'important matters,' I will tell you that Isabelle and I will leave on the morrow. I have been away from Talwar too long, already, and Chris must get back to Briarstone, as well."

"I'll do what I can regarding Sir Myles and the duke—" Hugh began.

"Nay, you do what you *must*," Justin corrected bluntly.

"Aye, aye, whatever I must, whatever Alexander must. Don't worry o'er the matter. Only tell me what you want me to say to Sir Myles. He wants to know what you intend."

Justin smiled again, baring his teeth this time. "Tell him that I intend to have everything from him that is rightfully Isabelle's and her brother's, everything that belonged to their parents, save the lands and titles, for Isabelle must be content with what I can give her in that regard, and Senet must make his own way when the time comes. Tell him that I will have Senet beneath my care before another fortnight has passed, and that he will not interfere in my collecting the boy from Sir Howton, unless he wishes to play quintain for my next bout of jousting practice."

"Justin, Justin," the earl said chidingly. "Such violence."

Placing his hands on the back of a chair, Justin leaned forward slightly, his eyes intent on his brother's face. "Tell Sir Myles that he will not try to contact Isabelle for any reason. I shall keep her well and busy, and if he misses the use of her particular skills, he may bethink himself that I am the one who will rightfully enjoy the benefit of them, i' faith, of all that Isabelle has to offer. Tell him that I wish him luck in finding a suitable husband for his lovely daughter, Lady Evelyn."

The earl made a *tsk*ing sound. "'Tis clear that you do not even know what you want with the girl, whether she will be your wife or your revenge."

"For now, she is both."

"Don't be a fool, Justin. You will only bring misery

down upon your own head. Leave revenge aside. Forgive Alex and me for loving you well enough to meddle where we should not, and forgive Sir Myles for being a greedy fool. If you want happiness for yourself and your good lady, heed me.''

"You are my brother, Hugh, and for that I owe you love. You are the earl of Siere, and for that I owe you respect. But you are not my liege, and I do not owe you my obedience. Isabelle and I will be happy because I will make it so. As for the other…you need not fear. I've no desire to make a feast of revenge. Not a feast, nay. Only a delicacy, which I will enjoy until the moment it begins to make me weary.''

Chapter Seven

"**J**ustin."

The sound of his name as he left his brother's working chamber stopped him midstride, and he turned to find Isabelle standing against the wall near the open door, her hands and body pressed against the smooth mortar as if it were her only support. Her face was pale, and her eyes were filled with fear.

"How long have you been there?" he demanded, turning toward her with more forcefulness than he knew. "How much did you hear?"

The words were harsh, angry, and he wondered, the moment he heard them coming out of his mouth, what he could mean by speaking them. It was obvious that she was afraid, standing there as if she'd committed some horrible crime, when she could have so easily run away and never told him that she had been there.

She had stayed to face him, he thought with sudden remorse. She had stayed.

"Will I be made to return to my uncle?" she whispered. "And Senet?"

"Nay," he said, shame making him unable to reach out to her as he wished, to be tender and kind after speaking to her so harshly. "I will not let him take you back. Senet will come to us, just as I promised."

"You want me because I can make you rich?" she asked, her widened eyes steadfastly held on his.

"Nay," he said again, knowing very well that she had good cause not to believe him.

"For revenge?"

His heart began to beat loudly in his ears and he thought, *Aye, this is what it will be with us. She must learn to trust me or we will never be content together.*

"You heard what I told my brother," he said, taking a step nearer to her, "and you know what I told you in Cambridge. I want us to make a good life together, to have children and happiness."

Her breath came out in a loud rush; she visibly swallowed, and the small color that had been in her face drained away, until she was as pale as the early dawn.

"Then I will go with you now and become your wife."

He was aware of the sudden silence in Hugh's working chamber, and reached out to firmly close the door, not caring what his brother thought of being so ceremonially shut inside.

"Isabelle." Justin reached a hand toward her, palm up, supplicating. "Will you come with me to the gardens?"

"Nay," she whispered, her voice thin and fearful. "Take me to your chamber, please, and make me your wife before it is too late."

He took hold of her trembling hand and brought it to his mouth, pressing her fingers lingeringly against his lips in an effort to soothe her. "Do not tempt me beyond reason, I pray." One hand stroked gently over her covered hair, down to her shoulder. "I dream of you saying these words to me when we are at Talwar, and because you desire to be my wife in every way. But not out of fear, Isabelle. Never out of fear."

She searched his eyes. "Speak the truth to me, my lord.

I beg it. Do you mean to set me aside, once you have satisfied your revenge upon my uncle? Because if you do—'' she grabbed his sleeve when, in shock, he pulled away ''—let me at least stay at your estate and be your steward. If you would only bring Senet to me and keep us safe from Sir Myles, I will do anything that you ask. I will make you wealthy. Only do not send us back to my uncle.''

He had thought that nothing, and no one, could hurt him as badly as Alicia Sherringham had once done. But he'd been wrong. Pushing free of her, Justin staggered back against the opposite wall and stared at Isabelle as if she'd just stuck a dagger in his belly.

"You think I will not take you to my bed because I mean to set you *aside?*" he asked. He was tempted, when she nodded, to drag her off to the nearest chamber and demonstrate how fully wrong she was. But why should she think otherwise, when all the world, it seemed, agreed that he was a crazed fool not to have made his claim upon her certain? Isabelle had been betrayed before, by her uncle, who had lied when he said that he would care for her and Senet and then done naught but make them as slaves. And her uncle had been a blood relative, while Justin was nothing better than a stranger.

Revenge. Justin hadn't cared about it, hadn't really thought about it until Hugh mentioned the word. Then his brother's reaction and his own anger had spurred him on, causing him to make more of the matter than it was. He wanted only to be left in peace, with no more invasions made upon his life and privacy. If he couldn't make his family, and Sir Myles and the royals, understand that now, then he and Isabelle would never be left to themselves.

But how could he make her understand that? He had taken her by force, had wed her by force. With her own ears she had heard him foolishly taunting his brother about revenge. He wanted Isabelle to trust him, but she had no good reason to do so.

"We are wed, and I will never set you aside," he heard himself saying, though his mind seemed divorced from the words. He was trying to see himself through her eyes, trying to see whether he was as some terrible, violent stranger to her, someone to be feared and appeased, rather than a man who craved her love and trust. "If you are not satisfied with my word, which I give you in honor, then I will take you to my bedchamber now and do as you have asked. I will make you my wife. If you wish to wait until we achieve Talwar, then we will wait. The choice must be yours, Isabelle, for I will not live the rest of my days bearing the guilt of having taken you against your will."

She said nothing, but wrapped her hands together tightly and pressed them against her stomach. Her eyes, he saw, were filled with dread, and his heart softened.

"Are you very afraid of what takes place in the marriage bed?" he asked gently.

Flushing deeply, she nodded, and whispered, "But I fear my uncle more."

He was across the space that parted them and had her in his arms before he even realized he was moving. "Isabelle," he murmured, holding her tight against himself, feeling her hands clutch at the tunic he wore. "Have I not given you my vow that he will never have you again? We will go to Talwar and make our life there. It is very beautiful, and you will come to love it as much as I." He kissed her hair, her cheek, where he tasted a salty tear. "And when you are no longer afraid," he murmured, taking her face in his hands and kissing her mouth, "we will be man and wife, and no one save God will be able to part us."

She stiffened when he kissed her more deeply, but she did not pull away, or protest when he touched her with his tongue. He had not kissed her so intimately since the night at the monastary, and when she opened herself to him, he made a murmur of pleasure before reverently taking the sweetness that she offered. A moment passed as she continued to hold herself rigid and tense, and then, as he strove to please her, she gave a tiny "Oh" and, with a sigh, put her arms about his neck.

He lifted his head, drawing in air. "Is it all right, Isabelle?"

"Oh," she said again, dazed. "Aye."

Much encouraged, he kissed her again, briefly. "It does not frighten you?"

Her reply was to pull his head down to hers again, but his lips had barely touched hers when the door to the chamber opened.

"Ahem," said the earl of Siere. "Forgive me, I pray, but I fear I have an unbending rule about not allowing such intimate public displays in the castle halls."

Smiling at Isabelle, who smiled back, Justin asked, "Except between yourself and Rosaleen, Hugh?"

"Aye," Sir Hugh admitted readily. "Just so. But I am lord here, and thus have certain rights. May I suggest," he added cheerfully, "that you children retire to one of your bedchambers to further explore this sudden interest in each other's well-being?"

"I think," Justin said, "that my wife wishes to walk in the gardens." Releasing her, stepping back only a small distance, he took her hand and kissed it. "Do you, my lady?"

"Aye, my lord, I should like it very much."

Walking with their heads together, talking and laughing with intimate pleasure, they left the earl of Siere standing alone.

"Gray hairs," he said, watching them go. "That's what I'm getting out of all this. Naught but gray hairs. I hope Alexander's satisfied. They're even more trying than Robert.'' Which reminded him that he needed the help of his capable steward, so that he might write responses to the missives that still lay in his working chamber, yet unanswered.

Chapter Eight

She fell in love with Talwar the moment she set eyes on it. The main dwelling was a small, square keep with a half-timbered manor house added to one side. A short distance away, but within the walled grass bailey, sat several smaller buildings, all seeming to be in good repair. Surrounding the estate was a tall, variously angled wall with four towers that were flying flags bearing what Isabelle thought must be Justin's coat of arms. Before this lay several acres of crops, neatly laid out and obviously well cared for, while beyond was a wide, slow-moving river and a thickly wooded forest.

"Briarstone is beyond the trees some few miles," Justin said as he rode beside Isabelle. "There is a road through the forest, although you cannot see it from here."

"Oh, my lord, it is beautiful. Just as you said it would be."

The words clearly pleased him. "It is small and simple, but a comfortable home. I hope that you will find it thus."

"I promise that I will," she assured him. If Sir Christian hadn't been with them, she would have dared to say more, to tell him what it meant to her, after the confusing, difficult years following her parents' deaths, to at last have a home of her own again. "It is more than I ever dreamed of having. Thank you, my lord."

"Look," Sir Christian said. "Your students are preparing to greet their new lady in the proper manner."

"Kayne will have had my missive two days past," Justin remarked, lifting himself up in his saddle to see better. "We shall see how well he has remembered his lessons."

"Kayne is the eldest?" Isabelle asked as they prodded their horses forward. He had told her about the boys who were in his care. They were all from Briarstone, Sir Christian's estate, which had been founded many years before by Sir Christian's brother with the aid of a variety of criminals and whores, all of whom had agreed to labor there without wages in the hope of a better life. These boys were the sons of some of those prostitutes, and Justin had agreed to train them for knighthood. It was a small way in which he could repay Christian for his help and friendship over the past many years, for, as Justin had told Isabelle, "If it had not been for Chris, I would never have had Talwar, for he was the one who helped me to win and rebuild it."

"Kayne is the eldest and most capable," he replied now. "I have set him over the others, and he has the charge of them, indeed of all of Talwar, when I am not here."

They were lined up outside the gates, five lads mounted on exceptionally fine horses that belied the plain, well-worn clothes they wore, which Isabelle realized must be the best that they owned. But these were well scrubbed, as were their wearers, each sitting tall and proud, with neatly combed hair that shone under the sun. The eldest, a handsome blond youth of perhaps ten-and-six years, had a freshly shaven face. When he rode forth to greet them, Isabelle was struck by the boy's masculine beauty. His eyes were distinctly blue against his blond hair and sun-darkened face, and his noble features were solemn and serious.

"My lord, Sir Justin." He greeted them with so much ceremony that Isabelle bit her lip to keep from laughing at how greatly he reminded her of Robert, the ever-proper steward of Siere. He bowed his head once, then turned to Sir Christian. "My lord, Sir Christian," he said with equal eloquence, bowing his head again. Then he turned to Isabelle, and in even deeper tones said, "My lady Isabelle, mistress of Talwar. We welcome you with full hearts and every gladness."

He sounded so miserable that Isabelle had to clear her throat to master her amusement before saying, in what she hoped were equally regal tones, "Thank you, Master Kayne."

His head lifted at the sound of his name, and his gaze sharpened.

"Sir Justin has spoken well of you," Isabelle added quickly, wanting only to put him at ease, "and often. Indeed," she continued, moving her horse a little farther on, "I believe I know all of you, already, from Sir Justin's words."

The next boy in line was dark-haired, like her brother, Senet, although much larger in both size and muscle, and had a scowl on his face.

"You are Aric," she said with a soft smile. "Ten-and-four, and capable with both sword and crossbow." He was the quiet one, Justin had warned her. A harsh childhood had left the boy suspicious and reserved, but unfailingly loyal to those few people whom he finally came to trust.

Aric inclined his head, never taking his eyes from her face, and Isabelle guided her horse forward to the next boy, a slender youth with hair and eyes the soft color of a sparrow's gray-brown wing.

"And you must be—"

"John," the boy answered, his wiry body straightening with taut energy. "John Ipris, m'lady, for wasn't I born at Ipris Inn, with no better name to make claim to? I've seen *you* before," he went on without taking so much as a breath, speaking in the thickly accented tones Isabelle had often heard in London. "Walking to Saint Paul's you was, with a fine-dressed gentleman and lady, and you walking behind, dressed in gray and about as lively as a dead cat, I vow. And wasn't it cold? God's teeth, it was. I saw you, all right, plain as a cock's tail from where I was, sitting under Fleet Street bridge and breaking me fast with a bun I'd swiped. Right there as ready as my own nose, I saw you."

Kayne, who had moved his horse forward with Isabelle's, gave John a stern look, which the younger boy blinked at twice before suddenly coming to himself.

"Oh," he said, then straightened again, like a soldier about to greet his commander. "Welcome to Talwar, my lady Isabelle," he blurted out with rigid solemnity.

"John has an amazing memory," Justin said from where he sat, his voice both gentle and proud. "He lived in London for many years before coming to Briarstone, and then to Talwar, and if he says that he saw you once, you may believe that he did."

John's face suffused with open pleasure at his master's words, although he correctly kept his eyes forward.

"I'm certain he must have," Isabelle agreed. "We did attend chapel at Saint Paul's, and the walk along Fleet Street from the Strand was our common route. I only regret that I did not see you, Master John Ipris."

He did turn his eyes then, briefly, to see Isabelle's smile and to blink twice again before forcing his gaze forward.

She moved to the last two boys in line.

"You will be Ralf," she said to the eldest, a towheaded youth who appeared to be just over ten years of age. "And you," she said to the last, a vividly redheaded nine-year-old, "must be Neddy. You are brothers, is this not so?"

The boys nodded silently, and Sir Christian said, "Their mother, Helen, manages the household of Briarstone."

Isabelle turned her horse about so that she could see each boy. They were a ragged lot, but as proud as any knighted men she'd ever seen.

"I have never had so fine or gracious a welcome," she said truthfully, "nor have I ever again expected to be treated with such perfect courtesy. We should have the truth between us, so that you may decide for yourselves how we will get on together. For myself, I should like very much to be companionable with one another, and friends, if it may come to that in time. I am no great lady, and would not have you treat me as such. My father was French, and was declared a traitor to the throne of our late King Henry, may God preserve his soul. For the past four years, I have lived beneath my uncle's hand, as his servant. That is the manner in which John Ipris saw me in London. I am only here at Talwar because of the kindness of your master, Sir Justin, and it is not my intent to play a role that is neither fitting nor right. I am only Isabelle, and only what you see before you now. If we may all be easy and kind with one another, I shall be most grateful. I pray it shall be so for all of you, as well."

There was total silence as each of the five boys stared at her, and as Isabelle steadily met their regard. It was a chance she had taken, she knew, and it had probably not been at all what Justin expected her to say, but this was the beginning of a new life for her—an entirely new life, with everything that she had once cherished of her past put aside—and she would not begin it with lies or misunderstandings. She was as much a refugee here as these boys were, and if they would accept her, then there must be nothing but the truth between them.

Kayne, the one she had least expected to accept her, was the one who moved first. He unsheathed the sword from the scabbard dangling from his waist and held it high.

"God bless our Lady Isabelle!" he cried, and the others followed suit.

Justin, his expression filled with pride and pleasure, rode his horse up beside hers and took her hand. Kissing it, he murmured, "Aye, God bless our Lady Isabelle."

Her new home was just as he had promised it would be. It was not grand, but it was comfortable and well kept. The manor house had been built after Justin gained ownership of Talwar, and had, he assured her, every modern comfort, from glass windowpanes to tiled floors covered with Spanish carpets to large stone hearths set in the walls. Gazing at the dwelling closely for the first time, Isabelle thought of the home she had lived in during her childhood, her father's grand estate, Castle Lomas, and of her uncle's palatial home on the Strand, and she knew, without a flicker of doubt, that she would be more fully content here than she had been at any other time in her life. Here, she and Senet would at last find peace.

"The boys live in the old keep," Justin said as he pulled her down from her horse. "In the soldier's quarters, which they seem to like very well. There is a separate kitchen that was finished more than two years ago, so you'll need never worry over food being cooked in the house." Taking her hand, he led her to the manor's large wooden doors, which were already open.

They walked in together, and were greeted at once by three women who stood in a formal line beside the entry. Isabelle forced her curious gaze away from the simple beauty of the dwelling's interior to smile at them.

"Welcome home, my lord, Sir Justin," the first said. She was a handsome older woman, her hair a dark gray and her eyes a bright blue. To Isabelle she said, with a bow, "Welcome to Talwar, Lady Isabelle."

"This is Mistress Gytha," Justin said with warm affection. "Gytha manages the household, and has been as good as a mother to all of us."

"Mistress Gytha," Isabelle greeted.

"My lady," Gytha said, taking the hand Isabelle offered

and holding it tightly. "We've praised God these past two days since having the missive our lord sent, telling us of his marriage. You are a gift sent from heaven, I vow."

Next was Meg, whom Justin introduced as the cook, a plump, smiling middle-aged woman whose two front teeth were missing.

"The best cook in all of England," Sir Christian declared from where he stood at the door.

Meg beamed and made a bow. "I've made a special meal for this eve, my lady," she said. "To welcome you to Talwar."

"Thank you." Isabelle set a hand against her stomach. "I am very hungry, and know I shall enjoy every bite put before me, Mistress Meg. I cannot believe my good fortune, to have so fine a husband, and so fine a home, with a fine housekeeper and fine cook." She glanced back at Sir Christian and the young men, who all stood within the entrance. "And such fine gentlemen for company, as well."

She looked expectantly at the girl who stood last in line and, moving forward, put forth her hand. The girl, whose blond head had been cast down, took Isabelle's fingers and held them, and at last lifted her face, revealing tear-filled eyes. Isabelle's smile died, and she stared at the pure beauty of the girl, at the wet tearstains on the girl's face. She had never seen such wretched sadness before.

"This is Birgitte," Justin said quietly as he came up beside her.

The girl's gaze moved to Justin. Her fingers slackened and fell away from Isabelle's, and she whispered, "Sir Justin."

"Birgitte helps both Gytha and Meg."

"I am pleased to know you, Birgitte," Isabelle murmured, but the girl only continued to stare at Justin.

"Greet your lady, Birgitte," Justin commanded gently. With a sob, Birgitte did as she was told. "Welcome to

Talwar, my lady,'' she managed brokenly, and then her sobs overcame her. Covering her face with her hands, she turned and stumbled out of the room.

''Oh, no...'' Isabelle began, thinking to go after the distraught girl, but Justin held her back with one hand on her arm.

''Nay, leave her be. She will be returning to Briārstone with Chris, I think.''

His expression matched the seriousness of his words, and Isabelle, fully bewildered, asked, ''But why?''

''It is best,'' he said, then smiled at her. ''Now that you have met everyone, will you let me show you all of your new home?''

He took her to her bedchamber first, which was large and airy and had obviously been prepared with meticulous care for her arrival. When he was assured that she was more than well satisfied with it, he showed her his bedchamber, which was joined to hers by a connecting door. Next he took her through the guest chambers—four in all—and even showed her the garderobes, which made her laugh and him blush, when he realized that he was proudly displaying the dwelling's latrines. He dragged her back downstairs to the large great room that made up most of the lower level, to show her all the wonderful modern features he'd had put into his home.

The manor house was connected to the elderly keep by a passageway located on one side of the great room. It was built in the same sturdy, modern manner as the house itself, and existed as much for protection as for practicality, Justin explained, showing her where the passage entrance was fitted with iron gates that could be locked in case Talwar became the object of attack by one of the mercenary armies that roamed England, causing so much trouble at smaller estates like Justin's.

''The keep is completely defensible,'' he said, pulling a lit torch from the wall and taking hold of her hand to lead her into the dark corridor. "If we were attacked, we would move into the keep and seal the passageway. The manor house would be forfeit, but there are enough supplies in the keep to maintain us even for a very long siege. Otherwise," he added with a smile, "the lads have a good time running back and forth and giving us all a scare when they rush unannounced into the manor."

It was something of a shock to move so suddenly from the warm comfort of the manor to the chilly, ancient severity of the keep, especially when the modern corridor gave way to the keep's dark, unmortared passageway. Torch in hand, Justin led Isabelle along with a quick stride that bespoke his confidence and long familiarity with what seemed, to Isabelle, a gloomy, daunting place.

"Were there many battles here?" she asked, her voice quickly softening when she heard it echoing off the soot-darkened bricks.

"Many," he said, stopping before a wide stone step and holding the torch higher, so that she might see the small, slender opening above. "This is where a soldier would stand to shoot out of the arrow loop. Here he would be out of the way while others used the passageway to run back and forth, carrying weapons and supplies. They are all along here, do you see? Here is another." He pulled her a few feet along, until they came to another raised step.

"It is so dark, though," she murmured. "The arrow loops are the only source of light. Would it not be difficult to fight in such darkness?"

"Aye, but such small openings provided greater safety, and a man could not crawl in through one. Talwar was not built for comfort, I fear, but for safety and war. It was never once breached, by any enemy."

They began to walk again, toward the soldiers quarters where the boys lived.

"How did you come to own Talwar?" she asked.

"I won it in a tournament six years ago," he replied. "Chris and I had come across it while we were hunting two years earlier, empty and ruined, and used the keep for shelter for several days. I thought little of it at the time, beyond feeling a certain sadness that such a fine castle had become so poor with neglect. But shortly thereafter I decided that I must have an estate of my own, for I could not live at Briarstone forever, and I wanted nothing that my elder brother, the lord of Gyer, would give me. Come up here, Isabelle," he said suddenly, taking her hand and leading her up a narrow flight of stairs that had appeared at the end of the passage. "Careful, my lady. 'Tis very old, and the steps are smaller than most. Are you all right?" He had released her to push open a small door.

"Aye," she said, and felt a delightful gust of cool air on her face. "Does it lead outside?"

"Yes. Come." Reaching back, he pulled her up and out onto the rooftop.

"Oh, Justin," she said with awe, turning about and taking in the beauty of the view surrounding them. "'Tis magnificent."

He put the still-burning torch in a holder. "You are pleased, Isabelle?"

"Oh, yes, my lord. Thank you." She said the words with heartfelt emotion. "Thank you for giving me such a wonderful home. I shall do everything I can to repay you."

He smiled and put his hands on either side of her face, kissing her gently before saying, "I feared that you would find it wanting, for it is not grand as your uncle's palace, but I love Talwar very well, and can only be thankful that you are content with it."

She thought he was going to kiss her again, but he seemed to recall that he had more to show her, for he said, "You have not seen all of it yet. Come." He pulled her to one side of the rooftop, toward the keep's inner courtyard. "It is not so fearsome on the inside as it is from the outside."

"A garden," she said with some surprise, gazing down at the large square patch of green below. There were several paths, some trees, and even benches. "It is lovely, Justin."

"Our children will like to play in it, do you not think so? There is the well, by the kitchen. Do you see? The water is uncommonly sweet and healthy, may God be praised. And there are more windows here, to give light to the inner chambers. Those are the soldier's quarters, where the boys live. And there is the chapel. 'Tis small, but in good repair. Hugo comes four times a year to give a proper mass, but one day we may have a priest of our own, should we prosper."

They would prosper, she thought silently. It was one of the reasons he had married her, and she would make certain of it. She would make Justin Baldwin the richest man in England, if she could. He would be able to support and maintain a dozen priests by the time she was done.

"The stables are over here." He walked to the other side of the roof, pointing down into the walled, grassy bailey. "It was built new, also. Completed but four years ago."

"So large," she noted. "You must have many horses, my lord."

He nodded. "Aye, and all good war-horses, suitable as mounts for knights. I could not train the boys so well without them."

"What is that smaller building?" She pointed toward the right of the stables. "Is it a smithy?"

"Aye," he said with what sounded like reluctance. "'Tis my smithy, where I make my swords and fashion other weapons that we need."

She found the idea that he was so skilled thoroughly amazing, but the way that he was looking at her, his expression almost challenging, as if he didn't wish to speak of the ability to her, kept the thought unvoiced. Instead, she said, "Talwar is all that you claimed it to be. I understand even more fully why you did not wish to lose it. Please tell me the rest of how you came to own it."

His gaze wandered toward the hills over which they had traveled earlier, and he rested his arms on the low wall that ran the roof's length.

"I had decided that I wanted Talwar because, as I said, I wished to have my own estate, and also because it is close to Briarstone and I liked the idea of living near Chris." He looked at her. "Of being neighbors with him, as well as friends. He is the only true friend I have ever had, and I value him greatly."

"Sir Christian is indeed a fine man," she agreed.

"It was Chris's idea to make an attempt for the property at a tournament. The land and castle, so we discovered, belonged to the duke of Barhaven, and the duke of Barhaven, so we further discovered, was about to hold a tournament, with the grand prize being twelve fine steeds and a purse fat with gold. I did not need the horses, for I had already bred several better at Briarstone, and I had plenty of gold from past tournaments that I had won. But at Chris's instruction I went to the duke's estate and participated in his tournament, and when I was declared the winner and about to be awarded the prizes, I said to the duke, before all the assembled, that I would far rather be given Talwar. I have never seen a man laugh so hard or long as that before." Justin smiled at the memory. "Even so, he was not inclined to give me the land, for he thought it a poor way of rewarding a victor. Then Chris told him that I desired the estate so that I might be able to woo a lady." His voice had grown wistful, almost sad, it seemed to Isabelle. "And that was true enough."

"Lady Alicia?" Isabelle asked, touching his arm lightly, with sympathy.

He nodded. "He gave me the land then, as well as the purse of gold to help pay for the repairs. I had the manor house built at once, and the stables and smithy. Then, as I was able, other repairs were made to the keep and walls. Not that any of it mattered, for she would not live here. She found the idea equally amusing and distasteful." He looked at her suddenly, as if he had only just remembered her presence, and his eyes narrowed. "How did you know of Lady Alicia?"

She was momentarily taken back by the curtness of his tone, and replied, timidly, "Evelyn spoke of your former betrothal. She is acquainted with Lady Alicia."

"I see." He lifted his gaze to the hills once more and was silent.

"Justin…" Isabelle began softly, but he abruptly turned and headed back toward the stairs.

"It will be getting dark soon."

"Justin, I'm sorry for having mentioned Lady Alicia, but—"

"I would ask this of you, Isabelle," he said, stopping by the stair entry, not looking at her. "Do not speak of Lady Alicia to me, or in my hearing. I will always try to speak truthfully and openly with you, but I cannot speak of her. It is very…difficult."

"Yes, Justin," she murmured quickly, pushing aside the sharp pain that the evidence of his love for another woman gave her. "I understand, my lord."

He held out his hand. "Come, then. I want to show you the soldier's quarters before we must return to ready ourselves for tonight's celebration."

In the cool of the early evening, while the night's feast was being prepared and while Justin closeted himself in his working chamber with Kayne to discuss all that had occurred in his absence, Sir Christian claimed Isabelle's company for a walk through the keep's inner garden.

"Do you look forward to your return to Briarstone in the morn, my lord?" she asked as they seated themselves on a small bench beneath the branches of a scraggly oak tree.

"Aye. It will be good to be home again," he replied. "Briarstone is a fine place, as well as one of the oldest castles in England. It was completed in the year of our Lord 1025, and was counted as one of the finest defenses in the land during William the Conqueror's time."

"You must be very proud to have such an estate," Isabelle said.

He nodded. "There is none other like it, I believe. Briarstone is a refuge for all the unfortunate. We are none of us well or highly born, and none smooth or polished. 'Tis a rough crowd, and yet the yield of our crops are so fine that brokers in London fight over the honor of selling them. Three years past we added five thousand acres to our holdings, and this coming harvest will yield twice what it did then. We have been very fortunate."

The mention of brokers and the London markets caught Isabelle's attention. Which brokers? she wanted to ask. She personally knew all of them in London, and had spent long hours discussing financial matters with most of them. She opened her mouth to launch into a discussion of current crop rates, which she had always found to be a fascinating topic, but Sir Christian spoke first.

"We owe most of it to Justin, of course. I doubt we would have prospered so well without him, despite the help we received from both the lord of Gyer and the earl of Siere."

"To Justin?" Surprise tingled all the way up Isabelle's spine.

"Aye, to Justin." Sir Christian leaned forward, resting his forearms on his knees. "I will speak the truth, my lady. I did not ask you to accompany me here simply to enjoy the cool night air. I wished to tell you something of Justin.

He has been my good friend these many years, and I would have him be content in his marriage. You do not yet know him well, as I do, but he was badly hurt once by a woman whom he loved, and I do not wish to see him hurt again. I do not think that such is your intent, but, perhaps, if I tell you something of Justin, you may be more…inclined to be kind to him."

"I mean to be kind to him," she whispered, horrified and embarrassed.

"Oh, my dear Lady Isabelle," Sir Christian said with quick and warm reassurance, "I did not mean to say that you did not. Indeed, have you not already been wonderfully kind in wedding yourself to a man who is nearly a stranger to you, simply to save his lands? But I have sensed this evening that all is not well. Only this afternoon there was contentment between you and, aye, even happiness, which existed since before we left Siere and which had given me great hope for your future together. But now it is all gone. You seem unhappy, and Justin seems confused. And here am I, ready to leave for Briarstone, where I will do naught but worry. I know Justin well, you see. He is too gentle in many ways, much to his own suffering. If you are unhappy with him, he will not know what to do, and if you do not understand him well enough to help him, my lady, then the knot may never be untangled."

Isabelle released a long breath and folded her hands together to keep them from trembling. "You are mistaken, I think, my lord. There is no knot. Sir Justin wed me to preserve his lands, and that aim has been achieved. There is nothing more to the matter."

"Is there not? I do not deny that he wished to keep his lands. And what man would not? But if that had been his only reason, he could have chosen any woman."

Isabelle looked at him sharply. "Very well. He also took me because he wished to hurt my uncle. For revenge, and for the skills I might bring him. He never would have chosen me otherwise.''

"It is not so, but I cannot think of the way to convince you of it. Will you let me tell you something of Justin, my lady? Perhaps, afterward, you will understand him better."

Silently, she nodded.

"Ten years ago, I was given the ownership of Briarstone by Sir Hugh Baldwin, who was not yet then the earl of Siere. The estate had once belonged to my elder brother, John, but he had foolishly gambled it away to Sir Hugh while they served together in France under King Henry, may God rest his soul. John was killed at Agincourt, and Sir Hugh returned to England to take up his place as the master of Briarstone. Fortunately, for those of us who lived there, he brought Lady Rosaleen with him, although none of us knew that she was the heiress of Siere, not even Sir Hugh, who mistakenly thought her a commoner. When all was at last settled between them, and when they had married and Sir Hugh had been made the earl of Siere, Briarstone was given to me, as I was my late brother's rightful heir.

"I was ten-and-eight years of age," he said, his voice wistful, "and fully afeared to find myself suddenly responsible for such a large estate and so many people. But Sir Hugh had ever been good to me, and he sent his twin brother, Father Hugo, as well as his youngest brother, Justin, to Briarstone to lend me aid. Justin and I are of a like age, and we became friends. I had never had a close companion before, and he had not, either. It was good to have someone to talk to, someone to listen and understand. Although our births were of a different order, he being nobly born and me being a bastard, we had shared similar childhoods. When I told him that I had lived much of my youth in fear, he knew very well what I meant. I will not speak of that, for if Justin would have you know more, he will tell you himself.

"We were strange young men, my lady. Quite strange and quite dull." Isabelle turned to look at him, and he gifted her with a warm smile. "We were solitary, and too serious-natured, I think. Justin would beat me senseless if he knew I told you this, but he had never even been with a woman before coming to Briarstone." He grinned at her. "The whores there had a wonderful time teasing him, and teaching him, too, i' faith, although I don't suppose I should tell you any of that. But it was truly most entertaining, if you could but envision such a thing. He was full grown, a man in every way, and, as a knight of the realm, had even killed other men, yet he would blush as readily as a shy young maid when one of the women would so much as wink at him." He chuckled, and Isabelle found herself smiling, too, for she could indeed see her handsome husband doing just such a thing.

"Those first three years were hard," he continued with a sigh. "So hard, my lady. We labored long in the fields so that we might pay our debts at harvesttime and have enough left over for all that was needed. More and more people arrived as word of Briarstone spread among the desolate and poor. We could not turn any away, as long as they agreed to share in the work, for how could we be so hard-hearted? But there were many mouths to feed, and never enough food. The castle was overflowing, and we required new buildings to properly house our people. We had once, before Sir Hugh had come, been forced to steal from our neighbors to survive, but Father Hugo would not allow such as that while he was there, and, in truth, we were all loath to return to the practices we had worked so hard to put behind us. For a time, we did let some of the women who wished to run a whorehouse."

Isabelle's eyes widened. "And Father Hugo allowed that?"

"He had little choice. He did not like it, but he liked much less seeing the children crying from hunger, their already small bodies growing thin and ill. It was not long after that Justin decided he must do something to bring sufficient money to Briarstone so that the whorehouse would not be necessary."

"Justin? Even though it was not his estate?"

Sir Christian nodded. "Even so. He decided that he would follow the tournaments in England, and whatever prizes he won would go toward supporting Briarstone, at least until the estate was profitable on its own. He did not have to do so, but he wished to help me, his friend, and he had come to love the people there as much as I did. Justin has a good heart, my lady." He held a fist to his chest as if to prove the fact. "A very good heart."

"The tournaments," she whispered. "He could have so easily been killed. Or maimed."

"Aye, s'truth," Sir Christian agreed. "I did not want him to attempt it, nor did Father Hugo, but we could not stop him. He was the only one among us who possessed the skills for such gaming, although he had undertaken to train me and several of the other men in the ways of war and fighting. You do not know your husband well yet, my lady, but he never undertakes to do anything save that he does so with his whole being. He went out to follow the tournaments—I went with him in the beginning—and he won the choicest prizes at each one that he entered. For three years he did nothing else, and not only did he keep Briarstone from ruin, but he also began to put a measure aside for himself, looking to the day when he would no longer be able to support himself through such gaming. It was during this time that he began courting Lady Alicia, and later determined to gain Talwar through a plan I had conceived."

"He would not speak of her," Isabelle murmured. "He

told me not to mention her name. How much he must have loved her.''

Sir Christian frowned ''Aye, he loved her, although I have never been able to fathom why. She was very beautiful, and a nobly born lady, but she was seldom kind to him, and usually unkind. But Justin has ever been one who dreams, and his dreams always seem very true and real to him. He believed that Lady Alicia loved him, and he believed that, once he had made Talwar perfect for her, she would be ready to wed him and live here. To Lady Alicia's credit, I cannot say that she ever purposefully led him to think that such things were true, but Justin had his dream and could not let go of it. When she left him to marry a wealthy commoner, he was grievously wounded. I cannot speak of those days, for the memory is awful to me. He was as one gone mad, and I think he wished to die, for he went back to following the tournaments and was reckless, disregarding every form of safety. His brothers finally had him disqualified from participating, and he returned to Talwar. He has lived here for the past four years as little better than a hermit, save for his occasional visits to Briarstone.''

''He has been content?'' she asked softly. ''He said that he did not wish to wed.''

Sir Christian's shoulder's lifted in a light shrug. ''He has been content, I believe. As to wedding, he did not wish to suffer again as he had suffered at Lady Alicia's hands. She told him that he was insufferably dull, you see, and that she would not be bound to a dullard. He believed her, my lady, and did not think another woman would find him any better. Until he met you, I vow. He set sight on you, my lady, and decided that the two of you could be very content together. I will speak the truth and tell you that I believe he is possessed of another dream. He has decided that you will be happy as man and wife, and he will not believe otherwise unless you give him cause.''

"But do you think it can be so, my lord?" Isabelle asked. "Could it be?"

"That depends upon you and Justin, my lady. You care for him, do you not? I have seen you look at him in such a way that gives me hope."

"I care for him," she whispered. "But he... I do not know if feels the same. He says often that his desire is for us to be content, but I do not know if he and I share the same meaning of the word." She lowered her eyes to look at the hands she held clasped upon her lap. "I do not know what to think. Or what to believe. You have truly given me much to think on, my lord."

He set a hand over both of hers, squeezing lightly. "It is all that I could hope, that you would consider these things before being so certain of Justin's feelings toward you. There is more that I could speak, things that, if you knew them, would lend you much assurance. But they are for Justin to speak of, if he will, and I will not abuse his trust. You are a fine, grand lady, Isabelle Baldwin," he said, standing and pulling her to her feet. "If Justin can find happiness on God's earth, it will surely be with you."

Chapter Nine

The evening was clear, and pleasantly cool for midsummer. Justin stood in his bedchamber by his favorite window—the one that opened toward the hills—and gave himself over to the deep pleasure of being home. He had always loved coming back to Talwar, but this time was different. Special. Better. This time he had brought a wife, and what had once seemed good now seemed perfect. Only one more thing was necessary to complete his happiness, but he knew he would have to be patient in waiting for Isabelle to bear him children.

He wondered if she was ready for him to come to her yet. A glance at the door adjoining their chambers showed that it was still partly open, that the candles were still glowing, and he was tempted to move quietly and peek through the tiny crack and see what she was doing. They had retired over an hour earlier, under the speculative interest of the boys and Christian, whom they'd left playing games before the fire in the great room below. Birgitte had followed to help Isabelle prepare for bed, and Justin had gone into his own chamber, where he had listened unrepentantly to the sounds of the women's voices as Isabelle undressed and washed and brushed her hair. He had attended to his own preparations, shaving and washing the dirt from their day's journey from his body with a cloth and a basin of warm water. He had even attempted to comb his long, unruly hair into some manner of order, although he doubted the effort did much good.

Birgitte had left Isabelle's chamber some minutes ago, and all had become quiet. Justin stayed where he was by the window, waiting. He did not think he had ever desired a woman as much as he desired Isabelle. Even Alicia, whom he had loved, had not haunted his dreams as Isabelle so constantly did. But then, Alicia had never been withheld from him. They'd become lovers almost immediately after they met, and he had merely had to look at her to have her. It was the one way that he had ever been able to please her. The only way—in bed, but never out of it, no matter how much he had wished it otherwise.

It would be different with Isabelle. He felt the truth of that in every part of his being. The first time he had caught her looking at him at Sir Myles's house, trying not to be seen doing so, he had known. She had looked at him the way he had always dreamed Alicia would, as if he were fine and good, as if he were…well, pleasing. It was no small thing to be regarded in such a way by Isabelle's beautiful blue eyes. He had understood the value of it at once, and he thought, now, that it must have been then that he began to want her for his wife, although he hadn't actually made plans to steal her for many days after.

He had been delightfully surprised—and pleased—by her calm, assured behavior earlier in the day, when they had first arrived at Talwar and she had so quickly and readily charmed first the boys and then Gytha and Meg. There was obviously a great deal more to Isabelle than he had realized, a great deal more for him to learn. Just as she had much to learn of him. But they had time now. Years. A whole lifetime, if God was gracious.

Pushing from the window, he walked to the adjoining

door, running his hands through his hair and hoping that she would find him acceptable to gaze upon.

"Isabelle?" he said softly before setting his hand on the knob. "Isabelle?" He opened the door and stuck his head around it to peer into her chamber.

She was sitting on the bed in her nightdress—the same one she had worn when he stole her. Her feet were bare and linked together at the ankles, her hands were clasped on her lap, her eyes were cast down. Her unbound hair hung over one shoulder in a smooth black waterfall that reached all the way to her knees.

"Good eve, my lord," she murmured.

She sounded sad, and Justin wondered if she was simply nervous or was still overset by his earlier refusal to speak of Alicia. Despite the fact that he had once been betrothed and was now married, he had not learned much of the ways of women. How long did such wounds last, he wondered?

He regretted deeply the way he had behaved earlier. It had been naught but cowardice to turn away, to tell her not to speak of Alicia to him, or in his hearing. For a horrible moment, he had heard his father's voice coming out of his mouth, speaking in the cold, despotic manner Justin had always hated. He remembered the shadows that had clouded Isabelle's eyes for the remainder of the day, even during the feast that Meg had so carefully prepared. She had grown reserved, and the warm intimacy they had enjoyed since their last day at Siere had vanished.

"Isabelle," he said, taking a few careful steps toward her. "I hope you have enjoyed your first day at Talwar. I am sorry if I have done...or said...anything to mar it."

"I have enjoyed it very much. You have been so kind to me, my lord, just as your people have been. I have been sitting here wishing that my parents could have known the good man I have married. My mother was so worried before she died about what would become of Senet and me.

How glad she would have been to know that Sir Justin Baldwin would make me his wife.'' She lifted her face to him at last.

She was not beautiful in the way that women who were called beautiful were supposed to be. Her hair was not blond, her skin was not pale, her features and form were not delicate. She would never be able to affect the commonly approved imitation of the much-painted Virgin Mary, as both Alicia and Lady Evelyn were able to do. Nay, Isabelle was none of those things. Her hair was as black and gleaming as a raven's wing, her skin was smooth, with the olive complexion that gave testament to her French heritage, her features were full and sensual, just as her figure was. Her eyes, set in the midst of all this, were so stunningly blue that he didn't believe he would ever grow used to, or weary of, looking at them.

"I am sorry to be so foolish," she whispered.

"You are not foolish. I also wish I could have met your parents. I wish I could have asked your father for his blessing on our marriage."

She colored brightly and looked away. "That is a kind thing to say, my lord, but it is not necessary."

She thought he only spoke out of kindness? If she had even the smallest idea of how glad he was to have her for his wife, she would know that he spoke the truth. And if she knew how much he desired her in that very moment, she would probably be rather afraid. Although not for long. It was the one sure confidence he had, that he knew how to make love to a woman. The whores at Briarstone had taught him well. But Isabelle was not simply a woman, she was also a virgin, and he had never bedded a virgin before. He tried to think back to his own first experience, to the daunting uncertainty and bewilderment. A memory of being teased by the women at Briarstone came to him—for, indeed, he had never had a woman until he went there to live—followed by the more pleasurable memory of what had come after the teasing. The women had taken their turns with him, each seeming softer and more delightful than the last. By the time they finished, he'd been too exhausted to move, and too giddy with pleasure to remember the fears that had once possessed him. That was what he wanted to do to Isabelle, he thought. Make her giddy with pleasure.

He moved about the chamber slowly, putting out each candle with care, watching Isabelle as she followed his movement with wide eyes.

"You must tell me if you want me to stay, Isabelle," he said as he neared the last candle.

"My lord?" Her voice was breathless, trembling.

"Do you want me to stay with you this night?" he asked, walking to her on silent, bare feet. The chamber was lit only by the flames in the hearth, causing the room's shadows to jump and dance. "Are you ready to become my wife?"

He held out his hand, and she put her own in it, letting him pull her to her feet.

"I thought…once we had reached Talwar…you said that we would…"

He set his hands at her waist, feeling how stiff and tense she was through the thin material of her nightdress. "I said that you would become my wife when we were at Talwar," he murmured, sliding his hands slowly downward, to her hips, and back up again, rubbing the cloth against her skin. Lowering his mouth, he placed a gentle kiss beneath her ear and pulled her body closer to his own, almost, but not quite, touching. "And when you wished it." His lips caressed the shell of her ear, softly tickling her with his warm breath as he spoke. "And only then, Isabelle." He kissed her ear with tender care, feeling a shiver run through her, hearing the small moan that escaped her lips. She pressed against him of her own accord, seeking instinctively the contact that he knew her body craved. His hands slid even lower, answering, curving slowly over her buttocks, lifting and pressing her more tightly against himself. She was warm and soft, moving against him in an awkward manner that bespoke her innocence, arousing Justin in a way that no more skillful touch could do.

"Will you become my wife, Isabelle?" he whispered, searching for her mouth. "Tell me."

"Aye." Her arms crept upward to curl about his neck, and she lifted her face to meet his kiss. "Aye, my lord."

The soldier's quarters were large and cool, built to house many more than the five young men who presently occupied one of the several sleeping chambers. One day, they all believed, when Talwar was a great estate, these chambers would be filled with fighting men—the army of Talwar—and they, having been the first among them, would hold places of honor. For now, the boys enjoyed the pleasure of living in the great stone keep and not having to share their privacy, even with their master.

"Well," Kayne said into the dark silence, as they lay on their pallets. "What do you think of her?"

Nobody needed to ask who "her" was.

"She's a surprise," Aric said stonily. "And she's not the one he went to get, that Lady Evelyn his brother wrote him about."

"I never thought he'd be so happy to wed," John said. "Not after what the other one did to him."

"He was full angered when he left for London," Ralf agreed. "But he came back smiling. I hope she won't change anything."

"I hope she won't change *him*," Kayne said vehemently. "Don't know what he needs a wife for, anyway. He's got us, hasn't he?"

"She's nice," Neddy's smaller voice put in.

Chuckling, John turned on his side. "You're just missing your mother, is what, Neddy. Any lady will do for that.''

''Not for our mother,'' Ralf returned hotly. ''And he's right. Lady Isabelle is nice. I'm glad Sir Justin married her and brought her here.''

''He could've had anybody,'' Kayne said. ''Why do you think he chose her? She's not really even beautiful.''

''I think she is,'' Aric said without shame.

''She reminds Aric of his mother, I'll vow,'' John said, laughing again. ''Dark-haired alike, aren't they?''

''Idiot.'' Aric tossed his pillow at him. ''Stop talking about mothers. You didn't even *know* yours.''

''Leave him be,'' Kayne told him sharply. ''I've told you before about that.''

''He's obsessed with mothers,'' Aric muttered, standing up to retrieve his pillow. John lay still and silent as the older boy plucked it away. ''And Lady Isabelle is beautiful. Any fool could see it, whether they had a mother or not.''

''She's not in the common way, I should have said,'' Kayne admitted. ''But 'tis clear that Sir Justin finds her comely enough. Did you see how he looked at her throughout the meal?''

''Aye,'' Ralf said. ''He had no mind for his food, s'truth. He seemed…besotted.''

A silence followed this, as each of the boys thought on how their master's newly married state would affect them.

''We must wait and see what happens,'' Kayne said at last. ''It may be that 'twill pass, like some sickness, and all will be as it ever has been. We have known Sir Justin a long while—longer than she has—and he wouldn't abandon us for a mere woman. All will be well.''

''Aye,'' John said quietly.

''No matter what does happen,'' Kayne added. ''I charge each of you to treat Lady Isabelle with all courtesy and due accord, as Sir Justin has taught us is right. We will abide by the code of chivalry.''

"You don't need to tell us," Aric said angrily. "We know how to treat a lady, especially Sir Justin's wife."

"See that you do, then," Kayne warned. "For if any man among you fails, he will not only meet Sir Justin's anger, but mine, as well."

In Isabelle's chamber, the lord of Talwar and his new wife lay together in the bed they shared, shaking with unrepentant laughter.

"But what did you mean by it, Isabelle?" Justin managed to ask, lifting himself up on his elbows. One look at Isabelle's wide grin sent both of them back into laughter, and he collapsed on top of her, helpless to stop.

"Oh, my lord!" she gasped after they'd calmed. "You're crushing me."

"Forgive me," he said, chuckling and rolling to his side. "God save me." He wiped his eyes and smiled at her in the darkness. "Never, in all my life..." he began, but renewed laughter brought the words to an end. Still laughing, he threw the covers aside and, naked, went to wet a cloth in a nearby basin. Isabelle was still grinning when he returned to the bed, her eyes gleaming with amusement.

"You said I'd enjoy it," she teased, "but I didn't expect that you meant this much."

He chuckled and sat beside her, pushing the covers aside to reveal his wife's lovely, unclothed body. "Ah, Isabelle," he said, leaning down to kiss her smiling mouth. "You are a jewel, and priceless. I have never in my life laughed so hard. We must be crazed, the pair of us." He kissed her again, gently and thoroughly, then pressed his forehead against hers and gazed into her eyes. "Did I hurt you very much, little one?"

"You know full well you did." She began to giggle, and Justin felt more laughter rising in his own throat.

"We *are* crazed," he said, sitting up with the cloth in his hand. "It shouldn't be funny. Let me wash the blood from you, beloved."

Isabelle clamped her legs together and said, with sudden embarrassment, "Oh, nay, my lord!"

With one hand, he gently persuaded her legs apart. "'Twill not hurt, I vow. Let me care for you, little one. I am your husband in full now." He bent and placed a quick kiss on her belly, then grinned up at her when she gasped. "There is no longer any need to be shy. I have seen all of you, and you have seen all of me, and we are very beautiful together. There, is it not soothing?" He carefully pressed the cloth upon her. "I am sorry to have hurt you. I have no experience with virgins, but I think you must have been very well fortified, Isabelle."

"Very…" she began, giggling, "*very* English."

It was what she had said when he was in the midst of making her his wife, and when the barrier of her maidenhead proved to be much more difficult to breach than either of them had expected. What had begun for Isabelle as the most shockingly pleasant experience of her life— with her husband's patient, gentle lovemaking discovering something in her nature that Isabelle could only think of as a hitherto-dormant, and French, passion—had become something altogether different when his several attempts to bind them together were frustrating for him and painful for her. Overtaken by tears and agony, afraid she was disappointing Justin past tolerance, she'd made an apology, telling him that she was sorry to be so very English. A moment later, her maidenhead had given way, and a few long moments after that, Justin had taken away all thoughts of pain. It was only after, as they lay together, damp and exhausted, that he began to laugh, and had asked her what she'd meant by the words. The foolishness of it made her laugh, too, and that had made him laugh even harder. Soon they'd been rolling with amusement, laughing uncontrollably.

Finishing his gentle ministrations, he tossed the cloth on the floor and crawled up over Isabelle, pulling her with him until they lay side by side, facing each other, snuggled beneath the covers.

"Isabelle." He said her name with a sigh, nuzzling the soft skin at the base of her neck and caressing her back with his fingers. "It will never be painful again, I vow. We shall have only goodness in our marriage bed." He kissed her mouth, tasting and teasing with slow strokes of his tongue. "No woman has ever given me as much pleasure as you have done this night," he murmured. "Did you find it agreeable?"

"Aye," she whispered, tentatively touching his chest, feeling how hot his skin was, how hard his muscles. "You are so beautiful, my lord."

He made a low, growling sound in reply, his dark head traveling downward beneath the covers, to her breasts.

"I am so glad," she said, gasping as she felt his mouth on her body, "so glad that you stole me for your wife."

"But I *love* you!"

Isabelle sat up with a start, panicked and confused, gulping down great mouthfuls of air. Several moments passed before she realized where she was—at Talwar, in her new bedchamber, naked and in her new bed. She felt for Justin and found only the warm place beside her where he had earlier fallen asleep.

"And you are very dear to me, also, Birgitte. Indeed, more than dear, for you have been so good to me—"

"Because I love you, my lord. Please don't send me away. Please. *Please.*"

Sobs followed this. Horrible, pain-filled sobs.

"I have a wife now, Birgitte, and I have vowed before

God to be faithful to her, to keep myself only to her. If you will stay at Talwar, you must understand and accept this.''

"You don't want her," Birgitte cried tearfully. "You *can't* want her. She's ugly and stupid! She won't know how to please you as I do. Please, my lord! Let me stay! I'll do whatever you ask of me. Everything I know that you like.''

"Nay, and I will not have you speaking thusly of your lady—''

"It's the truth! You're just too kind to speak it. Oh, please, my lord. Please. I know you want me. If not tonight, then tomorrow. Or the next day. Or next week.''

"Never," he said gently. "Put on your clothes and go. In the morn you will return to Briarstone with Sir Christian.''

Birgitte burst into even louder tears. "You can't send me away!" she wailed.

"It would be best," he said patiently. "You have been very good to me this past year, Birgitte, and I will not cease to be thankful, but you must go. I will share a bed now with no other woman but my wife. That is the way it will be.''

"But I'm with child, my lord. With *your* child!''

Hearing the words, Isabelle squeezed her eyes shut and set a hand to her mouth.

There was silence, save for Birgitte's woeful weeping, until Justin said, "If you are with child, then it is most likely not by me. You are aware that I have taken every care against such as that occurring. Howbeit," he went on quickly when she began to wail again, "if you are, I will recognize and support the babe. If you are not, I will yet continue to support you, even for the remainder of your life. You have naught to fear, Birgitte. I shall take good care of you, and you shall want for nothing.''

"But—''

Isabelle could hear his chamber door opening.

"All will be well, little one, and you know that Sir Christian will keep you safe and happy at Briarstone. Lady Isabelle and I will see you in the morn to bid you God speed. Good night, Birgitte."

There was the sound of a swift kiss, and then of the chamber door closing. Isabelle pulled her legs up to her chest and dropped her head forward to rest it on her knees.

Justin could hear Birgitte weeping as she walked away down the hall, even through the closed door, and he released a long breath. He regretted hurting the girl, but it seemed impossible to keep from doing so. She was a sweet, beautiful and sometimes foolish creature who would someday make another man an enchanting wife. But not him. He needed an entirely different sort of woman, and had been fortunate enough to find one. A woman who not only was beautiful and kind, but who would be the companion he had forever dreamed of having.

Isabelle.

The thought that she had heard what had taken place filled him with dread, and he walked noiselessly to the adjoining door. She was sitting up in the bed, huddled with her head upon her knees. He thought perhaps she must be crying, although she made no sound.

"Isabelle."

She lifted her head to look at him.

With a sigh, he crossed the chamber and sat on the bed, straining to see her face in the darkness.

"I would have spared you this, if I could have done so. Birgitte has been my leman, on occasion, for the past year. I have no excuse, save that I was not wed nor had any intention to wed. If I had, I pray you will believe that I would not have kept the girl here."

"You do not have to explain the matter to me, my

lord,'' she whispered, her voice so small that his heart ached for having caused her pain. "I knew that you were not…without experience. And it is an acceptable practice among men, is it not? My uncle has a leman. Her name is Bertilde, and I paid her debts and sent her an allowance every quarter. I will do the same for Birgitte, if you wish it."

"By the rood," Justin muttered, rubbing a hand over his eyes and thinking that Sir Myles deserved to be drawn and quartered for the contemptible care he had given his niece. "I would never ask you to do such a thing. Never. Isabelle…" He said her name with a groan. "I don't know how to make this better. What to say to you to keep you from pain. I didn't know that I would be getting married. And when I did know—when I received the missive from my brother about Lady Evelyn—I no longer shared my bed with Birgitte. For more than a month, until tonight, there has been no one. I have touched no other woman but you." He searched through the bedclothes for her hand, and grasped it tightly. "For all of our married life, I vow, I will never touch any other woman but you. It is the truth I speak to you, Isabelle, and I ask that you will believe me."

"I believe you."

She said the words, but he wondered if she really meant them. If he had discovered that she'd kept a lover for a year before their marriage, he would have been inconsolably desolate.

"What about the child, my lord?"

"The child?"

"Birgitte…said that she was with child."

"Ah." He nodded. "I do not know if she truly is or not. She has said that before, several times, to try and make me wed her. But time ever proved the truth."

Isabelle gazed at him solemnly, and Justin could hear

the echo of his words repeating themselves, even in the silence.

Time ever proved the truth.

"If there is a child, I will not neglect it." Reaching out, he gently cupped her face. "I am the same man I was an hour ago, Isabelle. Far from perfect, s'truth, but I will be as good to you as possible, the best man I can be. Can you not trust me, even a little?"

She covered his hand with her own, holding it against her cheek. "It is hard for me to trust any man," she whispered. "But I will strive to do so, for you have been kind to me, my lord, and I wish to please you."

"That you do easily," he murmured, leaning forward to kiss her, then to gather her close in his arms. "Most easily, Isabelle."

Chapter Ten

The account books were a horrible mess. Even after a week of laboring over them, Isabelle was beginning to wonder if she'd ever get Talwar's finances straightened into some semblance of order. Justin, she had discovered with some surprise, had such a dim interest in keeping count of his money that he hadn't even known where his accounts were. It had taken Isabelle and Gytha two days of searching before the books were finally found, at the bottom of a clothing chest in Justin's bedchamber. The last recorded entry had been made four years earlier, after which keeping the accounts up to date had obviously become a duty too tedious for Justin to bother with.

His lack of interest reminded Isabelle forcibly of her father, who had embraced a similar disinterest in what he regarded as a thoroughly soulless occupation. For her father, it had seemed much better to be involved in political intrigues; for Justin, the care and training of his young charges took preeminence, the task to which he devoted most of his day and self. Although not always. Sometimes—often—his interest was focused all on her.

Isabelle had always thought that the honey month that followed a marriage would be one during which a newly wed couple became better acquainted, although she'd never realized exactly in what manner this was accomplished. But Justin had known, and had evidently decided that they were going to be very well acquainted, indeed. His desire for the physical union was seemingly unending; Isabelle couldn't count how many times they had come together in the past week, in so many places, and during so many different times of the day. He didn't seem to care at all for the propriety of keeping only to their marriage bed. S'truth, he didn't seem to care for anything at all, save that there was some semblance of privacy, whether it be on a windy hillside beneath the shelter of trees where they had ridden to view his lands, or in the bathing chamber when he bade her wash his back and ended up washing all of her, instead, or in the working chamber where she now sat, remembering with hot cheeks and in vivid detail what he had done to her while they sat together in a single chair before the fire. Once, she had gone out to the stables to ask him about quarterly funds paid for dry goods, and after he sent the boys out of the building on some foolish task, he had quickly managed to drive all thoughts of both funds and dry goods entirely away. She hadn't even remembered why she'd first gone out to find him until an hour later, when she sat down at her working table again and realized that she must look as giddy as a drunken lunatic. But that was what he made of her, and so easily— a lunatic. With a kiss, a look, a word.

They had perhaps had an unfortunate start, with regard to the serving girl Birgitte, who had shortly admitted, after her arrival at Briarstone, that she had lied about carrying Justin's child, but the memory of that had quickly become distant and dim, forgotten by Isabel's heart entirely and held only by her mind as an event that had passed.

She'd never been so happy in all her life, or dreamed that there could be anything like this, waking each morn to find her handsome husband lying warm beside her, his dark hair disordered, his darker eyes closed in slumber.

Surely God had looked down upon her misery while she lived with Sir Myles and decided to be kind. How else could such a miracle have befallen her, that she should find herself married to the most wonderful man in England? She loved him so much that sometimes she felt guilty for it. Husbands and wives weren't supposed to love each other, for love was to be given to God alone, but if the Lord had found it fitting enough to bless her with Justin, Isabelle thought, then perhaps He would not mind it so much if she gave a part of her love to the blessing itself.

A soft knock fell on the chamber door, and then the door opened slightly as a head overwhelmed by tousled brown curls appeared around it.

"Your pardon, m'lady. Meg says there's hot cider, and I'm to ask if you're wanting some. And Gytha says there's a missive for Sir Justin that's just arrived from his brother, the earl." The missive in question was held up through the opening. "Shall I take it out to him or leave it with you, I'm to ask."

"Please leave it with me, Odelyn," Isabelle said, smiling as the girl rushed into the chamber to do her mistress's bidding. Odelyn had arrived three days before, with an escort from Briarstone and a missive from Sir Christian saying, "For Lady Isabelle, with every gratitude for her kindnesses to one whom I hold dear, an excellent maid to replace Birgitte and to lend you and your household aid. Odelyn is a precious jewel." And that she surely was. She was somewhat younger than Birgitte, being, Isabelle guessed, around ten-and-five years of age, although nobody knew for certain exactly how old she was. Odelyn had been found abandoned at Briarstone's gates nine years earlier, only able to point at herself and speak her own name. She had become everyone's child in the castle, growing up with dozens of mothers, fathers, sisters and brothers, and had come to Talwar already looking upon everyone there, save Isabelle, as a part of this large, informal family. She was as energetic as a child, happy and smiling and eager to please.

"Thank you. Sir Justin has been waiting for this to arrive. I shall take it out to him right away. Please tell Meg that I'll have some of that cider when I've returned."

With a quick curtsy, Odelyn left the chamber, running, as she usually did, and Isabelle turned the missive over in her hands, to find the earl of Siere's seal. This would be what Justin had been waiting for—word of whether her uncle had made the way clear for Senet to be removed from Sir Howton's care. Pushing away from her table, she closed the account book she had been working on and went in search of her husband.

She found him in the outer bailey, mounted on horseback and brandishing a blunted wooden sword in one hand and a much-dented shield of armor in the other. Facing him was Ralf, who was likewise mounted and armed.

"Don't worry about your steed," Justin instructed loudly, so that the other boys, who were mounted a little farther away, could also hear him. "A well-trained warhorse will know what's expected of it, especially if you don't confuse it with a lot of unnecessary handling. All your horse needs is an idea of direction and speed, nothing more. Let it do its part without any additional distraction, for mercy knows there will be plenty of that in battle. What *you* must concentrate on is keeping your shield before you, thus—" he set the heavy shield he bore tightly against his chest and belly "—and your sword high. Remember, never carry it below the level of your shoulder, for once you are engaged you must keep your weapon aloft to defeat your foe. He may come at you from the side with his weapon, but that is what your shield and armor are for. You attack from above, aiming for the most vulnerable areas in his armor, the head, neck and shoulders." He chopped sharply at the air with his wooden sword, causing Isabelle to grimace at the cold-bloodedness of the actions. "Hold the reins to your steed here, in your shield hand, but loosely, mind you. Jerking the horse about in the midst of a fight may cause it injury or you death, or both. Now, Ralf..."

He seemed to realize, by the direction of Ralf's gaze, that Isabelle was there.

"My lady." He smiled at her in the same manner he ever did when setting sight on her. It amazed Isabelle that he never seemed to be angered when she interrupted him, no matter what he was doing.

"I am sorry to disturb you, my lord."

"Oh, nay," he said, dismounting and leading his steed toward her. "Being disturbed by you is the most welcome occurrence I know." The wicked gaze in his eyes told her just how much he meant the words, and Isabelle grew hot with embarrassment. Over Justin's shoulder, she could see the boys grinning.

"This missive arrived from your brother, the earl of Siere." She waited until he had removed his leather gauntlets before pressing the parchment document into his hands. "Is it about Senet, do you think?"

"It must be." He broke the seal and unrolled the single page. His brows lowered as he read, and the line of his mouth grew set.

Isabelle's heart began to pound frantically. "What is it?" she asked, touching his sleeve. "Will my uncle let Senet come to us?"

Justin shook his head. "Sir Myles refuses to answer either of my brothers' missives, and Sir Howton has replied that he will not release Senet until he has word from Sir Myles. My eldest brother, the lord of Gyer, has appealed to the duke of Gloucester to intervene. Hugh asks us to be patient. To wait." He quickly rolled the document up and gave it to Isabelle.

"What will you do, then?"

"I gave you my word that your brother would be here at Talwar within a fortnight of our leaving Siere, and he shall be. Kayne!"

Kayne rode up at once. "Aye, my lord, Sir Justin?"

"You will ride to Briarstone full speed and ask Sir Christian to send a dozen of his best men back with you this day to guard Talwar and my lady for the next week. You may tell him, if he asks why, that we are going to fetch Lady Isabelle's brother from Sir Howton."

"Justin!" Isabelle cried. "You cannot!"

He paid her no heed. "Mind that you have returned to Talwar by nightfall," he told Kayne. "We will all want a good night's sleep before we start in the morn."

"Aye, my lord," Kayne replied obediently, his face flushed with excitement.

"Go, then, and tarry not."

With a nod, Kayne turned his horse about and rode full speed out the bailey gates.

"My lord," Isabelle said, striding to keep up with him as he walked back to the other boys. "You cannot mean to do this! The earl of Siere has asked you to wait. To be patient. Surely you cannot go against his wishes."

He uttered a laugh. "Can I not? I think I will find it exceedingly easy to do."

"But—"

"I have been more than patient with your uncle, beloved. But no more. He had full warning, and has no cause for complaint." To the boys, he said, "We are going on a journey, with the object of stealing Lady Isabelle's brother from a highly esteemed lord whose castle will be well fortified and his army well trained. It should be a very good lesson for you all. We'll leave at first light tomorrow morn. I want you to spend the remainder of the day preparing yourselves and your horses for a week of hard traveling."

"Aye, my lord," the boys murmured variously, pleasure

at this unexpected boon strong in their voices and expressions.

"Aric, I would have you prepare an additional horse for Lady Isabelle's brother to ride. Make it the chestnut gelding. He's strong and well trained. Here. Take Synn and have John care for him."

Taking the reins that Justin handed him, Aric obediently replied that he would do as his master bade him, and then, with the only smile that Isabelle had ever seen on the boy's face, rode away to join the others.

"And now, my lady," Justin said, putting his hands on Isabelle's waist and pulling her near, "you and I will retire to our bedchamber for the remainder of the day."

"But I wish to speak with you, my lord."

"Aye," he murmured happily, bending to kiss her. "That is just what I want, also, my dearest wife. I want to hear you speaking to me, constantly, so that I may carry the memory of your beautiful voice with me while we are parted. I want to dream of the things you say when I am loving you, deep inside you."

Her face grew hot at the words. "Do I *say* things then?" The idea was thoroughly embarrassing.

"Oh, indeed, yes," he murmured against her mouth. "Sweet, delightful things. Come with me, and I shall prove it to you."

Chapter Eleven

Isabelle shut the account book and shoved it away with a weary sigh. She couldn't work, couldn't concentrate. It was impossible with Justin gone. Three days had passed since she awoke to find that he and the boys had already left. Three days in which she had alternated between worry for their, and Senet's, safety, and fury that Justin had left without even waking her to say goodbye. Not that it would have made much difference. He'd exhausted her so thoroughly with his lovemaking that she doubted a herd of cows walking through her bedchamber would have woken her.

She pushed away from her working table and went to stare unhappily out of the chamber's east window, letting her gaze wander over the far hills and the blue sky. It was another hot late-summer day. She wondered if Justin was suffering from it, traveling beneath the hot sun, or if perhaps it was cooler wherever he was.

Wherever he was.

"He could have at least left a missive," she said aloud, folding her arms over her chest and releasing an angry breath. "Even a word or two." She'd had nightmares since he left. Nightmares of him being caught and jailed, or, worse, killed. What would happen to the boys, then, and to Senet? Would they be jailed, as well? Mayhap even punished? And what would happen to her? She doubted that her uncle would allow her to remain at Talwar, even though she was Justin's legal wife. Sir Myles was still her guardian; it would be a simple matter for him to have her returned to live beneath his hand.

Justin, she thought for the hundredth time since he'd left, *you should have done as your brother advised. You should have waited.* But that wasn't the kind of man that he was. Certainly not in regard to obeying his brothers. In truth, when it came to his family, he was obdurately stubborn.

She had learned that much about him on their last night together, when she had lain in his arms, her head upon his chest, contented to rest that way forever after the loving they had shared.

"What was your childhood like?" he had asked, and Isabelle had felt a small shock of surprise. People didn't speak of what was in their personal past, for life was short and only God and the future mattered.

"It was a usual childhood, I think," she had said at last, letting herself think back to the time when her life had been happy and secure. "My father and mother shared a deep affection, but they were different from each other. My father was very French, very passionate in all his dealings, while my mother was fully English, and much more reserved. They got along well, but it was confusing at times, especially when I was young. They seldom agreed on matters. Father believed that the heart must rule over all, while Mother felt the heart to be a rather poor and unstable instrument. She much preferred the qualities of the mind."

She had glanced at him, and Justin had smiled encouragingly.

"I was tutored at home," she continued, relaxing into the rhythmic stroke of his fingers across her bare back.

"My mother was the one who taught me mathematics. My first plaything was an abacus. Her abacus. Mother loved the mystery of numbers and passed that love to me. When I was five, I would sit on her lap and decipher tables from the *Almagest*." She smiled at the memory.

"Mother had several mathematical manuscripts of her own. We had four priests at Lomas, and although they did not wish to do so, Father bade them to make copies of the *Almagest*, and of *Arithmetica*, and of Leonardo of Pisa's *Liber abaci*. There were some smaller works by Archimedes, as well, and even one volume of Euclid's *Elements*, which Father had sent to him by one of the chancellors at Oxford so that it might be copied. It was wicked, I suppose, for they might have copied the Holy Bible, instead of works for Mother's pleasure, but indeed it was wonderful to have them. Being so English, she was a little horrified by my father's insistence about the books, even though she loved them so. But he had a passionate nature, as I have said, and was determined that she should know every possible pleasure in life."

"I begin to think that your father and I have much in common," Justin told her, teasing, and Isabelle laughed and said, "Much more pleasuring from you, my lord, and there will be naught left of me."

They both laughed, then, and he asked if her uncle, Sir Myles, had her mother's books.

She shook her head. "No longer. He gave them to a broker in London, who sold them with the rest of my parents' library. I invested the money that came from them in a salt mine in Droitwich. It returned a huge profit for my uncle."

He squeezed her hand in a brief, comforting gesture. "I'm sorry," he said.

"Me, also," she murmured. "The manuscripts that were my mother's bore her likeness. One of the younger priests was given to much artistry, and at my father's bidding painted small portraits throughout each book, show-ing my mother in many fanciful ways. He made her the Queen of Numbers," she said, chuckling. "'Twas all in much fun." His answering smile made her feel slightly dizzy. "I wish you could have seen them."

"As do I. Was your brother also taught at home?"

"Oh, nay. Father was already unhappy that his daughter should take such an interest in anything so dull and En-glish as mathematics. He wanted his son to be like him."

"Passionate?"

"Even so, my lord. Even so. For a time, he considered sending Senet to France for training, but Mother would have none of that. Finally, when he was eight, Senet was fostered with Sir Howton."

"A good choice. He is accounted one of the finest train-ing masters in all of England. Many great knights have been fostered by him."

Isabelle nodded. "I missed my brother badly after he was gone. We have not seen much of each other these past many years. After my father's trial, Sir Howton meant to give Senet over to my uncle, for he did not wish to succor the son of a traitor, but Sir Myles asked him to keep Senet as a servant, to labor there and earn his living."

"To labor?" Justin repeated with a frown. "He has not been indentured, I pray."

"I do not think so. Does it make a difference?"

"I cannot like it if, after being trained for knighthood so many years, he was suddenly made into a servant. Nay, I cannot like it. It is not fitting for a young man who has started in the way of knighthood to be so taken away from it. And made into a servant, by the rood! Sir Howton should feel naught but shame for enacting such a crime."

"Does it matter so much?" she asked worriedly. "He need not be a knight. If he could only live here, in peace, as you promised—"

"He will yet require proper training," Justin insisted.

"Whether he achieves knighthood is only his concern, but any man who wishes to make his own way, with some measure of respect, must be trained in war and chivalry. It is the way of things."

"I suppose this is the truth," she admitted, wondering if this was the time for them to speak of the journey he meant to take. But she was curious now, having spoken of her own past, and asked him the same question that he had asked of her.

"What was your childhood like, my lord?"

He hesitated, so long that she thought he might not answer, but at last he began to speak, slowly and without emotion.

"It was very hard. A matter of survival, more than anything else. My mother died when I was but a lad, almost too young to remember her. Everyone else in the household was at war with one another. My father was a violent man. A tyrant, and evil in his way. I remember most that he hated my younger sister, Candis, and blamed her for my mother's death. From my earliest days, I knew that if I did not protect her, he would kill her."

Isabelle rolled over onto her stomach, propping herself up on her forearms and gazing up into his stony face.

"Oh, Justin…"

"My eldest brother, Alexander, was the next object of my father's wrath, never able to please him, no matter what he did. With my other brother, Willem, it was much the same. Only the twins—Hugh and Hugo—managed to escape his wrath, and they were given free rein. You would not know it to see them now, but in their youth, Hugh and Hugo were as wild as untamed animals, and just as dangerous." He clenched one fist at the memory. "Living in Castle Gyer was as living in a battle, every day, trying to avoid my father, trying to avoid Hugh and Hugo. Fortunately, Candis and I were not given much care or thought, beyond being fed and clothed. We learned to live in the shadows, to move silently, to listen for our father's anger and to keep away. Days, sometimes weeks, would pass before Alexander or Willem would so much as say a word to either of us, even after my father had died and Alexander became lord. It was harder to avoid Hugh and Hugo and their wretched plots.''

"They were cruel to you?''

"Not purposefully so. But they were wild, and carried their wildness with them everywhere. There were always snakes and spiders, fires and poisons and sharp objects. They were poor companions for young children, especially for Candis, who only had me to guard her. But, for all the harm and destruction they wrought at Gyer, Hugh and Hugo seemed to feel some affection for us. Once, I caught one of our tutors fondling Candis in a lewd and unseemly manner, and although she cried, he would not let her go. I tried to make him, but he was drunk and struck me a hard blow, throwing me out of his chamber. I ran for Hugh and Hugo, and they came at once, threatening the man through his chamber door until he let Candis come out.

She was unharmed, but very frightened, and he asked forgiveness, begging us not to tell Alexander or anyone, and promised that he'd never touch her again. I do not know what Hugh and Hugo did to him, but something happened during the night, for in the morn the man was babbling with madness, screaming about a visitation he'd had. Alexander had to send him to an asylum, and a week later, or so we heard, he threw himself from a tower and died. The twins celebrated by hiding beef bones behind the tapestries in the great hall and letting all of Gyer's hunting dogs loose in there.'' He let out a breath. "What a spectacle. Alexander turned so red I thought he'd burst.''

She didn't smile, understanding the sadness the memory gave him. It should have been humorous—all those dogs, racing about, wreaking havoc, in such a refined setting— but she knew that he would never see it the way others might. He would only remember the fear he'd lived with every day and night during those days, even in such moments as that.

Reaching out, she pressed her fingers gently over his fisted hand, rubbing to take his tension away.

"I'm sorry," she whispered, echoing the sympathy he'd earlier offered her.

He gazed at her, and when he spoke, his voice was more even, shorn of its sadness. "It was not forever thus. A few years later, Hugh and Hugo stole some travelers as they journeyed through Gyer, and locked them away as prisoners in the castle before Alexander could find out. One of them, by fortunate incidence, was Lady Lillis, the daughter of my brother's greatest enemy, Jaward of Wellewyn. Alexander decided to keep her and her nurse, Edyth, who had been traveling with her, and later he and Lillis were married."

"Lady Rosaleen warned me that I was not the only bride to be stolen by a Baldwin," Isabelle said.

Justin grinned. "It does seem to have become a family tradition," he admitted. "But a happy one. Lillis and Edyth changed everything for Candis and me, and for everyone at Castle Gyer. They were our salvation, and loved and cared for us tenderly. We were safe then."

"May God be praised," she murmured.

His fist uncurled, and he caught her hand, holding it. "And Alexander and Lillis have been content and happy in their marriage. Just as I hope that we shall be, Isabelle. I should be ashamed at having stolen you, but I am not. In truth, I become gladder of it every day."

"I, also," she said. "Although I cannot think why you went to so much trouble, when any woman would have gladly gone away with you, if you had but asked."

His gaze grew intent, and he pushed her to her back, leaning over and searching her eyes. "Would you have, Isabelle? If I had come to your chamber in the dark of night and said, 'Lady, I am seeking a wife. Will you come away with me and be my bride?' would you have come?"

"I would have wanted to."

"But would you?"

She had to think on the answer before she could reply, honestly, "I would have been afraid, I suppose, to go with a man I hardly knew. I *was* afraid of you until we reached the monastery. But in my heart, I would have longed to say yes." With a hand about his neck, she persuaded him closer, and kissed him. "I am glad you did not ask me, and saved me from being very foolish."

The answer pleased him, for he slid his hands beneath her, bringing their bodies together, and said, "I shall remember that in future, my good lady wife, whenever you are being difficult."

"You will steal me again, my lord?"

"Oh, aye, beloved. Again and again and again."

But it wouldn't be necessary, she thought now, as she moved to press one hand against the sun-warmed windowpane. Just as it hadn't been necessary that night. She had given him, and would give him, anything he asked for, anything he desired. She loved him, and would never be able to deny him.

A movement in the distant hills caught her attention, something tall and dark, although the thickness of the glass pane made it difficult to tell exactly what. It was moving resolutely toward Talwar at a steady pace. Was it a man on horseback? she wondered, her heart lurching. Could it be Justin, returning already? Another figure appeared beside it. Men on horseback, she was certain. And another figure, and another.

"It must be Justin," she murmured with growing excitement. But the next moment it seemed as if an entire wave of figures flooded over the hill. *Hundreds* of men on horseback. And all of them heading for Talwar.

Isabelle stood paralyzed, staring at the relentlessly approaching army, unable to comprehend who they were, or why they had come. The size and scope of them was frightening. Overwhelming. It seemed as if Talwar would be swallowed up by a never-ending sea of men.

"My lady!" The chamber door banged open, and one of the men Sir Christian had sent to guard Talwar in Justin's absence stood there, gasping. "Sir Alexander Baldwin, the lord of Gyer, is approaching. It looks as if he's brought his whole army, God save us!"

Chapter Twelve

Sir Alexander Baldwin was just as imposing in person as Isabelle had always thought he would be, the kind of man whose inherent nobility was a thing that was seen, as well as known. He was a handsome man, tall and dark-haired, like Justin, but with eyes the color of new green leaves, rather than the dark, earthy brown that his younger brother possessed. He didn't have the same width of shoulders or the great muscle that Justin did, but for all that, he gave the impression of strength and danger. The way he stared down his long, aquiline nose at Isabelle made her knees shake beneath her skirts.

She met him outside in the inner bailey—after having spent one full, terrified minute in her working chamber, trying to decide whether she ought to instead find some place to hide—with the belated realization, after he'd already ridden through the gates, that she wasn't properly attired to greet a personage of the lord of Gyer's eminence. He was one of the most powerful, and certainly one of the wealthiest, barons in England, and probably not used to being greeted by a woman whose hair wasn't properly arranged or covered, and who was wearing nothing better than the plainest working clothes.

He left the bulk of his massive army outside the **gates**

and, accompanied only by two other men on horseback, rode to where Isabelle stood.

"My lord, Sir Alexander," she began, bending into a deep curtsy. "I welcome you to—"

"Where is my brother, Sir Justin Baldwin?"

The curt demand stunned Isabelle, so that she did no more than gape at him until he added, "Speak, woman!"

"He's…he's not here," she managed, swallowing down the fear she heard in her voice. "We did not know that you were coming to Talwar, my lord."

The expression on the Lord of Gyer's face grew so forbidding that Isabelle nearly turned about and took flight.

Sir Alexander's horse pranced daintily beneath his commanding grip as he brought the massive steed nearer. "*Where* has he gone?"

His tone was accusatory, fully condemning, and Isabelle instinctively raised a hand to her throat.

"Into Wales, my lord. To Sir Howton's estate."

The lord of Gyer's jaw tightened for the briefest of moments, hardly enough warning for the explosion of curses that followed. By the time he was done, Isabelle felt as if she'd been scorched by Hell's own fires.

"And *you*, I suppose," he said with tight anger, fixing her with that disturbing green-eyed gaze, "are the woman he stole. Isabelle Gaillard?"

Isabelle cleared her throat. "Isabelle Baldwin," she corrected.

The lord of Gyer made the same sort of breathy huffing sound that an angry bull might. The only thing he lacked to make the picture complete, Isabelle thought, was a puff of dust coming out of his nostrils.

"We shall see," he stated.

He dismounted and handed the reins of his steed to one of his men. "Wait for me here," he instructed, then said to the other, "Tell Sir Alain to set camp outside the walls. We will bide at Talwar this night." To Isabelle he said,

"Come. We will speak inside," and strode past her into the dwelling, without waiting for an invitation. Isabelle, feeling as if she were a naughty child, followed.

Gytha, Meg and Odelyn were lined up beyond the door, already bowing as the lord of Gyer walked in.

"Thank you," he said in reply to their murmured welcomes, then, as if he were their master, added, "Bring wine to the working chamber. I will speak with Lady Isabelle there."

The three women lifted their heads as the man walked away, meeting Isabelle's wide-eyed gaze with open sympathy.

Isabelle leaned toward Gytha as she followed Sir Alexander, whispering quickly, "The *best* wine."

Gytha nodded, and Isabelle, steeling herself, walked into the chamber.

Sir Alexander closed the door behind her.

"There is no need for us to exchange false courtesies, Lady Isabelle," he said without delay. "I will tell you plainly that I am displeased with my brother's choice in a wife, especially when I had already approved another, far more suitable, bride for him. You are the daughter of a traitor, and I will never be able to forget that. Howbeit, I cannot force my brother to set you aside if he does not wish to do so. You, however, might be persuaded to leave him, if given the appropriate incentive. Am I right in this?"

Bewildered, Isabelle shook her head. "What can you mean, my lord?"

"I mean, Isabelle Gaillard, that I don't believe my brother took you against your will. I mean that I believe you tempted him away from his rightful betrothed, Lady Evelyn, and schemed to wed a Baldwin in order to gain whatever power and wealth such a union might bring you. But you have not done so wisely, my lady, for you have not counted on me. I can make your life exceedingly unpleasant if you refuse to meet me in this matter of obtaining an annulment and setting my brother free. I am willing to be more than generous, of course. You will be provided with a small estate that you will own outright, and there will be a suitable allowance for both your brother and yourself that will continue for the remainder of your lives."

"*What?*" she sputtered in disbelief. "Surely you can't... *Surely* you don't mean what you say."

His expression remained impassive. "Are you with child, then? That makes the matter a little more difficult, but not impossible. I shall provide for the child, as well."

Oh, her temper, Isabelle thought remorsefully, even as the fury within her began to build. Her unfortunate, wretched temper. She very nearly told him that he could take himself off to Hades, but with an effort, she recalled that there were better ways to handle such men. She'd learned that well enough during all her financial dealings with the obstinate, insulting creatures, of whom he had been the worst.

"I am not with child," she replied, striving to unclench her fisted hands. "And I will not leave my husband. You insult both of us with such false accusations and unholy offers."

A gleam of unexpected appreciation filled the lord of Gyer's eyes. "You mean to make the best bargain possible," he said. "I can admire such a quality in a woman. Very well. I shall provide you with a household of well-trained servants, also with a sufficient number of field and livestock laborers." He thought a moment longer, adding, "And fifty head of fine cattle from my own herds. You must be responsible for all other livestock."

"I don't *want* livestock," she told him furiously. "I don't *want* any of it! I am no foul conspirator, such as you believe. Your brother stole me of his own determination. I had naught to do with it!"

The lord of Gyer sighed. "Very well. I shall provide a full complement of livestock, including fowl. I'll even supply a stock of fish, if you arrange to have a suitable pond dug."

"Are you deaf?" she demanded. "Can you not hear me when I say that I want *nothing* from you?"

"God's feet, but you're a demanding wench," he replied. "I'll go so far as to start your stable with six fine horses, but that is all. If you do not accept the bargain now as final, I will withdraw it and find another, much less pleasant way of removing you from my brother's house. This is no idle threat, my lady. I have the means to get rid of you, and I will use those means if I must. Do you agree to accept my offer in exchange for annulling your marriage to Justin?"

A strange sensation gripped Isabelle, a dizzying feeling, as if rage were pumping through her veins, rather than blood, rushing and throbbing and swelling, so that she began to wonder if her buzzing head was about to explode. She cast about her working chamber for something to throw at the man. Something that would smash his thick skull in.

"Well?" he prompted.

Her skirts whirled as she stopped her search to face him; her chest heaved with the effort to speak, and her voice, when she did speak, sounded foreign, as hot and evil as if she were breathing demon fire at Sir Alexander, rather than making words. The words themselves came out in spurts, between harsh, shaking breaths.

"I wouldn't—agree to anything—that *you* proposed— for all the riches on earth! Not even—for all the Italian silk—in the *Fair Helen*'s hold!" Breathing hard, she gave him a moment to comprehend her words. "Not that you— could offer me that—unless your exalted *means*—include raising ships from the depths of the oceans!"

Sir Alexander blinked at her as Isabelle stood across the

room, striving to calm herself. A knock fell on the door, and Gytha entered bearing a tray with a wine decanter and two goblets. Observing the tension, the older woman quickly put the tray on the working table and left. The moment the door closed, Sir Alexander spoke.

"How did you know of the *Fair Helen?* It cannot be that your uncle discussed his financial undertakings with you."

She laughed scornfully, her voice fully controlled now. "And to think that I once felt sorry for you because you refused to take my advice on that final venture. I *told* you the *Fair Helen* wasn't seaworthy for another journey so soon. I *told* you she needed repairs. But nay, you'd not pay heed. You believed that drunken lout you'd hired to inspect the ship, rather than me, with whom you'd already completed three successful undertakings!" She threw the last sentence at him angrily, remembering just how upset she'd been when she received his missive saying that he was going ahead with the journey, with or without Sir Myles's financial participation.

"But I'm *glad* now that you ignored my warnings. You're a haughty, unfeeling, miserable, *wretched* cur, and I can scarce believe you're even related to Justin, who has never failed to be all that is good and kind, even when he was in the midst of stealing me!" She stalked closer, lifting on her toes to shout into his face. "And despite being stolen and persuaded into such an unusual marriage, the only thing I regret about being wed to Justin is that I must now also be related to *you!*" This last word she punctuated with a one-fingered poke at his muscle-hardened chest, which, she realized belatedly, hurt her a good deal more than it did him.

The lord of Gyer was staring at her as if she were some unfathomable apparition.

"'I. G.,'" he murmured. "All of the correspondence that I carried on with your uncle's financial steward was signed 'I.G.' But that couldn't—" he was shaking his head "—that *couldn't* be you."

She stepped back to make a mocking bow. "But it *is* me, my lord. Isabelle Gaillard. My uncle wouldn't allow me to use my full name, as he didn't want you, or anyone else, to realize that he had entrusted all of his wealth into the care of a female. Only those who lived in London, the brokers and bankers with whom I dealt, knew the truth."

"And they," he said, "being sometimes dependent on your skills, wouldn't reveal that truth, either."

"Even so," she agreed.

His eyes narrowed as he contemplated her. "God's feet," he muttered, and pushed past her to fill a goblet with wine, which he drank before speaking again.

"I wrote your uncle after the disaster with the *Fair Helen*. Did you ever know that?"

Surprise took the place of some of Isabelle's anger. He was leaning over her working table, his back to her, all of his imposing manner gone.

"Nay, I did not. He never spoke of the matter, save to say that we would have no further dealings with you in the way of jointly funding ventures."

"You are right when you say that I should have listened to you regarding the *Fair Helen*. After she went down, I was full angered with myself for being so stubborn. Your advice in the former ventures that your uncle and I financed had been unfailingly correct, and I knew, the moment I had word of the Fair Helen's fate, that you had been right again. The other ship—the one you suggested we use instead of the *Fair Helen*—made the same voyage without mishap. Is that not so?"

"Aye," Isabelle said. "The *Capetian* arrived safely in Portsmouth with a full cargo. My uncle made a rare profit from the Italian silks we sold."

"Just as I had made three times before with the journeys you had arranged." He sighed, and turned to face her, his expression much softened. "I enjoyed the correspondence we had shared, you and I. There was a confidence and intelligence that I much admired, and humor, also, regarding life and the fates of gambling fortunes, which gave me much pleasure. I spoke often to my good lady wife of 'I.G.,' the fine gentleman whom Sir Myles was so fortunate to have as his steward, and said that I should be blessed to have such a man laboring for me. After the *Fair Helen* sank, I determined that I would have you for my steward."

"Me?" Isabelle flushed with helpless pleasure. Her former fury was gone, replaced by wonder that a powerful man such as Sir Alexander Baldwin had so admired her skills.

He nodded. "I wrote your uncle, offering anything he cared to name in return for your service. He replied that there was no sum or prize on earth that could make him part with you, and that he regretfully believed he and I should no longer deal together. Knowing now who you are, I can understand why he is striving so urgently to have you returned to him. I have had several missives from Sir Myles in the past few days, pleading for my aid in this. He is the one who convinced me that you had seduced Justin into stealing you away instead of marrying his daughter, Lady Evelyn."

Isabelle found the nearest chair and sat down, feeling as if someone had suddenly knocked all the breath out of her.

"I have felt shame many times in my life," the lord of Gyer said quietly, "but I do not think ever more than this moment. I have come here making judgment when there was no just cause, and I have spoken cruelly. The insult I have given you this day is unforgivable, but I would ask you to believe that I have acted only out of love for my brother. He was wounded once before by a woman—badly wounded—and I would not let him suffer such as that again.''

Isabelle stared at the floor, trying to think. Her mind had fixed on the fact that her uncle had asked for the lord of Gyer's help, and she could barely move beyond that to grasp the words he said. He was offering his apology, she thought numbly. The exalted lord of Gyer was offering *her* an apology.

''Why?'' she asked, thinking of the things he had accused her of earlier. ''Why should you believe me now?''

His expression filled with remorse. ''How could I not, when I know the person who guided me through three fortunate ventures to be one who is honest, forthright, and admirable in every way? I have missed 'I.G.' this past year, since your uncle declined my offer. I have missed the humor and advice. The longer I think on what has occurred this day, the more foolish I feel. I have known sadness at losing such a friend, and yet I come here, to that same friend, and accuse her of the basest motives. I do not expect your forgiveness, Lady Isabelle, but I tell you in all truth that I fully regret the things that I have said this day, and all that I have accused you of.''

''But…you even brought your army,'' she said with confusion.

''Half my army,'' he corrected. ''I brought them because I thought Justin might require a more compelling force in meeting with Sir Howton's skilled fighters. I only wish that he had waited for me to arrive, for together we might have claimed your brother without incident, but I seem to have misjudged Justin's desire in the matter.''

''You meant to lend him aid in gaining Senet, even though you thought me a devious fraud?''

Sir Alexander smiled. ''Not for that reason, I fear. I do not desire that my youngest brother should be killed while retrieving the son of a traitor. I knew it would be foolish to try to dissuade him from his chosen path, once he had set upon it. Justin is rather stubborn, if you have not yet realized it.''

"It appears to be a common trait in your family, my lord,'' Isabelle replied tartly.

Sir Alexander laughed. "S'truth, my lady. But you are a brave lass. 'I.G.' would not quail at such a daunting set of relatives, I vow.''

"'I.G.' is quailing,'' she assured him. "You made me lose my temper this day, my lord, and that is not easily done. I suppose I should ask your forgiveness for having spoken to you so boldly, but I will not. You deserved every word, and more.''

"Verily,'' he agreed when she looked at him with defiance, "this is so. I will give you the rest of the day to think of any further tirades you may wish to scold me with.'' He pushed away from the working table, moving to stand before her. "I will leave you now and see to the settling of my men. This eve I will return to share your evening meal, and we will speak more of Justin, and your uncle, and other matters.''

Isabelle's heart sank. "My uncle?''

"Aye, your uncle.'' His expression was solemn. "He wants you back at any price, and insists that Justin honor the agreement that my brother Hugh and I made regarding his marriage to Lady Evelyn.''

"But that cannot be!'' Isabelle told him. "I heard Sir Myles with my own ears, on the night he found us at the monastery, and he told Justin that the agreement to marry Evelyn was forever broken.''

Sir Alexander gave her a patient look. "In a moment of anger, a man will say things he later regrets, just as I have proven this day. But an alliance with the Baldwins, especially through marriage, is not a thing to be treated lightly. Having bethought his fortunes, your uncle has stated to myself, also to my brother, Sir Hugh, and also to the duke of Gloucester, that if **you are** returned to him, all will be forgiven as if it had never occurred. His desire is to see his daughter wed to Justin, and Lady Evelyn is evidently agreeable.''

"God save me," Isabelle said with a groan, setting a hand to her forehead. "They spoke of it often before Justin took me, of how fortunate they were to receive such a boon. My uncle meant to use his daughter's marriage to gain power, and Evelyn—" Isabelle dropped her hand and looked directly at the lord of Gyer "—Evelyn said she would only marry Justin if my uncle would help her to carry out affairs when she grew bored." Isabelle stood, feeling angry again. "She said that Justin is dull, but he is not! And I will never let her wed him and make a fool of him!"

Sir Alexander chuckled and put up both hands, as if to ward her off. "Do not become angered with me again, I pray. I am in full agreement that it shall not be so. And do you think, my dear lady Isabelle, that I would lose you again, after having so shortly found you? Now that you are my sister-by-marriage, I intend to make certain you remain so."

"If you will, my lord," she said, trying not to sound as desperate as she felt, "I will do whatever you ask in the way of financial matters. Any advice you want—anything—I will gladly be in your service."

Sir Alexander tilted his head to one side, regarding her with a slow smile. "Can it be," he said, "that you love my brother, Isabelle?"

She folded her hands together, nodding. "Aye, my lord. I do love Justin."

He took her clasped hands and pulled them both up to his mouth, kissing them. "Then have no fear, my lady. We will find the way to manage your uncle. I will set myself to the task, and you may believe that when I have embarked upon a chosen course, I am seldom defeated in it. On this, you have my vow."

Chapter Thirteen

Justin and his party returned to Talwar four days later, weary and hungry, but as triumphant as if they'd defeated the king's own army.

Isabelle had an early warning of their arrival from the guard serving as lookout, and spared a moment before she ran out into the bailey to greet her husband and brother to shout for Meg to prepare the welcoming feast they had earlier planned.

Justin dismounted the moment he saw Isabelle racing toward him, shouting her name and catching her up in his arms, twirling her off her feet in a wide circle before setting her down and kissing her on the mouth. "My beloved lady," he murmured, holding her so tightly that she could scarcely breathe. "I praise God that I see you again."

"You're home," she heard herself saying, clutching him, covering the side of his face with rapid kisses. "And you're alive."

He pulled back and grinned down at her. "Of course I'm alive. Did you think I might let myself be killed so soon after our marriage?"

He was ragged and filthy with dirt, and his dark beard was stubbly and rough, but Isabelle didn't think he had ever looked more handsome.

"What's this?" he murmured, wiping tears from her cheeks with the palms of his hands. "There is no need for tears."

"Aye, there is," she told him. "I'm so glad to have you home."

He chuckled and kissed her again—a short, hard, joyful brand. "Come and see your brother," he said when the other riders had dismounted. In a softer tone, for her ears alone, he whispered, "Do not let yourself be surprised by the sight of him, love. He has suffered much cruelty these many years."

He led her in the direction of a tall, thin, dark-haired youth whom Isabelle almost didn't recognize. The boy held himself stiffly, unsmiling, gazing at her with caution as she approached.

"Senet," she whispered, moving toward him with one hand outstretched. "Senet. Oh, I am glad to see you again. It has been so long."

He stared at the hand, flinching when she gently set it on his arm.

"Senet." She searched his face and touched his cheek with her fingertips. He had grown so tall since she last saw him. He had grown into a man, nearly, when in her memories she had always seen him as a boy. "Do you remember me?"

His blue eyes were filled with distrust, but he nodded once, and some of the wariness left him. Isabelle moved slowly, putting her arms about his rigid body and holding him in a light clasp. He made no move to return the embrace, but stood very still, enduring it. Isabelle, sensing his discomfort, pulled away. She tried to smile up at him in a reassuring manner.

"Now that we are together again, all will be well. Sir Justin has promised us a safe home here. No one will ever be able to part us again, or bring us harm."

He made no reply, but lifted his gaze to Justin, as if

waiting for that man to tell him whether he should speak or not.

"Why do we not go inside?" Justin suggested, setting his hand about Isabelle's waist and gently pulling her away from her brother. "We are all weary, and I know that the lads will want to tell you about their great adventure. They frustrated Sir Howton's skilled forces with ease, and took Senet without a moment's trouble. Is that not so, lads?"

Isabelle looked to where Kayne, Aric, John, Ralf and Neddy all stood holding their horses, their dirty, tired faces glowing with pride. They had only been gone a little more than a week, yet they all looked years older.

"And I want to hear every word of it," Isabelle told them. "Every word, and then I shall give you all of my thanks for bringing my brother to me. If I can find words that can tell you just how grateful I am."

"Go and stable your horses," Justin said. "Kayne, you take Synn, and Aric, you take Senet's steed—"

"Nay." It was the first word Senet had spoken, and Isabelle was stricken at the sound. His voice was hard and bitter, sharp as a blade.

"Very well," Justin said without pause, his hand tightening about Isabelle when she opened her mouth to disagree. "Come to the great room when you are done, and we shall drink a glass of wine together to mark the end of our journey. And after that, my boys, you will all have a thorough scrubbing. I shall tell Gytha to start boiling plenty of water."

Four hours later, Justin yawned and opened his eyes, stretching one arm up above his head and smiling sleepily as with the other he pressed his slumbering wife closer. The long shadows in the room and the deep gold of the sunlight coming through the windows told him that it was late afternoon, and that he and Isabelle had been asleep for some time.

She lay against him, naked and warm, her dark, silky head nestled between his arm and his chest, her breath brushing his skin in deep, slow, even puffs. He ran his fingers down the softness of her arm, tucking her nearer and reveling in the goodness of holding her again. Married life, he thought with drowsy satisfaction, was going to be thoroughly enjoyable. And now that he had brought Isabelle's brother to Talwar, there would be nothing else to bar their way to beginning that life in full.

Except perhaps for Senet himself.

Not that the lad would prove difficult, for despite the hard life the boy had lived, Justin knew that he would, given time and patient handling, eventually emerge from his darkness. Justin had dealt too often with just this sort of youth at Briarstone, where so many of the children had been spawned and abandoned on city streets, living and surviving in the harshest of conditions, and he felt confident that he knew how best to help Senet regain his humanity. But Isabelle, in her desire to make everything right, might make the matter more difficult than it needed to be, simply by trying to protect and coddle the boy. Senet would reject any such kindnesses too soon, even from his own sister, and Justin prayed that he would be able to make Isabelle understand. All that Senet required for a time was good food and drink, a secure place to sleep at night, a regular routine to follow during the day, privacy when he needed it, plenty of physical work, and a chance to become used to the changes in his life.

But it wasn't going to be a simple matter, Justin thought with a sigh. Already they had argued over the matter. Isabelle had wanted to know what her brother had suffered at Sir Howton's hands, and Justin had tried to be as honest as he could without revealing the whole of it, for he did not think that he would ever be able to tell her the worst of what Senet had experienced. Only he and Kayne knew the entire truth, as they had been the ones to enter and remove Senet from the cramped, filthy closet in which he had lived more like one of Sir Howton's dogs than a civilized being. The boy had been filthy, crawling with lice and vermin, his thin body scarred from what must have been several harsh whippings. It was clear that he had been made to serve his master and former peers in the most menial manner, as a slave—worse, as the son of a traitor—who was only good enough to carry out the lowliest, most repugnant tasks.

Justin knew without being told that the boy must have suffered a great deal of taunting, but despite every attempt to strip him of pride, Senet Gaillard had not yet been daunted. At their very first stop, after they had made their escape, Justin had taken his knife to the boy's hair, furiously slicing away the crawling, infested mass until all that was left was a short cap of thick black hair. Then he had bidden him undress and scrub himself in the river. Senet had removed his filthy clothing slowly, silently, as he exposed the ugly scars that marred him. With his chin high and his expression fierce, he had silently dared his onlookers to speak their disgust. But he had misjudged if he'd thought that the boys who had rescued him would be anything like the highborn sons he had lived with at Sir Howton's. Kayne and the others knew better than Justin himself did how to treat Senet; they recognized one of their own, a fellow being who'd suffered as they had, and at once, without speaking a word, had taken Senet into their own private fold. It was a place where even Justin, despite the reverence they gave him, was not invited to be. They did not offer Senet pity, or even kindness, but respect and understanding and, most important of all, silence. And Senet was silence itself. Justin had only ever heard him say two words: *Aye,* and *Nay.* Otherwise, he nodded or shook his head to make himself understood.

The boy would need time. He was filled with bitter hatred and distrust, and suffered even the smallest touch with nothing less than intense dislike. But John had been much the same when he arrived at Talwar, and, although it took time, he had eventually become the boy he was now—giving and cheerful and willing to be made a part of the whole among the other boys.

The thought of John made Justin smile. What would they have done without him when they made their plan to take Senet from Sir Howton's heavily guarded castle? The lad had been years away from London's streets, yet he retained the essential skills he had learned to survive there. He had slipped unnoticed through the gates—for who would take note of such a slender, grubby youth?—and had shortly memorized the castle's every detail, from how many men guarded the entrances to the precise location of the castle chambers. By the time he finished mapping it all out, everyone in their party had known where Sir Howton's weaknesses lay, and how they could be used.

The stealing itself had gone smoothly, almost laughably so. They had sneaked in one at a time during guard changes, and had blended in with the common castle folk until the evening meal. Then, with Aric starting a fire in the busy kitchen and Ralf throwing pebbles into the great hall's long windows from a safe distance and Neddy standing at the front gate bawling for his mother, enough soldiers were distracted for John to lead Kayne and Justin to where Senet was chambered. Senet had gone with them readily, speaking not a word and following behind as they crept silently out the kitchen gate, which the guards there had abandoned in favor of putting out the fire.

An hour later, they had all met at the agreed-upon place, and had mounted up and ridden as far and as fast as they could before stopping out of exhaustion. Justin doubted that Sir Howton had realized Senet was even gone before the next daybreak. Now, if he wished to follow all the way to Talwar and try to retake Sir Myles's nephew, he would be facing not only the wrath of the throne, but that of the entire Baldwin family.

The news that his brother Alexander had arrived at Talwar with half his army to assist him in taking Senet had made Justin feel strangely pleased. Remembering all that Isabelle had told him, Justin considered what it meant for his eldest brother to have done such a thing. It was not Alexander's way to speak of love or affection; he was far better at showing how he felt. They had not had much contact since Justin learned of the part Alexander had played in having him disqualified from participating in the tournaments; indeed, he'd had more discourse with Hugh, since Hugh refused to be ignored. He had not even spoken with Alexander since that time, but had only exchanged short missives with him. To know that his stoic eldest brother had come to help him now meant a great deal, and Justin regretted that he had not been at Talwar to greet him.

It was clear that Isabelle thought well of the exalted lord of Gyer. She had given him the highest praise possible, saying, "He understands money, and how to invest it. We are going to arrange a courier system between all of the Baldwin estates, including Siere, and I'm to have the deciding of each major investment." When he laughed, she'd declared insistently, "We shall work well together, I vow, and you will become one of the richest men in England. You'll see."

He chuckled at the memory, and kissed her forehead tenderly. He didn't care about being wealthy, but if it made her happy to play with money and finances, then so be it. He only wanted her to be content at Talwar; for all of them to be content with the good life to be had here, in this peaceful place, and with all the plenty that God had blessed them with. Life was too short for anything less, and Justin meant to rise every day with the intention of mining the most from it that he could.

* * *

"That's your pallet," Kayne said, pointing to the cot directly across from his.

With a nod, Senet put the pillow he carried in the spot where his head would rest, then unfolded the blanket Gytha had given him and spread it over the thin mattress. He was weary from the day's long ride, his stomach ached from having eaten such an unaccustomed amount of food during the small celebration feast, and his skin and scalp burned from the torturous lye scrubbing that Meg and Gytha had put him through in order to rid him of lice, but he would not let himself lie down. Not yet. It had been years since he had slept upon a mattress, and he had wished for it too often to grasp the miracle too quickly. This miracle, or any of the others. He was going to take his time. He was going to savor all of it, just as he had dreamed of doing. Then, if it was taken away again, he would at least be able to remember the small details, to appreciate as he had not been able to do before, when he took such comforts for granted.

The other boys moved about the chamber, putting their things away, some of them stretching out on their pallets with grateful sighs.

"'Tis good to be home again," he heard Ralf saying.

"'Twas good to eat such food again," Aric said in reply. "What a feast!"

"Aye," Kayne agreed. "That it was."

"Why did Sir Justin and Lady Isabelle retire so soon?" Neddy asked, yawning. "They hardly ate at all. They didn't even want any tri-cream."

Aric chuckled softly. "'Twasn't tri-cream they were hungry for, I vow."

"S'truth," John said with a laugh before imitating Isabelle in a high, squeaky voice. "'But don't you want more ale, my lord?'" His voice dropped to a low, heavy tone meant to copy Sir Justin's. "'Nay, I don't want more ale. I don't want anything but to leave the table.'" He laughed again. "And didn't he drag her up and off, after that? Without so much as another word? And wasn't she red as fire, our good Lady Isabelle? And him all smiling, like it was time for the rents to be paid, almost."

"You're daft," Ralf muttered, but the other boys laughed.

Senet stayed where he was, staring down at his pallet, silent. And remembering. He had been as they were, before. He had laughed with his fellows, and talked in such an easy manner. If he closed his eyes, he could nearly grasp the dim memory of when he had lived with the other boys in Sir Howton's castle. Aye. He had been one of them, and had held a place of honor, not only as the son of a great lord, but as one of Sir Howton's finest students. He could remember it. Almost. It was the same with everything that had come before his fall from grace. There were shadows, colors, voices, faces...but they were never complete, never finished. He knew he had lived a different life before he lived as Sir Howton's slave, but it often seemed more like a dream.

Just as Isabelle seemed like a dream.

She was his sister—he could recite that fact readily in his mind—but he didn't really *know* her. Her face was familiar, her voice was familiar, yet she seemed strange and foreign. He didn't know what to do with her, what to say. Sir Justin felt more real to him than she did.

"Here," Kayne suddenly said from beside him. "You'll need this until Sir Justin can send to Briarstone for clothes of your own." A heavy long-sleeved tunic landed on the bed. Slowly, Senet bent to pick it up, nodding once as he fingered a sleeve of the warm garment. His own lice-infested clothing had been left near the river where they first stopped after leaving Sir Howton's castle. The other boys had given him some of the extra clothes they had brought on the journey to wear until they reached Talwar, and now, having had his bath, he wore some of Sir Justin's overlarge garments. With a frown, Senet thought of the girl who had brought the clothes into the bathing chamber while he was suffering Meg and Gytha's scrubbing. She had been smiling when she first entered, her pretty face framed with curls, but one glance at the scars on his chest had sent her running back out, her hands pressed in dismay against her cheeks.

"Thank you."

He furrowed his brow at the sound of the words, at the strangeness of having spoken them. When Kayne's hand tentatively came to rest upon his shoulder, he tried not to flinch.

"You aren't beholden to any of us. Long as you do your share of the work, you'll have your place and no trouble. We take care of each other here."

"Isn't one of us hasn't traveled rough roads before," Aric put in from where he lay on his pallet. "Time is what you need, and time is what you'll get. Just don't be a sluggard about it. We all do what Sir Justin tells us, and no complaining. Idle off and you'll get what you deserve. From us."

Senet understood the warning, and, more, he understood the pride behind it. The knowledge soothed him as nothing after leaving Sir Howton's had yet been able to do. If work was all that was required of him, then Senet knew he would be safe here. Whatever task Sir Justin required of him, he would perform it tenfold; when these boys expected him to take his place in their ranks, he would not fail them.

With a breath, he lowered himself to the pallet, feeling the softness of the mattress beneath his weight before lying down flat. In his hands he still held the warm tunic, his fingers unthinkingly squeezing the fabric. He gave way to his exhaustion a few moments later, falling asleep even as his eyelids drifted shut, and slumbered so deeply that he never felt the extra blanket John put over him.

Chapter Fourteen

With one final effort, and a loud, unified groan, Justin, Kayne, Aric and Senet at last managed to heave the enormous Yule log into the great room's massive hearth.

"God's feet," Kayne said, straightening and brushing his hands on his tunic. "'Twill keep the manor warm, i' faith."

"'S'truth," Justin agreed, chuckling. "It may do more than merely warm us. We'll be sweating freely during our meals, and longing to stroll out in the snow."

"'Twill last until Twelfth Night, methinks," Aric stated with satisfaction.

"Aye, and that it will." Justin clapped the boy on the shoulder. "Mayhap even longer. You chose well, Aric." As Aric flushed with pleasure, Justin added, "Well done, all of you. Now, go and wash yourselves for tonight's feast. Your good lady will be displeased, should she find you at table wearing all this filth." He looked down at his own dusty clothes with a grimace.

An hour later, having tended to his own cleaning and change of clothes, he went in search of his wife. The manor house was cheerfully decorated with holly and mistletoe—Isabelle and Odelyn, as excited as children, had gathered several baskets full of each from the forest, insisting that all of it be used to decorate the dwelling. Odelyn had the excuse of youth to explain her excitement, but Isabelle's delight came from celebrating her first Christmas as the mistress of Talwar, rather than as her uncle's laborer.

She had changed so much in the past six months that Justin could scarce remember the shy, uncertain lady he had stolen for his bride. She was exuberant now, radiant, and so beautiful and loving that every sight he had of her seemed to make him feel breathless. The boys had long since fallen beneath her spell, and sometimes Justin even wondered if Kayne and Aric weren't perhaps a little in love with their mistress. Gytha, Meg and Odelyn all thought Isabelle was near perfect, incapable of doing any wrong, and where Justin had once held the place of master of Talwar, Isabelle now ruled supreme.

He knew where she was, and went directly to the working chamber that had become solely hers. She was sitting at her working table, he saw when he peeked through the door, and he leaned against the frame, contentedly watching as she scribbled in one of her account books. The chamber was warmed by a fire in the small hearth, making it a comfortable, inviting place in which to spend time. Isabelle kept it scrupulously neat and clean, and also simply furnished, with but the most necessary pieces of furniture: a large table on which she worked and four comfortable chairs. There were shelves for her books and atlases, and a large wooden chest where she kept her ink, writing instruments, sealing wax and parchment. One large window gave the chamber natural light during the day, and something for Isabelle to stare at when her mind was occupied with equations. More than once he'd found her just so, staring blindly out the window, and had come to recognize the concentrated look on her face that meant she wasn't going to hear a word spoken to her until she'd solved whatever troubling problem she was struggling with.

Since Alexander's visit of so many months before, she had been in this chamber daily, plotting investments and tallying accounts and being delightedly happy. Justin could only remember one day on which she'd been angered by her financial machinations, when she had come out to the smithy while he was forging a new sword and stopped him with the declaration, "Justin Baldwin! You're *already* wealthy!" He'd been amused, at first, that she was angry at something he considered to be so insignificant, but her obvious disappointment at not being able to make him rich had quickly had him putting aside his tools and taking her into his arms. It had taken quite a long while to get her mind off the revelation, but he, being a dutiful husband, had put every effort behind the task. By the time they emerged from the smithy, some hours later, they'd both forgotten their original reasons for being there, and it hadn't been until late in the night when he woke with a start, remembering the work he'd left unfinished.

The truth of his wealth had relaxed Isabelle to some degree, especially in regard to him. She no longer seemed to think that he had taken her as his wife for that purpose, and he was glad for it, yet there was still something—a curtain behind which she retreated—that kept her from ever quite fully trusting him. There were times when he thought that, perhaps, she loved him, for she never failed to smile at the sight of him, to greet him as if he were the finest thing in her world, to give herself to him in every physical manner. Not only in their bed, although she was a generous, exquisite lover, but also in conversing with him so honestly and openly, in thinking of his comfort and well-being. She was, just as he had known she would be, a wonderful wife. But there were other times when he wondered if perhaps she was only grateful to him for taking her and Senet away from Sir Myles, if perhaps all she felt was affection and...indebtedness.

He loved her so much that the simple knowledge of it made his heart ache with thanksgiving and joy—and with a longing to have that love returned. Every day, every moment, it seemed, the words were in his mouth, ready to be spoken, but he was too afraid to let them free. Did she love him? he wondered, gazing at the smooth bow of her neck as she bent over her work. He lifted a hand to rub the sweet pain in his chest. Did Isabelle love him?

She was to have his child. They had both wept when she told him about it. And then laughed like two giddy children, lying in their bed with their faces together. She was not far along; the child would come during the summer. Her belly had only just begun to swell, and each night, as Justin curved his fingers carefully over the place where his child grew, he longed for the day when he would be able to feel the babe moving.

He pushed the door wider, and Isabelle, hearing the sound, turned around in her chair. Her face, at the sight of him, lit with a welcoming smile.

"My lord," she said, abandoning her work and moving toward him with both hands outstretched. "I saw the Yule log. 'Tis perfect!"

She went into his arms and lifted her face, receiving his kiss with the eagerness that never failed to heat him all the way through to his bones. How many men, he wondered, were so fortunate as to have such a willing and affectionate wife?

"Mmm..." he murmured against her mouth. "If this is the manner in which I am repaid for a deed well done, I shall be chopping down trees and dragging them home to you every day, I vow." His hand slid across the velvet of the heavy winter surcoat that Alexander had sent her from London until it rested upon her belly. "How is our babe this day, good lady wife?"

Isabelle covered his hand with her own. "He is most well, as is his mother."

"You've not suffered your daily sickness? This is the fifth day that it has been so."

"I disremember ever feeling better than I do now. Gytha said the sickness would pass after the first few weeks."

"May God be praised," Justin said fervently. She'd been so ill in the beginning that he began to worry that she'd waste away to naught. "We shall have much to celebrate this night."

"Aye." She put both arms around his neck. "Where is Senet? He had no trouble helping you with the Yule log? He looked tired this morn, I thought."

Justin made a conscious effort to keep from sighing. After five months, Senet was still foremost in her thoughts, as well as in her worries. The boy had gained in both strength and confidence, so much so that he and Kayne now contended for being Talwar's most accomplished student, so much that Justin believed the boy was going to be an extraordinary soldier when he grew to be a man, and yet Isabelle still wanted to protect him as if he hadn't made any strides at all. It was the thing they argued about most—the only thing, really. She never failed to be angered when Justin required Senet to take his rightful part in what she believed were dangerous exercises, be it sword fighting or battle training or merely spending a full day wearing heavy armor.

It was well enough for the other lads to partake of such things, she insisted, but not Senet. Senet had suffered, and so must be treated gently; Senet was troubled, and so could not be expected to work so hard. But Senet, Justin knew, wanted every challenge that the other boys were given, and more, and was driven to perform every task better and more fully than the others. Justin doubted that he could force him to stop even if he tried. But Isabelle couldn't understand the truth of it. Senet was her brother, and she meant to take care of him, whether he wished to be taken care of or not.

"He had no trouble," he assured her, "and he did not seem weary in the least. I sent him and the others back to their chamber to prepare for tonight's feast. We were all dirty after fetching the tree."

She nodded thoughtfully, releasing him and moving back toward her working table. "I've been worried about him of late," she said, running her fingers lightly over the last entry she had made in her account book. "Odelyn seems to be quite taken with him, but Senet won't speak of the matter to me. I know that he is of an age to dally with women, but Odelyn is very dear to me, and I cannot like it if he should…treat her lightly." She bit her lower lip, reddening at the words, and glanced at him.

Justin had to think a moment before deciding what to say. The topic was clearly an embarrassing one for Isabelle, and if she knew the full truth, she'd most likely be horrified. Matters between Senet and Odelyn had progressed beyond dallying. Justin had caught them in the stables once, each of them half clothed, and they'd been involved in such a violent embrace that at first he wasn't sure whether Senet was trying to couple with the girl or kill her. Neither had occurred, since Justin had immediately called a halt to…whatever it was. Odelyn had been flushed and embarrassed at being caught, while Senet had been flushed and thoroughly relieved. After the girl assured Justin that it wouldn't happen again and ran away, Senet had straightened his clothes and said, angrily, "She'd best learn to leave me in peace. I don't want her following me about." It was the most Justin had yet heard coming out of the boy's mouth, and he'd been so surprised that Senet walked past him and right out of the stable before Justin was able to properly reprove him.

"I do not think Senet shares Odelyn's interest," he told her gently. "I realize she's become enamored of him, but he has given no sign that he returns the feeling. He seems mostly to want to be left alone.''

"Yes, I think that is so," she said with a nod. " I have spoken with Odelyn and received her promise to stop pursuing him as she does, but I was uncertain of Senet's regard. He has seemed not himself so much since his disagreement with Kayne."

Justin chuckled at her use of the word *disagreement*. It hadn't been a disagreement at all; it had been a full-out battle. He didn't think Isabelle had yet forgiven him for not putting a stop to the fight at once and, more, for holding her back when she would have gotten between the two boys to put a stop to it herself. But they'd needed to sort the matter out. The boys had been friends, and were better friends now, but the fight had been brewing for a long time.

Justin had seen it coming the first time that Senet unseated Kayne from his horse during jousting practice. No one but Justin had been able to unseat Kayne before, not even Aric, who was as skilled a fighter as many grown men Justin knew, and the sting of the insult had burned in Kayne's eyes even as he stood and dusted himself off. By the tenth time Senet had unseated him, the burning had turned into a raging fire, and Kayne had launched himself at the other boy with, Justin assumed, every intention of teaching the usurper a few things about keeping his place in the line of rank. With both boys dressed in heavy full armor, the tussle hadn't lasted more than a quarter of an hour, and had mostly been a farce of them swinging, knocking each other down by turns, then getting back up and starting all over again.

He'd decided to let them wear themselves out first, before sending them to spend the night together in the keep's jail, which was, Justin thought, a fitting punishment for breaking one of his strictest rules: no fighting without his permission. Isabelle hadn't been very happy with him about that, either. She hadn't shared a bed with him for a week, until she was assured that Senet hadn't taken any harm from his one-night sojourn in the damp cell, from which both boys emerged the next morn, fully reconciled.

"It may be that he is more himself now than he was before their…disagreement," he told her, moving nearer and setting his fingers gently on the back of her neck, rubbing at the tenseness he found there in a soothing rhythm. "He is beginning to come out of his silence, and the anger he has kept brewing this while is rising to spill out. I warned you that it would come, in time, beloved. There is much for him to be rid of, and there will be moments—perhaps many—when he will be angered and unpleasant. But we must be patient and wait. When it has all gone out, he will begin to learn contentment. It was the same with Kayne and Eric and John. They were once as bitter as Senet is, but you see how they are now."

"I know you speak the truth," she admitted, pressing her cheek against his chest and looping her arms about his waist. "But sometimes…he does not even seem like the boy I once knew. It is almost as if he is not my own brother, but some stranger. It is so hard."

"I know," Justin murmured, kissing the top of her head, where her smooth hair felt like silk. "In truth, he is no longer that young boy who lived with you at Lomas. He will never be that boy again. But he will always be your brother. In time, you will come to know him once more."

Isabelle nodded silently, hugging him, and Justin felt the contentment that he had come to delight in stealing over him.

"Come and have a cup of wine with me," he said, "while I prepare the Yule log for its lighting. There is not much time before Meg will be calling us to table."

"Oh." Isabelle lifted her head. "I must finish this before we begin the celebration. Sir Alexander's courier will arrive on the morrow, from Siere, and I must have all of the instructions ready for him to take to London. Profits from the coal mine have made it necessary that we have another boat built right away to expand the trade.''

Alexander's couriers had become a weekly part of their lives. The men on horseback arrived with the sort of regularity that both Alexander and Isabelle insisted upon.

"More boats," Justin said with a smile. "You'll be rivaling the Hansa soon."

"We *will*," she replied with perfect seriousness. "Indeed, I mean to recommend to Sir Alexander and Sir Hugh that we make plans to build our own warehouse in London, bigger than the one Hansa has, and perhaps even one in Venice, if we can do so. There's no good reason why the Germans and Venetians should make so much profit on their trade in London while the English merchants cannot do the same in their ports."

Except, perhaps, for the fact that the German and Venetian fleets wielded almost as much power as they did wealth, and would not welcome any more rivals for their commerce and trade. Isabelle wouldn't think about the dangers of such an undertaking, Justin knew, but he hoped Alexander would. He didn't want Isabelle drawing too much attention to herself, or gaining too many enemies. Sir Myles was yet causing more than enough trouble all by himself, with his continuous demands to have Isabelle returned to him. His latest efforts had involved beseeching John of Lancaster for help, but with the king's regent so occupied in France, Justin doubted anything would come of the petition. Especially now that Isabelle was with child. The only recourse Sir Myles could hope for was that Isabelle herself would decide to return to him, for she still retained that right, since she had been taken against her will. But that, Justin knew, would never happen. She was content to be his wife, and content to live at Talwar. Whenever he gazed into her face, he could see her happiness shining up at him.

"Finish your work then, good lady wife," he said, bending to kiss her lovely mouth. "And then we will begin our Christmas celebration."

Chapter Fifteen

The grand Christmas feast that Meg had prepared was long over, the Yule log had been lit with much ceremony, the games Isabelle and Odelyn had arranged had just ended, and now, as Meg and Gytha passed out goblets of hot spiced wine, everyone in the great room grew silent, waiting for the lord of Talwar to begin his yearly giving of Christmas gifts.

Isabelle watched with growing anticipation as Justin opened the large wooden chest he had earlier placed near the fire. She already knew what was inside, for she had helped him to fill it during the past month, adding each gift with care and smiles as they spoke of how the receiver would like it. Because he had no vassals of his own, borrowing workers from Briarstone to work Talwar's fields each season, Justin had made a habit of giving gifts to the boys, instead, as well as to his household servants, much to the delight of everyone involved.

Murmurs of appreciation and delight filled the room as Justin presented each gift, one by one. There were sharp new daggers set with real jewels for each of his "lads," all made by Justin's own skilled hands, and lovely, fine Scottish wool cloth for Meg, Gytha and Odelyn. There were new clothes and shoes for every member of the household, ordered and made to fit by the finest tailors and shoemakers Briarstone had to offer. Finally, Justin handed out little leather bags, each holding six gold coins.

"Oh, thank you, my lord," Gytha said, hugging her gifts against her chest. "God bless you."

The others joined in with thanks, and Isabelle thought that a few of the boys looked nearly overcome. Senet, she saw, was gazing at his new dagger as if it were the most beautiful, stunning thing he'd ever seen, turning it over in his hands to look at it from all sides and blinking his eyes rapidly.

"I am the one who is thankful," Justin said. "For all the blessings that God has given me, most especially for the fine women who keep my home and care for all of us. It is little enough to repay you in such a small way only once each year. And—" he winked at Isabelle "—I am not yet done with my gift giving yet."

"My lord!" Isabelle exclaimed as he reached into the chest once more. She hadn't expected him to give her a gift. He had already given her so much; surely she could not deserve anything more.

He lifted something large out of the chest, something wrapped in dark blue velvet and tied with gold silk cords, then he carefully carried it to where she sat, placing it upon her lap.

"I have waited a long time to see you open this, my lady," he said, kneeling beside her. With a brief caress of her cheek, he murmured, "See what it is."

She untied the cords with shaking fingers and pushed the velvet aside. And then, lifting a hand to her lips, she whispered, "Oh." Tears welled in her eyes, and she said again, "Oh."

Her mother's books. All of her mother's books. She blinked to see if they would disappear, but when she opened her eyes again, the books were still there. Right on her lap.

"You are pleased, Isabelle?"

"Oh, aye. Aye." She couldn't seem to stop the tears. They were streaming down her face now. "Oh, Justin. How did you—?" A sob stopped the words, and she ran a hand over the leather binding of the first book, the *Almagest*.

"I wrote Alexander and asked him to do whatever he must, use his every power, to find them for you. He was glad to do so when I told him how much your mother's books meant to you."

She sobbed again, then uttered a teary chuckle. "The lord of Gyer has been a busy man, it seems. Senet." She lifted her head to gaze at her brother, who was frowning at the books in her lap. "Go into my working chamber, please, and open the chest where I keep my accounts. Bring me what you find there. It is wrapped in a velvet darker than this is."

With a curt nod, Senet pushed away from the wall against which he'd been leaning and went into her chamber.

"Look," Isabelle said when he had gone, opening the *Almagest* to the first page. "Have you seen the paintings, yet? This is my mother. Oh, Justin…"

Justin smiled down at the illustration of a beautiful, fair woman whose hair and dress were skillfully drawn to represent an elegant number one. "That is your mother, Isabelle? I thought she would have dark hair." He lifted a hand to wipe the tears from her cheeks, and when she looked at him, the expression of love shining in her eyes made his heart thump painfully in his chest.

"Nay, she was very fair, like an angel. Senet and I have our coloring from my father. We all thought she was so beautiful. I cannot tell you how good it is to see her again, to have her books. Thank you, my lord." She caught his hand and pulled it to her mouth, kissing his palm fervently. "Thank you."

"Isabelle." The strange sound of Senet's voice caused everyone to turn toward him. He stood at the door of her working chamber, his face as pale as the snow that fell outside, holding something long and slender and wrapped in purple velvet.

She smiled at him encouragingly, and held out her hand. "Bring it here, Senet. If you have guessed what it is, I know that you, like me, will want Sir Justin to have it."

"Aye," he murmured as he strode toward her. "I do."

He placed the object in Justin's hands and stood back, watching as Justin unwrapped the velvet to reveal a finely crafted sword, ornamented at the hilt with seven large sapphires forming the shape of a cross.

"God's mercy," Justin said reverently, and the rest of the boys drew around with awe.

"'Tis beautiful," John whispered.

"'Tis very fine," Kayne agreed.

"'Tis the finest sword I've ever set sight on," Justin said, lifting the heavy, elegant weapon into the air. "I have never before seen its like."

"It was our father's," Isabelle said softly. "And his father's before him. I knew where my uncle had sold it, and asked Sir Alexander to use the profits that were my part from the coal mine to find it and buy it back. I thought, with your own love of making weapons, that you would like to have it."

"Like?" he repeated, gazing at the sword with disbelief, then shaking his head as if to clear it. "But Senet should have it. It was his father's."

"Nay," Senet stated flatly. "I do not want it. Isabelle is right. If it is any of mine, then with a full heart I join her in giving it to you, my lord."

"I will cherish it," Justin replied solemnly. "I will cherish it every day that I live."

"Just as I will cherish having my mother's books," Isabelle told him. "I have never had so fine a gift before. Senet, look. Do you remember?"

Senet knelt and leaned forward to look at the illustration she pointed to. He was silent, staring, and at last lifted a finger to touch the tiny face on the parchment.

"Mother," he whispered, then drew in a shaking breath. "I remember. I—" He drew in another breath, sharper this time, and surged to his feet.

"Senet!" Isabelle called after him, but Justin set a hand on her arm to silence her as the boy strode toward the passageway that joined the manor house to the keep.

He didn't care about the snow. It felt good on his hot skin, soothing. He gripped the icy stones of the low parapet wall and leaned forward, striving to calm his breathing and the strange, aching sounds that were fighting their way out of his chest despite his efforts to subdue them. Streams of wet heat streaked down his face, and he wiped them away with a punishing hand.

I remember.

One sob managed to escape, burning, sharpening the ache.

Isabelle, I remember.

He bent his head low, letting the agony in. He hadn't wished for his parents since after the first week of his servitude at Sir Howton's. They had laughed at him when he wept during the first few days that followed his father's conviction, and then had beaten him until the tears stopped. He'd spent every waking moment in his cell praying for his parents, wanting them so badly. On the day that his father was executed, they had dressed him in women's clothing and made him dance in the great hall for the entertainment of everyone present, while they laughed and threw coins. But he hadn't smiled while he danced, as they insisted he do, and Sir Howton had taken out his whip, ready to force him to it. He had not given way. After the tenth strike on his bare back, he had finally, mercifully, fainted. When he awoke in his dirty cell, he discovered that he could no longer remember his parents' faces. Or anything about Isabelle, save her name. And not remembering them had been a blessing, for he'd no longer had any reason to weep.

But now, at last, he remembered. His mother, and his father, and Isabelle. He embraced them in his thoughts with all the same longing that he'd felt during that first miserable week so long ago.

Turning, he slid against the parapet into the snow, resting his face against his indrawn knees. And he let himself weep. The heat of his tears soaked his knees, a biting contrast to the numb chill of the rest of his body.

"Senet?"

He groaned at the sound of Odelyn's soft voice. He didn't want her to see him like this. Not like this.

"Senet." She sounded closer, more concerned. He heard her footsteps crunching through the snow as she crossed the rooftop. "You should not be here," she murmured. "'Tis so cold."

The heat of her body enveloped him as she knelt and put her arms around his stiff form. "'Tis so cold," she repeated. Her hands pulled him closer, and he went unresistingly into her warm embrace, uncurling and gripping her fiercely, pulling her nearly into his lap, pushing his face against her neck.

She held him, murmuring and stroking his hair, and he loved her so much in that moment that he couldn't even think of the words to tell her. She'd spent the past five months pursuing him, heaven only knew why, and he'd spent the past five months running, because Odelyn was beautiful and good and he wasn't. He was only ugly, with his scars and his violence, and he knew that he would hurt her if she didn't stay away from him, no matter how sweet and gentle she was. He would hurt her.

He tried to say her name, but it came out only as "Oh—" before a sob cut off the rest. Then, shuddering, he pushed her away, gulping for air and struggling to his feet.

Odelyn stood, too, still holding him, her whole body pressing against him. Senet let her do it, though he didn't return the embrace. He stood very still, looking over the parapet into the outer bailey, trying to calm enough to tell her to go away. But somehow, even when the tears had stopped and the sobs had ceased, he didn't tell her anything, and they stood thus, together, listening to each other's breathing while the silently falling snow gathered on their hair and lashes.

It was the muffled sound of horses approaching that brought Senet to his senses, and he realized that his arms had somehow slipped about Odelyn's waist to hold her to him, that he had rested his head against the top of hers.

"What is it?" she asked when he suddenly straightened.

"Listen," he said. "Horses."

"In this darkness? And snowfall?"

"There. Look." He pointed over the parapet to where three riders stood outside Talwar's gates, one of them ringing the bell. The sound of it echoed loudly across the empty bailey.

"Who could it be?" Odelyn asked.

"I do not know, but there is no good reason for any man to be out on such a night. We had best return to the manor." He took hold of her hand. "Come."

The silence in the great room was so complete that only the sound of the fire in the hearth made itself known. Isabelle tried to speak, to move forward toward their suddenly arrived visitor, but her mind was bereft. She couldn't think of a single word to say. She felt Justin's hand at her waist, warm and still, and realized that he was as absolutely stunned as she was.

It was Evelyn who finally broke the silence, standing where she was, dripping-wet and dusted with snow, gazing at everyone in the great room with a thin smile and narrowed eyes. "What, Cousin, no greeting? Will you not even welcome me to your home?"

Isabelle opened her mouth. "I..."

"What are you doing here?" Justin asked in a low voice. "You arrive uninvited, my lady. Has your father come with you?"

Evelyn's smile tilted up slightly, mockingly. "Nay, I am come alone. The men who delivered me have already left to return to Briarstone." She nodded toward the wet bags that lay nearby, which Aric had carried in at her command before he went to stable her horse. "I had nowhere else to go, and brought all that I now possess with the hope that you will let me remain until the snow passes. A few months, until spring comes, and then I will leave." Her gaze, stony and somber, locked with Isabelle's. "I will beg you if I must. I have nowhere else to go."

"How can this be, Evelyn?" Isabelle asked with disbelief. "Your father, Sir Myles—"

"Has disowned me," Evelyn replied tautly. "He has blamed me for bringing ruin down upon his head, for driving you away and for failing to wed with Sir Justin. He sent me away in shame, with nothing but my own possessions and the jewels that were mine from my mother. I had no money, and so used the jewels to secure an escort here to you. Those two men who have just ridden away have taken all that I had left of my mother's legacy. Now I have nothing save my clothes." She took a step farther into the room and pulled the hood from her head, revealing the beautiful face that Isabelle remembered so well. "I have come knowing that there will be no welcome for me here, and accepting that you owe me naught, after the misery you suffered at my hands, and at the hands of my father. But I come, Isabelle, because I am desperate. I will labor for my keep, if you wish it. I will be your servant, if you will but let me remain until the spring arrives.''

"Why the spring?" Justin asked suspiciously.

"I will write to whatever friends I have remaining, and ask for their aid. There are several men who, although they will no longer want me for their wife because of my lack of a dower, may be inclined to take me as a leman.'' She ignored the disapproving sound that Gytha made. "But I will need time to decide what will be best. That is all I am asking of you, Cousin. A little time. I do not merit such consideration from you, and yet I ask it. If you wish me to leave, I will go in the morn. I beg you, as an act of Christian charity, please do not make me go out again this night. I am full weary, and so cold that I think I shall never be warm again. I will surely die if I cannot rest at least this one night.''

She did look as if she were about to collapse, Isabelle thought with a sudden rush of sympathy. She had never seen Evelyn in such a state before, shivering and bedraggled, her lips blue and her skin raw from the wind and snow. She was weak and vulnerable now, no longer the dominating woman who had made Isabelle's life a very hell.

"Of course you must stay this night," Isabelle said, moving forward with outstretched hands, unable to feel anything but sorrow for her fallen relative. "Come and sit by the fire, and remove this wet cloak. God's mercy, 'tis wet all through.'' Having pulled it from Evelyn's shoulders, Isabelle tossed the offending garment to Odelyn, who caught it with a grimace. "Meg, bring hot wine, and quickly,'' she instructed as she brought Evelyn to a comfortable chair near the hearth. "Your hands are as ice, Evelyn. Gytha, heat water for a bath, I pray you, and Odelyn, hurry and make the upstairs chamber ready. We will have you comfortable shortly, I vow,'' she assured her cousin.

"Thank you, Isabelle." Evelyn leaned forward, her hands shaking as they reached toward the flames. "I do not deserve such kindness. God bless you." Her voice was filled with emotion, such as Isabelle had never heard from her cousin before, almost as if Evelyn might weep.

Justin moved to stand before her, staring down at his former betrothed with a frown. "You may stay this night," he stated bluntly. "But no more than that. In the morn, whether the snow has stopped or no, I will take you to Briarstone."

"Briarstone?" Evelyn repeated shakily.

He nodded. "Sir Christian will keep you safely until you have made some determination of where you will go."

"But, Justin—" Isabelle began.

"It is for the best," he told her. "I do not blame your cousin for the trouble that your uncle has caused, but I do not think it wise to let her remain at Talwar for long." He held up his hand when she opened her mouth to argue. "Nay, Isabelle, it will be as I have said. Lady Evelyn may stay with us this night and be welcome, but in the morn, she will leave."

Chapter Sixteen

The snowfall had stopped during the night, and the world surrounding the three travelers was beautiful, with a white blanket that made everything seem fresh and new.

They were silent as they rode, for which Justin was grateful. He didn't want to converse with Lady Evelyn, and he didn't particularly want her making an effort to converse with him. It had been hard enough to leave Isabelle this morn, to disentangle himself from her alluring warmth, especially after the night of loving they had shared; he wasn't going to make it worse by reminding himself that it was on her cousin's behalf that he'd had to do so. Escorting Lady Evelyn to Briarstone was the last manner in which he'd planned on spending the day. It was all too rare when he and Isabelle had an entire day to themselves, to do what they pleased, rather than tend to duties. He had looked forward to Christmas this year for just that reason—so that he might have Isabelle all to himself, instead of sharing her with her account books or his lads.

He wasn't very happy to be burdening Chris with the care of Lady Evelyn, either, especially now, when the people of Briarstone would be tending to their own celebrations. But he knew that his friend would do him this favor and take the woman in, despite the fact that Chris had so disliked Lady Evelyn. Justin, at least, had been able to admire her beauty, wit and intelligence, even despite her scheming, while Chris hadn't found any redeeming qualities in her whatever.

She was, truly, quite beautiful, Justin thought, glancing briefly at Lady Evelyn's proud profile. It was a pity that such a cold heart lay beneath that lovely countenance, but he had learned long ago which of the two elements was more valuable. Isabelle's beauty would never fade, not even when she had grown old. Justin would always think her the loveliest woman he had ever known. Her warmth and generosity to her cousin the night before had proved the fact to him again. Despite the cruelty and contempt that Lady Evelyn had ever treated her with, Isabelle had been gentle and kind to her. Later in the evening, when they were alone in their bedchamber, she had even asked Justin to let her cousin stay at Talwar, insisting that Lady Evelyn's presence would not upset her. But Justin didn't possess a nature quite so forgiving as his wife's. Every time he thought of how Isabelle had suffered at her cousin's and uncle's hands, he was filled with renewed fury.

And yet, he thought, looking at Lady Evelyn again, she did not appear to be quite the same woman he had known in London. Despite the proud tilt to her chin, she seemed tense and uncertain, perhaps even a little fearful, and quite pale. As he watched, she grew even paler, and suddenly lurched forward in her saddle, setting one hand over her stomach.

"My lady, are you ill?" he asked, moving Synn so that he could take hold of her steed's bridle.

The hand that was on her stomach moved up to cover her mouth, and Lady Evelyn, wide-eyed, nodded violently.

He could see that there wasn't much time, and quickly dismounted, grabbing Lady Evelyn by the waist to pull her to the ground. She made a sound of distress and shoved away from him, stumbling to the side of the road toward some bushes, collapsing to her knees while her stomach emptied itself.

"My lord?" Kayne said, having turned back to see what was amiss.

Wanting to spare Lady Evelyn further embarrassment, Justin waved the boy forward. "Wait for us ahead. We will follow shortly."

Kayne nodded and turned away, and when he was out of sight Justin went to Lady Evelyn, bending beside her in the snow and setting one hand on her back.

"Gently, now," he said soothingly, waiting for her body to cease its wrenching. "Gently. All will be well."

She was shaking, trembling violently. She tried to wipe one gloved hand over her mouth, but wasn't able to control her limbs enough to do so. Placing the hand back on the ground, she knelt where she was, bent over, and began to sob.

"Here, sit up," Justin instructed calmly, taking her shoulders and pulling her upward. Somehow she turned into him, and somehow he was holding her while she wept, shaking and pressing her forehead against his neck. She was feverish, he realized, feeling the heat of her skin against the chill of his own. And she was weeping as mournfully as a babe, as if her misery were too great for her to bear.

"There, now," he murmured, holding her, stroking one hand over her covered hair to calm her. "You will be better now, my lady."

"Nay," she managed. "I will not."

"Certainly you will," he assured her. "You are but weary from so much traveling, and upset because of all that you have endured. 'Tis likely that you should become ill from it."

A painful sob shuddered through her, and she shook her

head. "It is not because of that. It is because they…the men…they…"

"The men?" Justin asked. "The ones who brought you?"

She nodded. "They r-raped me." She spoke in a horrified whisper, choked with tears. "Oh, G-God save me. I th-think I am with child."

Justin felt as if he'd been poleaxed. "They *raped* you?"

"Each n-night as we t-traveled. They threatened to l-leave me if I did not do what they asked."

"The bastards!" he snarled furiously, gathering her slender body more closely into his embrace. "I will hunt them down like the dogs they are and *kill* them!"

"What am I to do, my lord?" She clutched his cloak with desperate hands. "What am I to do with a child? No man will take me now, while I am breeding. Where will I go? If my father should discover it, he will have me publicly shamed before the king's regents. Oh, God—" she raised her voice, pleading "—have mercy on me!"

"Do not be afraid," he told her. "No harm will come to you, I vow. You will stay at Talwar until the child is born, and then we will decide what is best to be done. You will have naught to fear."

"My father…"

"He cannot touch you there, while you remain beneath my protection. I will not allow him to so much as threaten you."

Gingerly, she pushed out of his embrace and gazed up at him, her face wet and puffy. "But you don't want me at Talwar. Not after all I've done to Isabelle. Last night you made it clear that I'm not welcome. How can you take me back there and let me stay?"

Justin wondered the same thing, and could find an answer only in the pity he felt for her. Lady Evelyn had fallen far from the perch where she had once been worshiped by so many. He didn't think he could have felt anything for that hard, cold woman, but for the miserable, wretched creature sitting before him now, he couldn't do otherwise. He only wished it was something more noble than mere sympathy that he felt.

"You are Isabelle's cousin," he told her, "and for that, also for the sake of the child you carry, I owe you my care and protection. At least until the child has come. After that, you must decide where you will go, and I will lend you my aid."

"Thank you," she murmured gratefully, sniffling and wiping her face. "Thank you, Sir Justin. I will do whatever you ask of me, and will not make you sorry."

He stood and held out a hand to pull her to her feet. "Come. Let us return to Talwar before you are ill again. Isabelle suffered badly during the first weeks that she carried our child, and if I remember aright, you will be wanting a bed and slumber soon."

"My lord," Evelyn said, stopping him when he would have turned to the horses. "Please, may I ask a great favor of you? I would beg you not to tell Isabelle that I am with child. Not yet, I pray you."

He looked at her curiously. "She must know soon, as will the rest of the household. And she will want to care for you while you are sick."

"Oh, please!" She took hold of his hand with both of hers, pleading with him. "I am so ashamed. I cannot bear for anyone save you to know of it yet! Please give me time, only a little while, to pray for God's strength and to become ready for what will come. Can you not tell her that I am only ill? Please, my lord, I beg it of you."

"'Tis foolishness not to speak the truth," he told her. "I do not like it, and I will not lie to Isabelle."

"You need not lie," she said. "Only tell her that I am ill, for is that not true enough? You need not tell her why. Oh, please, Sir Justin, promise me that you'll tell no one that I am with child! If, perchance, I should lose the babe in these early days, then my great shame need never be known.''

It was true that many babes were lost early on, Justin thought. It had been his greatest fear when Isabelle first realized she was with child. And it was equally true that Lady Evelyn was fully distressed, and he didn't wish to be the cause of such as that. If she kept the child, the truth would be known, and only she would have to answer as to why it had been kept from the others.

"The child is yours," he said, "to speak of if you will, until the matter becomes evident. I will not tell anyone of what has happened, if that is your wish."

"It is!"

"Then I will not speak of it. Howbeit, you also keep me from seeking justice for the men who raped you, for I cannot hunt them out and be silent both. Is this what you wish?"

"I wish for them to be drawn and quartered," she answered vehemently, "but that will not help me now. I must have time to think, to consider my shame and prepare for it. That is all I can hope for until God has given me peace."

Justin nodded. "Then it will be as you have said. I give you my solemn vow not to speak of the truth until you give me leave to do so."

Fresh tears glimmered in her eyes, and the gaze she held upon him shone with gratitude. "Thank you, my lord. You are the kindest man on God's earth, and I know I do not deserve such from you. Thank you."

She bent to kiss his hand, but Justin, with a grimace, pulled free of her touch. "Do not speak thanks to me yet, my lady. I am willing to let you live at Talwar so long as you cause no trouble. If I should see my lady Isabelle made unhappy by your presence, in any manner, then you will surely know my displeasure, and that I vow before God."

Chapter Seventeen

With a long sigh, Isabelle set her quill aside and put her face into her hands, rubbing at the headache that throbbed behind her eyes. She'd been having more of them lately, this past week, and couldn't fathom why, save perhaps that it was something new from carrying the babe. She'd never suffered such aches before, not even when she spent all her waking hours laboring on her uncle's behalf. Of course, she was laboring almost as hard now, caring for not only Justin's moneys but for the lord of Gyer's and the earl of Siere's, as well. And at the pace that their combined wealth was growing, she wasn't certain that she'd be able to handle it all much longer. The responsibility was becoming more than she could bear. Perhaps that was why she was so plagued with headaches of late, although Isabelle suspected the source was much closer than that.

As if knowing her thoughts, the reason for Isabelle's worries suddenly knocked on the door to her working chamber, and the next moment Evelyn's head appeared.

"Meg's just made fresh burrebrede cakes," she said, "and they're delicious! Would you like me to bring you some while they're warm? There's spiced cider, too."

No matter how kindly Evelyn spoke to her, nor how

thoroughly sweet her manner, Isabelle simply couldn't bring herself to trust the woman. She was far too changed from her former behavior, far too...strange. But it was wrong to be so suspicious, Isabelle thought guiltily. She should at least give Evelyn a chance before condemning her as a counterfeit. Surely no charlatan could have kept up such a false front for more than an entire month, and in that time, Evelyn had been unfailingly sweet and helpful. She took on duties without being asked to do so, and did whatever she could to help both Meg and Gytha. She was friendly to one and all, without being overly so, and had made every attempt to be a pleasant guest. Except for that first week when she was ill, after Justin brought her back to Talwar only an hour after he left to escort her to Briarstone, she'd been consistently cheerful and active. And yet, Isabelle felt uneasy. Sometimes, watching her beautiful cousin go about her day, she wondered if she really knew Evelyn at all.

"No, I thank you," Isabelle replied, standing slowly from her chair. "I have only just finished the cup of wine you brought earlier, and am not hungry. But if you will ask Meg to prepare a basket and a tankard, I will take some out to Justin. He will be glad of sustenance, having labored so hard in the smithy all morn."

Evelyn's perfect smile widened. "Do not worry over Sir Justin, Cousin. I've already prepared a basket to take out to him. You shouldn't be walking in the snow while you carry the babe. I know Sir Justin worries that you might fall and harm yourself or the child."

"Even so," Isabelle said firmly, the throbbing in her head growing worse, "I wish to bid him good-day, and will take the basket to him. Bring it here to me, please."

"You don't look well, dear," Evelyn said, her eyes falling on the open account book on the working table. "Have you another headache? You shouldn't be working so hard. I'll speak with Sir Justin about the matter, and he will force you to your bed, I know. He's told me often enough how he wishes you would rest more.''

"You will do no such thing!" Isabelle said angrily, lifting a hand to try and rub the throbbing away. The worst part was, Evelyn spoke the truth. If Justin knew how often she suffered such aches, he would most certainly forbid her to continue her work, and she couldn't put it aside now. Not when so much was at stake in the London markets. "Very well, then," she said, defeated, feeling wretchedly miserable. "Take it out to him, if you must." She sat in her chair and turned away, not looking at Evelyn's satisfied expression, and felt like weeping.

"I'll bid him a good day for you, Cousin," she heard Evelyn say, and then the door closed.

"God's mercy," Isabelle murmured, bending forward as the pain grew worse. With an effort, she made herself stand again, and went to the window, looking out just in time to see Evelyn merrily tromping through the snow, a basket tucked in one hand and a tankard held in the other.

This was what she hated the most, this was what ate away at her, more and more as each day came and went. Evelyn and Justin, too often together, laughing and smiling at each other, sitting by the fire and talking as if they alone existed. Isabelle had known before just how well and how easily Evelyn could charm a man when she determined to do so, but she had never thought that Justin would fall prey to such as that. He'd seen through everything Evelyn gave him in London, but now—now he readily accepted all of it. He thought her fully wonderful, and spoke of her often with admiration. Wasn't Evelyn witty? And charming? And talented? The very memory of his praises made Isabelle start rubbing her forehead again. Evelyn's perfection even followed them into their bed at night, when Justin would suddenly laugh out loud, recalling something humorous that Evelyn had done or said earlier in the day.

Isabelle groaned and went back to her chair, falling into

it with a thump. She couldn't compare to Evelyn. Evelyn was beautiful, and skilled in all the feminine arts, while Isabelle was plain and only good at mathematics. Evelyn could sing beautifully, ply a needle perfectly and manage a household with ease, while Isabelle's singing made people cover their ears, her needlework was always a disaster, and managing even a small household like Talwar seemed beyond her grasp. In truth, if not for Gytha and Meg and Odelyn, Isabelle knew very well that she never would have managed at all. This was the only place where she was of any value to Justin. Here, in her working chamber, where she could at least make him a wealthier man than he already was.

"So." The unexpected sound of Senet's voice made Isabelle jump. "You let her get Sir Justin to herself again."

He stood just inside the door, an expression of displeasure on his handsome face.

"Senet, I did not hear you come in."

"That's evident," he said with a snort, and closed the door. "Are you ill, Isabelle? You're as pale as death."

"Nay," she said, rubbing her head. "It is just this ache. 'Twill not go away."

With a frown of concern, he moved nearer, setting his hand upon her shoulder. "You should be in your bed."

"I cannot." Her hand dropped to rest upon the account book. "There is too much work to do, and Sir Alexander's messenger will be here on the morrow. I must have instructions for the London bankers written out."

"Justin would not allow you to weary yourself with such work if he knew that you were not well. You have not told him about the headaches, have you, Isabelle?"

She shook her head.

He squeezed her shoulder lightly. "And you let our cousin make her way with him, as freely as she pleases. Can you not see what she's about, Isabelle? She means to lull him from you, always putting herself in his company while you lock yourself away with your books in this damned chamber.''

"Is that how it seems to you?" she asked tightly, while angry tears stung her eyes.

"It is how it seems to all of us, save you, I vow. How can you let her get away with it? Why did you let her go out to him just now?"

"My lord seems to want her company," Isabelle replied shakily. "And so he may have it. He is the master of this place, and should do as he likes. He did not bring me here out of love, but only to be his wife. I'll not keep him from doing whatever pleases him best."

With an irate gesture, Senet paced away from her. "You're a fool ten times over, Isabelle. Is it any wonder that he should enjoy the company of a woman who so diligently seeks him out, when his own wife will not stir herself to as much as take him a basket of cakes?"

"That is not the way of it!" she insisted. "I wanted to take them to him, but Evelyn would not let me."

"Wouldn't let you?" he repeated. "Isabelle, 'tis *you* who are mistress here, and not her! Do you think Justin knows how she bends you to her will with her clouded threats? Indeed, I know very well that he does not. And Evelyn fills his head with the same manner of speech, not quite the truth, not quite a lie, until he begins to think you do not care for his company at all."

Furious, Isabelle stood, pressing one fisted hand against her rounded belly. "I care for his company! I *love* him!"

"Then prove it!" Senet flung back. "Don't let Evelyn so easily take what is yours. It is not Evelyn he wants, but if Evelyn is all he sees, he will soon begin to believe that she is all he can grasp. Has Sir Justin not proved to you over and again how deeply he cares for you, Isabelle? But no man will keep throwing his heart into the hands of a woman who does not seem to want him in turn."

"And what would you know of such things?" Isabelle demanded.

Senet's expression hardened. "I know what it is to lose all that you hold dear. I know what it is to be alone."

Isabelle clamped her mouth shut, knowing full well that she had no right to compare what she had suffered at Sir Myles's hands to the hell that Senet had lived at Sir Howton's.

Wordlessly, she walked to the door and opened it.

"Where are you going?" he asked.

"To fetch my cloak," she replied. "It is too cold to go out of doors without it."

With one last blow, Justin finished hammering flat the metal for the new sword he was making, and then, wiping his sweat-soaked brow with the back of his hand, he lifted the piece high to inspect it.

"A little more, I think," he murmured, just as the door to the smithy scraped open, bringing in a fresh, cold gust of wind.

"Good day, my lord," Evelyn called gaily, smiling as she pushed her way farther in.

Setting the blade on the anvil and putting aside his hammer, Justin moved to help her. "Good day, my lady." He opened the door with one hand and relieved her of the tankard she carried with the other. "I have just been in want of some of Meg's hot cider, and here you come to bring it, like an answer to prayer. I thank you."

She smiled and made an elegant curtsy, just as if she were dressed in all her London finery, rather than the simple clothes she had worn since coming to Talwar. "It is my great pleasure, Sir Justin, to serve you. And look, here are some burrebrede cakes, still warm." She lifted the basket up until he could smell the delicious treats. "Howbeit," she teased, pulling the basket away when he would have taken it, "you must dress before I let you eat them."

Her gaze fell pointedly on his bare chest, which glistened with sweat. "I could not in good conscience let the lord of Talwar eat unclothed. And you must be cold."

He shut the smithy door with the flat of his hand. "In truth, 'tis hot as the Fiend's own fires in here, no matter how cold it may be outside. But you are probably chilled from your walk. Come in and be warmed, Cousin." He moved back to his work area and snatched up his tunic, wiping himself dry before slipping it over his head. "Sit." Justin motioned her over to a stool near the fire. He didn't get company too often in the smithy, and it was always pleasant to take a few moments from work to rest with a good companion. The boys usually only came when he was teaching them the craft of making weapons, and Isabelle came only when there was some urgent matter to speak to him about. Like Alicia, who had found his favorite pastime laughable and dull, Isabelle didn't seem to want much to do with his sword making. He had given up hoping that she would ask him about it or, better still, spend time with him in the smithy. She was ever too busy with her books and numbers. If he wanted to see her during the day, he had to seek her out in her working chamber.

"How does the day find you, my lady?" he asked as he sat down on his working bench, drinking deeply from the still warm cider.

"Very well, I thank you, my lord," Evelyn replied happily. "Meg and I have been busy in the kitchen, as you can see."

When she smiled in just such a way, Justin thought, he had a difficult time remembering the sort of woman he had once believed her to be. If she had been scheming and cruel in London, then it must have been because of her father's wicked influence, for since she was at Talwar, Lady Evelyn had proven to be only kind and well behaved. She was a delightful companion in every way. A delightful woman. And she possessed a rare interest in matters that most women found lacking. She liked to sit with him in the smithy, learning about how swords and daggers were made. Indeed, her interest was so great that he oftentimes had difficulty answering all of her many questions. And she never seemed to grow weary of asking him about Talwar's history, of how it was run and what his plans for it were, or of exclaiming over how perfect his home was. It sometimes left Justin feeling rather amazed that he had once assumed she would never be happy living in such a simple place. In all truth, she seemed to love Talwar better than Isabelle did.

"And there will be a fine feast for the evening meal, which I vow you will enjoy," she said, tilting her face up in a charming, childlike manner. "Lamb, roasted with herbs, and pheasant with currant sauce. I shall be hungry all day, only thinking of it!"

She laughed, and Justin couldn't seem to help but laugh, too. She was truly an enchanting companion.

"You must take care not to weary yourself so early on while you carry the child," he told Evelyn, pulling one of the small, flat sweet cakes out of the basket. "You do too much now, as it is. Why did you not have Meg or Odelyn bring the basket out to me? Or Isabelle, even? She would have been glad to do so, being past the time of worry with our babe."

Evelyn's smile died away, and she began to look embarrassed. Her gaze skittered away toward the door. "I am feeling well, my lord. You must not worry for me or the child. And Isabelle was...too busy to come to you herself."

Justin swallowed the bite he'd taken and looked at her with surprise. "You asked her?"

Evelyn nodded. "Aye, my lord. But she said that she was too busy to stop her work for something so foolish as to take cakes and cider to her husband. She bade me bring them to you, and indeed—'' she lifted shining eyes to him, filled with affection ''—I am more than pleased to do so. You have been wonderfully kind to me, my lord, and I am glad to serve you in any way that I can.''

Justin stared at her. ''Isabelle said that?''

''She did seem most busy,'' Evelyn assured him softly, leaning forward. ''My lord, you know how hard she labors to help your brothers....''

''Aye!'' Justin spat out, tossing the unfinished cake into the basket and shoving it away. ''My brothers! God save me.''

Standing, he ran his fingers through his hair in agitation and paced a few steps back and forth, at last kicking over an empty water bucket. ''Damnation!'' he swore.

Evelyn jumped to her feet and went to him, putting her hands on his arms. ''My lord, I beg you, do not distress yourself. Please don't be angered with cousin Isabelle. She is only doing what she knows best, and what she enjoys most.''

''She is my *wife*,'' he said. ''Am I to ever be lesser to her than her damned numbers? How much longer must I wait before I mean anything to her at all?'' He put Evelyn away from him and went back to his working bench, sitting down and bowing his head into his hands. After a moment he said, miserably, ''Nay, that is unjust. I should not have spoken thusly. Isabelle has been everything that I could crave in a wife, and more. She did not deserve that. I know that her desire is to be helpful to me, even though I cannot seem to make her understand that I do not care for wealth. But it makes her happy.'' He sat up, rubbing at the dull throbbing that had begun at the place between his eyes. ''And I brought her to Talwar so that she might be happy.''

''Indeed, and so she is,'' Evelyn assured him, placing her hands upon his taut shoulders and rubbing in a soothing manner. ''She was never so content at my father's house as she is here with you. Will you not drink more of the cider, my lord? 'Twill help to calm you, I vow.''

He didn't really want more, but drank it to please her. Her hands on his shoulders felt good; no woman had ever done something like this for him before. Bowing his head, he relaxed beneath her coaxing hands.

"Thank you," he said. "You are very kind, Cousin."

"If I am, 'tis only because I wish to repay your goodness in letting me stay here, and for keeping my secret so well. I am more grateful than I can ever speak." She tugged at his tunic. "Here, take this off, if you think you will be warm enough, and I shall be able to help you better. You are very tight here." She patted his shoulders.

Obediently, glad to be relieved of it in the heat of the smithy, Justin pulled the tunic over his head and tossed it on the working bench. Evelyn's hands did feel more effective on his bare skin. She dug her fingers into his muscles, rubbing and kneading until he began to wince.

"It will not be much longer before the secret is made known," he said. "I wish you would agree to let me tell Isabelle the truth."

"Oh, nay!"

"She will understand. Why will you not believe me? Isabelle will never turn you away. You cannot help what has happened. Can you think her so coldhearted?"

"I think Isabelle the most understanding creature on God's earth," Evelyn replied. "But my shame is so great. After all she suffered at my hands, how can I put such a burden upon her?"

The smithy door creaked, suddenly, and then flew wide open. Both Evelyn and Justin turned to find Isabelle standing in the doorway, holding her cloak wrapped tightly about herself in defense of the cold.

Justin's heart filled with gladness at the sight of her, and he stood, saying, "Isabelle!"

Evelyn stepped back, away from him, repeating, in a more horrified tone, "Isabelle!"

Justin glanced at Evelyn, wondering why she made it sound as if they'd been caught doing something wrong, but she was too busy gathering up the basket and tankard to meet his gaze.

"I'm sorry, Isabelle," Evelyn murmured guiltily, confusing Justin even more. "I'd best go."

"Evelyn," he began, but she had already lifted her skirts and scurried past Isabelle and out the door.

The early months of childbearing, he thought with a shake of his head, could certainly cause women to behave strangely. Isabelle had suffered several distressing moments, he recalled, but, thankfully, all of that had passed. Although she looked as if she felt badly at the moment. She stood in the open door, her face white as the snow outside and her eyes half circled with darkness.

"Beloved," he murmured, striding toward her. "Are you not well?"

She moved away from him as if he carried the plague, holding even her cloak free of his touch. "Do not," she said in a tight voice. "I'll not be the cure for what troubles you now."

"For what troubles me?"

"If 'tis ease you want, then chase after Evelyn! I'm sure she'd be more than pleased to put out the fire she's begun."

"The fire she's—?" He stopped, suddenly realizing what she meant. "Isabelle, by the rood! You cannot think that your cousin and I … that *Evelyn* and I were … *trysting*." The idea was so foolish that he nearly began to laugh, fully expecting Isabelle to laugh, too. But she did not, and only stood where she was, damning him with her eyes. It struck him, like a sharp blow to the side of the head, leaving him almost dizzy from the force, that she truly believed it. And of him. That he had plotted unfaithfulness, or perhaps even carried it out already. The cold air seeping in through the still-open door made him shiver, and he didn't know whether to laugh or weep.

"After all we have shared together," he said at last, unable to keep the hurt from his tone, "and after all I have done to prove myself to you, can you think this of me, Isabelle?"

A spark of something passed through her eyes, and he realized that she was striving to keep her own tears at bay.

"I cannot think otherwise when I come upon my husband nearly unclothed—" she nodded toward his bare chest "—and my cousin's hands upon him. But I vow, I should have expected such as this. "

Releasing an angry breath, he turned to retrieve his tunic. "You do not know what you speak. My shoulders are weary from my labors this day, and Evelyn did no more than offer comfort."

"Indeed?" Isabelle countered, moving to stand in front of him. "Is comfort all she offered?"

Justin had run across Isabelle's temper before this, and had always done what he could to assuage her. But now, knowing how callously she had refused to do so small a thing as to bring him a basket of cakes and some ale, he was ready to meet her fury head-on.

"Nay, not all," he returned. "She offered companionship, and brought me food and drink. 'Tis more than another in this household has ever done—my own wife!"

"I would have brought the food and drink to you!" Isabelle told him. "But I'm glad now that I did not! You've made your preference for Evelyn more than clear these past many days, and if 'tis Evelyn you want, 'tis Evelyn you may have!"

"God's mercy!" Justin raged wrathfully. "I don't want Evelyn!"

He tried to turn away, but Isabelle rounded on him. "Only think, my lord, how great a mistake you made in taking me from my uncle's house, when you might have had the woman you truly want, if you had been more patient!''

His head was beginning to throb, and shouting at Isabelle only heightened the pain. When she raised the palm of her hand and pressed it against her forehead, closing her eyes, she seemed to mirror his own agony.

"I do not want Evelyn," he repeated more calmly, striving to contain his fury. "I admit I've enjoyed her company since she has been at Talwar, but only because the woman I should rather be with cares more for her books and numbers than in being with me."

"That's not so!" Isabelle cried.

"Is it not?" he asked scornfully. "Always locked away in your working chamber, giving all your attention to making my wealthy brothers even wealthier. When have you ever once come to me of your own accord? Simply to greet me during the day, or to spend a few moments with your husband?"

Surprise possessed her features, and her mouth dropped open. "But I didn't wish to disturb you," she told him earnestly. "You brought me to Talwar to care for your fortune. I did not wish to become a burden, or an annoyance."

"God save me!" He moved away from her, his fury renewed. "I don't give a *damn* about being wealthy! How many times must I tell you before you finally believe me? I wouldn't care if you took those cursed account books and threw them down the well, or if you used them to fuel the hearth! The only reason I let you play with them is because you *want* to do so, because you enjoy doing so, and I had vowed that you would be happy here."

"Then perhaps," she suggested, the line of her mouth growing stubborn, "you made a mistake in choosing me. Perhaps you should have waited for Evelyn."

"Perhaps I should have!"

"Then why didn't you?" she demanded.

"Because I thought I wanted you!" he shouted back, enraged beyond care. "Because I thought you might want me, as well. But I can see now that I was wrong. Oh, aye, how wrong I was. A blind fool could have seen better than I that you would never come to trust me, no matter what I did to earn your faith! I brought your brother to you, Isabelle, and gave you back your mother's books." He set his hand against his forehead, trying to push away the lancing pain. "I've been a damned fool! I wish I *had* taken Evelyn for my wife. At least she craves my company!"

The words shocked them both, and filled Justin with sudden horror. The look on Isabelle's face was worse than death. "I didn't mean that," he said quickly, sick that his anger had made him so reckless. "Isabelle—"

She backed away from him, weeping, one hand pressed against her temple and the other against her stomach.

"I didn't mean any of it, Isabelle, I swear it!" He reached out to take hold of her, but she crumpled, falling onto the straw-covered earth with a cry of pain.

"Isabelle!" He dropped to his knees beside her. "Oh, God." He tried to put his hands beneath her to lift her up, but she gripped his arm.

"I trust you," she sobbed. "I believe in you, Justin."

"I don't care if you do, or if you never will," he told her truthfully, his heart in his throat as he pulled her precious, seemingly weightless body into his arms and cradled her with desperation. "I love you, Isabelle. What have I done to you? Forgive me."

But her eyes were closed, and her head fell limply against his shoulder, and Justin's heart filled with dread. Rising, holding her with all the care that he possessed, he pushed out of the smithy and ran toward the manor house, shouting for Gytha every step of the way.

Chapter Eighteen

The chamber was darkened when Evelyn sneaked inside, with only the fire in the hearth to light it. Isabelle slept soundly in her bed, suffering the effects of the poison Evelyn had been feeding her these past several days.

"Cousin," Evelyn murmured, moving silently to gaze at Isabelle's still form. It had taken longer than she expected for the poison to take its toll, just as it had taken longer for the one that she herself swallowed to work its magic on the day Justin attempted to escort her to Briarstone. More than an hour had passed after they left Talwar before she finally felt the effects of the double dose she'd taken, and by then she'd nearly given up hope of being able to convince Justin that she was with child. Afterward, at Talwar, she'd been so truly ill that she almost began to believe the lie, herself. She could only pray that when she truly did carry Justin's babe in her belly, she would not suffer so badly. For if she did, she would get rid of the child right quick. Or just as soon as she had Justin's ring upon her finger, and his signature upon their marriage contract. Once she had that, a great many things were going to change, and most eminently their place of residence.

She wasn't going to live in this rustic hovel for the rest of her life. It amazed her that she'd managed to stand it as long as she had, regardless the cause. No, indeed. Once she and Justin were wed, they would build the finest palace in all of London. One that would rival even her father's. And there would be servants, and every comfort that his riches could buy, and if Justin didn't approve, she would threaten to *never* give him children. The fool wanted them badly enough to learn obedience right quick, she knew. He was laughably ecstatic about the child Isabelle carried. So much so that Evelyn almost regretted bringing the child's life to an end. Almost. She would make the loss up to Justin somehow. He was easy enough to please, the lackwit. Lady Alicia hadn't exaggerated just how dull the man was. His preference for living a peasant's life was beyond understanding, and his love of sword making was so foolish that she didn't know how much longer she'd be able to pretend an interest in it without exposing her true feelings for such a filthy, lowly occupation. If it weren't for Justin's well-favored looks and his wealth, Evelyn never would have suffered so much to gain him for a husband.

Isabelle murmured in her sleep, and Evelyn sat beside her, pulling a small vial from out of her surcoat.

"Only a small amount will rid you of the child," she told her sleeping cousin. "A very small amount." She uncorked the glass bottle and lifted the edge to Isabelle's parted lips, carefully, and slowly, dribbling the contents into her mouth. "Ah, 'tis bitter, I know," she murmured when Isabelle coughed and tried to turn away, "but you must drink it, dear little mouse. I only hope it will not kill you, for if you should die, Father would be most displeased."

With her fingers she wiped the few remaining drops from Isabelle's lips, then replaced the cork and slipped the vial back into the folds of her surcoat. "It will be painful, Isabelle, as you lose the child, but I will give you no sympathy. You stole the man who was rightfully mine, and

have made Father's life a misery.'' She stood from the
bed, leaning to whisper, ''You deserve to suffer.''

He was in the smithy, just as he had been for the past
few hours, since delivering Isabelle to her bed, and just as
Evelyn expected, he was suffering from more than simple
remorse. Lying on the straw, Justin had one hand pressed
to his head, suffering the effects of the same poison she
had been giving Isabelle in smaller doses. It was good that
he should react so strongly to his first taste of it, Evelyn
thought. She would have no difficulties with him once
he'd drunk the sleeping potion she had brought with her.

Summoning up the sweet voice that had pleased him so
well these many weeks, she said, with concern, ''My lord,
Sir Justin! Are you ill?''

He groaned as she knelt beside him. ''My head aches,''
he whispered, as if the words alone caused him to suffer.
''It is my just due for speaking so badly to Isabelle. God
has rightly punished me.''

She touched his forehead with gentle fingers, smoothing
his dark hair away from his brow. ''Nay, my lord, it is
not so. Please, I have brought you this wine to drink, to
soothe your suffering. Drink it, I pray you, and let me do
what I may to bring you ease.''

He pushed her hand away. ''How is Isabelle? Does she
rest? I must go to see her.''

''She is sleeping gently, and well. You must not fear
for her, my lord. She would not want it so. You know it
is the truth I speak. Drink this wine and let me rub your
aches away. When you are rested, you will wish to speak
with her and be of good mind, will you not?''

''Aye.'' He sounded fully miserable. ''I want to beg her
forgiveness for speaking to her so falsely, for making her
ill. If she should lose the child because of me…''

''She will not lose the child,'' Evelyn lied reassuringly,
''but she will worry if you are ill when she awakes. Come,

my lord, and drink this before my hand grows weak and I spill it. Let me help you.''

He sat up a little when she put her hand behind his head, and drank when she put the cup to his lips.

'''Tis bitter,'' he murmured when he lay down again.

'''Twas the last in the barrel,'' she told him, moving until she knelt behind him. Putting her hands to his temples and rubbing gently, she whispered, ''Close your eyes, my lord, and I will make the aching go away. 'Twill all be better soon, and you shall sleep. When you awake, you will speak with Isabelle, and all will be well.''

''I should go to her,'' he said, his eyes drifting shut. ''I do not want her to be alone when she awakes.''

''She'll not be,'' Evelyn said softly. ''For you will be beside her. Now rest, my lord, and let your mind be at ease. All will be well, once this pain has gone away from you.''

The potion lured him into slumber quickly, and Evelyn heard his breathing calm, growing deep and even. Beneath her hands, she felt his muscles relax, and an hour later, when Isabelle's screams began to fill the night air, dimly echoing in the outer bailey, he did not stir.

Someone would come to fetch him, Evelyn knew. She had been looking forward to this moment since the day she and her father planned it. She scooted downward, tossing her cloak away, and began to unlace his leggings. She tugged until the garment was down about his knees, unrepentantly admiring the way God had made him. Her potion left him useless for the moment, but he would be a welcome lover when they were at last rid of Isabelle.

Quickly, before they were discovered, she unlaced the top of her surcoat and pulled it down to her waist, baring herself to the cold of the night and praying that someone would come before she began to freeze. Justin's body was warm as she straddled him, and she wished that she had been strong enough to remove his tunic and bare his flesh to hers. His warmth would have been that much greater to soothe her, and the effect on their certain intruder would have been more useful. But his shoulders, heavily muscled from his work in the smithy, were too heavy to lift without aid, and she would have to suffice with what she could. Arranging her skirts so that his lowered leggings were clearly shown, Evelyn huddled against his clothed chest, gathering what warmth she could, and listened for any sound that she might hear above Isabelle's screams.

At last it came. Hurried footsteps and loud, distraught breaths.

Evelyn pushed up on her arms, making certain that whoever came in would see that she was naked from the waist up, and began to move her hips on the lifeless Justin as though they were coupling.

"Oh, my lord," she cried loudly, moaning in a way that had never failed to convince her lovers of her sincere passion. "Oh, yes, my lord."

The smithy door squeaked open, grinding against the dirt as it moved inward, and Evelyn prayed that whoever it was would simply go away again, for if the person moved any closer, he or she would surely see that Justin's eyes were closed in nothing more than slumber, and all would be lost. Out of the corner of her eye she thought she saw Aric, standing with one arm held against the door as if he were made of stone.

"Oh!" Evelyn cried out, moving in a greater frenzy and striving to be heard over Isabelle's increasing screams. "Oh, Justin!"

With a passionate toss of her head she saw that it *was* Aric, his usually somber face filled with shock and revulsion. And that was perfect, she thought, even as the boy turned and fled, pulling the smithy door closed behind him.

Absolutely perfect.

She climbed off Justin with a sigh and a laugh, patting

him after she pulled his leggings back up and retied his laces.

"Perfect," she said happily, sliding her arms back into the sleeves of her warm surcoat and lacing the front until she was as modest as a nun once more.

"Aric will never forgive you," she murmured as she lay down beside Justin's slumbering body, covering both of them with her heavy wool cloak. "Never. He loves Isabelle too well for that." She slipped her arm about his waist for warmth and snuggled close.

Isabelle was only crying now, but weakly, and wearily, and could barely be heard. Evelyn hoped her cousin would not die, but if such an unfortunate event did occur, she knew exactly how to comfort Justin Baldwin. In a few months, whether Isabelle lived or died, he wouldn't even remember who his first wife had been.

Chapter Nineteen

Justin came awake slowly, his head feeling as thick as if it were filled with tree sap.

"God's mercy," he groaned, trying to push away the weight that lay half on him.

The weight, which rolled over at his ungentle prodding, groaned in reply.

"Is it morn?" Evelyn asked sleepily, yawning. "Have we been here all night?"

The light hurt Justin's eyes when he opened them, telling him that it was, indeed, morn. With an effort, he pushed into a sitting position and blinked at the now freezing-cold smithy. The fire that kept the small building warm while he worked had long since died down to naught but embers.

"How did we come to be here?" He brushed a hand through his hair, trying to rid it of straw. "Isabelle," he said with sudden remembrance, and struggled to his feet. "She will be wondering where I am." Staggering, he turned to Evelyn. "Did you come to fetch me? Why did you not wake me? Is Isabelle all right?"

She, too, was pulling straw from her hair, brushing it from her surcoat. "She was well when last I saw her," she told him. "She was sleeping peacefully. But you were suffering from an aching head when I found you here. Do you not remember?"

Shutting his eyes, he pressed a hand over his face, striving to lift his mind from its sleepy fog. "I remember...you brought me a cup of wine, and rubbed my forehead. I must have fallen asleep. But why are you still here, Evelyn?"

"I could not wake you," she replied innocently, gazing up at him wide-eyed. "And I was afraid you would freeze to death alone."

"You stayed to share your warmth?" he asked, deeply touched by this selfless gesture. "I am grateful to you, Cousin, but you should have sent one of the lads in your place. There is no need for you to suffer such discomfort."

Evelyn gave a little shrug and smiled. "We were warm enough to sleep. 'Twas not so bad." Lifting her hand, she let him pull her to her feet. "But we must return to the keep, for Isabelle will be worried, and the others, as well."

"Aye." He released her at once and started for the smithy doors, pulling them open with force. He was groggy yet, but driven by the need to see that Isabelle was well. She would think him crazed to have fallen asleep in the smithy, but he would tell her about the ache that had plagued him, and of his remorse for the words that had passed between them the day before.

There was no one in the manor house when he walked inside, and the silence and stillness filled his heart with dread. The last bit of sleep left him, and his every sense sharpened. Gytha and Meg and Odelyn should be busy here in the great room; the lads should be breaking their fast. There was only one reason why they would not be here.

"My lord?" Evelyn's questioning voice came behind him, but Justin was already running for the stairs, taking them two at a time, toward Isabelle's bedchamber.

They must have heard him coming, for the door opened before he got there, and Aric stepped out.

"Aric," Justin said breathlessly, grabbing him by the arm. The sight of the boy's face stunned him—he had never seen Aric cry before, never, not even after the lad first came to Briarstone, beaten almost to naught and abandoned outside the castle gates and left for dead. "Aric?"

Aric glared at him with eyes filled with hatred. Jerking free, he shoved past Justin and strode to the stairs, wiping his face with his forearm.

Heart pounding, Justin pushed the chamber door wide and walked inside. The window had been covered, and the room was dimly lit. He could see Kayne and the other boys standing at the far end, all of them staring at him with faces made of stone. Senet held a weeping Odelyn in his arms, but over her head his gaze locked with Justin's, as hard and unwavering as if they were enemies.

Gytha and Meg were bent over Isabelle's bed, but at the sight of him Gytha rose and came to him, pushing long stray strands of hair from her face. She looked years older than she was. Her face was filled with sorrow.

"She is past danger, my lord," she told Justin quietly, the soft words filling the chamber as if she were shouting rather than whispering. "The bleeding has stopped. She is not going to die."

"Die?" Justin repeated with sick horror. "What do you—?" He pushed past her, surging forward to the bed. "Isabelle!" Meg moved away when he knelt, and Justin gazed at his wife, who lay so still, her face drained of all color. "Oh, God. Isabelle."

Her lips moved, parting slightly that she might breathe, then whisper, as lightly as a feather's caress, "Justin."

He took one of her cold hands in his, bringing it to his mouth and kissing it fervently. "Aye, beloved. I am here."

"I didn't think…you would ever come."

"I am here," he repeated, weeping suddenly. "God forgive me, Isabelle. I fell asleep in the smithy. My head ached, and I... It doesn't matter. Forgive me, I pray. Forgive me.''

She didn't open her eyes. Only her lips moved, as if she were dreaming and speaking of what she dreamed.

"I called for you," she whispered. "I wanted you."

"I was asleep," he said mournfully. "Oh, God above. The babe has gone. Is it not so? You nearly died, and all the while I slept!''

He pressed his face into the bed, holding her hand, and wept. Isabelle slowly opened her eyes, and with an effort pulled her hand from his clasp and set it upon his head, stroking as if she would soothe him. Her fingers plucked at a piece of straw, and, weakly, she lifted it, staring. Past the straw she saw Evelyn standing in the doorway, and she watched, almost too weary to keep her eyes open, as her cousin lifted her own hand and, with a smile, lifted a similar piece of straw from her own hair. Evelyn held it aloft a moment, long enough for one and all to see what it was, and then she dropped it upon the floor and turned and walked away. Upon the bed, Justin sobbed disconsolately, as if he had lost everything he held dear. Isabelle set her hand upon his hair again and stroked once, twice, before her eyes drifted shut and she fell asleep.

"Oh, no, you don't," Senet growled, grabbing Aric by the collar and shoving him up against the nearest wall. "You aren't leaving.''

"Get your hands off me," Aric warned in a low voice. "You're not my master.''

"You're not leaving," Senet repeated. "I don't care what you think—''

"Think? I *saw* them!" Aric shoved Senet away forcibly, breathing hard. "Going at each other like two dogs in heat.'' He sneered. "Lady Isabelle's saintly husband and that swine she calls 'cousin.' Do what you like, but I won't stay and watch them kill her.''

"It doesn't matter what you saw," Senet told him, moving to stand between Aric and his pallet, where he had been packing his things. "Or what you think you saw. Sir Justin deserves better than such a quick and final judgment."

Aric gaped at him. "Do you think I'm blind? I'm telling you that I saw them. And heard them, as well. Don't you care for your sister at all? You should be up there beating the man to dried salt—" he nodded toward the roof "—not down here arguing his innocence."

"If I didn't love my sister, I'd let you leave Talwar with my blessing, but she needs you. She needs all of us." Senet's gaze swept the chamber, taking in the other boys before returning to rest on Aric. "I could have sworn you, more than any other, would not desert her in her time of need."

"Senet's right," Kayne said quietly from where he stood in the corner. "No matter what Sir Justin may have done, Lady Isabelle needs us now."

"If I stay," Aric said, "I'll kill him! The bastard. Telling us what's right and wrong all these years, when he's no better than the lowliest knave on London's streets."

Senet's hands curled into fists. "You can speak of him so after what he's done for you, for all of us? I have been here only a short while, but the rest of you—" pacing away, he flung a hand out at the others "—have been here with Sir Justin many years, learning beneath his hand, eating the food of his table. Taking your rest beneath the comfort of his roof and letting him pull you up from poverty and want. And all the while, has he asked anything of you but trust and obedience?" He turned, facing them. "Until this day, would any of you have spoken a word against him?" At their silence, he shook his head. "One fall from grace, only one," he said softly, "and you are ready to turn your backs on the man who has given you the very way to climb out of the pit you once lived in. So then, go!" he shouted at Aric, suddenly furious. "Take everything he's taught you and make your way! It won't be so hard for you now, as it once might have been. Sir Justin's cleared the road for you. I have no doubt you'll be the kind of fighting man he's trained you up to be. Why should you stay and make his life wretched with your ingratitude and faithlessness?"

Breathing hard, Aric stared at him. "I know what I owe Sir Justin, but I won't stay and watch him hurt Lady Isabelle. And I'll not stay at Talwar if Lady Evelyn is to be mistress here. I'll not answer to that bitch. *Ever.*"

"She'll not be mistress here," Senet assured him. "Sir Justin loves my sister, on this I would set my very life."

"Oh, loves her, does he?" Aric said with a snort. "So much that he's been following Lady Evelyn about like a devoted dog this past month?"

"It's Lady Evelyn's been making herself so welcome with Sir Justin's company," John put in, moving to stand beside Senet and setting his fists on his hips in an angry gesture. "Senet's right enough about Sir Justin. He's been good to us, and good to Lady Isabelle, too. Better than most men are to their ladies. And Lady Evelyn isn't to be trusted, I vow. I remember her and her father from London, and a more common cat you won't find. She's not what she puts on to be here at Talwar."

"I agree," Kayne said. "I don't trust her, and never have. If Sir Justin fell, 'twas she who was the cause of it. He's made his feelings for Lady Isabelle certain these past many months. Is there any one of us who'll say that he hasn't?"

Aric set his mouth, looking stubborn.

Senet regarded him soberly. "If you had stayed this morn, you would have seen his remorse for not being with Isabelle while she lost the babe, and how he grieved for the loss of the child. There was no falseness in his tears."

At that, Aric's eyebrows rose. "He wept? Sir Justin?"

Senet nodded. "Like a child. Never have I seen a man more desolate."

"He said he fell asleep," Neddy said, and they all turned to look at the boy. "That's what he said."

"Neddy's right," Ralf maintained with wonder in his voice. "He *did* say that. And sounded as if he spoke the truth."

"You've known him many years," Senet challenged. "Could he have stayed away from Isabelle for any reason, hearing her cries throughout the night? Knowing that she might be losing the very babe of which he has spoken to us so often with longing and pride?"

"Nay," Kayne said thoughtfully. "Not if he heard her cries, which he must have done in the smithy, for she was that distressed. He would have killed an army to reach her side, if he'd heard her calling for him."

"And if not for love of Lady Isabelle," John added, "then surely for the child. He's done naught but crow over it, and haven't we all heard him, time and again?"

"But I *saw* them," Aric insisted. "Even while Lady Isabelle's cries filled the bailey. They were going at it through all the noise, not caring."

"But what did you see?" Senet pressed, taking a step toward him.

Exasperated, Aric ran a hand through his thick black hair. "They were lying together in the hay. She was on top, and Sir Justin beneath. What more do you need to know? Shall I describe the whore she looked, with her dress about her waist, or the way she sounded, like a cat howling in heat?"

Senet grabbed his sleeve. "She was on top? How do you even know Sir Justin was sensible? Did you see his face?"

"See his face?" Aric gave a disgusted laugh. "His leggings were down around his knees, and Lady Evelyn was jumping up and down faster than a rabbit, moaning like a dockside whore riding the king's regent and knowing she was about to be well paid for the performance. Why in the name of all that's holy would I need to see his face?''

The other boys exchanged glances.

"Oh, come along," Aric chided. "You think she was taking her pleasure of him and he wasn't having any? That he wasn't even awake?"

"Was he moving?" Kayne asked. "Or just lying there?"

"He didn't need to do any moving," Aric replied tartly. "She was doing enough moving for both of them, and a couple more. Why would he need to weary himself while taking his pleasure so free?"

"Verily," Senet returned. "Why would he? Save that he has never before been the kind of man who would do such a thing while listening to his wife's tortured screams, has he?"

"Nay," John said firmly. "Never."

"Even if he might have readily coupled with Lady Evelyn, he'd not have done so at such a time," Kayne agreed. "Not if he was aware enough to hear Lady Isabelle crying for him."

"He has proved time and again to be a man of honor," Senet stated. "He saved Isabelle from my uncle's cruelties and gave her his name and his home. He has devoted himself to raising all of you up farther than you might otherwise have dreamed. And for me," he said, setting a fist against his chest, "he came while I lived in darkness, and risked everything he possessed to bring me out of it."

"We all came," Aric argued. "We all took risks."

"S'truth," Senet admitted. "But you did not all do it only for the sake of your lady wife, as Sir Justin did. He did it for Isabelle alone. Can you stand there, then, and say that he does not care for her?

Silent, Aric turned away.

"I cannot so easily throw away my gratitude," Senet

murmured quietly. "If he had not come for me, I would
yet be living in the darkness that had become my Hell.
But here I stand, free, in the presence of others whom I
have learned well to respect and hold dear. Because of Sir
Justin Baldwin." He unsheathed the dagger belted at his
waist and lifted it into the light. "The man who labored
long to create these for each of us when he might so easily
have given us naught is a man whose heart is tender and
good. I do not care if he has proved to be human, as the
rest of us are, even if he has fallen from the heights where
we worshiped him, and has betrayed the vows he took with
my sister. I will not desert Sir Justin. Surely not while that
foul witch who is my cousin plots against him. Aye, and
against Isabelle and the rest of us."

"Nor will I," John declared. "I stay at Talwar and with
Sir Justin."

"I, also," Kayne said.

"And I," Ralf added, putting a hand about his younger
brother's shoulders. "And Neddy, too."

"Aye," said Neddy. "We've got to get rid of Lady
Evelyn." He looked sternly at Aric. "We've got to do it
together."

"You're a crowd of fools," Aric told them, scowling.
"But I'll stay, if only to make certain no harm comes to
Lady Isabelle. It's clear enough Lady Evelyn's set her aim
on Sir Justin, and I don't trust her not to do whatever she
must to get our good Lady Isabelle out of her way."

Senet clapped him on the shoulder, clasping him in the
way of an honored comrade. "It does not matter why
you're staying, Aric, but only that you are, and that you
stand with us."

"Neddy has spoken truly," Kayne said, moving forward until they all stood in a circle. "We must work together to rid ourselves of Lady Evelyn. 'Twill be no easy
task, but we will find the way. Let us set ourselves to it,
and determine just how we shall go about succeeding."

Chapter Twenty

"Come away, Justin. The night is nearly upon us, and you've been here since afternoon. Come away."

"I'm all right, Hugo," Justin replied. "I wish to be alone."

Lifting the skirt of the dark robe he wore, Hugo sat cross-legged beside his brother, who had spent most of his recent days here beneath the tree where his lost child was buried. It was mid-March, and the grassy ground was, thankfully, no longer wet from the recent rains.

"You cannot bring her back," Hugo said quietly, placing one large hand on the back of Justin's neck. "She has been with God this past month, and will not return to this place. You must accept it."

"I have."

"Then what is it that troubles you so? Surely you no longer blame yourself for the loss of the child. You and Isabelle were both ill. Neither of you could have stayed the hand of God, nor done anything to change its course."

"I know." Justin pulled in a shaking breath, wiping away a single tear. He was full weary of crying, and yet every memory of the lifeless little girl, so tiny, but perfectly formed, readily called forth an unending well of tears. His child, his daughter, if she had but lived...

"Is it not a mercy that the sickness did no more damage?" Hugo asked, squeezing the back of Justin's taut neck in a soothing gesture. "You might have died, as well, or Isabelle. Others at Talwar might have taken ill with the disease and died of it."

Justin shuddered. "God forbid."

"Can you not be glad, then, that you were spared such loss, and think on that, rather than on the child?"

"I will try," Justin answered, closing his eyes and letting his head fall forward to rest upon his indrawn knees. "I would give anything to go back to that day. Even if I could not have stayed the loss of the babe, I would at least be able to stop the things I said to Isabelle."

"Is that what haunts you?" Hugo asked. "But you know that Isabelle does not set any blame at your door."

"Nay, she does not. She has been very kind, when she should do naught but curse me. If I had not spoken to her in such a way, giving her such lies, she might never have become so ill." Lifting his head, he rubbed at the stinging beneath his eyelids.

Hugo gave a long sigh, and patted Justin's back. "Now you begin to play at being God, my brother. I have no doubt that whatever passed between you and Isabelle that day had nothing to do with what came after. If you spoke wrongly to your good lady wife, then you must ask her forgiveness, and afterward, you must forgive yourself. Then both you and Isabelle must begin to go on with the life that God has given you. A month of grieving is enough. More than this, and you court the sin of indulgence."

"You speak truly," Justin admitted, releasing a long breath and settling his gaze on the valley below. After a moment, he said, calmly and quietly, "I am a great fool."

"Nay, not a great fool," Hugo countered. "Only a little one, as all men are from time to time. You should resist the temptation to make yourself better or worse than your fellow man, Justin. We are all fallen creatures, dependent only on God's grace. Now.'' He pushed up onto his feet. "Return with me to the keep, where the evening meal awaits us. You will speak with Isabelle and ask her forgiveness, and put all that is past behind you.''

"I do not know how to speak to her," Justin said. "If she should turn me aside, I will no longer wish to live.''

Hugo lifted his eyes heavenward and shook his head dismally. "Such tormented feelings. I'm glad I married the Church, rather than a woman. They seem to be a great deal of trouble.''

As they made their way down the hillside, toward Talwar, Justin said, "I have a request to make of you, Hugo. It may be grievous, yet I will ask it.''

"Speak,'' Hugo encouraged. "Ask what you will.''

"When you leave Talwar, I want you to take Lady Evelyn with you. I would have sent her away before you came, if I could have done so, but there was no safe way to manage it. If she goes with you, however, I will have no cause to worry, for no one could give her better care.''

"She will be safe in my hands,'' Hugo agreed. "And I will be glad to take her with me. Indeed, your decision encourages me. I have not been pleased to know that you have taken Lady Evelyn in, when it was she and her father who made Lady Isabelle's life such a misery. I have not forgotten, nor will I ever forget, Sir Myles's behavior on the night you married Lady Isabelle.''

"I had no choice but to offer Lady Evelyn a home when her father sent her off with no manner of support,'' Justin told him. "She is my responsibility by marriage. I had my fears, as well, but you can see that she is nothing like her father. Indeed, she has proved to be altogether different than what I had once imagined.''

Hugo glanced at his brother in surprise. "Isabelle does not seem to share your feelings. She has been clearly unhappy to have Lady Evelyn living at Talwar.''

"That is why I am sending her away. Isabelle has not yet been able to forget all that she suffered while she lived with her uncle, but I fear she has unjustly judged her cousin. Whatever she may have been before, 'tis clear that Evelyn has changed. She has been a blessing since she came, doing whatever she can to serve us all."

Hugo put out a hand and pulled Justin to a stop. "Are you in love with the woman?"

"Nay!" Justin's tone was filled with disbelief. "How can you ask me such a question? I love Isabelle, and ever will. Evelyn is as nothing more than a sister to me. I care for her in the same manner that I care for Candis."

"And do you think Lady Evelyn understands this?"

"Certainly she does," Justin assured him. "How could she not? There has never been anything improper between us. I do not know why you and the others should think there has been. Even Isabelle accused me of dallying with her, but there is no reason for it, I vow."

"Is there not?" Hugo asked. "When Lady Evelyn follows you about most of the day, smiling and speaking sweetly and doing everything she can to make you comfortable? You are with her more than your own wife, and yet you are surprised that we should find that odd? Perhaps you are blind to it, my boy, but Lady Evelyn does not behave as a sister toward you, but like a lover."

Justin gave a snort of disdain. "You do not know what you speak of, Hugo, and I fear that you insult my wife's cousin beyond bearing. Evelyn has not once done an improper deed, nor spoken an improper word, while she has been at Talwar. I will tell you what she is like. The night Isabelle was so ill and lost the child, when I was also suffering badly, Evelyn stayed with me in the smithy where I had sought silence and refuge, keeping me warm throughout the night. She never once thought of her own comfort, but only of what she might do for me. She was as kind as a sister to me that night, and I will not stand quietly while you, or any other, openly malign her. If it were not for Isabelle's unhappiness, I would not consider sending the girl away. 'Tis more than wrong to treat her as if she has committed some grievous crime, when she has done naught but act with kindness.'' He released a taut breath. ''I wish it were not necessary.''

''Hear me well, Justin,'' Hugo advised. ''It bodes no well for you and Isabelle while you so openly favor another woman. I will ask you this, and you must answer in truth. If it were Isabelle who had such a one to follow her about each hour, a fine and handsome fellow, who cared for her where it was your right to do so, and spoke with her when you wished to do so, smiling and whispering and teasing until she smiled and whispered and laughed in turn, not at you, her husband, when it was all that you craved—would you not be wretched? And perhaps angered?''

He would be, Justin thought silently, but said, ''I would trust Isabelle with such a man, to keep the vows she had taken with me. I would *always* trust her.''

''There is no question of that,'' Hugo said. ''Isabelle is eminently trustworthy. But what of the man?''

''I'd kill him,'' Justin admitted tautly.

''Ah.''

''It is not the same!''

''Is it not? You should ask Isabelle and see if she agrees.'' Hugo looked at him consideringly.

Justin lowered his gaze, staring hard at the ground. ''I do not need to ask her. She has been unhappy, and whether there is any cause for it or no, I will send her cousin away. It is unfair that Lady Evelyn should be the victim of such unfounded jealousies, but I love Isabelle, and will not have her suffer for any reason. She is what matters most to me in this life.'' He looked at Hugo, daring him to speak against such blatant heresy. ''And if God is jealous, then so be it. I cannot stop the love I feel for her.''

Hugo lifted his hands palm up in a placating gesture. "I will give you no argument, my brother. Does not God himself command that a man should love his wife? If the Church condemns such a thing, I, at least, do not."

Justin nodded. "I will speak with Evelyn this night and tell her that she must go."

"Shall I take her with me to Briarstone, when I leave on the morrow?"

"Nay, I can't send her to Chris. He hates the woman. He would not even speak with me when he came to see the child buried, he was so angered that she was here."

"I thought Sir Christian seemed strangely unsettled. Then I must return for Lady Evelyn when I have finished my duties at Briarstone, another ten days during which she must yet remain beneath your care. Have you in mind a suitable place for the woman to go?"

"I do, but first, there is something I must tell you. I promised Lady Evelyn that I would not speak of this matter, and so you must take the secret I reveal and keep it in confidence, as a priest of the Holy Church, and not as my brother. Will you give me your word on this?"

"I will."

Briefly, Justin related what Evelyn had told him about the rape she had suffered at the hands of the men who'd brought her to Talwar, and of the child she now bore.

"God's mercy," Hugo said afterward. "I am sorry for the girl, and honor your kindness to her, but it is well that you send her away now. 'Twould greatly pain Isabelle to watch her cousin grow heavy with child when her own has gone to heaven."

"Aye," Justin murmured. "I have thought on this, also."

Hugo put his hand on his younger brother's shoulder. "It would be best for Lady Evelyn to be settled in a goodly place where she can be cared for until her time is due. I suppose she must go to Hugh and Rosaleen."

"That is what I have decided, as well," Justin said. "But I fear that Hugh will make a mere mouthful of the poor girl. You know what he is. She'll be the sparrow to his lion."

Hugo smiled. "I'll make him behave. Leave our brother, the mad earl, to me. He'll treat Lady Evelyn as if she were the queen of England."

Justin made a face. "That's what worries me. Better to have him treat her like a common whore. He's ever had a softness for the poor and desolate."

"Would you rather that I take her to Alex? She'd not last a full minute in Castle Gyer before the heat of his fire burned her to cinders."

"Nay, nay, take her to Siere," Justin said quickly. "Surely Hugh will feel some responsibility, as he was the one who chose her for my bride."

"I will return for her, then, ten days from the morrow. Tell Lady Evelyn to be ready when I come to fetch her. And when I have returned, I will perform the ceremony to sanctify Lady Isabelle. Enough time has passed since she lost the child, and I would have her churched so that she may again attend mass, also so that you may resume your marriage in every way, and make your new beginning together."

"It is what I desire above all else," Justin said. "We were content and filled with every happiness before Evelyn came. Mayhap you are right about these matters, Hugo. If by sending Evelyn away, Isabelle and I can regain all that we have lost, then I will be glad to have her gone."

"You want me to leave Talwar?" Evelyn repeated, staring at him with wide eyes. She clutched the shawl she had brought with her to the smithy more closely about her shoulders. "You asked me here to tell me this? That you want me gone?"

"Aye," Justin said with a nod. "It is for the best, Evelyn. You have been good to us while you have been here, and Isabelle and I are grateful, but I would ask you to go. My brother, Father Hugo, must journey to Briarstone in the morn, but in ten days he will return to escort you to Siere."

"You gave me your promise," she whispered. "You told me that I could remain at Talwar until the child was born, that you would help me to decide what to do." Her mouth began to quiver, and her eyes grew moist. "You gave me your solemn vow."

It seemed strange to Justin that he should feel disappointed in her for saying such a thing, for not readily accepting his decision, as he'd expected her to do. He'd spent the evening meal watching Isabelle dabbing at her food, seeing how pale and sad she looked, and the knowledge that Evelyn must leave had gripped him even more firmly. She must go. For Isabelle's sake, and for his.

"You'll be content at Siere. My brother, the earl, and his wife, Lady Rosaleen, will see to your every comfort. They will care for you tenderly until the child comes, and then will lend you aid in determining your future afterward. I give you my vow—"

"Your vows!" she cried, tears spilling down her cheeks. "Do not speak to me of vows, when yours have proven to be naught but false!"

"Evelyn." He took a step toward her, pushing away the desire to take her in his arms and give her comfort. "Do not, I beg you. I will miss you when you have gone, for you have been a dear friend to me."

"Will you miss me?" she asked, sniffing loudly. "Do you care for me, Justin?"

"Of course I do," he began, but the next moment she pitched against him, holding him tight with both arms wrapped about his waist.

"I *knew* you did," she said, with a tear-filled fierceness

that surprised him. "Just as I care for you. Do not make me go away. Please, my lord. I beg you to let me stay with you here. Please do not make me leave Talwar."

He set his arms about her in a light embrace and thought of Isabelle's unhappy face. "You must. I am sorry, Evelyn, but that is the way it will be. I would ask one thing of you before you go." With a finger, he lifted her chin so that he could look into her eyes. "I would have you tell Isabelle about the child you carry. I know it is much to ask, but I want her to know why I have let you remain at Talwar so long. She has begun to think there is another reason, and I would not let her continue believing any such falseness."

"I cannot," she said, shaking her head. "Oh, Justin, do not ask it of me."

"I wish you could be spared the telling, but Isabelle should have known the truth long ago. I had thought that the babe would make itself known before this. It is only right to speak the truth now. Surely you agree that it is so. You would not leave Talwar letting Isabelle think what she does?"

"I don't care what she thinks!" Evelyn told him, sobbing. "How can you send me away because of her?"

Justin stiffened. "How could I not?" he asked. "She is my wife, and I love her. You are dear to me, Evelyn, like a sister. But you are not my wife."

She pressed her face against his chest and wept miserably, and Justin stroked her hair with a gentle hand, waiting patiently for her to master herself.

"Very well," she said at last, pushing away with sudden anger. She wiped her face and glared at him, and the expression in her eyes made Justin tense with unaccountable unease. For a moment, she looked as if she were capable of committing murder. "I will tell Isabelle the truth. Before I go with Father Hugo, I'll tell her every-

Chapter Twenty-One

From her chamber window, beneath the light the full moon provided, Isabelle watched Justin leave the smithy, without Evelyn, whom he had taken there, and stride purposefully toward the manor house. In only a few moments he was entering the front doors, and a few moments later she heard him opening and closing his chamber door. Then she heard very little else. The door that adjoined their chambers was almost always kept closed now; she couldn't hear him moving about as she'd used to do when it had always been kept open.

With a sigh, she moved to sit on the edge of her bed and waited for Odelyn to come and help her undress. Justin and she had once performed such tasks for each other, but no more. Not since she had lost the babe. He hadn't touched her since that night a month past. He had been as civil and kind to her as a husband should be to a wife, but he'd not touched her. There were times when Isabelle thought that perhaps only death might be worse.

There had been a few strange nights when she came awake suddenly, thinking that Justin was with her, when she was so certain he was standing in her chamber, or sitting on her bed, speaking to her in his soft whisper, stroking her hands and kissing her face. But each time she'd awaken to find herself alone, her chamber dark and silent, save for the fire in the hearth.

Such dreams and longings were a torment, but worse was his absence from her bed. Isabelle had never before known that a woman could want a man so much, or that it was possible to love so deeply and fully that she didn't care for anything but to be with him again, even for a small time, just to hear his voice or feel his kiss. But Justin no longer cared to share her bed, or even to be with her if he could instead be with Evelyn. Sometimes, during those few occasions when he spoke to her, he didn't even bother to look her in the eye. It was as if, she thought sadly, he had come to dislike her so much that he could not bear to see her face.

"I must go," she whispered softly, hearing the words aloud as she had thought them in silence so many times. "He does not want me anymore."

If only the child had lived, she thought. How wonderful it would have been. Even if Justin had decided to keep Evelyn at Talwar as his mistress, Isabelle would at least have had his child for comfort, and she yet would have been his wife. Surely he would not have sent her away. Not when she had given him a daughter whom he would not wish to see made illegitimate. And he might have continued to visit her bed in the hopes of conceiving an heir. Now, perhaps, Evelyn would be the one to give him children, if he made her his wife in Isabelle's stead.

And he would take Evelyn, she thought miserably. Why should he not do so, when he clearly loved her?

"And what will happen to me then?" she said, putting her fingers against her eyes to keep the tears away. She had cried so many tears for her lost babe, and was weary to death of the pain. "And to Senet? Will he send us away? Will he let us go to Sir Alexander?"

Sir Alexander would take them in; he would give them a home if she agreed to labor as his steward.

But, oh, God above, would Justin make her leave? Would he tell her, in that kind way of his, that he had been wrong to take her in Evelyn's place? That it was Evelyn he wanted now, and not her? Not her...not when he could have a wife so beautiful and clever.

The adjoining door suddenly opened, and Isabelle stood from the bed just as Justin came into the room.

"Isabelle?" he said tentatively, as if seeking her permission to be there. Then, seeing her, he repeated, "Isabelle," and moved toward her with one hand stretched out. "Are you weeping?"

"Nay," she said, but his fingers, touching the wetness on her cheeks, contradicted the word.

His hand gently smoothed over her skin, then her hair. His expression was filled with the tender concern that she had come to know in him. But it was an expression he might have held for anyone whom he pitied.

"You are weary," he said. "And not yet recovered from your illness. Let me help you get ready for sleep."

"It is not necessary," she said, her heart aching from the thought that he would perform the familiar task without the desire he had once felt for her. "Odelyn will be here in a moment."

"Nay, she will not," he said with a small smile. "I told her that I would attend my wife this night, that she was not to come. I hope you will not be angered with me." His fingers moved to the laces at the leather belt around her waist.

Isabelle swallowed. "How could I be? You are the master of Talwar, and may do as you please."

He tossed the belt to the bed behind them. "Aye, and so I am," he murmured, loosening the laces on the front of her surcoat. "Does it displease you to have your husband perform this service for you?"

Isabelle lowered her head. "Nay," she said.

"I have missed doing it," he told her, turning her by

the shoulders so that he might more easily pull the heavy wool garment from her shoulders, until she remained clothed only in her chemise. Setting the surcoat beside the belt, he gently pushed her down onto the bed to sit, and knelt before her, reaching his hands up beneath her skirt to unlace her undergarments.

"Hugo will leave in the morn to journey to Briarstone," he said after an uncomfortable silence had stretched between them. "In ten days, he will return, and many things will change." He pulled the undergarments free of her legs, and put them on the bed. Still kneeling, he looked up into her face. His hands were warm on her bare legs, gently kneading her calves and ankles, sending pleasant sensations tingling up Isabelle's spine. "Hugo is going to take Evelyn with him to Siere, but before they depart, he is going to—"

"Evelyn!" Isabelle repeated. "She will be leaving Talwar?"

Justin nodded. "And Hugo will properly church you, so that we may be man and wife again."

Isabelle was so relieved and pleased at the idea of Evelyn leaving that she barely heard what Justin said about being churched again, fully purified after the loss of the babe and allowed to enter a holy sanctuary once more.

"We cannot lawfully resume our marriage until that time, as you know," Justin said, his hands warm and caressing. "But, when the time has come, and if it is your wish, I will keep to my own chamber even after you have been purified. You must only let me know what you desire, and it will be so."

If it was what she desired? Isabelle thought numbly. Was it what he desired? Was he hoping she would release him of his obligations as a husband?

"Justin..." she began, but he stopped her.

"Let me tell you everything, first, before you speak. I've been afraid of this moment, so much that I've put it off like any craven coward, but now it is here I must speak all that is in my heart." The words came out haltingly. "There is much for which I must beg your forgiveness, Isabelle. This past month, I have lived in torment, remembering the foul words I spoke to you before you lost our child. They were lies, wicked and untrue. Every word." He lowered his head. "And by speaking them in my anger, I hurt you badly, and perhaps—" he drew in a shuddering breath "—perhaps I caused you to lose the babe."

"Justin, nay," she said gently, setting her hand upon his cheek and lifting his face. The misery she saw written there tore at her heart. "How could you think such a thing? I had no idea that you did so, else I would have put an end to such foolishness. If either of us is to blame, it is me. Never you, my lord. The words I spoke that night were far worse than yours, but to the sin of speaking them I must also add the sin of faithlessness, for never did you deserve that from me."

"You were unhappy," he told her, taking her hand in both of his and holding it tightly. "I would not listen to you, nor accept the truth of what was before my own eyes. And now, I am sorry. So sorry." His kissed her fingertips reverently, keeping his eyes closed as he asked, "Will you forgive me, Isabelle?"

The ache inside her was eased by a rush of tenderness and love. "I am the one who should ask forgiveness of you." She stroked her other hand over his soft hair. "If there was any reason or need to forgive you, my lord, then know that I have done so long ago."

The taut line of his shoulders relaxed slightly, and he nodded. "It is enough for now. Thank you, Isabelle."

She smiled and prayed that he would stay with her. If he would lie beside her, holding her through the night, then she would know that all was well.

But he only kissed her hand again and pushed to his feet. "I will leave you to find your rest. I would ask of you, before I go, that you consider in what manner you wish our marriage to proceed once you have been churched, whether we shall go on as before, or if such would be distasteful to you. I beg that you will have no fear in making your decision, Isabelle, for whatever it may be, I will honor your wishes.''

He left her sitting on the bed, staring at the door, which he had closed after him, with a thousand conflicting thoughts whirling through her mind. Had he only come to receive her forgiveness? Because he felt guilty for wanting to put her away, or because he wished to put the past behind them before they went on? He had not spoken of love, nor had he told her what his own desire for the future of their marriage was. He had only been gentle and kind, as he was to everyone, and had asked her forgiveness, just as he would ask it of anyone he felt responsible for.

''I do not care how it may trouble you!'' Evelyn told her father hotly, one hand fisting about the reins of the steed as it restlessly pawed the ground. ''You'd best be ready to take Isabelle before ten days are gone, or you'll not be able to take her at all!''

''Calm yourself, Evelyn.'' Sir Myles's calm tone was a stark contrast to his daughter's. He stood facing her with a composure that belied their location, as if they were conversing casually in their London home, rather than in the midst of the forest of Talwar and in the dark of night. He pulled his cloak more tightly about his neck in deference to the night's chill, and cast a glance at his men, who stood a short distance away with their horses. ''How difficult can it be to make Sir Justin change his mind? It's too soon for me to take Isabelle, unless you can somehow make her ready more quickly. She's to come of her own will, remember, else our plan fails altogether.''

''Our plan is going to fail at the end of ten days,

whether she is willing or not!" Evelyn told him. "I want her gone from Talwar. She's ruining everything!"

"Is she?" her father replied with interest. "You told me at our last meeting that you had matters well in hand, and that Sir Justin was nearly at your feet and ready to do your bidding. Has that changed, so soon? Have you not yet managed to take the man into your bed?"

"Only because of Isabelle," Evelyn said tightly. "Justin is too honorable a man to consummate his love for me while he is yet married to another. But he has set Isabelle aside, and has not visited her bed this past month, nor done so much as to touch her. 'Tis only *me* he wants now."

"If that is so," Sir Myles commented calmly, "then why does he send you away?"

"Justin wants me to be rid of the child he believes I carry, and needs time to rid himself of Isabelle. He has not said it openly, for he is too kindhearted, but he is planning to send for me when the time is right and all is well, so that we may be man and wife, as it was meant for us."

Sir Myles gazed at his daughter doubtfully, but Evelyn went on. "Can you not see, Father? If you take Isabelle out of the way now, then I can tell him the truth, all of it, that there is no child, and that I am willing to be his wife in every way. Once he knows that there are no barriers between us, he will let me stay at Talwar."

"You do not think he will be angered to know that you have lied to him?"

"Oh, nay," Evelyn said with confidence. "Never. He loves me too well, and wants me too much. Just this day he told me of how deeply he cares for me. When he realizes that we can be together, that all I have done has been for him, he will only be glad. And then we can be wed and come to London to be with you."

"But not too soon," Sir Myles cautioned quickly. "I will need time to settle Isabelle in her new home, and to make certain that she cannot be found if Sir Justin should not believe that she willingly left him.''

"He won't care for that!" Evelyn cried. "Justin will never search for her. He is like me, and only wants her gone! And I'll not wait forever to come to London. I'm sick to death of living in that disgusting hovel, surrounded by such disgusting people! I want to go home!''

"Very well, my dear," Sir Myles said soothingly, putting a finger to his lips in an effort to quiet her. "Very well. I know that these past many months have been more than unpleasant for you, but we are almost at the end of our goal, and if we move too soon, or without care, then we may lose everything, and all of your suffering will have been for naught. You do not wish that, do you?''

She shuddered at the thought. "Nay."

"Then let us be wise and act with caution. You have done well, my daughter, and will be rewarded tenfold for all that you have suffered.''

"I want more than that," she said. "I want Isabelle to suffer as I have. I want her to pay for all that I have been made to endure. Promise me that, Father, and I shall do whatever you say.''

He nodded. "I give you my word that your disobedient cousin will be punished for all of her sins. Fully punished. Have no doubts on the matter.''

"Will you take her away soon, then? Before I must leave Talwar?''

"I will take her if you can convince her to willingly come away with me. Sir Justin must have no doubts about her desire to annul their marriage. I do not want him following hot after me to take back his wife.''

"I'll find a way to make Isabelle want to leave," Evelyn vowed. "Justin will not follow after her. When I have finished dealing with my dear cousin, she'll gladly go with you, and Justin will *never* want her back.''

* * *

Late into the night, Justin stood in the shadows of his wife's chamber, watching Isabelle slumber. He hoped she would not be angry if she ever knew he was here, or that he came every night, watching as she slept, sometimes touching her or kissing her face, wanting her and loving her and praying that she would somehow find the way to forgive him for the angry lies he had spoken. How many nights had he stood just so, thinking of how it would be when he finally found the courage to speak to her of the matter? He had envisioned her being merciful, as she had proved to be, but he had not dared hope for such a sweet reprieve. With a few gentle words and the stroke of her hand, she had taken away the darkness that had haunted him since the loss of their child. And now he berated himself for not having known how it would be. Isabelle was too generous to do anything but what she had done, forgiving him as readily and easily as if there were almost no need for it.

But forgiveness was only a part of what lay between them. Even with it gone, he could not yet fathom how they would work their way across the gulf of acceptance and make their lives together as husband and wife. Whatever happiness they had known before seemed to have gone away with the child, or perhaps even before that. Aye, before that, in truth, else they would never have exchanged such harsh words with each other in his smithy.

Justin could no longer deny the thought that had come to him over and again during the past two months.

Isabelle was not truly content to be his wife.

She could blame it on Evelyn's presence, and he could blame it on her devotion to her account books, but neither of those things were the real cause. It was the way that they had begun, and the way that they had gone on. He had stolen her for his own gain, she had agreed to be his wife out of gratitude, and he had foolishly believed that if he only gave her whatever she wanted—her brother, her mother's books—then they would be eternally content together. Their marriage had consisted of nothing more than want and gain and gratitude, and that, as they had discovered to their regret, was not a solid enough foundation upon which to build a life.

This time she would have her say in what she wanted, whether she wished to be his wife or not, whether she wished to stay with him at Talwar or not. And whatever she decided, Justin vowed, he would honor it.

But, God in heaven, how he prayed that she would decide to stay. He could not fathom life without Isabelle, and these past weeks had been nothing short of torment. She had hardly spoken a dozen sentences to him in all that time, or touched him, and every time he tried to approach her, she'd dropped her eyes and moved away. She had almost looked afraid of him, as if he might do her some harm, as if he were going to hurt her again the way he'd hurt her in the smithy. The knowledge was a bottomless source of pain, worse than death. He could not bear to have her looking at him in such a way, not when she had once gifted him with joy and open smiles.

Slowly, silently, he approached the bed, and slowly, with great care, sat beside her upon it. She was always beautiful, but slumber added a peaceful grace, an innocence that made her look almost childlike. But the covers, which were lowered and settled about her waist, gave testament to the falseness of the impression. She was no child. Her full breasts strained against the thin cloth of her chemise, the round nipples showing darker through the white cotton. She was very sensitive to touching, everywhere, and had learned to tell him what pleased her best during their lovings. She loved to be kissed and suckled, so much so that she had once shyly asked him if such a strong desire was sinful. He had taken great delight in convincing her that a man and wife could be as good and loving in their marriage bed as they wished, pleasing each other without fear of incurring God's wrath.

There had been nights when he came into her chamber and gave way to temptation, touching and kissing her and savoring the sleepy response she made. Fear had always driven him away before she fully wakened; desire had pulled him back the following night, time and again.

He didn't touch Isabelle tonight, or kiss her. There were tearstains on her cheeks, making him know that she had wept after he spoke with her earlier. And she had looked full weary as he helped her to undress. She must sleep undisturbed, gathering the rest she needed for the coming days. Her decision would be made, and Justin would take no chances on letting weariness sway her one way or another. If she stayed, she would do so of her own free will, and he would know that she was ready to be his wife in every way, forever. And if she went away, he would accept her decision without a word. No matter what his heart told him to do—to keep her at all costs, even if that made her his prisoner—he would let her go.

Chapter Twenty-Two

"Thank you for helping me pack, Isabelle." Evelyn slanted her eyes sideways to give her cousin a considering look. "I hope you're feeling well enough? I don't wish to weary you."

"I'm fine," Isabelle answered, folding one of the beautiful surcoats that she remembered Evelyn wearing in London—a surcoat Evelyn hadn't worn once while she was at Talwar, favoring instead simple, plain clothes that she'd have disdained before. "I'm glad to help you in any way I can."

Which was the truth, Isabelle thought, setting the garment on the bed, beside the others she had already folded. Only two days remained before Evelyn would be gone. Two days before everything at Talwar would begin to be what it had once been, and for that Isabelle would have gladly done all of Evelyn's packing by herself.

The past few days had been promising. Justin had been unfailingly kind and affectionate, seeking her out and spending time with her as he had not done for many weeks, and each night he came to her chamber and helped her to undress in preparation for bed. He had not kissed her yet, not spoken of desire, but his lingering gaze and gentle hands made his feelings well-known. As soon as she had been properly churched, and as soon as Evelyn was gone, Isabelle knew that he would come to her bed again. Everything was going to be wonderful then. Perfect. She could hardly wait to once more be his wife, and to show him how greatly she loved and desired him.

"It is very kind of you," Evelyn said, separating various undergarments into piles. "You have been so kind to me these past months, despite everything that has happened. I'm sure I'll never be able to repay my gratitude. And I know that Justin has made his pleasure in your excellent behavior well-known."

Isabelle looked at her curiously. "I suppose that he has," she murmured, disliking the familiarity Evelyn used when speaking of Justin.

"And now that Senet and Odelyn are to become betrothed, you'll no longer need to worry about your younger brother. They shall be content to remain here at Talwar until Senet is able to make his own way. You know that Justin will take good care of both of them until that time has come."

"Yes, of course he will," Isabelle agreed.

Evelyn sighed. "I'm so content. I never knew how wonderful it would be. And I'm so fortunate that you are so understanding, Cousin. You must care very deeply for your husband's happiness."

Isabelle added another surcoat to the pile. "I care more for my husband, and for his happiness, than for anything else in life."

Evelyn was silent a moment. Then, with a smile, she glanced at Isabelle and said, "I am glad to know of it, my dear. I only hope that you will remember that declaration in days to come. Many wives are not so understanding as you regarding these matters. But Justin has told me often that you are perfectly malleable and would never deny him the wishes of his heart, and now I know that he has spoken the truth. It was rather foolish of me to doubt him."

"Evelyn," Isabelle said curtly, growing angry, "I do not understand what it is you speak of, but I wish that you would—"

Evelyn suddenly gasped and put a hand to her temple, swaying forward.

"Evelyn?" Isabelle threw aside the surcoat she was folding. "Here, to the bed," she instructed, slipping her arm about Evelyn's waist to keep her from falling. "Come and sit."

"Oh!" Evelyn said. "I felt so dizzy, suddenly. It is better now. Only give me a moment." She drew in a deep breath and exhaled it slowly.

"Are you ill?" Isabelle asked with worry, peering into her cousin's face more closely. Evelyn didn't appear to be either pale or flushed; indeed, she looked perfectly healthy.

"Oh, nay," Evelyn said with a small, happy laugh. "'Tis only the babe, but you will understand that without my telling you. A small discomfort for the joy the child's presence brings me. I have not really been ill at all, may God be praised."

Isabelle stood straight, and backed away a few steps, staring at her cousin.

"Babe?" she whispered. "A child? You…are with *child?*"

Evelyn's expression grew bewildered. "Certainly. But, Isabelle, I thought you knew. Hasn't Justin told you?"

Isabelle suddenly felt as if she'd been tossed into the icy depths of a frozen lake. Blackness welled up about her, overwhelming and engulfing. So great was her shock that she nearly didn't make it to the chair into which she collapsed.

"He *did* tell you, didn't he?"

Evelyn's voice sounded as if it were coming from across a valley. Isabelle set a shaking hand to her forehead and tried to force herself into control.

"Nay," she said, her voice rough and cracking. "He

said naught.'' She thought of Birgitte, suddenly, and remembered how relieved she'd been to discover that the girl was lying about carrying Justin's child.

"Isabelle, forgive me,'' Evelyn said from where she still sat on the bed. "He said he was going to tell you the truth before I left for Siere. I thought that he had already done so. I wanted him to wait until after I had gone, but he assured me that you would want to know the truth as soon as possible, so that you might make a decision about what you want to do.''

"What I will do?'' Isabelle whispered, numb everywhere.

"Whether you will remain at Talwar or let Justin put you in your own home, where you will not have to see the child. Of course, I realize that you will continue to give Justin children, if you are still able to do so after what you suffered so recently, but you cannot wish for our children to be raised together, can you? For me, I would rather not do so, although I will bow to your wishes in the matter. Justin has assured me that you will not prove difficult, and I know he is right. You have just said that his happiness is most dear to you.''

Isabelle closed her eyes, fighting the rush of nausea that threatened to overtake her. "But Justin is sending you away. He's sending you to Siere.''

"Yes,'' Evelyn admitted sadly, "and we are going to miss each other very much, although he has promised to visit me there often until our child is born, and will bring us back to Talwar as soon as you have been settled elsewhere, if you agree to go, as he has said you will. Otherwise, he must have a separate dwelling built nearby where the child and I will live. I will be content either way,'' she said, "but surely you realize, Isabelle, that Justin will choose to live with me, and not with you. I cannot think you will want to live here at Talwar alone, when you might have a comfortable house elsewhere.''

Isabelle was shaking her head, and trembling violently in her limbs. "It is not true. None of this is true. He said we would start anew once you had gone. He is sending you away!"

"It *is* true," Evelyn said more sharply, standing. "Don't be a fool, Isabelle! You're not blind. You know that Justin and I have been lovers nearly since the day I came to Talwar. We love each other in ways that you, with your silly books and foolish ideas, could never understand. And we will not be parted simply because Justin made such a mistake in wedding you. He regrets that now, and you know it very well. You've known it from the beginning, haven't you?" She moved closer, towering above Isabelle. "Haven't you? Did you ever think that he would desire you above me? Has he not proved these past months who he prefers? He hasn't shared your bed, even when he could have done so, because he's been with *me*. Every night, and during the days, whenever we're able." She knelt, grasping Isabelle's hand and forcing it against her stomach. "Feel, Isabelle, where his child grows within me. Can you deny the proof of that?"

Isabelle snatched her hand away. "It's not true!" she cried.

Evelyn slapped her with a vicious snarl. "You stupid little bitch! Is it any wonder Justin can't wait to be rid of you? Do you know when he put this child within me? Do you?" She leaned forward, speaking in a low, hot tone. "On the night you lost your own babe, Justin and I were in his smithy, joined together. He planted his seed within me during the very hour that your own babe died. That's why he wasn't with you, not even when you called out for him. It was because he was with me, and nothing, especially not *you*, could make him leave the woman he truly loves. You think of that, Isabelle, when I've gone to Siere." Evelyn pushed to her feet. "And if you still don't believe me, then go and ask Aric. He came running for his master to bring him to you, and intruded upon us while we were yet joined. Or, better yet, ask Justin. He'll not deny the presence of the babe that I carry. He'll tell you of it himself, and gladly.''

Isabelle found Aric working in the stables, brushing down his horse after the hard ride Justin had led him and the other boys through earlier in the day. He looked up when Isabelle pushed through the stable doors and, seeing her, fell still with his arms lifted and a brush in one hand. He froze that way, staring at her.

"My lady," he said, in a voice so dismayed that Isabelle realized she must look as frightful as she felt. "What is amiss?"

She told him what Evelyn had said, forcing the words out past trembling lips, struggling to keep herself under control and not give way to the pain and fear that tided within her.

"Only tell me if it is true," she begged him on a sob. "Please, tell me."

His arms lowered slowly to his sides, and he clenched the brush so tightly that his fingers whitened. "I do not know what is true and what isn't. My lady, I do not want to give you pain." He closed his eyes, and when he opened them, Isabelle could see within his own suffering and sorrow.

"Oh, God." She lifted shaking fingers to cover her lips, even as hot tears coursed down her cheeks. "Oh, God."

"My lady!" He caught her as her legs gave way, and gently lowered her to the straw, kneeling before her. "I pray you, do not. What I saw is what Lady Evelyn has described to you, but I cannot swear that what I saw is what she claims it to be. At first, I thought it could be nothing else, but Senet has made me understand—"

"Senet!" she cried. "He *knew* of this?"

Aric reddened with remorse. "I told him, and the others.

Please forgive me!'' he said quickly, when she tried to jerk free of his hands.

''Am I the only one at Talwar who never knew that my husband was bedding my cousin!'' she demanded, weeping. ''All this time, you've known. You've spoken with me, shared a table with me, and known—all of you!''

''I'm sorry,'' Aric said pleadingly. ''Oh, my lady, my lady, please do not! What can I do to help you? Only tell me, I pray, and I will do whatever you ask.''

''Stay,'' she managed, gripping his hands tightly. ''Only stay…a moment.''

''As long as you will it, my lady.''

They sat together in the straw until Isabelle had grown calm. Her face was yet stained with tears, red and puffy, but her breathing was even, and her mind was clear. By the time she left Aric alone in the stables, she had secured two things: his promise to lend her aid when she at last left Talwar, and the composure that she required to face her husband.

Kneeling before the largest of the wooden storage chests in his chamber, Justin ran one hand over the last of the ornate account books that had only just arrived with the courier who came from Gyer every week.

They were beautiful books, twelve in total, all fashioned to Justin's exact specifications in the finest leather, richly ornamented in an elegant design made of etched gold and studded sapphires. On the front page of each book were the initials *I. B.*, beautifully painted in the illustrated style that was currently so popular. Isabelle would like them, he hoped, and when she had filled each one to its capacity, he would order new ones, even more beautiful than these. The next books, he thought with satisfaction, would have Isabelle's portrait in them, just as her mother's books had. He would hire the finest painter in England to come and do the work, and when their children were grown, they would smile with the same love over their mother's beautiful face as Isabelle and Senet now did.

Only two more days. Two more days, and Isabelle would be churched and ready to make her choice about their marriage. But he already knew, from the sweet and open affection she had gifted him with these past several days, what her decision would be. They would be man and wife again, and all would be as new.

It had been hard to keep his distance since that night when he asked her forgiveness. With his wretched behavior put behind them, they had once more begun to embrace the closeness that had meant so much to him and, Justin believed, to Isabelle, as well. The nights had been endless, lying in his chamber so close, wanting her, aching with the need to love her, even just to set his hand in hers and know that she was there. But the days had been wonderful; sitting with her at table and conversing again, as they used to do; playing chess in the evenings before the fire, smiling and speaking in low voices, teasing and laughing. Twice in the past week she had come out to the smithy and stayed an hour and more—only to be with him, she said. His happiness had been an almost painful pleasure, and he had thanked God that he should know such goodness in his life.

The books would be his first gift to her, given as soon as Hugo and Evelyn had ridden away from Talwar. The second gift would come later, after he had shown her, with the worship of his body, and told her, with the words of his mouth, how very much he loved her. She would be more than pleased with it, he thought, with the house in London he had bought for her. It would serve as their residence each winter—a fine dwelling where she could practice her love of finances as closely as she pleased, while he refined his love of sword making at the special smithy he would have built.

Later, when they had children to care for, he would

spend his days in London educating them in the ways of God and man, for London, despite its many failings, at least had that to offer—enough of churches and charities, of the rich and the destitute, to provide a suitable knowledge of such things. His lads would come with them, if they wished, or they could remain at Talwar. Soon enough, his boys would be leaving him to begin their own lives, taking with them all that he had been able to impart, and Justin would fill their places with new lads, eager to learn and grow. For that alone, he and Isabelle must remain at Talwar for most of each year, but he would not deny her the pleasure that a month or three in London would bring her. It would only become something looked forward to in their lives, never regretted.

Through the adjoining door, Justin heard someone entering the other bedchamber, and he quickly placed the book inside the chest and closed the top.

"Isabelle?" he called out as he stood and moved toward the door.

She gave no answer, but he heard the unmistakable sound of the bed curtains being pulled aside, and he pushed the adjoining door wide in time to see Isabelle lying down on the bed, facing away from him.

"Good day, beloved," he said, stepping into the room. "Are you going to nap?" It was something she had done nearly every day since her illness passed. He had recovered much more quickly, and had suffered much less, from the strange sickness that had seized them both.

"Yes," she said, her voice dull and weary.

He sat beside her on the bed, placing a hand upon her arm. "Are you feeling unwell?"

"Only tired."

"Shall I stay with you until you have fallen asleep?" With his fingertips, he began to stroke along the sleeve of her surcoat, from her shoulder to her elbow. He was tempted to kiss her, to press his mouth against the smooth, curving skin beneath her ear, but knew the temptation to do more would be too great. Already his body had begun to harden with desire, simply from being so near her.

"Nay. I wish to rest alone."

He frowned at the sadness of her tone, and leaned forward to peer into her face. "Have you been crying? Isabelle, what's wrong?"

She was silent. He pressed his hand against her arm and repeated, "Isabelle?"

Her voice, when she spoke, was a solemn whisper. "Evelyn told me about the child she carries."

"Did she?" he asked softly, torn between relief that the truth was finally known and worry over Isabelle's strange behavior. "I am glad that she has done so, for I wanted you to know before now. I'm sorry if the news has upset you, but I felt you should have the truth of why I have allowed Evelyn to stay at Talwar, and also why I am sending her away."

"Don't send her away."

"What?"

She drew in a breath and released it shakily. "I said, do not send Evelyn away. There is no need."

The words surprised Justin. He almost couldn't think of how to respond. "Isabelle," he began tentatively, "I understand the concern you bear for your cousin, but you have not been happy with Evelyn's presence, and I believe it will be best for her to go to Siere."

"I will try to be happy," she said. "I'll not be the cause of any difficulties, I vow."

"Oh, my dearest, I did not mean that you would," he assured her quickly. "It is you I think of in sending Evelyn away. Do you not know that your happiness is important to me?"

"But what of Evelyn? Surely you desire her happiness above all things, especially now. You cannot want her to leave."

"I wish Evelyn all good things," he admitted, "and pray that God will be kind to her. But what I *want* is for you to be content again, for us to have peace together."

"But you do not want her to go."

The laughter that formed on his lips at such a foolish consideration died unuttered, and he began to wonder at her insistence. "It does not matter to me, in truth," he said.

"Keep her here," Isabelle countered. "Write to your brother, Father Hugo, at Briarstone and tell him to go on without her. You have been good to me, my lord, and I'll not repay such kindness with base ingratitude. You need never worry that I will interfere in your happiness, or Evelyn's. I shall always be thankful to you for what you have done for both Senet and me."

He was silent, struggling to push away the suspicions that her words gave rise to. Straightening, pulling his hand away from her arm, he said, "You are my wife, Isabelle. I put no one's happiness above yours, nor will I ever. Evelyn will leave, and I will not regret her absence."

"It is not fair to either her or the child," Isabelle replied stonily. "Or to you. I should be the one to go, and I will willingly do so. If it would not shame you, I will go to your brother, Sir Alexander, and will take Senet if you do not wish him to remain at Talwar."

He stood, then, as the dark suspicions became clearer and more fully understood. Isabelle yet believed that he had betrayed her with her cousin. She believed that she wanted Evelyn, and none of his efforts to prove his love these past many days had made a moment's difference. She did not believe him. She would never believe him. The pain of that knowledge was as nothing that Justin had ever before known, and he felt hollow, suddenly, so empty and hollow that he could see no reason why his life should go on.

"I want to go," she continued, her voice absent of emotion. "Sir Alexander has ever appreciated my love of numbers. He understands me well. Just as I think you and Evelyn understand each other. You and I both know now what a mistake it was to take me rather than to wait for her, but it is a mistake, by our fortune, that can easily be made right."

He was a fool. When would he accept the truth about himself? Isabelle didn't want him, just as Alicia hadn't. Somehow—perhaps it had been born in him—he lacked the way of winning a woman's heart. Everything he had done to show Isabelle what he felt for her seemed foolish to him now. All the plans he'd made were useless. Worthless. She had rejected all of it, all of him. And now she wanted to go. He felt like weeping, but thought that if he let himself so much as shed one tear, he would go mad with his pain.

"I...I want you to know," she said, her voice cracking like hard ice, shuddering with a sob that he realized she had been striving to keep at bay, "that these months with you have been the m-most wonderful I've ever kn-known."

She covered her face with both hands and gave way to a mournful, wracking grief that shook her entire body. Justin stood where he was, frozen, unable to offer her comfort in the face of his own hurt. He stayed where he was until she had calmed, some moments later, her ragged breathing loud in the chamber's silence.

"I do not want Evelyn," he told her, struggling to keep the words even and steady. "I have never wanted her, and have never betrayed you with her. I've told you this before, but you've determined, for whatever reasons must seem good to you, not to believe me." He swallowed against the sharp ache in his throat. "I have only asked this one thing of you since we wed, that you trust me, even a little. I cannot think of anything that I have done to deserve less than that from you, except perhaps for the words I once spoke to you in anger. But you have forgiven me that, or so you said. And now, if, after the months we have had together, you have such little faith in me, then you are right. It was indeed a mistake for me to choose you over every other woman, and you must go to my brother, whom you clearly trust more fully.

"But heed me, Isabelle. I will yet send Evelyn away, for I will never again be able to look upon her face without remembering what her presence here has cost me. I thought once to be kind to her, to be honorable as a knight of the realm, but if I had known that by giving her shelter I would one day lose you, I would never have let her stay. Although perhaps that is a foolish thing to say, for even if she had not come, you never would have given me your trust, or your love. Would you?"

She fell so still that he almost thought her breathing had stopped, but the next moment she pushed up on her arms and swung toward him, her face wet with tears and filled with shock.

"Justin," she said, her eyes wide upon him.

He felt dead within; she no longer had the power to hurt him, not more than she already had.

"I will write Alexander within the hour, and ask him to send an escort to take you, and Senet, if he desires to accompany you, to Gyer. Forgive me if I am not here to bid you Godspeed, but I fear that urgent business will keep me from Talwar for some time. I wish you happiness, Isabelle. May you find it with Alexander as you were not able to find it with me."

He left the chamber, shutting and locking the adjoining door, and ignored Isabelle's pleading from the other side as he wrote a missive to Alexander and then packed a traveling bag. An hour later he had given the boys their instructions and, without speaking a word to anyone else in the household, mounted Synn and ridden out of Talwar.

Chapter Twenty-Three

"But why did Sir Justin leave in such a way?" Odelyn asked, setting her head more comfortably against Senet's shoulder. "He seemed so unhappy."

Senet pressed his mouth against her forehead in a gentle kiss before murmuring, sleepily, "I do not know. He and Isabelle must have had an angry spate, for there was surely no warning. And my sister has never looked more downcast, although she will not tell me what troubles her so. She spent most of the day closeted together with Evelyn, and that is not like her."

"Nay, 'tis very strange," Odelyn agreed, stretching out a hand to place it over the place where she could feel Senet's heart beating. "I wish you would make me your wife now. Why can we not be handfasted?"

Smiling into the darkness of the stable, where they lay together, warm and comfortable, in the loft, he replied, "If you think it is because I do not want you, then you are far wrong. 'Tis the most difficult thing I have ever done, keeping myself from taking your maidenhead. But we will wait." He kissed her nose. "I love you too well to get you with child before you are full ready, also before we are wed."

"I am nearly too old!" she chided. "Most girls my age

have at least one child or more. I shall be mocked as useless.''

Rising over her, he said, ''Never,'' and kissed her mouth. When he lifted his head, he teased, ''I can think of many good uses for you, my pretty wife-to-be. I will weary you from being such a demanding husband.''

She slipped her hands beneath his tunic, pressing him closer to herself. ''Senet, please...''

''Sweet Odelyn, do not tempt me so,'' he murmured against her lips, taking them again with his own, and then once more, even more fully. ''I want you so much I dream of you even when I am awake.''

''Then why will you not take me?''

''I will, I vow, an hour after we have been wed.'' He stroked the backs of his fingers across her cheek. ''But not before then. You will not know dishonor because of me, sweet Odelyn, for I love you more than my own life, and will never bring you shame. It is bad enough that we meet here in the stables so often, sneaking about as if we were thieves. I should be stronger and resist such temptation, but it is impossible. You have given me so much, my very life...''

She turned her face to kiss his fingers. ''I love you, Senet.''

His expression filled with wonder. ''And that most of all, that you should love me, when I am all that is wrong, so unsightly and ill-favored.''

''You are not!'' she insisted with great indignation.

''I have been a slave,'' he reminded her. ''And am scarred from head to foot.''

Her fingertips, wandering beneath his tunic, found one of the scars he spoke of and caressed it with gentle care. ''I would take them from you, if I could, but only because they bring you sorrow,'' she said. ''For me, I think you are very beautiful, everywhere.''

He laughed lightly. ''I beseech you, my dear lady, never

to say such as that in Aric's or Kayne's hearing. They would tease me until the end of my life, I vow."

She joined him in laughter, though it died away with his as their gazes held fast.

"Odelyn," Senet whispered, lowering his mouth to hers with reverent care, "I love you so."

He did not know how many minutes passed before the sound of the stable doors opening brought him to his senses, but when he lifted his head at last, he was full dizzy with sensation. Beneath him, Odelyn moaned her dissent and tried to pull him back down.

"Wait," he whispered, and put a finger against her lips to warn her to be silent.

"Hurry!" It was Evelyn, clearly irate and nervous. "Come along! Why are you so slow? Do you *want* to be caught?"

"Nay."

At the sound of Isabelle's weary voice, Senet and Odelyn exchanged surprised glances.

"Then come along! Help me to get the horses saddled."

Sitting up, Senet silently crawled to the edge of the loft and peered down. In the darkness, he saw both his sister and his cousin, heavily cloaked, each of them working to saddle a horse.

"Are you certain Kayne won't stop us? He's always so vigilant when he's taking his turn as guard."

The heat of Odelyn's arm pressed against Senet's as she joined him at the edge. He spared a glance toward her, meeting her gaze swiftly in an exchange of shared disbelief.

"Kayne won't even know we've gone, I promise you," Evelyn said with satisfaction. "And Aric left earlier, taking your missive to Briarstone, did he not? Senet and the others will be soundly asleep, so we've no need to fear. Hurry!"

The women continued to saddle their steeds, until they were nearly done, and Isabelle suddenly stopped.

"What's the matter with you?" Evelyn hissed. "We need to get on our way, and quickly! Sir Christian won't wait for you forever, but will come to Talwar in search if we tarry too long."

"But what if Justin went to Briarstone?" Isabelle asked worriedly. "Perhaps he will be angered that I asked for Sir Christian's help. And Father Hugo will not know what to think if I am not here when he arrives on the morrow, especially if Justin has not returned by then...."

"I've told you over and again that Justin waits only for you to leave Talwar before he returns to it. He told me himself, before he left, that you had decided to leave for Gyer. What's the matter with you? Why are you looking at me that way?"

The full moon shining through the stable windows gave light to the play that passed on the faces of the women below. Senet clenched his fist at the sight of his cousin rounding on his sister, who was clearly confused and upset.

"Justin denied ever touching you," Isabelle said faintly, closing her eyes as if striving to remember something very important. "I'm not certain that I should leave like this, without him knowing... He said he would write to Sir Alexander."

Evelyn's expression took on a demonic fury, and Senet, watching her, drew in a breath. He had seen such as that before, and knew to be wary.

"Did Justin deny that I carry his child?" she demanded. "Did he ever deny that, Isabelle?"

Miserably, Isabelle shook her head. "Nay, he only said that he was glad I knew of it at last."

"And so he is, just as I told you he would be. Surely you do not think a man so noble as Justin would admit to anything that would hurt you? Has he ever failed to be

kind to you, or to keep you from harm if he could do so?"
Evelyn pressed, her voice kinder, more beguiling. She
moved to finish the work that Isabelle had begun, saddling
the horse, yet keeping her attention on Isabelle. "You
want him to be happy, Isabelle, do you not? Don't force
him to choose you over me, simply because he is so honorable and you are his legal wife. He will never be able
to set you aside so long as he feels responsible for you.
Let him be happy. Give him his freedom, as you know
you must. It is the only way that you can fully repay him
for all that he has done for both you and Senet."

"Yes, I...I suppose it is," Isabelle admitted haltingly,
her fingers closing about the reins that Evelyn set in her
hands. "I only wish that we had not parted as we did."

"There's no time for you to worry over whatever foolish remark you said that upset him so," Evelyn told her,
swinging onto her steed with remarkable ease. "Now you
must only do what you can to set things right. Only think
how pleased Justin will be to return to Talwar and find
that he need no longer worry over you."

"Aye," Isabelle agreed softly, making two futile attempts before at last, with her skirts tangling beneath her
legs, managing to stay seated in the saddle. "Evelyn," she
said, stopping her cousin when she would have ridden out
of the open stable doors. "You do love Justin, do you not?
You don't simply want him as you did in London? Only
for those things that he possesses?"

Evelyn uttered a short laugh of disdain. "I love Justin
Baldwin more than you could ever imagine doing. I vow
before God that I would give my life only to maintain his
happiness. Does that satisfy you, Cousin?"

Isabelle nodded silently, then prodded her steed forward
and followed Evelyn out of the stables. The moment they
were gone, Senet leaped for the loft's ladder and rapidly
climbed down.

"Senet! What will you do?" Odelyn called after him, descending as quickly as she could.

"I must follow behind and see where they go. Hurry, Odelyn." He took her by the waist as she neared the floor and set her on her feet. "Run and wake the household, everyone, and tell Kayne and the other boys to dress at once and meet me here. I will have the horses ready. Run!" he commanded, pressing her through the door. "We cannot risk losing their trail in this darkness!"

Not more than ten minutes later, John, Ralf and Neddy came racing through the stable doors, still lacing their tunics and running their fingers through their hair.

"Kayne's been drugged!" John shouted above the noise as they all quickly mounted. "Odelyn found him on the rooftop, where he had been keeping guard."

"God," Senet said. "We cannot leave Talwar so fully unmanned. Ralf, you must remain and do whatever you must to guard the keep until Aric returns. Neddy—" he moved toward the youngest boy, his expression sober "—ride to Briarstone and find Aric, bringing him back with as many men from there as can be spared. Can you do this?"

With a curt nod, Neddy said, "I'll do it," and the next moment set his heels into the horse's flanks and rode for Talwar's gates.

John followed the boy out into the darkness, while Senet sent one last look at Ralf, who had already dismounted. "Rouse Kayne as quickly as you can and discover what happened. When Lady Evelyn returns, lock her in her chamber and do not let her out until you've had word from me or Sir Justin. Not for *any* other reason. Believe nothing the witch says."

"Aye, Senet. Godspeed."

They would need God's help, Senet thought grimly as he followed John into the night and out onto the open road leading away from Talwar, especially if they were to find and follow Isabelle and Evelyn. Even with only a few minutes' lead, the women might be impossible to find in this darkness.

"Damn you, Justin Baldwin," he muttered as he quickened his horse's pace to catch up to John, adding, more prayerfully, "Merciful God, bring him back soon."

It was Aric who showed them which way to go, when he suddenly appeared out of the darkness and waved them onto a nearly hidden path heading straight into the woods. Once concealed in the darkness, he put up a hand to bring them all to a halt.

"Lady Isabelle and her cousin are just ahead," Aric whispered. "We must be silent, else we give ourselves away. Several mounted men went in earlier."

"What are you doing here?" Senet demanded, his anger evident despite his low tone.

"I'll explain later," Aric promised, dismounting. "We must hide the horses and go in on foot. Hurry."

A few minutes later, moving stealthily through the trees, they neared a clearing where several torches, held aloft by armed soldiers, gave off clear light.

"I'm disappointed, Isabelle," Sir Myles was saying. "Are you not glad to see your loving uncle?"

Isabelle seemed not to know who to look at, either her cousin, whose beauty was marred by a graceless smirk, or her uncle, who was clearly well satisfied with himself and the situation. Swinging her gaze from one to the other, Isabelle demanded, "What have you done with Sir Christian? He was to meet me here. If you have brought him some harm..."

"Have no fear for the lord of Briarstone, Cousin," Evelyn replied. "He never received the missive you wrote, asking him to act as your escort to Gyer. The missive I gave into Aric's care was for Father Hugo, telling him that there is no need for him to come to Talwar on the morrow, and to go on to Siere without me. I hope you will not mind that I signed your name to it, but I could not take the chance of forging Justin's signature, should Father Hugo be familiar with his brother's written hand.''

Both Senet and John turned to look at Aric with accusation, until, with a sly smile, Aric silently pulled a rolled parchment document from out of his tunic and held it up for them to see in the darkness. His meaning was clear—he had never delivered the false missive—and Senet released a breath of relief before returning his attention to his sister, who was staring at Evelyn as if she had never seen her before.

"It was all lies," she said, clearly stunned. "Justin said that he had not betrayed me. The child is not his, is it?"

Evelyn laughed with delight. "What child, Cousin?"

"God's mercy," Isabelle uttered faintly. At the distress in her tone, Senet surged forward, held back only by John and Aric each putting a hand on his shoulder. Isabelle looked at her smiling uncle. "You did it to bring me back?" she asked, shaking her head slowly. "But Justin will know. He'll realize that I have not gone to Gyer, and he'll come looking for me."

"Will he?" Evelyn asked. "When you had such little faith in him, and left of your own accord?"

"He expected me to go to Gyer!"

"Foolish mouse." Evelyn sneered, prodding her steed closer to Isabelle's, so that she might speak into her face. "Justin is well rid of you, I vow. Do you think I shall have any difficulty convincing him that you left Talwar on your own, keeping your destination a secret, even though I tried to stop you? And who will disprove me? Aric didn't know what was in the missive that you sent Sir Christian, and Father Hugo will be on his way to Siere by tomorrow. By the time Justin's priestly brother hears that you have gone, perhaps many months from now, he will only conclude that you sent him on his way out of goodness, so that Justin and I might be together.''

''Senet...'' Isabelle began.

''Is sleeping soundly,'' Evelyn told her. ''And will be as confused by your absence as the others when he arises in the morn.''

''Then Kayne will surely know something is amiss,'' Isabelle argued insistently. ''He was serving as guard this night, and will know that you have been gone, as well.''

''Kayne, I think, will only feel some shame and regret for drinking too much wine and falling asleep at his post. I took him the wine myself, well mixed with a sleeping draught. He drank only a little, to serve him credit, but I can easily persuade him that he drank much more, and soon became insensible. Guilt will keep him from pressing the matter more. No one will see me return to Talwar, and no one will know that I have ever been gone. In the morn, I shall be as distressed as the rest of the household, and more than ready to comfort Justin when he returns to find you gone and lost. Not that he will suffer long, since he already wanted you gone. Oh, he will want to know where you are, I grant, for he will feel responsible for you yet. But when he realizes that you cannot be found, he will forget you soon enough, and he and I will find the happiness that you tried to deny us.''

Isabelle held her cousin's gaze. ''Do you love him, Evelyn? In truth?''

''I didn't lie about that,'' Evelyn told her. ''You need not fear that Justin will ever be unhappy, for I would gladly kill to make sure of it. And you already know that he loves me.''

''Nay,'' Isabelle said sadly. ''He told me that he does not. I wish I had believed him instead of you.''

''He does love me!'' Evelyn cried, raising a fist to strike her cousin.

''Not now.'' Sir Myles reached out and grabbed his

daughter's hand before it could descend, steadying his horse as it bumped against hers. "Leave Isabelle to me."

"She's mad!" Evelyn shouted furiously, pulling herself free of her father's restraint. "She's crazed if she thinks that any man would choose her over me. A plain, ugly, *stupid* mouse!"

"Very well, my dear," her father agreed placatingly. "Very well. I shall take care to punish her thoroughly for stealing your rightful husband from you, and give you my word that she will learn sorrow. You must keep your thoughts on handling Sir Justin, and not worry o'er Isabelle. And you must return to Talwar before you are missed."

Evelyn glared at her cousin, who sat solemn and still in the cold night air. "Only make certain that you do as you have said, Father, for if I find that she has been living in luxury and comfort so that you might better win her efforts on your behalf, I will ruin everything for you. I vow it on my mother's soul."

Without another word, she backed her horse a few steps, then turned and rode away.

"Where are you taking me?" Isabelle asked, her gaze moving over the men her uncle had brought with him.

"It is none of your concern, Isabelle. Only be thankful that I have let you live, for by rights I should kill you for the slight you have given your cousin and me."

Isabelle leaned forward in her saddle, pinning her uncle with a steady gaze. "You should kill me, then, for I will be of no better use to you alive. I will not labor for you again. You have nothing left with which to make me obedient."

Chuckling, Sir Myles tapped Isabelle's pale cheek with two lifted fingers. "Oh, you will, my girl. Never doubt it. If you value Sir Justin's life, which will now be under Evelyn's command, you will do exactly as you're told."

Isabelle leaned away from his touch, her face twisting

with disgust. "Evelyn would not kill him. She is many things, but she could not do anything so vile."

"Could she not?" her uncle mused aloud, leaning to pull the reins of her steed from her hands. "Think well, Isabelle, and wonder how it is that you were so ill, and how you came to lose your babe." Ignoring her gasp, he continued pleasantly, "If your memory serves you well, you will soon understand that Evelyn played her part in both. And she drugged the boy named Kayne, did she not?"

"Merciful God," Isabelle uttered, horror and shock thickening her voice. "My baby..."

"And so you see, my dear," Sir Myles went on, as the horses set forth into motion, and as he pulled Isabelle's mount after his, "you must be a very obedient and dutiful niece if you don't want Sir Justin to meet with a similar fate. Wish him a long and happy life, and luck in keeping Evelyn content, and do nothing, my girl, to make me regret my care of you. Despite her declarations of love, I could easily persuade Evelyn to do my will with but the promise of a few well-purchased rewards. Never forget it."

John and Aric waited until the riders were well away before at last releasing Senet, who stood bolt upright with a furious oath. "Bastard!"

"Aye," Aric agreed, coming up beside him. "I thought something was amiss when Lady Evelyn put that missive into my hands, instead of Lady Isabelle. We agreed that she could not be trusted, did we not?"

"She's a murderer," John murmured as he, too, stood. "She poisoned Lady Isabelle and made her lose the babe."

"We cannot think on that now," Senet said, "or we'll lose sight of all else in our anger. Has Sir Justin not taught us better than that?"

"S'truth," Aric agreed as they began to return to the horses. "What should we do, then?"

"Go after my uncle and his men and discover where they're taking Isabelle, and then return for Sir Justin," Senet replied. "We must hurry. Aric, you go back to Talwar while John and I follow Sir Myles."

"No."

Senet threw the other boy an angry glance. "There's no time to argue. Someone must go back and tell the others what Lady Evelyn is about, and I'll need John to remember the way we go so that we can readily lead Sir Justin there."

"I'm going," Aric stated stubbornly. "Lady Evelyn won't be causing any trouble until we get back. She'll not want to overset Sir Justin, and will behave well enough until she's found out. But you'll need every man possible following after Sir Myles. Three of us together will fare far better than two."

"He's right," John put in as they reached their steeds, swiftly untying them and mounting. "We've no money and no arms, save the daggers Sir Justin gave us, and only these clothes, hardly fit for traveling. If we don't get caught and charged for stealing horses like dirty thieves, won't we be glad enough just to keep pace with Sir Myles? We need Aric. He's the best among us in a fight, isn't he? I say, God's word, he *is*."

"You speak the truth," Senet admitted. "And this is no civilized tournament we're entering, nor even a war with rules of combat, such as Sir Justin has taught us." With a nod to Aric, he said, "Thank you."

"I'm not doing it for you," Aric replied brusquely, "nor even for Sir Justin. 'Tis Lady Isabelle I think of."

"It is well enough," Senet said. "Kayne will be pulling his hair from his head, wondering where we are and what he should do, but he will have to do his best until Sir Justin returns. God be with him, and with all of those at Talwar."

"God be with us," John added softly as they set off into the night, where a thick, hanging mist had already made the start of their journey both treacherous and cold.

Chapter Twenty-Four

Justin returned to Talwar four days later, in a foul mood. If the presence of several soldiers from Briarstone seemed strange to him, he did not stop to take note of it, but rode through the front gates and up to the doors of the manor house. He dismounted the weary-looking Synn, tersely instructed two of Sir Christian's soldiers to take care of him, then walked into his home without any concern for how his filthy, unshaved, unkempt appearance might seem to those inside. He was greeted by the sight of Sir Christian, his brother Hugo, several men-at-arms, and Gytha and Meg, all of whom had stopped what they were doing and turned to gape at the man who'd so suddenly entered the house.

"Where's Isabelle?" he demanded. "I want to talk to her now!"

"Justin," Sir Christian began, taking a step toward him. "Where have you been? I've had men out searching the countryside…"

"I don't have time for that," Justin snapped, waving his friend aside as he started for the working chamber. "Isabelle!" he shouted. "Isabelle! I want to talk to you! You're not leaving Talwar, and I don't care whether you agree to it or not!'' The sight of the empty working chamber wrought a curse from him, and he flung the door shut.

"Justin!" Hugo said sternly.

"Not *now*," Justin told him, and, striding across the room, began to take the stairs toward the upstairs bedchambers two at a time. "Isabelle Baldwin! Do you hear me? *I said you're not leaving Talwar!* I don't care what you think about your cousin and me, but I'll not let you leave me for it! I'll lock you in your chamber if I have to! Because I damned well love you, and I'll go to Hell and back before I'll let another man have the care of you! Do you hear *that?* Isabelle!''

He disappeared down the hall, and those standing below in the great room could hear him going through each chamber, shouting Isabelle's name and slamming doors. At last he appeared at the top of the stairs.

"Where is she?" he demanded. "And what are you all doing here? Hugo, I thought you'd have Evelyn at Siere by now. Where are my lads?" He began to descend the stairs, shouting, "Kayne! Aric! Senet! Attend me!"

"Justin, will you be still a moment and let me speak?" Christian demanded, just as Kayne came running out of the passageway that joined the manor house to the keep, with Neddy and Ralf at his heels.

"My lord," Kayne said with open relief, "you've come back!"

Justin looked about him, at all those in the room, as if seeing for the first time their faces and realizing that something was amiss.

"Aye, I have," he said. "Kayne, where is Lady Isabelle? What has happened while I've been gone?"

They all descended upon him at once, Kayne, Christian and Hugo, speaking so rapidly that Justin held both hands up to make them stop.

"I've been riding night and day to return to Talwar," he said, collapsing into a chair, "and am full worn. Gytha, bring me food and drink before I faint, I pray, and Chris, you speak. Slowly. Tell me first where my wife is, and if she is well."

"I cannot," Christian replied quietly, "although I wish that I could." Choosing his words with care, he told what he knew of Isabelle's disappearance, and of Lady Evelyn's part in it.

"God's mercy," Justin murmured grimly, wearily rubbing his exhaustion-ridden face with both hands. "Where could she be, if Aric never arrived with the missive, and if you did not give her escort? Could she have gotten to Gyer with the help of some other?"

"I do not know."

"Sir Christian has been good enough as to send messengers to both Alexander and Hugh," Hugo put in. "We have not had a reply from either of them yet."

"Kayne, are you certain that you were drugged?" Justin asked. "You did not simply drink too much wine?"

Kayne's face flushed with the heat of grave affront. "My lord, I did not. You cannot think it."

"I do not think you would do so apurpose," Justin admitted, "but any of us may make such a mistake and perhaps not realize it."

"Lady Evelyn brought me a cup of wine without my request," Kayne insisted. "I drank but a few sips, only because she asked it of me and I did not wish to be unmannerly. Also, to speak in truth," he added with greater irritation, "I wished to be rid of her, and it seemed the most expedient way."

"He was drugged, Justin," Hugo attested. "He had not yet been roused when Christian and I at last arrived with Neddy, and he slept on until the middle of the next day. 'Twas no drunken stupor the boy suffered."

Odelyn had come into the room, and Justin saw her standing in a corner, looking pale and drawn. "Come here,

Odelyn.'' He waved her forward. "Tell me what you heard in the stables.''

Obediently Odelyn stepped forward, and obediently told all that she remembered.

"She said the babe was yours, my lord,'' she said softly, casting her eyes to the floor. "I heard her with my own ears.''

"That's impossible,'' Justin countered irately. "I know Isabelle had some wrong idea about Evelyn and me, but it was not true. None of it. Evelyn would have no cause to lie to her about such a thing.''

"Would she not?'' Christian asked pointedly.

Justin let out a taut breath, rubbing his eyes and fighting exhaustion. "I find it hard to credit. All of this.''

"She *did* say it,'' Odelyn insisted. "I heard her, my lord, and so did Senet. He'll tell you that I speak the truth when he returns. Lady Isabelle sounded heartbroken.''

"Aye, indeed,'' Justin admitted, staring thoughtfully at the fire in the hearth. "It explains many things, if she truly believed such a lie. But where has she gone? Evelyn has said naught?''

"She has refused to speak until you returned,'' Christian said. "I have kept her locked in her bedchamber, for I trust her no more than I would a wily fox left to guard a brood of hens. Senet himself left word with Ralf that she shouldn't be released until either he or you sent word, and 'tis clear he knows more of this matter than any of us here, despite his absence. I saw no good reason to doubt his order.''

Gytha returned to the great room with a tray bearing meat, bread, cheese and ale, which she set upon the table. Justin rose at once and hungrily began to eat, not speaking again until he had nearly sated his painful hunger.

His mouth filled with bread, he asked of Kayne, "There has been no word from Senet, or the other lads?''

"Nay, not even from Aric. We do not know what has

become of him, my lord, although we have searched for miles and found no sign. Senet and John left with the purpose of following behind Lady Isabelle, wherever she went. This is what Ralf understood.''

Justin pushed the tray aside, standing from the table. ''It is well done of Senet, also of John, to have followed. There is something fully amiss, and I begin to think I know what it may be.'' He met Christian's gaze, then glanced at his brother. ''Did not Sir Myles vow in our hearing that he would have Isabelle back one day?''

''Aye.'' Sir Christian bit out the word angrily. ''And who better to send as his accomplice than his own daughter, who had as much a reason for vengeance as he?'' He took a step forward, flinging a gloved hand out in a furious gesture. ''How could you have taken the deceitful bitch in as you did? How could you *ever* have trusted her, after all that we learned of her in London?''

''It was a mistake,'' Justin admitted. ''Not the first I've committed since Evelyn came to us, nor even since I met the woman, but one I mean to correct as soon as may be.'' With his mouth set in a grim line, he headed for the stairs. ''Gytha, bring hot water to my chamber. I will bathe as soon as I've finished with Lady Evelyn. Hugo, write again to Hugh and Alex, tell them that I need them and their armies, as many men as they can bring, as fast as they can bring them. I have grown past weary attempting to be civil to Sir Myles,'' he said as he began to climb upward. ''Now, I am ready to fight.''

Evelyn was standing at the window, looking expectantly toward the door when he opened it, and Justin realized, as he stepped into the chamber, that she must have heard him unlocking it.

''Justin!'' she murmured, a glad smile lighting on her lips. ''You've come home, at last!''

The next moment, she launched herself across the room,

throwing her arms about him and burrowing her head against his chest.

"Oh, I'm so glad to see you! You'll not believe what I've been made to endure these past days at the hands of your brother and Sir Christian. I have prayed for your return, knowing that you would set all to rights."

Stiffly, taking her arms in a hard-fingered grip, Justin forcibly unclasped her embrace and set her away from himself.

"I want no soft words of welcome or pretty looks from you, my lady. I only want to know one thing. Where is my wife?"

Evelyn stared up at him, her expression fully bewildered, before she at last uttered a laugh.

"Justin! You tease me, surely. You cannot have believed whatever *they* may have been telling you! Have you not come to know me better these past months than to believe such lies?"

"I begin to think that I do not know the half of you, Evelyn Hersell."

Her smile faded. "We have been friends," she said. "Good friends. I have learned to trust you in all things, but I can see that you will not accord me the same courtesy. I admit that I helped Isabelle leave Talwar, but only because she begged me to do so, and because I didn't want her to go alone into the dark of night. But, for the rest of what I am accused, I will not accept blame. If Aric wants to run away, leaving no word, how can I prevent it? And if Kayne drinks too much wine and becomes insensible by it, why should I be blamed?" She gazed pleadingly into his eyes. "How could you believe them over me, Justin?"

"How can I not?" Justin replied tautly. "You lied to Isabelle. You told her that the babe you carry is mine. For that alone I should wring your neck."

"I did no such thing!" Evelyn declared hotly, shoving free of his painful grip. "Odelyn has hated me from the start, you know that she has.'' Her mouth curved into a malicious smile. "The little bitch only lies about me now to keep from being pressed about what she and Senet were doing in the stables. I'll wager you've not thought of that, have you?''

"Odelyn has no reason to lie, or even to be ashamed,'' Justin told her. "She and Senet are nearly betrothed, and you know as well as I that the law considers them hand-fasted, as good as wed except for the matter of an exchange of gifts. If they had wished to share a chamber together openly, no one would have so much as looked awry.''

"Then Odelyn is mistaken in what she heard,'' Evelyn insisted stubbornly. "I never told Isabelle that the babe I carry is yours. She knew the truth, and was determined to leave you whether I stayed at Talwar or no. She *wanted* to go, to leave you for the sake of her beloved numbers.''

Justin was shaking his head even before she finished speaking. "I do not believe you, Evelyn. On the last day that I saw my wife, she was fully overset for believing that you and I were lovers. She asked me not to send you away, and said that she would go instead. I didn't understand at the time, but it was because you had told her that the child is mine. Isabelle didn't want to leave me. She was doing it only so that you and I and the child could be together, and I, like a damned fool, gave her even better reason to go.''

"Then perhaps you should thank Isabelle for being so wise. Perhaps she knew better than either of us what is best.''

Justin opened his mouth to speak, but then, without uttering a word, fell silent and stared at her consideringly, a frown upon his face. Evelyn, mistaking his reaction, moved forward to set her hand upon his arm, speaking more softly, and with great care.

"Only think, Justin. Isabelle isn't the wife for you. She

never would have come to you of her own free will, if you'd not taken her by force, and she only stayed out of gratitude, because you proved to be kinder than my father. You know that I speak the truth. Has she not proved it by leaving you so readily, by believing you guilty of such falseness? But she has gone now, of her own accord, and you and I can be together, as we should have been from the start.''

Justin's lashes lowered as his gaze fixed upon the hand she yet held on his arm. "Is it what you want, Evelyn? You would be happy here with me?"

"Oh, yes!" She pressed closer, touching his cold, darkly stubbled cheek with her fingertips. "It is what I want more than anything in life. I love you, Justin, and I know that you love me. We can be more than content together, if you will only give us the chance."

"But what of Isabelle? I do not even know where she has gone, and I must at least see to her welfare."

"Surely she has gone to your brother, the lord of Gyer."

"By herself? All alone?"

Evelyn stroked his cheek lightly. "She must have done so, since Sir Christian has come to Talwar."

"Do you not think that odd, when she had sent Aric to him with a missive?"

"Well, we *did* think it odd, certainly, when we arrived at the place where we were to meet Sir Christian and he was not there. Isabelle was most especially distressed, as you can imagine." She began to play with the front of his dirty tunic, plucking at the laces with her fingertips. "But she would not listen to me when I begged her to return to Talwar, nor would she let me go on with her, but insisted that she must press on alone."

He was thoughtful for a moment. "Do you think, my dear, that perhaps she and Aric found each other and went on together?"

Evelyn lifted wide eyes to his, and with a nod said,

"Indeed, my lord, it must be so. I had not thought of it, but it would explain Aric's absence, would it not? They must have been at Gyer by yesterday, already."

"Mmmm..." Justin replied, lifting his fingers and gently taking a few strands of her golden hair, twining them about caressingly. "Perhaps. It would depend upon where they started, I should think. Where, exactly, was Isabelle to meet with Chris?"

She smiled. "On the hill overlooking Talwar, where the oak trees grow. You can see the place from my window."

He smiled down at her in turn. "But that is south, Evelyn, and Ralf said that Senet and John rode north, toward the forest, following behind you."

"He must have been mistaken," she replied evenly. "He is quite young, yet, and easily confused. We went to the hill and waited. Why, I should never have left her alone, otherwise, save that she was so near to Talwar and in a place so safe that no harm could come to her. It is the truth I tell you, Justin."

Dropping her hair, he pushed her away. "The truth as you know it, mayhap, but not the truth as I desire it of you. There are so many lies coming out of your mouth that I doubt you know what you speak."

The shock that possessed her delicate features lasted only fleetingly, and then her eyes narrowed. "Don't be a fool, Justin Baldwin, as you were when you took Isabelle in my place. She is gone now and we can finally be together."

"Never. Isabelle is my wife, and I love her. It will be so for as long as I draw breath, and neither you nor your father will ever be able to separate us. If you have imagined that I might ever feel something more than a familial affection for you, my lady, then you have been far mistaken." He moved closer, leaning to speak to her. "I took Isabelle because I *wanted* her, and because I loved her."

"No!" she cried furiously. "You only did it to punish

me! Because you wanted me for your wife and I would not come to you so easily. You wanted *me!*"

"Never once, since I set sight on you, did I desire you. I was appalled at the wife who had been chosen for me, and would not have married you. I continued to court you only so that I might find a way to have Isabelle. She is the reason why I remained in London and played the part of the devoted suitor. The *only* reason."

Venomous wrath filled Evelyn's eyes, and her hand flew up to strike him. Justin caught her wrist in midair, without ever moving his gaze from her face. She reeled beneath the squeezing force of his fingers, and cried out, "Cease!"

"Tell me where my wife is, Evelyn, and I will do no more than give you over to the mercy of the king's regents. If you do not, I will exact my own vengeance once I have found Isabelle, and it will not be so kind, I vow."

"She was on her way to Gyer!" Evelyn shouted. "That's all I know!"

"With the help of your father, mayhap?" He pressed harder against the slender bones in her wrist, until her knees buckled from the pain and she was bent beneath him, held up only by his strength.

"My father has nothing to do with it! She was on her way to Gyer! Oh, God, release me!"

His hand opened, and she fell upon the floor, breathing hard, pushing away from him.

Justin stood over her, merciless and without emotion. "If she doesn't arrive at Gyer within the next two days, and if I discover—"

"'Tis not my fault if she doesn't arrive!" Evelyn asserted angrily, glaring up at him. "She could be waylaid by robbers, even killed, and never arrive at all. I have no control over such things, and you cannot lay the blame at my door."

"You didn't let me finish," Justin said calmly. "If she doesn't arrive at Gyer, and if Senet and John return and tell me that your father has, in truth, taken Isabelle with your aid, I will see you hanged from the north tower before I set out to bring her back, and will not consider the consequences, though I doubt that the king's regents will ever hold me at fault.''

Evelyn stared at him. ''You can't do such a thing. My father is a baron. You cannot do it.''

''I will do it. Understand and believe that, for I mean what I say. If you bethink yourself that you have anything to tell me about my wife's location, you may yet save yourself. I am still ready to hand you over to the king's regents, if you tell me where Isabelle is. Think on it, Evelyn, long and well, and send for me if you have anything to speak of.''

He left her then, and locked the chamber door behind him.

In his own chamber, he found the tub filled with hot water and, pushing his exhaustion aside, removed his filthy clothing and bathed and shaved. He dressed again when he was dried and even put his boots on, thinking that he must go out and begin his search. Wherever Isabelle was, she would be frightened, and perhaps in pain, or hungry and cold. The idea of what she might suffer at Sir Myles's hands was unthinkable. But he could barely keep his eyes open after his many days of riding, and knew that he wouldn't be able to stay awake, much less sit a saddle.

He lay down on his bed with the thought that he would only slumber for a short while, even a few minutes, but a deep weariness quickly crept into him, making it impossible to move while his mind struggled to find peace.

''Isabelle,'' he whispered, closing his eyes, thinking of her, seeing in his mind her face as he had last seen it, filled with tears and sadness. ''Why didn't you trust me, even a little? I meant to let you go...but now I shall have to steal you all over again.''

Chapter Twenty-Five

Justin knew something was amiss even before he opened his eyes. There was a scratching sound outside his chamber door, weak and barely discernible but accompanied by a louder, anguished groan. He lay on his bed for a spare moment, staring at the canopy above his head, grasping knowledge as it came. He was stiff, nearly paralyzed, and cold. Light coming through the open chamber window told him that it was morn, that he had slept without motion for many hours.

"My lord," he heard, spoken so mournfully, so softly, that it was more like a breath of sound than a voice.

"Odelyn," he murmured, sitting up and moving with clumsy, sleep-ridden steps to the door, which he flung open.

Odelyn slid into the room, onto the floor, with a small gasp. Blood, bright red, colored the front of her dress in a wet, rapidly increasing stain, and coursed down one of her arms, falling from her fingertips in thick droplets. A trail of blood led down the hall, covering the short distance between the open door of Evelyn's chamber to Justin's room.

"Odelyn!" Justin knelt beside the girl, carefully setting his arms beneath her.

"Oh, Sir Justin," she managed, drawing breath in short gasps and grimacing when he lifted her in his arms. "I let her go. I was taking her a tray of food...she had a knife. Now she's gone...my fault. I'm sorry." A sob, pain mixed with grief...racked her slender body. "So sorry, my lord."

"Don't think of it, little one," Justin murmured, setting her gently upon the bed. "Lie still and be quiet. I'm going to fetch help."

His shouts woke the entire household, and brought everyone running. Christian arrived first, with Hugo fast on his heels.

"God's mercy!" Christian moved to the bed, horror in his voice. "Odelyn."

Tears coursed over the girl's cheeks, and she gazed at her former master with despair. "Am I to die, Sir Christian?"

"God, no!" Christian knelt beside her, taking her bloodied hand in his tight clasp. "Oh, no, Odelyn. Dearest Odelyn."

"Let me tend her," Hugo said gently, nudging past Christian, trying to make him let go. "Send Gytha and Meg to me," he told Justin, who stood in the doorway. "I will do all that I can," he promised, then added, more severely, "You must find Lady Evelyn and bring her back to answer for this evil crime."

Christian stood, bending to kiss Odelyn's forehead with tender care before straightening and following after Justin, who had gone to shout for Meg and Gytha. At the head of the stairs, Christian grabbed his arm, roughly turning Justin about.

"You let that she-wolf into your home, and now see what she has done," he said tightly, his face drawn into a mask of rage and fury. "The right to deal with Lady Evelyn is now *mine!* I demand that it be so."

Justin nodded. "It will be so. Let us find her quickly."

Kayne pushed through the manor's front doors, breathing hard, and met them at the bottom of the stairs.

"The guard in the stable was found with his own knife in his throat," the boy told them in a tumultuous rush. "She killed him, and tried to ride over the guards at the gates before they got out of her way."

"The bitch has gone mad," Christian muttered, traversing the great room with rapid strides that continued as he crossed the bailey. "How long ago did she ride out, Kayne?"

"Only ten minutes, at most. Heading north. How is Odelyn?" He voiced the question timidly. "Will she live?"

Justin set a hand on the boy's shoulder as they entered the stables, squeezing it briefly before moving to saddle Synn. "We must pray that she will. It is all we can do for her now."

"Save to avenge her," Christian said tightly. "And I swear by God that I shall, or find my own death in the attempt."

It was a sight such as Senet had never seen in his life, and had never expected to see. They had been riding hard, relentlessly, day and night, resting only when the horses couldn't go on and pushing ahead as soon as they could, with reaching Talwar again as their only goal. Since dawn was first signaled in the sky, they'd begun to feel something other than weariness and hunger; a simple joy, knowing that they were only a few miles away from their destination, that they would soon be able to dismount their exhausted steeds and tell their tale, fill their bellies and quench their thirsts and sleep for a few precious hours on the comfort of a bed. Aric had actually smiled twice in the past hour, and John had begun to chatter in the nervous, restless manner that defined him. Less than a half hour of riding remained, and then they would be home.

But the early calm of the beautiful spring day was shattered by the shocking spectacle of Lady Evelyn, mounted on horseback, flying toward them with the compelling madness of a demon being driven out of Hell.

"God's feet!" Aric shouted, sharply jerking his horse aside just in time to avoid being run down by Lady Evelyn's hard-driven steed. His mount whinnied in distress, and danced precariously at the edge of the road.

Senet and John were likewise required to settle their mounts, but had barely had time to do so when three more riders came thundering headlong toward them.

"What's amiss!" John demanded furiously, impelling his unhappy steed into the trees again to keep from being trampled. "They're crazed!"

"Sir Justin!" Senet shouted above the roar of hooves. "Kayne!"

"Sir Christian!" Aric added as that man went flying past, bent low over his horse's neck and intent on his prey, not so much as glancing at the three boys calling to him. Only Kayne took a moment to address them, as he raced past, shouting what sounded, to Senet, like Odelyn's name.

"Now what?" Aric asked as they encouraged their nervous horses back into the road.

Senet nodded toward where the other riders had gone, saying, "Let's go."

With a nod of agreement, the other two turned and followed, riding back in the direction from which they had just come, pushing their horses as hard as they dared to catch up in the chase.

She hadn't gone far, they discovered when they finally followed the trail to where the others had dismounted at the edge of the woods. Lady Evelyn had evidently decided that she couldn't outrun her pursuers, and had abandoned her steed in favor of traversing the thickly wooded forest on foot. Senet and the others dismounted, following the sounds of voices as they drifted back from the edge of a sheer drop that overlooked the valley, and at last came out into a clearing where the trees gave way to a rugged stone shelf. Lady Evelyn stood at the edge of it, facing Sir Christian with a bloodied knife in one hand, her chest rising and falling with harsh breaths, her unbound hair and cloak billowing around her in the wind that flew upward from the valley, buffeting the rocks with whistling gusts.

"Accept the truth, woman," Sir Christian advised against the harshness of his own breathing. "You cannot escape down the mountainside, and there is nowhere else for you to go. Put down your weapon and submit, and I will yet take you before the regents and give you the chance of an honorable death."

"Honorable?" she repeated, laughing scornfully. "My name will be disdained throughout England if all that I have done becomes known. Better to die now and shield the sanctity of my title than to become the object of public disgrace."

She was mad, Senet thought. Fully crazed. He could see it in her eyes, in the wildness of her stance.

"At least do what you can to right some of your wrongs," Sir Christian advised, "and go to God with one less stain on your soul. Tell us where Lady Isabelle is, and what has become of her."

Smiling, she shook her head. "Oh, no, my lord. That I will not do. Isabelle will never be found, and she will suffer all that she has deserved. By the time my father and his men have finished with her, there will be nothing left to take back. What do you say to that, my fine lord, Sir Justin?" she asked, sneering. "Will you want your precious lady back after she's been made to play whore to a hundred men?"

"Evelyn..." Justin said, taking a step forward and stopping when she took a like step back, closer to the edge.

"Fool!" she snarled at him, precariously balancing to keep her foothold. "You might have had *me* for your wife!

The most beautiful woman in England! A jewel to possess, to display for all you knew to see and admire. Anyone seeing me at your side would have praised your great fortune and considered you a man among men. Oh, aye, I would have allowed you that great honor, yet you threw it aside as if it held no worth, and took that ugly mouse in my place. Isabelle Gaillard!'' She spoke the name with dark hatred. "I'm *glad* she's going to be ruined for you, just as she ruined everything for me."

"It matters not," Justin said. "A hundred men, or a thousand, or whatever base evil your father may visit upon my innocent wife. I am the only man who will possess Isabelle's heart. She can never be ruined for me. Tell me where she is, Evelyn."

"Nay. I will take the knowledge with me, and make my death the sweeter by it."

"It is not necessary that she speak," Senet said, hearing the thinness of his voice with some surprise, for he did not sound like himself. "We know where Sir Myles has taken my sister. John can easily guide us back to the place."

The smile on Evelyn's face faded away, and a tremor ran over her slight body. She looked, suddenly, like a young girl about to burst into tears of childish upset.

"It is so unfair," she murmured, lowering the hand that held the knife. "I should have had every good thing, but you have all worked to bring me down to this. I'm glad I took my vengeance while I yet lived. The child, and Odelyn..." Opening her bloody fingers, she let the knife fall to the ground, then lowered her head, shaking it sadly. "I only wish that I had killed Isabelle when I had the chance. She does not deserve to live and be happy, when everything has been taken from me. It is so unfair," she repeated softly, then closed her eyes and lifted her arms, leaning backward into nothing.

Senet stared at the place where she had been, sick to

his very soul at what he had witnessed, but driven by sudden, sharp fear to push the horror away.

"Odelyn," he murmured, his gaze falling to the bloody knife. "What did she mean?"

It was Sir Justin who turned to him when the others seemed made of stone. The grim, set lines of his face made Senet's heart turn over in his chest.

"She was yet alive when we left Talwar to follow after Lady Evelyn, but I do not know if—"

Senet turned and fled, racing toward the road and the horses. Sir Justin ran close behind him, shouting, but Senet could not stop, or think of anything beyond reaching Odelyn. She was alive, he told himself, ignoring the pain in his chest as his lungs demanded breath, pushing himself on through the trees as if Satan himself pursued him. Odelyn was alive. She would not die. It was impossible.

He lunged for his horse the moment he cleared the trees, but a strong hand jerked him back.

"Take Synn!" Sir Justin shouted, shoving him toward the large black destrier and nearly throwing him into the saddle. "Go!"

The horse responded to the hard slap of his master's hand on his flank with a forceful leap. Senet barely held fast to the saddle as the huge beast hurtled forward in a full-out stride, heading for Talwar.

Chapter Twenty-Six

Leaving Christian and the others to collect Evelyn's body, Justin rode for Talwar, arriving only moments after Senet. Climbing the stairs of the manor house, he found Hugo standing in his bedchamber doorway, gazing solemnly into the dimly lit room beyond.

"Hugo?"

His elder brother lifted his head, looking older than his years, weary and infinitely sad. He shook his head in response to the unasked question, and Justin let out a slow breath.

"God's mercy," he murmured.

"She is not gone to our Lord yet," Hugo told him, his voice low, as Justin moved to stand beside him. "I have just now performed her last rites. She is at peace."

Justin looked beyond him into the chamber, where Senet knelt upon the bed beside Odelyn, bent over the hand he held in both of his. Tears dripped down the boy's face; his agony seared Justin all the way through to his soul. But Odelyn, as Hugo had said, was calm and peaceful, gazing up at Senet with a gentle, shining love. The bleeding had been stopped, and she had been washed and clothed in new garments and covered warmly with blankets. Her curling hair was brushed back from her face, and if it had not been for the paleness of her cheeks and the blueness of her lips, she might have merely been a young woman taking her rest.

"You must not grieve, Senet," she said in a voice soft and whispery. "I do not want you to grieve."

Senet was weeping inconsolably, gripping her hand more tightly and pressing her fingers with desperate movement against his lips, as if he might somehow suffuse life into her there and keep her from death.

"Who will ever love me?" he asked, pleading with her. "Who will ever look at me as you do? I need you so. Don't leave me here alone."

Her eyelids fluttered and drooped, as if she were very weary, but she smiled at him, and said, "Nay, you'll not be alone. You have suffered so much of it before now. God will be merciful to you. There will be a beautiful lady to love you, better than I could have done. And you will come to cherish her as dearly as your own life. More so."

"Nay." He shook his head. "Nay."

"You mustn't push her aside when she comes to you, Senet. You must love her and let her love you, no matter how difficult it may seem. Promise me that you will do so."

"I cannot."

"I want you to be happy. It is all that I ask. Promise me, Senet. 'Twill give me peace."

He drew in a long breath, calming, wiping at his tears with his sleeve, never letting go of her hand. At last, with a nod, he said, "I promise, Odelyn."

"I'm glad." She made a sound, half a yawn, half a sigh. "You have made me so happy, Senet. I loved you the moment I saw you, just as she is going to love you. The very moment she sets sight on you."

"Odelyn," he whispered.

"I'm so weary," she said. "Will you stay with me while I sleep?"

"Aye." He began to blink against the new tears welling in his eyes. "I'll stay here beside you. Can you not feel my hand in yours? Sleep, and know that I love you. Always."

She smiled at him again, her eyes drifting shut. Senet bowed his head low and was silent. Hugo put his hand on Justin's shoulder, murmuring, "Let us leave them alone together. He will bear her company as she passes, and it is what Odelyn would wish."

Nodding, Justin allowed his brother to pull him away.

She was buried two days later, on the hill beside Isabelle and Justin's unborn child. Hugo presided over the solemn ceremony, and Senet was the one who threw the first fistful of dirt into the grave. When it was done, Justin tried to put his hand upon the younger man's shoulder in a gesture of comfort, but Senet shrugged away from his touch, turning to him.

"I want only to find Isabelle now," he stated fiercely, and then walked away. It was the most Justin had heard Senet say since he came out of the bedchamber where Odelyn died. He had been fully changed, silent, as he used to be when he first came to Talwar, but without a trace of youthfulness left in his features. It was almost as if he had left the other boys behind, leaping across the years and away from them, to become a man. Despite that fact, however, the bond between himself and the others had only become more firmly forged, and in their loyalty they had closed ranks around Senet, sheltering him constantly. Even now they followed behind him as he descended the hill, matching his long strides, as well as his silence. Justin watched them go, one by one, torn between pride in their honorable behavior toward their comrade and pain at the anger they directed toward him.

"Give them time," Christian said beside him. "For all they have suffered in their young lives, it is yet a hard lesson to know how evil man—and woman—can become."

Justin shook his head. "I am the one who has disappointed them," he said. "I do not know if they will ever forgive me—" he lifted his head "—or even if you will."

Christian frowned. "We have been friends for many years, Justin Baldwin. There should be no need for us to speak such things to each other. You did not know what Lady Evelyn was, or how maddened. I do not blame you for Odelyn's death."

"Do you not?" Justin countered. "You and Senet both could rightly do so. I should have accepted the truth of what everyone around me knew of Lady Evelyn. She poisoned Isabelle, killing my child, nearly killing Isabelle, and all the while I defended her." With a hard fist, he thumped his chest. "God have mercy, I *defended* her."

"You could not have known," Christian repeated more firmly.

"I was a *fool!* She said it rightly to me before she threw herself off the cliff."

"Listen to me," Christian said gruffly. "You offered kindness to that evil she-wolf, because you are a good, kind man. You gave to Lady Evelyn what you have given to all whom you meet, to your wife, to your lads, to me. Trust and kindness you give in full measure, and pray God that more of His people would do the same!"

"That is well and good," Justin replied angrily, "but I doubt that Isabelle or my lads will ever see fit to absolve me for such a reason."

"If you truly believe that, then you hand them an insult they do not deserve. I do not say that they will not suffer anger for a time, and pain, aye, but none of them is so blind as to blame you for what Lady Evelyn and her father have done. Don't heap coals on their misery by wallowing in self-despair and forcing them to prove their devotion to you now. Keep your mind on finding your wife. Lady

Isabelle must be living in horror, if Sir Myles is anything like his daughter.''

"I have thought of nothing else," Justin murmured.

"My lord!"

Both men turned toward the soldier who hailed them.

"An army approaches, from the east!" the man cried, rapidly climbing up the hill to them. "You can see them from the other side."

Justin and Christian scrambled past the grave sites, running to where Hugo already stood, looking down on the road that approached Talwar.

"It's Hugh," the priest said. "My twin has wasted no time in answering your summons, Justin. Look at the size of his forces!"

"A frightening thing, it is, to give such a man charge of so much might," Justin murmured, his chest rising and falling with painful emotion. If Hugh had ever wished to prove that he cared for his youngest brother, he had just done it. "But I praise God he has come. We will leave in the morn, at first light, and send a messenger to Alexander, telling him where to meet us as we journey north. Sir Myles will not be expecting such an invasion, but that is well. He has brought evil down upon my home and family. It is my right to exact vengeance, and I swear by God that I shall."

Chapter Twenty-Seven

It had been two days since she ate. Two days, and she was so hungry that even dreaming of food made her want to weep.

With cold, aching fingers, Isabelle scratched out the final tally beneath the column of numbers that she had been recording all morn. She set the quill upon the wooden table beside the lone candle that her uncle had deigned to provide, pushed the ledger away and sat back in her chair, closing her eyes. She had only been locked away in the castle for a week, and already she wondered how long she would be able to survive. Her chamber was at the top of a crumbling tower, damp and without heat, light or even air, since her uncle had boarded shut the only window in the room. That was just as well, however, for the ceiling leaked when it rained, and she didn't need the additional wet chill that the uncovered window would bring. During the summer, if she hadn't yet managed to escape this God-forsaken prison, she knew that she would crave whatever view the window might afford, and light and air. For now she was content to merely stay dry.

They were near Scotland, she thought, although she wasn't certain. Her uncle and his men had kept up a relentless pace, and Isabelle had become so exhausted toward the end that the last day of their journey passed as nothing more than a dazed, bewildering blur. She'd been half-asleep when they finally arrived, and her uncle had dragged her off her horse and into the castle, then up what seemed like hundreds of stairs to this chamber. She'd had only a fleeting impression of thick gray fog and drizzling rain before he pulled her into the rotting structure, an impression that was confirmed by the few glimpses that the crumbling and missing parts of the tower afforded as they climbed ever upward, and of trees, which made Isabelle wonder if the small castle wasn't built on a mountain or hillside. Not that it mattered. Justin would never find her here, even if he decided to look for her, which, considering the way she had left him, and the words she had said, Isabelle believed unlikely. He was probably glad to be rid of her, glad to be done with her faithlessness.

"Justin," she murmured, her voice small in the thick, damp air, "I pray God that you would know how sorry I am. Somehow, that you would know it."

The last words that he had spoken to her had haunted her relentlessly since he left Talwar, even before she, herself, so foolishly listened to Evelyn and left, as well.

You never would have given me your trust, let alone your love.

But, oh, how wrong he had been. Faithless she might be, but she loved him. So deeply, so fully... How could it be that he had never realized? Had she been so incapable of showing him what she felt? Too afraid to do so? She knew that she had never spoken the words aloud, not wanting to place a burden upon Justin that he might not want or, worse, that he might feel uncomfortable bearing. He hadn't taken her for love, after all, but only because he had needed a wife. Hadn't she told Senet that once, long ago? But on that last day, Justin had seemed hurt because he had believed she would never give him her love. The memory made Isabelle shake her head. If he had only known, if she had only *told* him, perhaps none of this ever would have happened.

"I love you, Justin," she whispered, wishing that the words might somehow be carried to him across the miles that separated them, that he might somehow know the truth of them and be soothed, even as he began his new life with Evelyn. "I will always love you."

He had deserved so much more from her when they were together. He had deserved so much better. Would he be happier with Evelyn? She was a murderer, a liar, but it was true that Evelyn and Justin had enjoyed each other's company during the months that passed. Perhaps, by some miracle, Evelyn would come to love Justin enough to be good to him, to put his happiness before her own. Isabelle prayed that it would be so.

But what if Evelyn couldn't be trusted? Isabelle had known her cousin long and well enough to feel a measure of despair at the thought of Justin's heart being put in Evelyn's care. There was only one thing Isabelle could do at the moment to ensure that Evelyn behaved, and that was to work very hard to please Sir Myles. And she would do so, at least until she found a way to escape and make her way to Sir Alexander at Gyer. Somehow, she would manage to get away, despite the army of men that Sir Myles had posted about the castle to guard her.

If she could survive living in this cold, damp chamber until the summer arrived, and if she could bide her time patiently until Sir Myles was forced to return to London...then surely a way would become clear for her to get free. And once she had done so, she would not demand that Justin take her back as his wife, if he proved to be content with Evelyn. She wouldn't even reveal the truth about the part Evelyn had played in murdering their unborn child, but *only* if Evelyn continued to make Justin perfectly happy. Then it would be Isabelle who held the key of control over her cousin. Evelyn would do what she must to please Justin, else she'd find her father and herself paying dearly for their crimes.

The lock in the chamber door began to rattle as the key was worked to open the ancient fixture, and then the heavy bolt, which had more recently been added on the outside of the door, was pulled back with a loud, sweeping *thwip*.

"Good day, my dear," Sir Myles greeted as the guard before him pushed the door wide. "How have you progressed?" Behind him, a servant hovered on the final step, bearing a tray of cheeses, bread and ale. The sight made Isabelle's empty stomach twist painfully with want.

Silent, she put a hand out to shove the closed account book a little farther away on the table, in her uncle's direction.

"Finished, have you?" he asked, strolling across the room and flipping the book open. Perusing it for a few moments with a smile of satisfaction, he at last gave a curt nod. "Very good. You may eat, then, and have the afternoon to rest." He waved the servant in, picking the large book up and stepping back so that the tray could be placed on the table. "I shall return this eve to discuss plans for a venture I should like to undertake. You returned a tidy profit for Sir Alexander and the earl of Siere with the coal boats you had running from their mines to London, and I want you to arrange a similar transportation system for the mines I own. I mean to push the lord of Gyer and the earl out of the competition entirely, and want you to bend your every effort toward the task. With what you know about their arrangements, it should be a simple matter for you to accomplish."

God's mercy, Isabelle thought with disgust. After all the hard work she'd put into organizing Sir Alexander's and Sir Hugh's various businesses, working now to destroy them would be a bitter chore, indeed.

"Still no words?" Sir Myles asked softly. "I grow weary with such foolish insolence, Isabelle. Must I give you another day of hunger to make you behave as you should, with the obedience I demand?''

Tilting her head up and to the side, Isabelle gave him a look that said better than a thousand words could about what he might do with his demands.

A slow smile drew up the corners of Sir Myles's mouth. ''Or shall I give you another lesson in humiliation? Despite Evelyn's jealous utterings, you were once a lovely creature, Isabelle. I had a good many marriage offers for you, though you were not aware of them.''

Marriage offers? Isabelle thought with a frown. For her?

''I felt it best to never let you realize how appealing you were,'' Sir Myles went on softly, ''but I need not worry over such as that now.'' With a quick hand, he reached up and pulled away the cloth with which she had covered her head, tossing the ragged piece of linen onto the table and laughing as Isabelle scrambled to grab it and cover herself again.

''That's better,'' he said with smug satisfaction. ''That's more of what I want from you, my dear. Fear and distress, which are far more appropriate to your circumstances than this useless determination not to speak a word. Now you listen very carefully to me, my girl.'' He placed one hand flat upon the table, leaning forward until his face was nearly level with Isabelle's. ''If you think that what I've done to you thus far is the worst there can be, you are far wrong. I'm willing to leave you in peace, so long as you behave well and do your work, but there are a great many men guarding this castle who would gladly and willingly lend me aid in forcing you to comply, should you continue to prove stubborn. When I return this eve, you will speak to me with all the respect and deference that is my due, else I will invite my guards to visit you here, one by one, and use you as they please, until you give way. You think on that, Isabelle," he advised, straightening. "You think on it long and well before deciding what you will do."

He left, striding past the guard who followed behind, shutting and locking the door. Isabelle sat where she was, shuddering at the visions her uncle's words wrought. She hated being forced into speaking to the wretch, and despised herself for being so weak, but Isabelle knew, without needing to consider the matter long, that she would give way. It would be far less disgusting to speak civilly to Sir Myles than to suffer the bestial embraces of his men.

Ravenous, she began to eat, quickly at first, ignoring the cramps in her stomach as it rebelled at being so suddenly filled, and then more slowly, savoring the taste of the simple fare even as exhaustion crept over her. At last, finished, she stood and, with unsteady, aching bones, made her way to the pallet in the chamber's corner, as far away from the leaking roof as she had been able to manage placing it, and lay down. She covered herself with the bundle of blankets Sir Myles had provided and closed her eyes, letting herself dream of Justin, and of the days that she would forever cherish, when she had lived as his wife.

Swiping rain out of his face with one hand, Justin bent and pushed his way into the tent where Alexander and Hugh sat around a table, drinking wine and making plans. Hugo, reclining restfully on a low pallet, greeted Justin with a smile, while in the far corner, Christian stood with his arms crossed over his chest, looking both aggravated and impatient at the conversation the other two men were having.

"Sir Myles's main guard is concentrated here, at the southern gate," Alexander said, thumping a map that John had drawn from memory after having bravely slipped around the castle walls during the dark of night, avoiding Sir Myles's soldiers, in an effort to locate each castle gate.

"We will attack from all sides, concentrating on breaking down the eastern and northern gates, here, and here."

Hugh was shaking his head. "We'll lose too many men. Better to attack with a small force of men at the north and make them chase us. Once they're distracted, 'twill be a far easier matter for the main group to take control of the gates and subdue Sir Myles's forces."

"If we attack from all sides at once, the elements of surprise and confusion will be ours," Alexander argued. "They'll be overwhelmed."

"But not quickly enough," Hugh countered. "There would be more than ample time for Sir Myles or another to make Lady Isabelle their surety by threatening her life against our withdrawal. It is a chance we cannot take."

"A chance we *will* not take," Justin added, shaking his dark hair to rid it of raindrops.

In his corner, Christian sighed loudly.

Hugo sat up on the pallet, reaching toward a low table to fill a goblet with wine.

"Will you take wine, Justin?" He lifted the goblet in Justin's direction. "'Twill warm you, and you look chilled through, i' faith."

"Thank you," Justin said with a nod, accepting the cup. "'Tis indeed a sorry place Isabelle's been brought to. I only pray that her uncle has been kind enough to keep her warm." He took a sip of wine before adding, "I'm sorry that you had to come all this way just to keep on eye on Hugh, Hugo. Not enjoying it overmuch, are you?"

Hugo gave a good-natured shrug. "If I don't take care of him, who will? And how could I refuse dear Rosaleen, who asked so sweetly in her missive to me that I keep our venerable brother out of trouble and make certain he behaves himself?"

"Wise of her," Justin murmured, glancing at Hugh, who was scowling.

"The woman's getting fussy as a mother cat," said the

earl of Siere with great affront. "I don't know why she thinks I need watching, like the veriest child."

"*Very* wise of her," Justin amended, setting the cup back upon its tray and approaching the table. "If you two have come to some manner of agreement, I would like to go now and fetch my wife."

"We'll attack at first light tomorrow morn," Alexander said.

"Nay, we will attack now," Justin replied calmly. "I waited until John could give us the information we required to make a successful attack, but I will wait no longer."

"The rain…" Hugh began.

"Will as like be here in the morn as it is now," Justin stated. "We are six to one against them, and the castle itself is so rotted that two men shoving with their shoulders on any of the gates would force them to give way. If you will command the attack on the south side, Alex, and you on the north, Hugh, then Chris and my lads and I will make our way in through the east."

"I agree with Justin," Sir Christian said. "The land is too heavily wooded here to require any such advance planning. 'Twill be a surprise attack, no matter how we make our approach. And Lady Isabelle will be suffering every moment longer that she is made to remain inside that rotting pit."

"Nay," the lord of Gyer said emphatically. "It is not well done. There must be a strategy. I cannot like such confusion."

"Alex speaks truly," Hugh put in. "No battle was won from such a lack of preparation. We must outwit our enemy as best we may, with care and planning."

Hugo, bending to straighten the blankets on his pallet, said, "Humph."

"Then my lads and I will go fetch Isabelle on our own. Chris, do you stand with me?"

"My men and I, both," Christian vowed.

"Damnation!" Sir Alexander slammed a fist on the small table, nearly shattering it. "I do not allow either of you to do anything so foolish. Sit down and be silent." He pointed to the two empty chairs on either side of himself and Hugh.

"Alex," Hugh said in an advising tone, "calm yourself. There's no need to act the tyrant just now. Justin, Chris, come, sit and speak reasonably. Hugo, bring us more wine, will you?"

Justin's eyes narrowed. "I am not indifferent to what I owe you both for your aid in helping me to free Isabelle. Indeed, my gratitude is boundless. But if you think that I will sit by in idle fashion, sipping wine as if naught were amiss, while my good lady wife lies imprisoned, suffering at the hands of her uncle, then you, my dear brothers, may take yourselves to Hell."

Sir Alexander stood slowly, his face burning with heat.

"God's sweet mercy," Hugh muttered, squeezing his eyes shut and rubbing the bridge of his nose as if there were an ache there. "Justin, will you *never* learn to guard your tongue?"

"I will not countenance such words from you," Sir Alexander said, directing a hard stare at his youngest brother.

"Will you not?" Justin returned just as stiffly. "And I'm done with being managed by the pair of you. First you had me expelled from the tournaments, then you decided to force me into marriage…"

"For *that*," Sir Alexander stated, "you should be thankful. You'd never have married Isabelle otherwise."

"Ha!" Justin retorted furiously. "I almost didn't have her because of you! You would have shackled me to a *murderess*. A foul, evil witch who would have gladly murdered me in my sleep if she'd but had the—"

"My brothers, be calmed," Hugo demanded loudly, holding both hands up and moving to stand in the midst of them. "I cannot think this bickering will aid Lady Isabelle. I want you to think a moment, Alex, and you, also, Hugh, as to what your feelings would be if it were Lillis or Rosaleen who was imprisoned in yon castle, rather than Isabelle. Would either of you then be so willing to wait and argue while your good lady wife lay captive in such a foul place, and at the mercy of such a man as Sir Myles?"

A silence ensued, during which every man stared at Hugo, who calmly returned to lie down upon his pallet. Alexander and Hugh exchanged glances, and then Hugh stood and checked the readiness of his sword.

"Let's go," he said, to which Alexander agreed with an "Aye."

The four men left the tent together, moving quickly to gather their forces for attack.

Chapter Twenty-Eight

Isabelle knew she was dreaming. It was exactly what she had done at her uncle's house, before Justin stole her. He would come to her while she slept, gazing at her in just such a way, with love shining in his eyes, and would approach her, slowly, silently, her father's magnificent sword in one hand, his handsome face covered with sweat and streaks of blood...

She blinked, shaking away the last part of the dream, which wasn't at all how it was supposed to go. But nothing changed. He kept coming toward her, slowly, saying her name, gripping her father's sword in one hand, his much-loved face covered with sweat and blood.

"Justin," she murmured sleepily, levering herself upward with a hand, trying to focus her blurred vision through the darkness of the room. He couldn't really be here. It was impossible. She must have gone mad with her longing to have conjured him up so. But he kept coming, closer and closer, until he stopped before her and slowly, so slowly, knelt, gazing fully into her eyes.

"Lady," he said, "I am seeking a wife. Will you come away with me and be my bride?"

She seemed to move without conscious thought, her

body propelled forward and into his arms by an unseen force, and she gripped him, tightly, and began to weep.

"Justin," she sobbed, trembling fiercely. "You're here. You came."

His arms crushed her with their strength, so hard that she thought he meant to somehow meld their two bodies into one.

"I came," he murmured, pressing kisses against the top of her head. "Could you think I would not? That I would not follow after you, no matter where you were taken?"

"Aye," she admitted against her tears. "I did not think you would want me again, after all that I said, after my faithlessness."

"I do not care about any of that, nor of the words I spoke to you before I so foolishly left you alone at Talwar. Now or ever again. I love you, Isabelle, and must have you with me, whether or not you ever come to trust or love me. I am sorry if it isn't what you wish, but I cannot be parted from you, else my life becomes worthless to me. I have come to steal you away again," he murmured more softly, taking her tear-streaked face in his palms and turning her up to meet his gaze, "and to keep you with me always."

Isabelle swallowed, and her mouth quivered into a smile. "You spoke truly when you said that I did not know how to trust, but you were wrong when you thought I did not love you, for I do, and have always loved you. From the time I met you, I have loved you. And if you will let me come home to Talwar and be your wife again, I will prove it to you in every day that remains of my life. Oh, my lord, I promise that I will."

His eyes lit with bright, sudden joy, and he searched her face with a hopefulness that filled her heart with aching for all that he had longed for and been denied.

"Isabelle," he whispered, lowering his mouth to kiss her gently, lovingly. "It is the most precious gift I could ever receive, your love. I will cherish and tend it carefully, all of my life. Take mine in turn, and we will begin anew, in the manner that we should have done if I had not been so foolish as to steal you away in the beginning. Is it as you would wish?''

"Oh, aye,'' she replied fervently, hugging him. "Aye, Justin. If it is what you truly wish.''

"There is nothing I want more,'' he said, and then lifted his hand to touch the cloth that covered her head. "Isabelle, what has your uncle done to you?''

She remembered suddenly, and with a gasp pushed away, setting both of her hands upon her head and staring at him wide-eyed.

"Oh! Don't look at me!'' she cried, horrified that he should see that her hair had been shorn away in the manner of fallen women who were convicted of crimes.

"Isabelle,'' he murmured, insistently pulling her hands down to her lap before tugging at the head covering to reveal her near baldness. "Oh, God.''

It was the first thing that Sir Myles had done to her after they arrived. Forcing her to kneel before him in a manner of penitence, he had pronounced her as being needful of a lesson in humility, and had hacked her hair away by the handful, leaving only short clumps of black hair tufting in odd and various lengths over her scalp. Isabelle knew how ugly she looked now that her only minor claim to beauty was gone. Ugly, and disgusting to gaze upon. No man would want a wife who bore the ultimate mark of shame, having had the crown of her glory cut away. So deep, so full, was her humiliation that Isabelle would have crawled away to hide if she thought Justin would have allowed it. As it was, she waited in silence for him to speak, dreading both his pity and his repugnance.

"Do you know when I first decided to make you my wife?'' he asked softly, ignoring her resistance and pulling her back into his gentle embrace. "It was on the very day that I presented myself to Sir Myles and Lady Evelyn. You were sitting in the corner of the room, where you always were, laboring on your uncle's accounts, but your uncle called you away from them for a moment to be introduced to me. Do you remember?"

She nodded against his chest. His hand smoothed lightly over the back of her neck.

"You had the most beautiful eyes I had ever seen, and the way you looked at me... I think I fell in love with you even then, for you made me feel as if I were the most desirable man alive."

"You are," she whispered, sniffling.

He chuckled, and said, "Your hair was beautiful, and I am sorry that your uncle visited such a vile manner of torment upon you, but, my beloved one, I would have loved you no matter how beautiful you were, or whether you had hair at all, simply for the way that you looked at me. I spent many years craving a woman to look upon me in such a way, and I could not let you go, once I had found you."

"But it looks so ugly," she said miserably. "Oh, Justin."

"Don't cry, Isabelle," he murmured, wiping his palm across her cheek when tears began to spill over them once more. "Your hair will grow again, more lovely than before, and until it has returned in its glory, you must embrace this state as one that proclaims your bravery in the face of great suffering. I am proud of you, Isabelle, and will ever be so."

How good he was, she thought, and how easily he eased her fears and filled her heart with peace.

"I do not deserve you, Justin," she began, but his fingers pressed against her lips to stop the words.

"Never," he said, "have more foolish words been spoken, especially between those who love. We deserve each other in every way that God and man can know, and so we shall be together, never again to be parted by deceit.'' He tilted her face upward, against his shoulder, and looked into her eyes. "If there is blame to be placed for all that has befallen us, then it should be placed upon me. I trusted Evelyn, blindly and stubbornly, and because of that, we not only lost each other, but also our babe.''

"You know?'' Isabelle whispered. "She poisoned both of us, making us ill, and then took our child's life.''

He nodded. "I blame myself as much as her, for I made the way easy, and now our child is gone. Can you ever forgive me, Isabelle? Will you ever be able to look upon me and not remember that I lost something so precious to us both?''

"If you can forgive me for having such a lack of faith in you, then how could I not forgive you for believing Evelyn's lies? We neither of us sinned with purpose, but in ignorance. Let us forgive each other and ourselves, and go on, just as you said that we should.''

He lowered his head to kiss her, but Isabelle suddenly became aware of the sounds of shouts and fighting that drifted upward from the stairs. Pushing up and out of his embrace, distressed, she looked over Justin's shoulder, toward her open chamber door.

"Is it a battle?'' she asked. "My uncle…?''

"Your uncle has been placed in bonds, although Senet and I both wished to kill him outright. My brother Alexander has claimed the right of taking him to London to face judgment.''

"Sir Alexander!''

"Aye, and Hugh and Chris, as well, and all their men.'' He smiled, and ran the backs of his fingers over one still-wet cheek. "You see, my beloved, how greatly you are valued? Three armies joined together to find and free you. Your uncle's small forces never could have stood against so large a venture.'' His smile faded, and he regarded her more soberly. "Isabelle," he said, "there is much I must tell you about your uncle and Evelyn. Much has happened since you were taken away from Talwar, much that will bring you great sadness, I fear. Our lives were not the only ones touched by sorrow."

"What has happened?" she asked fearfully, his words filling her with dread.

"I will tell you when I have got you safely back at our camp," he promised. "For now, only trust me and know that I love you. All will be well."

"Aye," she murmured, lifting his hand and pressing it against her cheek, turning her face to swiftly kiss his grimy palm. "I trust you, Justin, and I love you, and as long as I am with you, I know that all will be well."

Chapter Twenty-Nine

The end of the harvest season brought cool weather, a colorful world, and joy among the residents of both Talwar and Briarstone for the coming months of feasts, celebrations and greater leisure; Michaelmas, St. Crispin's Day, All's Hallow Even, All Saints', All Souls', and Saint Catherine's days, Christmas and Twelfth Night. The workers that Sir Christian had sent to tend to Talwar's small crops had already enjoyed the feast that Justin and Isabelle gave to thank and reward them, and had accepted the gold coins Justin handed out, packed their things, and returned to Briarstone with smiling faces.

On the rooftop of the keep, Justin and Isabelle stood together, his arms wrapped loosely about her slightly protruding belly, her head resting upon his shoulder as she leaned against him, savoring his embrace.

"It has been so long since Odelyn died," she murmured, her gaze fixed upon the hilltop where three tall figures, barely discernible from this distance, stood beneath the tree where her child and Odelyn were buried. "Do you think Senet will ever come to accept the loss of her?"

"He will," Justin answered. "In time."

"He has become so hard," she said sadly. "I worry

about him going out to make his way just now. What will people think of such a man, so cold and disdaining as he is? I wish he would stay at Talwar until some of his anger has left him.''

"The lads must all go one day," Justin said, comfortingly kissing the top of her head, where her thick black hair had grown back to make a soft, curling cap that he found thoroughly enchanting. "I cannot shelter them here forever, and each man must find and travel his own road. My lads will do well, for they have learned well and are ready now to live as men, rather than boys. The new ones that Chris has just sent to us will grow and leave, as well, and others will come to take their place. That is the way of things."

"But Senet and Kayne and Aric," she murmured, squeezing his hands. "You have loved them all as if they were your own. I thought that Kayne and Aric, especially, would stay with you forever. I know you will grieve for the loss of them."

"For a time, I think, I will, and when they have seen something of the world, they may come back to us, if it is what any of them desire. For now, it is good that they go out and discover what the world may have to offer. And I will not have time to sorrow long, for my new lads will keep me busy, and so will this little one, when you have given him life." He pressed his palm over her belly. "Or her. And John and Ralf and Neddy will be with us yet for some years to come, so we'll not be deserted all at once."

"But I shall miss them so very much."

"Aye," he said with gentle sympathy. "But they have promised to come to us at Christmas, when we are in London, and to visit us here when they may. We will not lose them altogether."

"But why must they go now? So soon before the feasts to come, with winter fast approaching? Could they not come to London and stay with us until next spring? 'Twould be so much better, and the house you have bought for us there is so grand and large that there would be room aplenty.''

"Nay, I do not think they will wait so long. Senet would have gone many months ago if he had not wanted to make certain of you, that you are well and content, and for Sir Myles to receive a just reward for his many crimes. Now that your uncle has been sent to God for his final judgment, your brother feels that you are safe enough for him to leave in my meager care. I do not think he will ever forgive me for having left Talwar, abandoning you to Evelyn's evils.''

"He should understand better than anyone else why you left as you did, and the pain you felt when I so much as accused you of betraying me.''

"Leaving you in a fit of rage was as childish a thing as I have ever done,'' Justin replied. "Senet has the right of it. I should have locked you in your chamber until you came to your senses, and I should have taken Evelyn by the neck and thrown her out the castle gates.''

"I do not blame you for leaving,'' she said, twisting her head upward to look at him. "But do you know, Justin, you have never told me what made you come back? I thought you meant to stay away until I had gone to Gyer.''

He smiled. "I have not spoken much of those days after I left, because they shame me so greatly. I spent the first two days riding as far away from Talwar as Synn could take me, and as fast as he could do it, with the goal of not returning until I was able to live in my own home without thinking of you every minute of the day. I was in such a foolish rage that I seldom stopped long enough eat or rest. By the third day, Synn and I were so weary that to stop was a necessity, but no sooner had I unsaddled him and arranged a sleeping blanket for myself on the ground than I was set upon by robbers.''

"Robbers?" she repeated. "Justin!"

"They weren't very *good* robbers," he amended with a grin. "Weary as I was, even the most unfit knaves should have been able to best me, but I must have been a sight to behold, for I think it was the wild look of me that scared them away so easily, although I did draw my sword to defend myself. After they had run off, I sat upon the ground with my sword in my hand, and I realized, suddenly, despite everything that had passed between us, that you must care for me, and perhaps even love me."

She looked at him with surprise. "Being set upon by robbers caused you to realize such a truth?"

"In a way," he admitted. "It was because the sword I held in my hand was the one you had given me. Your father's sword. And the knowledge struck me, like a much-needed blow against my head, bringing me to my senses, that you went to a great deal of trouble to give me such a precious gift, just as I had done in order to have your mother's books returned to you. I had undertaken such an effort to show you that I love you, but it had not occurred to me, until that moment, that perhaps you went to so much effort for the same reason. Because you love me."

"Aye," she said with a soft smile. "Indeed, that is why."

"And then I remembered what you had said to me before I left, that the months you'd had with me were the most wonderful you'd ever known. And I realized, suddenly, that if that was true, then you didn't really want to leave. That somehow you felt you must go for the sake of my happiness, not your own. Until that moment, I thought that you simply wished to be away from me, that you preferred to serve as my brother's steward, rather than as my wife."

"Never," she murmured.

"Once I understood the truth of it, I also understood

that you didn't know that I loved you, either. That somehow I had to make you know and believe it. I couldn't let you go if you loved me, no matter how hardheaded you might be.'' He grinned, and Isabelle laughed.

"So you got back on Synn and came back to Talwar to lock me in my chamber until I came to my senses?''

"No,'' he confessed with a measure of embarrassment. "I was so weary that I fell asleep where I lay, not on my blanket, but on the cold ground. I doubt even the robbers could have roused me, if they'd decided to return. Fortunately, I slept in peace and woke several hours later. *Then* I mounted Synn and headed back for Talwar, stopping only long enough to buy bread and ale once before continuing on.''

"Would you truly have locked me away?'' she asked.

His smile returned full force. "Aye, and with me your fellow prisoner, devoted to convincing you that we belong together. I was going to keep you captive until you admitted that you loved me. I had already stolen you once. It seemed a likely step to take.''

She turned more fully, sliding her hands upward and about his neck. "And what methods would you have employed to bring such a confession about?''

He kissed her long and fully before replying, "The most merciless that I could invent. I planned to lay a long, dedicated siege, you see.''

"But I was already gone,'' she said, sobering. "I wish I had stayed, and been here when you returned.''

"As do I,'' he agreed, "but it is long ago, and we cannot spend our lives sorrowing over things that cannot be undone. We must go on and take our happiness as we may, just as Senet and Kayne and Aric must now do.'' He lifted his gaze to the hill beyond. "They are riding back. Senet has finished saying his last goodbyes to Odelyn. It is well, I think. This is the place where he must begin to find his soul again, beginning now.''

She turned in his arms to watch as the three mounted riders carefully descended the steep hillside.

"They have grown into men so quickly. Look at them, Justin. So proud and strong they are, so steadfast and able. How very proud you must be."

"Indeed," he murmured. "I love them well."

"We must go down to meet them," she said. "To say goodbye. Only another hour, and they'll be gone."

"But not forever, beloved," Justin reminded, tipping her chin up and kissing her mouth. "Our lads will come and go as they may, but you and I will be here, waiting and ready to receive them, to welcome them home whenever they arrive."

"Aye," Isabelle said, smiling up at him. "We'll be waiting for them here. Together, and with joy."

"Together," he murmured, kissing her again. "And with joy. I love you, my beautiful wife."

"As I love you," she said with a mischievous grin, "my handsome, and most wonderful, thief."

* * * * *

HARLEQUIN WOMEN KNOW ROMANCE WHEN THEY SEE IT.

And they'll see it on **ROMANCE CLASSICS**, the new 24-hour TV channel devoted to romantic movies and original programs like the special **Harlequin®** Showcase of Authors & Stories.

The **Harlequin®** Showcase of Authors & Stories introduces you to many of your favorite romance authors in a program developed exclusively for Harlequin® readers.

Watch for the **Harlequin®** Showcase of **Authors & Stories** series beginning in the summer of 1997.

If you're not receiving ROMANCE CLASSICS, call your local cable operator or satellite provider and ask for it today!

Escape to the network of your dreams.

Take 4 bestselling love stories FREE

Plus get a FREE surprise gift!

Special Limited-time Offer

Mail to Harlequin Reader Service®

3010 Walden Avenue
P.O. Box 1867
Buffalo, N.Y. 14240-1867

YES! Please send me 4 free Harlequin Historical™ novels and my free surprise gift. Then send me 4 brand-new novels every month, which I will receive before they appear in bookstores. Bill me at the low price of $3.69 each plus 25¢ delivery and applicable sales tax, if any.* That's the complete price and a savings of over 10% off the cover prices—quite a bargain! I understand that accepting the books and gift places me under no obligation ever to buy any books. I can always return a shipment and cancel at any time. Even if I never buy another book from Harlequin, the 4 free books and the surprise gift are mine to keep forever.

247 BPA A3UR

Name _____ (PLEASE PRINT)

Address _____ Apt. No. _____

City _____ State _____ Zip _____

This offer is limited to one order per household and not valid to present Harlequin Historical™ subscribers. *Terms and prices are subject to change without notice. Sales tax applicable in N.Y.

UHIS-696   ©1990 Harlequin Enterprises Limited

Let's Celebrate!

LOVE & LAUGHTER™

invites you to
the party of the season!

Grab your popcorn and be prepared to laugh as we celebrate with **LOVE & LAUGHTER**.

Harlequin's newest series is going Hollywood!

Let us make you laugh with three months of terrific books, authors and romance, plus a chance to win a FREE 15-copy video collection of the best romantic comedies ever made.

For more details look in the back pages of any Love & Laughter title, from July to September, at your favorite retail outlet.

Don't forget the popcorn!

Available wherever
Harlequin books are sold.

 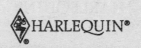 

HARLEQUIN®

HE SAID

♥

SHE SAID

Explore the mystery of male/female communication in this extraordinary new book from two of your favorite Harlequin authors.

Jasmine Cresswell and Margaret St. George bring you the exciting story of two romantic adversaries—each from their own point of view!

DEV'S STORY. CATHY'S STORY.
As he sees it. As she sees it.
Both sides of the story!

The heat is definitely on, and these two can't stay out of the kitchen!

Don't miss **HE SAID, SHE SAID.**
Available in July wherever Harlequin books are sold.

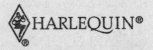

HARLEQUIN®

As Seen on TV!

Free Gift Offer

With a Free Gift proof-of-purchase
from any Harlequin® book, you can receive
a beautiful cubic zirconia pendant.

This stunning marquise-shaped stone is a genuine cubic
zirconia—accented by an 18" gold tone necklace.
(Approximate retail value $19.95)

Send for yours today...
compliments of ◆HARLEQUIN®

To receive your free gift, a cubic zirconia pendant, send us one original proof-of-purchase, photocopies not accepted, from the back of any Harlequin Romance®, Harlequin Presents®, Harlequin Temptation®, Harlequin Superromance®, Harlequin Intrigue®, Harlequin American Romance®, or Harlequin Historicals® title available at your favorite retail outlet, together with the Free Gift Certificate, plus a check or money order for $1.65 U.S./$2.15 CAN. (do not send cash) to cover postage and handling, payable to Harlequin Free Gift Offer. We will send you the specified gift. Allow 6 to 8 weeks for delivery. Offer good until December 31, 1997, or while quantities last. Offer valid in the U.S. and Canada only.

Free Gift Certificate

Name: _____

Address: _____

City: _____ State/Province: _____ Zip/Postal Code: _____

Mail this certificate, one proof-of-purchase and a check or money order for postage and handling to: HARLEQUIN FREE GIFT OFFER 1997. In the U.S.: 3010 Walden Avenue, P.O. Box 9071, Buffalo NY 14269-9057. In Canada: P.O. Box 604, Fort Erie, Ontario L2Z 5X3.

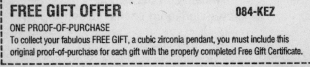

FREE GIFT OFFER   084-KEZ

ONE PROOF-OF-PURCHASE

To collect your fabulous FREE GIFT, a cubic zirconia pendant, you must include this original proof-of-purchase for each gift with the properly completed Free Gift Certificate.

084-KEZR